ACKNOWLEDGEMENTS

I wish to thank Lynn Vannucci and all the staff at Water Street Press for the courage they have shown in publishing this novel. Also, thanks to Sharon Thompson for her early and helpful readings of the manuscript, and for all the readers and editors who offered their encouragement when I most needed it. And finally, in gratitude to the Sisters of St. Joseph of Carondelet for their dedicated and humane efforts to educate me. Thank you all.

Some rise by sin and some by virtue fall.

William Shakespeare
Measure for Measure

1

IT WAS DURING MY pinched Italian phase, when I took to wearing tapered pants, black vests and pointed shoes, that I became known as the Virgin Queen.

It wasn't always so. During my first year at St. Lucy's School for Boys, those put in my charge called me no worse a name than Virgy, and that chirped in pubescent falsetto from the safe anonymity of their adolescent groups. I acted as if I hadn't heard, all knowing that I had. It was better thus. Virgy was not so bad, almost friendly. Better innocent diminutives than the names they coined for my colleagues: Bull Belloli, Greek O'Grady, Mother Murphy, Flash Fagan.

Most of you are by now familiar with what the New York tabloids have said of me. Try, if you may, to forgive those men of the press. Like the Cardinal who eggs them on, they suffer from paranoid delusions. Certainly, I am not the anarchist they make me out to be. It was never my intention to destroy the educational institutions of this city. On the contrary. I entered the schools to salvage what I could. Like Margaret

Mead, that courageous advocate of educational reform who preceded me, I would have kept the buildings, some of them, at least.

It is to teach and not for revenge—or, as some would say, an unnatural thirst for notoriety—that I shoulder my sandwich boards and head uptown to share my story with the people, abridged, of course, and as lightly expurgated as the times allow. I am driven to take my message to the streets because the publicity my enemies fear is the only weapon left to my disposal. A dissident's feet are scored with blisters and his soul is scarred from persecution. Teenagers armed with Magic Markers illustrate my story with crude obscenities. Policemen nudge me on with nightsticks.

Nonetheless, I march on. The saints who guide me expect no less, for just as they set me up for my first assignment and applauded along with the rich and famous as I rose to the top of my second career, so did they launch my third.

I remember the occasion well. It was a bright, crisp morning in late October, a fine day for job hunting. I rose at six, bathed and selected a severe black suit, pearl gray tie and signature black vest, an outfit appropriate to the occasion. A block down the street I stopped at the corner store for coffee light and a hard roll. After breaking my fast, I strolled toward a destination yet to be revealed to me. At the corner of Fifteenth Street and Broadway, I entered the dark canyon leading to St. Lucy's. Just as I was passing the church I felt the Hand. A power not my own directed me up the steps and down the aisle to a side chapel holding a life-size statue of a regal woman seated on a throne. In her left hand she held a bouquet of metal lilies and in her right a salver holding two glass eyeballs. I was instantly transported in spirit to the chapel of St. Lucy in Omaha, my hometown, where St. Lucy of Palermo sits enthroned in martyrdom, wearing a gold crown and robed in a golden cloak, sitting on her gilded throne just as she was now. I was stunned by the coincidence, that I should be directed to perhaps the only church in New York City housing a figure of St. Lucy. I looked for St. Philomena, with whom Lucy is often portrayed, and the namesake of another woman who has figured strongly in my life, and there she was, just half the size of Lucy, standing in the shadows, chained to the anchor the pagan emperor of Rome used to drown her in the Tiber, just as she stands in the chapel in Omaha. Portentous, I thought, this link to my past, but of events fortunate or dire, I had no way of knowing.

Most know St. Lucy as the patron saint of those afflicted with failing vision, but I would not learn until sometime later that she also looks after those whose worldview has been warped by circumstance. As I stood at the side chapel contemplating the holy woman, the milk glass eyes misted over. Droplets of water rolled down the lidless eyes to pool in the silver saucer. Just as the church bells began to toll, calling the faithful to morning prayer, I heard the holy woman speak.

"You are wondering, Virgil Quinn, why I weep. I will tell you. Evil times have beset the school that bears my name. Violent men have invaded my classrooms and usurped the role of teachers. You have been chosen, from many nominees, to rectify this situation."

The saint paused, apparently waiting for whatever objection I might raise. I raised none. I was penniless. Expelled in shame from my first career, I had abandoned my second, vowing never to return to the frivolous world of fashion. I had burned my bridges. The rent was due. I assumed that reformers who worked within the system got paid.

"You accept," the saint said. *"I expected no less of you. It's time to begin. Behind me you will find a stairs descending to*

the crypt. Take it. Behind the altar of the crypt you will find a tunnel. Take it. It will lead to the cafeteria of my school. Cross the cafeteria and ascend the stairs at the further end. This will lead to a corridor. Follow the hall to the first door on your right. This is Brother Principal's office.

"*And here I leave you. You are now on your own.*"

With a rustle of silk skirts, the saint hurried down the hall, paused mid-stride, and spoke over her shoulder. "*Good luck, my son,*" she called with a smile. "*You're going to need it.*"

And so it was, forewarned but not forearmed (as Sister Philomena was fond of saying), that I began to teach. Replacing blackboards of years gone by with sandwich boards relating my tale, I will teach again. I will prevail. The people of this city must know why I, Mr. Virgil Quinn, teacher of history and moderator of St. Lucy's Forensic Club, became known to the boys he taught and those millions in the tabloid world as Virgil Quinn, the Virgin Queen.

2

I'M NOT AT ALL sure it was the students who thought up the nasty sobriquet the New York tabloids like to couple with my name. More likely it was Bull Belloli. He had cause sufficient. Now, as I record my thoughts, I feed my anger by conjuring up the initial scene of my humiliation. Was this the way it happened? In the locker room full of freshly showered boys, with Bull Belloli slapping asses as athletes do?

"Good game, huh, Coach?"

"Great game, men, great game. But you, Figliano. You ain't gonna be on this team unless you pass history, Figliano. School rules. You gonna pass history, Figliano?"

"I don't know, Coach. Mr. Quinn, he's tough."

"What ya studyin' in his class, Figliano."

"Queen Elizabeth, Coach. They called her the Virgin Queen."

Laughter reverberates ominously around the tiled shower room. Probably that little stud Muldoon. The others giggle.

"None of that, men. No dirty language on my team. You, Figliano, better pass the Virgin Queen's history class"—the coach pauses for laughter—"or I'll break your legs."

That's how such things begin. Spite. Sister Philomena, my third grade teacher back in Omaha, taught me that. "There's nothing," she used to say, "more valuable than one's good reputation. Guard it, and guard the reputation of others."

Sister Philomena, plucking black lint from her snow-white bib, elaborated upon her theme: "To destroy another's good reputation, children, is a terrible sin, almost unforgivable. Not absolutely unforgivable, only despair is that, the sin of Judas. To destroy another's reputation is the sin called calumny.

"There was once a spiteful woman," Sister Philomena continued—she had a mesmerizing narrative style, "who had fallen into the sinful habit of telling tales about her neighbors. She repented her sins and went to the Curé of Ars to ask forgiveness. Curé, children, is a French word for priest. The Curé heard her confession, and when she asked him what she could do to restore the good names of those she had injured, he said to her, 'Tomorrow bring me a pillow filled with down.'

"The woman did so. The Curé of Ars took her by the arm and led her up to the belfry of the church. The day was windy, the sky dark. He took a penknife from the pocket of his soutane—that's French for cassock—and slit the pillow end to end. He shook the feathers into the wind and immediately they were caught up and carried over the town. The feathers settled on the rooftops and on the streets, some dropped into the river and were swept away. Some sunk.

"'For your penance,' the Curé said, 'collect the feathers and return them to the pillow from which they came.'

"'But that's not possible,' the woman said. 'They have scattered too far. Most are surely lost.'

"You see, children,"—ah, my beautiful, gentle Sister Philomena—"restitution for such a sin cannot be made. The feathers could not be found. Tales can't be untold. Destroying another's reputation is a terrible thing. Only the fires of purgatory can burn away the sin."

"Sister," I asked, waving a pudgy hand in the air. "What if all the tales were true?"

"That, Virgil, would make no difference. Who are we to judge?" And sister smiled her loveliest smile.

I learned a great deal from Sister Philomena—not arithmetic and such; Sister didn't spend much time on material of that sort—but about the saints and other eccentric people and how we can learn from their experience. Today, attacked from every quarter by vicious gossip, I repeat the simple Curé's tale. It gives me solace, induces recuperative sleep.

Gossip, they say, is nearly dead in the city's public schools. If so, size killed it. I'm told that thousands of students might be enrolled in a single public high school. Size engenders anonymity, anonymity indifference. Good gossip thrives on intimacy, and that St. Lucy's had a lot of. With a student body of four hundred and six and a faculty of only twelve, including Brother Principal, we all came to know each other well. Too well, the tabloids now suggest.

Rumor would later have it that it was not Bull Belloli but Mr. Fagan, or Flash Fagan as the boys called him, who coined the term that would one day become my epitaph. I never believed it. Mr. Fagan was a kind of jack-of-all-trades at St. Lucy's. Besides his strictly honorary title of Chairman of the History Department—he had done nothing to earn it— he taught one period of World History, two of Cultures in Conflict, one of Earth Science, served as guidance counselor and part-time librarian and, beginning in my third year at the school, taught a course called Domestic Economy. Mr. Fagan, I believed then and still do, simply lacked the imagination to come up with an epithet so nastily appropriate, considering the obvious play on my name, my nobility of bearing, my reputation as a history scholar, as the Virgin Queen. The rumor might, however, contain a kernel of truth. Mr. Fagan had his reasons for slandering me. It was I who unmasked the man, a story that bears telling and will be told at its appropriate time, if only to demonstrate the extent of the man's incompetence.

A courageous man makes many enemies. Kevin O'Connor, my student and friend and the most gifted boy ever to attend St. Lucy's, believed that Greek O'Grady launched the campaign that changed my name from Virgy to the Virgin Queen.

"He is the only teacher in the school," Kevin reminded me in a voice loud enough to be overheard, "resourceful enough to have thought it up, and the only one vicious enough to mouth it about."

I glanced about me. We were seated in Tina's, the tiny coffee shop around the corner from the school. Other students frequented Tina's eight- table café. I didn't want it to be said that I encouraged students to demean their teachers. But the place at that hour was empty except for Tina herself, who seemed more interested in her copy of the *National Inquirer* than the gossip of her neighborhood school.

Greek O'Grady taught trigonometry and calculus as well as Greek and Latin. Kevin was the first junior in the history of St. Lucy School to take three of O'Grady's four demanding courses simultaneously. He made room in his crowded schedule by studying French and American History under a tutorial arrangement with Mother Murphy and me.

"The rest of them," Kevin added, "wouldn't know the Virgin Queen from the Virgin Mary."

"Such cynicism, Kevin, is hardly appropriate to your age."

Pomposity was a vice I had yet to work on. So was hypocrisy. During the past months I had spent more time with the faculty of St. Lucy's than I had with any group since I'd left the nuns to attend, after a sojourn in my second career, Fordham University, and I couldn't recall a half-dozen instances where a teacher's conversation touched on matters relevant to his field of study. I had come to the same conclusion that Kevin had. But to admit as much would have been disloyal to my social class, and at that time I had not yet gone beyond bourgeois revolutionary thought.

So I was Virgy for only a year. If I had wished to place comfort above virtue, I might have remained so always— Virgy to my students, Virgil to my peers, rising always in the eyes of my superiors to become the appointed Chairman of the History Department with power over three, assuming in due time the role of Dean of Discipline. And who knows? If the Cardinal had negotiated in a spirit of compromise, not spite, I might have accepted the ultimate honor and had no need to record these events. I might have sat in just severity behind the Great Desk to receive those who entered in fear and trembling to beg a favor or humbly accept their punishment from Principal Quinn, first layman of the Diocese of New York to bear that title.

And never heard that base sobriquet lisped from the mouths of innocents—"That's him, Mr. Virgil Quinn, better known as the Virgin Queen."

St. Lucy died for virtue's sake and so may I. Those pagan men of Sicily plucked out her eyes. Forever after, the sculptors of Christendom would depict the virgin martyr standing relaxed but vigilant, holding her plucked-out eyeballs on a saucer for all to see the awful consequence of righteousness.

According to a collateral version of the virgin's tale, St. Lucy is portrayed eyeballs in hand to symbolize her heavenly medical specialty. Just as a pawnbroker hangs three silver balls above his door to indicate the nature of his trade, St. Lucy's eyeballs attest to her special interest in the affairs of men. She's a lobbyist, so to speak, before the Secretariat of Miraculous Cures, pleading for a speedy restoration of failing eyesight to all who invoke her name in prayer. The saint herself, the legend runs, suffered from acute myopia. I sometimes offer up a prayer to her myself requesting the cure of my astigmatic vision. I detest the effect glasses have on my appearance and refuse to wear them.

Myopic or heroic, St. Lucy stands just so in the Sixteenth Street foyer of her school, a cheaper copy of the sumptuous marble image occupying her chapel in the church. She gives me strength. If the students had been especially cruel one day, I would pause a moment before her statue, touch my fingers to my lips and press the kiss still lingering there to the two milkglass spheres with azure irises staring up at me from the painted plaster saucer.

3

UNFORTUNATELY, I BROUGHT QUALIFICATIONS to my third profession that would make it difficult for me to find true contentment at St. Lucy's. I made no boasts upon arrival, but it's no mean trick to hide light under a bushel. Baskets have cracks, and word of academic honors, of which I took more than my share, preceded me down from Fordham.

"We've heard of you, Mr. Quinn," Brother Principal began, "and our sources tell us you did very well by the Jesuits." Brother winced ever so slightly at the mention of the men most recently in charge of my education, revealing a hint of envy for an order that counted great saints and noted scholars among its members while his own community, the Little Brothers of Divine Grace, could come up with neither. "You have character references, I presume?"

Brother Principal had stood when I entered and now sunk into the high-backed, black leather armchair that sat behind an immense mahogany desk bearing the scars of a century of use. He dressed entirely in black. Today he wore a soutane buttoned to the neck, making him a near match for my recent teachers, if one overlooked the lack of a Roman collar that, as a lay brother, Church rubrics forbade him to wear.

I reached into my satchel and extracted a bundle of handwritten letters attesting to my character. I presented these glosses, all but one composed by myself and inscribed by friends, to Brother Principal. The letter vouching for my religious orthodoxy was authentic and came from Father Liam Hallahan, O.P. Father Liam owed me a favor. It was I who found him in civvies, ten years after he took the pledge and held to it without a slip, preaching a confused sermon on the evils of drink in front of the County Cork, a tavern I sometimes visit on a Friday afternoon. I got him off the street and into his rectory without anyone being the wiser, and for this simple Good Samaritan act, Father would have put me up for canonization.

"Impressive, Mr. Quinn. It appears that a good many people think very highly of you." Brother Principal shuffled the letters, shifted them to his left hand and used his right to pull at the distended lobe of his ear. Reading from the letter on top of the stack, he went on.

"Father Hallahan. A great speaker. You've heard his famous sermon on the evils of drink? Yes? And taken it to heart?" Brother paused to let this admonition sink in. "He says here that you are 'a bold thinker who grounds his social thought on papal bulls and encyclicals.' Now that's what I like to see in our teachers here at St. Lucy's." Pausing only for a moment, Brother demanded, "Give me an example of that, how you put a bull to work, so to speak?"

Apparently, no pun was intended, for Brother Principal didn't follow up his words with a smirk or a smile. Bulls, like grand operatic arias, are known by their opening phrase. In Latin. Now name one, Virgil, and be quick about it! *Carpe diem, Caveat emptor, Epluribus unum.* You've got to do better than that; the man's not a fool....

"Take *Splendide mendax Virgilorum,*" I shot back, hoping I got it right. It was the term Sister Philomena used to describe 'the splendid lie' of my first career, an escapade she got me into and, when it didn't turn out as planned, abandoned me to face my shame alone. I was confidant that among the hundreds of papal bulls broadcast over the centuries, Brother would not identify mine as a fake. I had rolled off Philomena's Latin phrase using an extravagant Italian accent. Brother Principal Brian McMahon, B.A., probably knew no more Latin than I, and no Italian. I was banking on his not understanding a word I said, but he would want to appear as if he did and, later, if he tried to recall my bull, words would fail him.

"The original document has been lost," I continued, "or misfiled in the Vatican archives, but we know from bulls that have come down to us through oral tradition, that if it were not for Holy Mother Church and her faithful servants, the priests, nuns and brothers who carry out her work, and the dedicated laymen who have chosen at great economic sacrifice to teach in her schools...."

I was prepared to go on in this fashion for as long as it took Brother's ear to numb, which was sooner than expected. He began to fidget in impatience, which prompted me to reach for my bag to retrieve further evidence of my qualifications to teach. Brother waved me off with a little flurry of fingers with nails bitten to the quick and jumped immediately to the subject of salary, naming an amount so low that I knew further subterfuge to be unnecessary. Six thousand a year? Little more, I presumed, than the salary paid the city's lowest civil servant. Who other than the chosen or the grossly unqualified would work for such a sum?

And so it was that in the fall of '68 I joined the faculty of St. Lucy's School for Boys. I was not asked for my résumé, heavily abridged as it was to exclude experience somewhat more exotic than that customarily expected of a schoolteacher. Nor was I asked for my transcript of credits, bona fide, that I carried in my bag. I was not surprised by either omission. Until quite recently, before membership in accreditation associations became the fad, parochial school administrators considered material proof of qualifications to teach the young a wasteful formality. They held similar views on the need for courses in education, practice teaching, even, if we go back a decade or two, in the bachelor's degree itself. Such documents were the amusing paraphernalia of the public school systems that had the time and personnel to waste filing away such things. How much more trusting to hire by ear. A few minutes of conversation to establish the presumption of literacy and evidence of religious orthodoxy, and you were in. A practice which, although I was forced to circumvent the latter requirement, I would be the last to censure. If Brother Principal had scrutinized my past too closely, I might not have been hired, and the winds of reform would not have swept through the halls of St. Lucy's little school on West Sixteenth Street.

Alas, this refreshingly unbureaucratic approach to faculty recruitment is changing. The diocese is sending these new nuns and brothers through administration courses required by the state. They come back demanding all sorts of paper-proven quality, even teaching certificates, and end up co-opted by the very force parochial schools were set up to contravene, the fundamentalist Protestant state. Or worse, join the state in the unholiest of alliances, the Whore of Babylon bedded down with the Moloch of secularism. Emmet Hughes, first bishop of Baltimore and builder of the American monument to Irish stubbornness, would wince with disgust to see his schools so defiled.

Oh, the sadness of it all! If only there was someone, some great visionary as appalled by the fate of the bishop's dream as I was... And I would sink, reflecting upon the bishop's dream, into a state of idle melancholy.

As I said, word preceded me, and quality, as the foreign observer de Tocqueville saw as early as 1840, would never be accepted by a society of egalitarian and therefore mediocre men. I doubt that few if any of my fellow teachers were familiar with the remarkable Frenchman's observations on American society. Nonetheless, they were out to get me from the start. How to do it perplexed them. Dull men themselves, they stood in spiteful awe of brilliance. At one time, these semi-literate sons of the working class would have directed their anger against the traditional enemy, the ruling Protestant elite. Their willingness now to devour their own was demonstrated by the vigor with which they searched my character for some small fissure into which to pour the acid of their slander and erode the only obstacle to their pursuit of gross incompetence and reckless brutality.

I WAS HIRED in October, five weeks after the term began. Four teachers had preceded me into those six classes of forty-eight boys each. I was met with smug grins and insolent glares: We got four; we'll get you, too.

Pity the innocents, so little did they know. Virgil Quinn neither adhered to the slap-'em-down school of discipline practiced at St. Lucy's nor had he come fresh from the effete courses in child behavior required of those preparing to teach in the public schools. Growing up in Omaha, I had been trained by a master, Sister Philomena of the Sisters of Mercy of Baton Rouge, an order that gave no quarter and could pride itself on never drawing blood.

I ignored their smirks and began the lesson.

"We shall begin with Chapter Six, Volume Two of Morrison and Commager, Fifth Edition. The text assigned to this course is simplistic, juvenile and more suitable for instilling patriotic ideals in the minds of grade school children than in teaching boys of your age and intelligence the history of their country. You may put the assigned text in your lockers until June. If you do not possess a copy of Morrison and Commager, eliminate Cokes and cigarettes from your budget for a week and buy one. Cokes destroy the satin texture of a young man's cheeks, cigarettes befoul his breath. Vanity, like faith, makes sacrifice a simple task. If you choose to destroy the only years of beauty many of you will ever know, the reference sections of your branch libraries carry copies of the text. I've checked with Central, so don't dispute me.

"American History II is a course required by the state. You are seniors. No one who fails this course will graduate.

"You will take notes—constantly, always, without being told each day to do so. You are now young men, not children. Only children must be told repeatedly what's good for them.

"I took the time—my time, Saturday, for which I received no compensation even at the paltry fee I'm paid—to check your IQ scores. Some of you are quite bright. I'm brighter.

"On Friday I observed St. Lucy's in operation. Brutalizing boys seems acceptable here. I do not strike boys. Unless provoked by brazen insolence. I have other methods. The curious among you will discover them.

"Brazen insolence must, of course, be checked at all costs. If such an act occurs, which it will not, the student will be informed that he has committed a brazen act and will be told to step into the hall. Refuse and I'll have you expelled by Brother Principal. The door will be closed behind us. Once outside, the student will put his hands to his sides and lift his eyes to mine. Then I shall strike him, once, with open left hand on the student's right cheek. I am right-handed. Using my left will demonstrate that the disgusting if necessary act is meant to mortify, not maim. The student will then precede me into the classroom.

"We will begin, as I said, with Chapter Six, 'The Passing of the Frontier.' I lived for a time in the American West and am an authority on the subject.

"The Frontier, boys, holds an importance in the psychology of America out of all proportion to its duration. The Frontier, as we speak of it here, refers to those few years between the first anti-draft riots in America and the acceptance of Lillian Russell as the nation's first sex symbol. It marks the death of the American Experiment and the rise of the American oligarchy. Democracy, boys, died with Jesse James. Jesse James, Butch Cassidy and Billy the Kid were not the outlaws so frequently portrayed by Hollywood and television. On the contrary, they were the last democrats fighting the reactionary forces of oligarchy and militarism, forces currently in control of the republic.

"It was the time and place the world now refers to as the Wild West. It was the age of the six-gun. The six-gun—a revolver first patented by Colt in 1873, called a six-gun because of its revolving chamber holding six cartridges of forty-two grains, each capable of being fired in rapid succession—can be compared in the history of American democracy to the flintlock of 1776. Both were the instruments of revolution. Just as the Minuteman left his plow rusting in the fields to raise his flintlock against the British oppressors, so did the last democrats, Jesse James, et al., abandon their sedentary pursuits of cowpunching and gold panning, to fire their six-guns against the new oppressor, Wells Fargo. Wells Fargo, boys, was a bank. It was but the symbol of an oligarchic system that oppressed the workers of farm and city alike. Your ancestors and mine were the men and women who built this city in which we live, and made it rich. Did we reap the harvest to their labor? No. Never. New York City, our city, was systematically robbed of its wealth by Fifth Avenue oligarchs who live today in their million-dollar condos and ride down to Wall Street in black limousines.

"The rich grow richer and the poor grow poorer. It's a law of history. You will learn more about the laws of history as we proceed through this last year of your secondary education—You back there! Silence! Or leave the room. Leave the room and fail for the marking period. The geographical area of which we speak when using the term, the Last Frontier, is properly called the Plains, or to employ the term favored by geographers, the North American Steppe. Early recorders of America's progress referred to that vast land between the Mississippi and the Rocky Mountains as the Great American Desert. Some modern historians, myself among them, define the word 'desert' spiritually rather than materially. In this sense of the word, all the populated regions of present-day America might be collectively classified under the term desert. The word 'arid' is essential to either definition, geographic or cultural. America, boys, is spiritually arid. To borrow a word from your own patois—a patois, as some may know, is a mongrel language—what America lacks is soul.

"The reason of course for the death of America's soul is the death of democracy and the rise of the oligarchy. We are ruled today by the Anglo-Saxon rich, the would-be aristocracy of modern America, and its parvenu. Parvenu is a French word meaning tacky. Most of our recent leaders, certainly the one presently occupying the White House, are parvenu.

"And so in closing, boys—the bell for your next class will ring in precisely three minutes—we can conclude from Chapter Six, 'The Passing of the Frontier,' that just as the patriots of 1776 were compelled to take up arms against their Anglo-Saxon Protestant oppressors, so were the guerrilla fighters of the last Frontier compelled to defend democracy against the Wall Street robber barons.

"History, boys, is a continuum. History, some say, repeats itself. If this is true, we must determine the role each of us should play in current affairs. What role do you think we should play in the struggle against the Wall Street Rich? Yes, young man. What is your name?"

"Coogan."

"And your first name?"

"Andrew."

"I prefer first names, Andrew. Let's break the militaristic habit, so popular at St. Lucy's, of addressing each other by surname only. Would you like to answer my question, Andrew?"

"I didn't hear it. Would you repeat it…please?"

"Certainly, Andrew. I asked what you think your role should be in the continuing struggle against the Anglo-Saxon oligarchic oppressor."

"Kill the commie bastards!"

"Hmmm. Run over to Barnes and Noble and get your books tonight, boys—I had them order in an adequate stock. You can skip Chapter Six. We've covered it in class today. Go on to Chapter Seven, 'Transportation and Its Control.' It's all about the Eastern capitalists railroading the Western farmer, the narrow backbone of America. There will be a quiz tomorrow morning covering today's lesson.

"Have a pleasant day."

4

CONTRARY TO THE NORM at St. Lucy's, I rarely closed the door to my classroom. Word would reach me through student confidants that my colleagues, from Brother Principal down to Flash Fagan, the chairman of my department, so-called, stood outside my door, just out of sight, listening. Fine. Perhaps they came to learn. They certainly were in need of enlightenment, and my lectures went well beyond their notion of history. The dedicated teacher accepts without discrimination all who sincerely wish to learn. You might say, "Mr. Quinn, you're being naïve." Perhaps. But who was I to question their motives? Paranoia is the dry rot of reason. I came to teach. History, correctly interpreted, frees man from the prison of the past. My fellow teachers, all Roman Catholics and thus heirs to one of the world's great sensual traditions, had fallen prey to the arid ethos of the Puritan State. They sensed this and came to stand humbly outside my door in hope of discovering the way to liberation.

I did, however, take the simple precaution of seating Primo de Popalano near the door of each of my sophomore year classes he attended. Primo, and cooperative students in each of my other classes, agreed to indicate by a pre-arranged signal (a loud blowing of the nose), the presence of visitors lingering without. A precaution that I used on several occasions to guide my lecture adroitly into matters less open to misinterpretation by ears cupped to pick up evidence of heresy.

Primo and I had become friends—well, if not exactly friends, we had at least gone beyond the typically antagonistic teacher-student relationship. I hadn't taught at St. Lucy's a month before I realized that if I was to survive the year, unlike my several predecessors who had each fled within a week of entering the classroom, I must pick out the leader of each clique and win him over. I began with Primo. His large student following overlapped three of my six classes. The boys worshipped him because of his good looks and bold impertinence, traits that made him a frequent target for the anger of Bull Belloli and Greek O'Grady. Primo, when I first met him, was not a discriminating boy. In his disdain for authority, he had somehow confused me with all the rest. I would change that.

Charm is an illusive quality. Some have it; no teacher can afford to be without it. Teachers who lack charm must resort to violence.

I began my campaign to win Primo over by calling on him to answer questions the dumbest boy in class could answer without hesitation. "Good, Primo. Exactly. You've done your homework." I flattered the boy while setting myself up as a teacher gullible enough to think Primo had prepared for class when everyone, students and teachers alike, knew he hadn't cracked a book in weeks. It took the edge off his irascibility. I fed him this diet of public praise and recognition, attentions he had already got too much of from his classmates and probably didn't get enough of from parents with too many kids, until I had him hooked. He would now be vulnerable, I hoped, to my offer of friendship and expectations of collusion. He would not get one without agreeing to the other.

Two weeks into my campaign I asked Primo to stop by after class, "To study your progress," a phrase both of us would have ridiculed if a wary paranoia, inherent in all student-teacher confrontations at St. Lucy's, had not prevented us from being frank with each other. "I take a special interest in students of Italian heritage."

Primo frowned in suspicion. "You prejudiced or something? You've got no right to expect more from me than any of the other guys."

"Oh, but I do, Primo. Much more." I paused again. He would want to tape to memory this glaring example of ethnic discrimination. If sometime in the future I found it necessary to fail him, he could claim bias as evidence against me. Resourceful students are no different from any other oppressed minority. To survive they learn how to manipulate the system.

"You see, Primo, my grandmother was a de Popalano—no relation to your family—and as Italians…" Primo broke into laughter. "Don't be fooled by my family name, Primo. It wasn't always Quinn. The family was once called Quinella, a good Sicilian name like your own. My grandfather changed it."

Primo stared at me, first in disbelief, then suspicion, and finally with a look I thought to be fear. I intended when I called Primo in to drop some personal revelation, however fanciful, that would imply he enjoyed a special relationship with his teacher even as I maintained the aura of mystery I used to heighten my authority. The less students know of their teacher, the fewer weapons they have to use against him. As Sister Philomena repeatedly told us, "Intimacy breeds contempt." She was advising against close friendships. "They are all," she said, "without exception, near occasions of sin." Coming from a woman as young and beautiful as Sister Philomena, her fear of intimacy was understandable. She would have been perfectly cast as the nun in *The Bells of St. Mary's,* a role won by Ingrid Bergman, Philomena's near contemporary and a woman who also wore the habit well. Sister did, however, in violation of her convictions, make an exception of me. I saw our intimacy as just that, an exception, and being something of a belle myself, I adopted Philomena's advice and made it the first principle of a teacher who wished to maintain order without resorting to violence.

"Why did your grandfather change his name?" Primo's question was direct, demanding an answer.

"Oh, he wasn't anti-Italian or anything like that," I answered hurriedly. "Granpapa just wanted a shorter name."

"No other reason?" Primo fixed me with black eyes slightly protuberant behind their fringe of luxuriant black lashes, the face of a Florentine prince executed by a Renaissance master.

Too late I recalled Sister Philomena's warning that lies, like little acorns, grow into trees. This whole thing was getting out of hand. I was not prepared to answer probing questions. Although I am skilled at improvisation in the classroom, put one to one I tend toward a naïve honesty. I searched for an explanation that would both satisfy the boy and allow the subject to drop.

"I think it had to do with a family feud, back in the old country. You see, my grandfather loved my grandmother, but there was something about her family. Trouble with the law or something. So my father changed *his* name and…"

Stories like this, I reassured myself, are never clear. Much is lost in transmission from one generation to the next.

"Trouble with the law?" Primo asked, obviously alarmed.

"Something like that. Now let's get on to what I asked to see you about, your academic and behavioral progression."

I spoke in my clipped classroom voice until Primo's suspicions—fears?—were buried beneath a load of ed psyche jargon I dredged up from the single course in the field I was compelled to take in my first career and which discouraged me from ever taking another. When the boy was sufficiently confused, I reverted to a confidential tone better suited to my purpose.

"Primo, you are one of the two or three boys here at St. Lucy's whom I find truly outstanding, the kind of boy I would like to get to know a good deal better than our classroom situation permits. I'm curious, for example, to learn of your outside interests, how you spend your time away from school."

Primo became defensive. "I've got lots of interests," he insisted. "I'm never bored."

"Oh, I'm sure you're not," I reassured him, and then pressed for more information. "Like what," I asked.

"Well, I follow all the teams, football, baseball, hockey..."

"Those are worthy distractions, of course, for people without talent themselves. Spectator sports provide a sense of achievement, vicarious though it might be. I was thinking more of activities aimed at developing your own potential. You are, as you must know, the most—" I could not tell Primo that he was beautiful or handsome, not even graceful. Teachers are expected to support the mores and taboos of the society that employs them. To have commented on Primo's remarkable physical qualities might have led to a confusion of intent on my part. I sought safety in pious abstractions. "God has blessed you with a body of near perfect proportions. The Russians excel at dance because the Bolshoi selects only those with perfect bodies for training. Have you considered the dance, Primo? As a showcase for your, ahh, physical attributes?"

"Dancers are fags," was Primo's simple reply.

"That, Primo, is neither true nor relevant. Dance is as old as man. When Adam and Eve were banished from the Garden, they spent the night, according to some authorities, dancing to celebrate their release from the righteous boredom against which even their Maker could not prevail. These same authorities state that Jesus sometimes danced on water to draw a crowd. We know for a fact that Alexander the Great danced after electing himself to the Olympian Hall of Fame, that the Inca danced to celebrate his divinity, and that Pizzaro and his men, after stealing the Inca's gold and destroying one of the world's great civilizations, danced the flamenco in what today is commonly called drag to immortalize the then-revolutionary phrase, God is Dead. Of all the men of history who aspired to divinity, only Hitler refused to dance. It is thought by some that his reasons for not doing so…"

Primo began to shuffle in impatience, bringing to even so simple a movement the grace of a dancer.

"In brief, Primo, dancing is divine. I dance. Indeed, I dance very well. Sister Philomena—my first, and only, great teacher; the rest were mere echoes of the nun—urged me to go professional. But fate, divinely ordained, assigned me to teach. Everywhere, all the time. I will, therefore, teach you to dance.

"On the first Saturday of the month, I hold a dancing class in my apartment for a select group of young men showing exceptional promise. Would you care to attend?"

"Well, if it's just dancin', nothin' fancy…"

Once a student is properly informed, he invariably comes around.

Primo, needless to say, went on to become my star pupil. So rapid was his progress that I surrendered the class to him. I had by then taken up hatha yoga and found that I didn't have the intellectual focus necessary to pursue such contrary disciplines as yoga and ballet.

5

I WAS FIRM WITH THE boys my first year of teaching; had to be to survive. I threatened physical punishment and used it on a single occasion. After tapping Coogan lightly on the cheek with the fingers of my left hand, the boy smiled at me and said, "Is that all?"

Impudent boy. The pain I felt was profound, akin to the loss of innocence. I fell into such a state of depression I never repeated the act. I concentrated instead on heightening my presence to the point where no boy wished to challenge me, preferably out of affectionate respect. In those few instances where I failed to win over the boy, I learned to cool his adolescent temper with an icy reprimand couched in the clipped diction I had learned from Sister Philomena.

Unfortunately, I lacked the self-assurance then to attack the abuses of authority I observed too often in the halls of St. Lucy's with the same unequivocal condemnation I leveled against the American power structure.

My acquiescence to institutionalized brutality seems to me now no less than cowardly, and I would rather not talk about it. But confession properly timed lends credence to the man: My first year at St. Lucy's—from fear, no doubt, and a life time of conditioning—that first year at St. Lucy's I saw boys struck and did nothing.

To have seen, stood by and done nothing! The dull thud of a boy's head striking the plaster wall... I can't remember now whether it was Kevin O'Connor or Primo de Popalano who became the agent of my fate. I often saw the two together though a year apart in school—Kevin a junior, Primo in his sophomore year. St. Lucy's odd couple, so very different in looks, personality and interests, they had crossed the barrier of class year and age to become friends. Perhaps both victims were involved in closely separated incidents. But the name of the man who would move me from apathy to resolution is burned deep into my memory: The brute was Bull Belloli, the Brooklyn Hitter.

Certain details of the day come back to me now. It was late in the first semester and I was racing through three chapters a day of World History II, desperately trying to reach the Battle of Waterloo before time ran out, when I found myself bogged down in the final battles of World War II, unsure just how I got there. On the day of my shame I had just rung down the curtain on Nazi Germany with a resounding denunciation of a nation whose exaggerated respect for authority caused the people to confuse good citizenship with blind obedience. I ended my lecture by quoting the courageous German patriot and resister, Pastor Niemöller. "And when they came for the Jews, I did nothing because I was not a Jew. And when they came for—" But I rarely lectured from notes and could not recall the many groups Hitler came for, so I cataloged a number of oppressed minorities of our time—Blacks, gays, Indians, whoever came to mind—and left it at that, ending with the ringing salutation, "And then they came for me!"

"Who could blame 'em?"

I heard it. The voice came from the back of the room. I ignored the comment because of its source, the depraved, if clever, Principe Mangora, one of Greek O'Grady's clique. His snide remark did not reflect the attitude of the majority of boys, I was sure of that, boys who sat in hushed admiration until the bell woke them from the spell I had cast.

The boy to be struck—yes, I remember now. It was Kevin O'Connor and not Primo de Popalano. Kevin was the last to leave the room. I was delayed a moment, and Kevin had reached the end of the nearly empty hall when I entered it. I saw Bull raise his hand to swing, saw the boy duck his head, heard the thud.

And I did nothing. I wished to act, to throw myself between Belloli and his victim, but between the willing and the doing, procrastination won the day. I waited until Belloli entered his classroom and closed the door behind him before approaching the boy.

"Why did Mr. Belloli strike you?" I asked.

His eyes were wet with unshed tears. An ugly welt swelling over his left cheekbone marred the soft lines of his adolescent cheek. He reached up and touched his head where it had struck the wall and winced.

"He didn't like my hat."

The cap responsible for sparking Belloli's outburst lay on the floor at Kevin's feet. It was a black and white Gatsby check, and probably, judging from Kevin's style of dress, a vintage piece.

"You know, Kevin, wearing hats in school is forbidden. If we allow hats—" I broke off, ashamed of my cowardice.

Kevin looked at me with the expression of a boy betrayed.

"But an infraction of the dress code," I added to salvage what I could of my integrity, "is no excuse for brutality."

For those of us taught to respect authority as the earthly expression of divine order, the spectacle of men in power running roughshod over human rights can create a dilemma that for some is insoluble. If the decision had been mine to make that day I looked into the eyes of a boy betrayed, I would have resigned. What could I, the most junior member of a faculty prone to violence and protective of its prerogatives, do to correct these abuses? And why me?

In search of answers I crossed the gymnasium and took the tunnel leading to the church facing Fifteenth Street on the downtown side of the block. I found my way through the darkened church to the side chapel housing the other, a more precious and sentimental rendition of the statue of St. Lucy than the one standing in the foyer of the school. I dropped to my knees before the saint and begged her to tell me what to do.

I got no answer. It had been a long day, and while continuing to beseech the saint, I dropped my head to the velvet padded shelf of the prie dieu, closed my eyes and nodded off listening to the church bells toll the hour.

With the last toll of the bell the saint spoke. She was not of much help.

"*Do,*" she said in a voice so clear that in my dream state I saw myself turning to see if any of the several old women kneeling in the pews behind me had heard, "*do what you were sent to do.*"

"They are all joined against me," I whined, "in a conspiracy of silence."

"If the job required an army," Lucy replied, *"we would have sent Joan of Arc. When I faced those pagan men of Sicily, I stood alone."*

"And they gouged out your eyes."

Lucy gave me the fatuous stone cold smile that never left her face even as she spoke in a voice apparently only I could hear.

"I have been taught to respect authority and order," I continued, "not to destroy it." I wanted to ask the saint, but dared not, how long it had been since she'd left her sanctuary for a walk around town. Did she know what was happening out there? If we brought down Bull and the Greek, was she prepared for the anarchy to follow? Probably not. Lucy had led a too sheltered life altogether, locked up behind the rood screen of her chapel. I did not tell her these things, although I suppose she read my thoughts.

"You've been taught by some of the best teachers the Church has produced," St. Lucy assured me. *"Search their words for the way to righteousness."*

I awoke to the tug of a gnarled hand pulling at the skirts of my blue blazer. With my head still resting on the kneeling bench I opened my eyes to look into the jaundiced eyes of a wrinkled crone dressed all in black and so short and stooped my eyes met hers at kneeling height. Lifting my head from the prie dieu, I looked around, getting my bearings. St. Lucy looked down from her marble perch, her silent lips still parted in the inane smile typical of saints chiseled in stone.

"You can't sleep here,' the gnome creature cackled. "This is a church, not a flop house. If you want to sleep, go up to Grand Central and crash with the rest of the bums."

MY METAMORPHOSIS FROM critical observer to man of action was not painless. The habit of correct moral decision is never easy to acquire. The line between prim disapproval and righteous indignation is more frequently drawn by intellectual esthetes than by battlefront soldiers. St. Lucy's opinion of my teachers not withstanding, I could find little in my eighteen years training in the art of moral vivisection to prepare me for the crude problems I encountered at St. Lucy's. True, all learning contains the seeds of obsolescence, but today I look back upon the hypothetical situations we were asked to probe during my Fordham years as just a trifle esoteric.

Take the puzzling case Father O'Beirne assigned to our Introduction to Ethics class:

Mary Flynn and her husband John have never used forbidden forms of birth control. Rhythm, in their case, hasn't been successful. Mary's menstrual cycle is irregular and John, although well-intentioned, tends to depression during long periods of abstinence. They have eight children. John is employed as a shipping and receiving clerk at three dollars an hour. Mary keeps house and tends the children. Her doctor, a non-Catholic, has warned her that if she again conceives, she is certain to die in childbirth. Neither Mary nor John has relatives willing to take the children in case of Mary's death. Mary conceives.

The case is further complicated by the tardy discovery (during the eighth month of pregnancy) that the baby Mary carries in her womb rests in the breech position.

Should Mary and John accept the advice of their physician, an agnostic who strongly recommends that the head of the baby be crushed and the lifeless child pulled from Mary's womb with forceps? Or should they ignore the doctor and leave Mary and the child in the hands of Divine Providence.[1]

Obviously, there is no solution to Mary and John's dilemma that is both morally correct and serves justice all around. Should the innocent child be murdered to save the life of a mother of eight and the wife of an incontinent, three-dollar-an-hour clerk (no longer young) who, although in obvious need of a woman's comfort, could hardly find a mate (not on his wages) to replace his beloved Mary and assume the responsibility for so many motherless children?

We tried and tried, my class did, to work out a solution to the perplexing case Father O'Beirne had posited. Most resolved to hope for the best, urge Mary to carry the baby to term and leave the rest up to God. Doctors are not omniscient, they said. Those students got A's. A few said 'Crush the baby's skull, save the mother.' These failed. I argued that the problem was not moral so much as political. Day care centers and decent wages would reduce the problem to its essence—a life for a life. Our socioeconomic system had robbed John and Mary Flynn of free will. Without free will, as Thomas Aquinas would be the first to assert, ethics is irrelevant. I received a C in the course.[2]

Although I developed my moral method in Father O'Beirne's classes, formal ethics holds little interest for me. The thud of Kevin's head against the wall... Sound moral

---

1 Reprinted from a blurred mimeographed copy still in my possession. I was unable to get the permission of the author, Father O'Beirne, but have chosen to reprint it anyway.

2 Never underestimate the Jesuits. Consider the case of Teilhard de Chardin, the famous Jesuit paleontologist. The Society of Jesus silenced the heretic for seventy years but did not burn his manuscripts.

principals, like a good roux brun, come from constant cooking. Morality is an extract drawn from the stew pot of history. Pile the totality of man's experience into the thick skillet of a good mind and simmer. Simmering is to the kitchen arts as contemplation is to the soul: Truth lies in reduction.

My fellow teachers, mostly educated at the takeout counters of higher education, never grasped this principle. They could not taste the porridge for the peas. How often I listened to their complaints, sniping at this rule or that regulation while never admitting that if education is to be relevant, it must be shaped by those who make it, students and teachers, and not those fey men over in the Chancery. If only my fellow teachers would—

Why, I nearly forgot! I must run down to the fish market. I'm expecting a friend for dinner and I plan to serve Filet of Sole, Bonne Femme. It's my signature dish and I'm told it compares favorably with those served in the very best French restaurants. A lady friend of mine proclaimed it to be one of the two or three best dishes she ever tasted. After eating my fish, Monica suggested we should marry. I declined, graciously, and mentioned my spiritual betrothal to Sister Philomena. I don't think Monica really understood.

RUPERT COULDN'T MAKE it. An important business deal demanded his presence. He promised though to send a little something in compensation. If he's generous, I'll record the gesture in my Black Books; if not, his name will be scratched.

VIOLENCE HAS ALWAYS perplexed me. Growing up in an Irish ghetto of South Omaha caught in the last throes of its own

Hundred Years War did little to resolve the conflict I felt, even at an early age, between my own nonviolent instincts and the rest of mankind's immutable urge to aggression. Our neighborhood, but no one from my immediate family, had waged war on the other Southside ethnic clans for as long as anyone could remember. Fearful of the appeal barbarism has to the young, my parents sent me at the age of nine to Band of Angels School, located in a part of the city distant from our own, to be civilized and perhaps saved by the Sisters of Mercy of Baton Rouge. My first day of school, I promptly fell from my chair, dazed by a four-pound volume of *America, Yes!* wielded by Sister Barbara, an aged and dour nun with yellowed parchment skin, when I snickered at her inability to pronounce the word 'statistics.' Each time she tried, she stuttered, finally substituting 'numbers' instead. I was called before Sister Mary Superior to explain my behavior and did so in a pious little homily on the need for peace and harmony 'in a world torn by strife,' both words and theme lifted from TV reruns of Monsignor Sheehan's favorite Sunday sermons, the words of which I now knew by heart. Sister Superior, like Sister Barbara, was not amused. She justified the harsh discipline Sister Barbara upon occasion meted out by drawing attention to the anarchy rumored to exist in the tax-supported schools of our city. At a later age I would have questioned the effectiveness of Sister Superior's reasoning by reminding her that if civilization is to be meaningful, it must be elected and not imposed. But even a child as precocious as I had no such command of temper and language. My response, when Sister allowed me to make one, was spontaneous and from the heart. "Sister," I said, and touched my temple gently with the fingers of my right hand, "my head feels just like it did when that white-trash, public-school kid clubbed me with his book bag."

For expressing this honest though reckless remark, Sister made me stay after school and clean every blackboard in every classroom for a week. Punishment, I would say, neither cruel nor unusual, and sufficiently humane to indicate that modern social thought had reached at least the leadership of the Sisters of Mercy of Baton Rouge.

Later, in senior high school, I was taught by the Little Brothers of Divine Grace. They employed all the common forms of discipline plus some new to my experience. Sister Philomena had by this time decided the next step in my career, one that would require me to grow my hair long so that later on there might be something to shear. Sister forbade me to tell anyone of her ambitions for me. When my hair reached my shoulders and Brother Aloysius told me to cut it, I could only reply that his request ran counter to "orders received from powers I'm in no position to ignore." Brother Aloysius was a man of little faith and, in response to my impertinence, implied that an orifice rather than pendant flesh occupied the intersection of my legs and torso. Brother's genitalia were conveniently concealed beneath the ample fall of his soutane, roguishly cinched to his hips by the low-slung line of a knotted cincture. John Wayne or Greta Garbo? Who's to know?

The community of the faithful I belonged to in my youth told me that we were the last bastion of decency and order. Ah, the incense and the shadows. Gold-toned tenors chanting the Mass in B flat major. The citadel of civilization in an otherwise barbaric world. I tell myself now—Oh, what went wrong? In pursuit of what sectarian ambitions did the spirit of humanism abdicate to the likes of Brother Aloysius?

When I first came to New York City, I read of classroom incidents in the public schools that made those rumored to occur in parochial schools pale by comparison. TV and the daily papers reported frightening examples of student anarchy. They still do, each successive article marking an escalation in terror. Recently, right here in Manhattan, the morning tabloid described the actual burning of a chemistry teacher by his disgruntled students. An auto-da-fé of our times, although aborted. The torched victim survived.

The students used lighter fluid for fuel. I pictured the wretched boys dancing around the terrified man, each squirting fluid from a Ronson can, yelping in ecstasy as their teacher burned. Every schoolboy's dream come true.

For these reasons I had to ask myself why the boys of St. Lucy's suppressed their wildest fantasies. Was it because of Bull Belloli, the Brooklyn Hitter? Or Greek O'Grady, the Great Intimidator? Or was it out of admiration for Virgil Quinn, Prometheus Unchained.

Excessive delicacy, I thought, might account for my revulsion with the hall scene. Perhaps my feelings were an affectation, and more indicative of my own moral shortcomings than instinctive proof of institutionalized brutality. Prim distaste or just wrath? Making fine distinctions is maddening to a man of my sensitivity, yet my disposition compels me to draw more than my share. A martyrdom of sorts, the consequence of doubt, the sin of the apostle Thomas. It is for this God punishes me. Once, when custom ruled my life, morality was a simple matter—I confessed my sins and reserved my wrath for Republicans in power. Now...oh, ours is a terrible time!

When asked if his parishioners still confessed their sins, one of those reformist Dutch priests replied, 'not many.' Then asked what use he made of the confessional boxes lining the walls of his ancient church, he answered, 'they make fine broom closets.' So much of what I once believed seemed similarly obsolete.

Yet I did not despair. Be creative, I told myself. Find new uses for old disciplines. God sent you to this cul de sac of education for a purpose. Discover how to accomplish that goal, then pray for the courage to see it through.

It is all too easy in times of grave disorder to resort to violence. Humane response to bizarre behavior requires constant study and reflection.

True, the boys of St. Lucy's could be provocative. Think of an entire class of forty-eight young men breaking wind simultaneously. But what boys are not gross? And sons of the working class besides, where men who have acquired proper parlor manners are more often mocked than praised for their refinement. A resourceful teacher learns to retaliate in ways befitting the behavior that provoked him. Take the time Andrew Coogan froze my lecture on the Suffragette Movement in America by calling out, "There's something awful in the wastebasket."

"Awful? In the wastebasket? What could be so awful and escape my attention?"

"Disgusting," Coogan replied in horror, when I knew that absolutely nothing disgusted the boy other than my attempts to civilize him.

I could have prudishly ignored the incident and bullied the class to attention by striking the insolent boy who dared interrupt the course of learning. That's what too many of my colleagues would have done. But I would not strike without need and I could not tolerate, not if I was to retain my dignity, a class of forty-eight sixteen-year-old snickering boys for the remainder of the hour.

Draped over the edge of the otherwise empty wastebasket was a used prophylactic. I was shocked at its freshness.

How? Where? In an all-boys school? St. Lucy's boys might talk about sex with girls, but they confined their growing need for release to autoerotic experimentation. Coogan, of course. Late for class. Perverse child! So young, and already adding kinky aberrations to stolen moments of pleasure.

I was attentive to the perennial student demand for relevancy in education and decided to take this opportunity to demonstrate the interdisciplinary dependence of science, art and social studies. Without further delay I slipped the tip of my pointer beneath the repulsive thing and lifted it from the basket for all to see. I carried it at eye level before the boys sitting in the first row. Then a quick venture down the center aisles, swishing the nasty thing about.

"Take notes," I snapped, "on what I'm about to say." I smiled pleasantly.

"The item you see dangling from the black rubber tip of my pointer is properly called a prophylactic. P-R-O-P-H-Y-L-A-C-T-I-C. You know it perhaps by one of its more common names—condom, rubber, or even scum bag. The prophylactic—the word is derived from the Greek *prophylacktikos*, itself a derivative of the infinitive *prophylassein*, to guard against"— I felt a pang of sadistic pleasure here, observing their futile efforts to spell the Greek and keep up with my lecture—"is an elongated elastic bag constructed from highly tensile rubber. It is, of course, difficult to discern the original design from the specimen you see before you." I gave the pointer a little shake, causing the condom to jiggle obscenely. "I will sketch an outline of an unused prophylactic on the board."

My ability to execute accurate line drawings without interrupting the even flow of a lecture is well known and has been of great help to me as a teacher. Unfortunately, teaching American history provides few legitimate opportunities to develop one's skill in describing the human anatomy. My sketch of the penis erect lacked proportion: Standing back to admire my work, the corona seemed grossly exaggerated; the prophylactic to the right of it, however, with arrows indicating the method of fitting it to the penis, bore an obvious relationship to the drawing of the human organ to the left.

"It's even more difficult," I continued, "to discern the ingenuity of the condom's design from the one hanging from my pointer. Once used, the seminal discharge causes the fragile rubber membrane to cohere into the pale amorphous glob you see before you.

"As you can see from my three-dimensional drawing, the prophylactic is designed to slip over the penis. The manufacturers package their product rolled, from base to tip, in such a way that the resulting disk, about the size of a half-dollar, a coin no longer in circulation, can be quickly fitted by simply placing the disk on the head of the erect penis and unrolling the stocking-like device down the length of the hardened muscle.

"The purpose of the receptacle we have before us is obvious from its sad condition. Do you wish to tell the class, Andrew, what that purpose is? Yes, Andrew? Speak up!"

"Ah…Mr. Quinn, I'd…ah…rather…."

"I understand, Andrew.

"The purpose of the condom, despite the lies printed by its manufacturers on men's room dispensers, is to prevent conception—or as you no doubt phrase it, knocking the girl up. Unless ruptured by the fornicator's too strenuous movements, this objective is achieved. The semen gushing from the penis at the moment of ejaculation is caught in the bulbous end of the disposable bag you see before you. The used condom, and that half of the potential human being contained therein, is

subsequently flushed down the toilet. Never dropped care-
lessly into a wastebasket, Andrew, or discarded on tenement
rooftops or on isolated roadsides—those places in every community made sacred by the timeless ritual of defloration...."

I paused a moment to let the boys catch up with their
notes.

"Designs vary," I continued. "What you see here is the standard American model. There are others. The French tickler—no
doubt conceived by the French but developed, marketed and
used primarily in America, not France—contains short nibs
of hard rubber near the rounded head of the prophylactic. A
rapid raking movement of these small protuberances"—here
I spiked the tip of my blackboard drawing with a number of
short quills—"against the walls of the vagina"—which I rapidly sketched—"are added to this more sophisticated version
of the prophylactic to extract, presumably, a frenzied reaction
from the female. Such effete embellishments of the quite cleverly sculpted penis, *au naturel,* are if not indecent, then at least
superfluous.

"But then I'm neither a Francophile nor am I Japanese. As
in so many fields of frivolous manufacture, the Japanese com-
pete with our own imaginative designers of sexual toys. They
have, I've heard, perfected a prophylactic capable of extension
beyond the natural length of the male organ. I don't know
how this is accomplished, having no need myself for such
artificial aggrandizements. These more expensive Japanese
models come in a wide variety of dayglow colors.

"The condom, however, has become somewhat passé in the
urban West. Educated in parochial schools all your life, where
virginity is still considered the loftiest virtue a young man
can bring to marriage, you are probably only aware by hear-
say of the preference for 'the pill' among the young pagans of

our society. Just as well. Surveys show a shocking increase of VD among American youth of your generation. This is due to the heightened pleasure but total lack of hygienic protection—remember: *prophylassein*, to guard against—offered by 'the pill.' I will not go into the details of this chemical contraceptive other than to say that both the Holy Father and the WLF—the Women's Liberation Front, of which I'm an auxiliary member—condemn 'the pill' for reasons moral, political and biochemical.

"In closing I would suggest you stick with masturbation,"—and I glanced at the beet-red face of Andrew Coogan—"but if you must indulge, then you should know that prophylactics come in three sizes—regular, large and jumbo. Mr. Nader, or whoever is looking out for the consumer nowadays, should see to the proper labeling of the condom—small, medium and large. Until he does, I recommend Trojan regulars. If you find even these too large, just roll down the top, much as your grandmother does her stockings."

I thought this one of my better lectures, but then extemporaneous speaking has always been my special province. And so much more effective than overworked lectures based on research.

The following day I quizzed the boys on the matter. Coogan, I was amazed to learn, passed the quiz with an 85. I had reached the boy at last.

Bold challenges to my authority, like the Condom Incident, took more out of me than I dared to reveal to my students or wished to admit to myself. I have always been a man who prefers to be in control of his situation. As examples of absolute authority become increasingly rare, even in the Church, holding on to any authority at all requires progressively more imaginative approaches. The truly great teacher is not content with knowing the truth; he must also learn how to render his audience receptive. To do both requires great resources of spiritual and moral insight.

Prophets labor under a lot of stress. Every artist worth the name pictures John the Baptist as a wild-eyed neurotic, preaching an unwanted message to a conservative crowd. The Baptist and I had a lot in common. Both of us expected kudos for our revolutionary message and got instead brickbats and demeaning epithets. Both of us have known exile—he to his desert, I from my classroom.

No one seems to know how St. John dealt with stress. We do know, because of his untimely death at the hands of Salome, that he did not turn to women at the end of a hard day's preaching. Locusts and honey? Perhaps. Health food friends of mine tell me that over-indulgence in sweets is a habit common to high-strung achievers and use Adolph Hitler as the classic example. Although none of my friends could name a study done on the nutritional content of the desert locust, all insisted that locusts were preferable to Valium, so why not give it a try? Insects, as Monica, my health food guru, pointed out, were an excellent source of lowfat protein and therefore an ideal complement to a high-sugar diet of honey. Unfortunately, I couldn't follow their advice. It would have violated my dietary laws. I hadn't eaten sweets since the age of eleven and the onset of puberty. Yes, eleven. I was a precocious child.

Discipline. The survival of the species depends on it. We live in an age where the feminine aesthetic is synonymous with emaciation, yet half of our women sport Rubenesque figures. So do the men. I don't mourn these statistics. Natural selection did not cease when the first ape stood upright to reach for yet another banana. If Darwin were alive today to determine who should flourish, who should perish, he would measure man's girth, not weigh his brain. Measuring my waist, a trim twenty-nine and one-half inches, he would mark me down as a survivor.

I learned will power under the tutelage of Sister Philomena. "Virgil," Sister told me one day after school when I offered to clean the blackboards, "you're getting spots." I had never heard the word 'spots' used in such a context, and I waited for Sister to explain. "Here," she said, and tapped her dimpled chin with her forefinger. "God gave you skin women will envy," she said as she stroked my cheek with a forefinger (I remember the smell of chalk dust). "Repay Him by preserving it as long as you can." I hung my head in mock humility. I had discovered vanity.

"Lent begins in one week's time," Sister continued. "But for you, Virgil, it will not end on Easter Sunday. First come spots, then fat. Starting on Ash Wednesday, you will give up sweets—forever."

"But Sister," I cried, tears coming to my eyes as I thought of a lifetime of ascetic denial. "I can't! It will be too hard. Everyday I pass three bakery shops on my way to school. I pass them again on my way home." Jam-filled Danish pastry, not Coca-Cola, was my particular addiction.

Sister was firm. "The Lord spent forty days in the desert tempted by more than cream puffs and chocolate eclairs. *He* did not give in. When you weaken, think of Him. To make it easier, avoid the proximity of sin. The shortest way home is often the longest way around."

When I was a child, nuns nearly always talked in maxims. I became skilled at cracking their codes.

Vanity is a powerful motive to self-improvement. Great teacher that she was, Sister Philomena never used the word but recognized my ambition, even at the age of eleven, to look my best. With the arrival of Easter Sunday I had broken the sweets addiction, and I had done it cold turkey. Sitting down to Mother's traditional Easter brunch, I dismayed the dear woman by rejecting her sticky buns, famous throughout our neighborhood, in preference for whole wheat toast, dry. I went on to reject grease and soda pop as well.

Leaving school the day of the Condom Incident, I wished that Sister Philomena had said something about dealing with stress. She rightly foresaw the consequences of over-indulgence, but failed to identify a proper antidote to the inner turmoil that plagued me even from an early age. Add to that the manic high that inevitably follows a great performance such as my handling of the Condom Incident, and I was in need of a little something to calm my nerves. Turning the corner into Eighth Avenue, I entered the proximity of sin. The sweet smell of bourbon wafted through the open doors of the Rose of Sharon Bar & Grill. *The shortest way home, Virgil, is often the longest way around.* I turned to walk uptown and out of harm's way. Midpoint in the next block, blinking neon shamrocks beckoned to me from the County Cork. McMahon's stood opposite, inviting me in for 'Happy Hour/ Shot and a Beer/Two for One.' When Sister spoke of avoiding the proximity of sin, she had obviously never been to New York City.

I joined the men of the County Cork standing shoulder to shoulder the length of long bar, working men mostly, floating away their cares on clouds of Irish Mist. Just one to quiet my nerves, I promised. Tomorrow I'll take the pledge…well, maybe nothing so absolute as that, but sign up for a course in stress management. Maybe.

Standing at the bar waiting to order, my eyes lingered on my image reflected in the backbar mirror. A single flaw marred the face confronting me. I took comfort in the slight break in the line of my chiseled nose, the consequence of a youthful mishap, a scandalous incident that I will relate in good time if only to correct Sister Philomena's stubborn mis-reading of the event that caused our near parting of the ways. A broken nose lent character to my perhaps too perfect features and made me feel more one of the boys, surrounded as I was now by men of rugged mien.

"What are you drinking, Mac."

It was not the bartender who asked, but the man standing next to me, as short and muscled as I was tall and lean. Working class; I liked that. Men like Mike took me back to my roots.

"Shot and a beer. What about yourself?"

"Sounds good to me," and we went through the charade of buying each other drinks, he paying for mine, I his, he mine, back and forth. It was Friday after all. No harm in making a night of it.

"My place or yours," Mike asked when remaining upright for either of us required the support of the bar.

The cabby pulled up to my building and I opened the curbside door to get out. Mike twisted around to follow me out of the cab. I reached in to give him a hand and, leaning on each other for support, we made our way up five flights of stairs to my apartment, an indiscretion I would never have allowed if I'd been sober.

6

M Y FELLOW TEACHERS, PRUDES that they were, disapproved of my teaching methods. Among themselves they approached things pubic with giggles and double entendres exactly as did their students. My frank and nonviolent response to classroom pranks designed to embarrass the teacher and diminish his authority both shocked and confused these men. Presented with the Condom Incident they would have resorted to primitive forms of discipline more suited to a barracks than a classroom. Because physical punishment was the method upon which they most often relied, they had first to identify the boy responsible for the disruption—brutalizing an entire class might well have sparked a riot. To find the boy, they terrorized the class with threats of mass punishment until the prankster, out of a sense of honor not shared by his teacher, delivered himself over to be abused or sent to the office for suspension.

My colleagues never learned the alternative uses of power. Their education had not even taught them where to turn for instruction. When Mother Murphy, for example, was having more trouble than usual with his class of French II boys—someone had set off a string of firecrackers in his classroom, which, given the criminal state of the streets, caused Mother to flee the room in hysterics—I advised him to read Machiavelli's *The Prince* and study the Great Florentine's methods of asserting control over unruly subjects. In the discussion to follow, Mother consistently referred to Prince Matchabelli, confusing Machiavelli's classic work on political tactics with the popular perfume advertised on his TV soap operas, and he wondered aloud if it made good business sense for corporations to market products so dissimilar as textbooks on discipline and exotic scents. Amidst such confusion there was little I could do to help, and so I remained the only teacher at St. Lucy's to master the art of student manipulation, a skill no disciplinarian can afford to be without.

I was alone except for the brilliant Greek O'Grady, who not only competed with me in knowledge of subject matter, but surpassed me in his ability to control troublesome students. Greek was a master of control. He knew the art and chose to pervert it, surpassing even the remarkable Bull Belloli in the number of boys ill used in any given week.

Besides his grasp of higher mathematics, O'Grady was thoroughly grounded in the classical languages. We were alike in that we had both passed through the hands of the Jesuits. There the resemblance ends. O'Grady mastered the language of the ancient Greeks while utterly failing to grasp the humanistic thrust of their civilization. I, on the other hand, chose to read Homer in translation, freeing me to reflect upon the ethic that raised the Greek pedagogical system to heights unique in the Western world. O'Grady concentrated on language, the better to scribble provocative lines from Greek lyricists on the term papers of favored students.

But I don't wish to mislead. If O'Grady chose to squander his talents, that was his affair. His public behavior, however, would have been sufficient cause for his dismissal. How many times had O'Grady ruined my lunch and stolen minutes from the precious few I had to eat it in! Always, day after day, I was forced to listen to his harangues against defenseless minorities.

"Tripping through the Rambles in sneakers and tight white chinos. Trying to look half their age. If the fuckin' cops in this town had the balls, they'd bust the whole flitting swarm of them."

Language like this from a man steeped in the poetry of Virgil and Homer.

"What right has he to single out a few unfortunates for persecution?" I directed my impotent protest to Mother Murphy, expecting a sympathetic response. Greek O'Grady, six foot three, bullet-headed and hard-eyed, recalled too graphically the feared and hated Brother Aloyisus from my high school days to attack him directly.

"You'd think they were Jews," Mother Murphy murmured, referring to those the Greek chose to persecute.

Greek O'Grady was a typical example of the colonial mentality prevalent at St. Lucy's. Sons of the ghetto trying to demonstrate their right to full citizenship by surpassing the overlord in degree of oppression. And what, by the way, was O'Grady doing in the Rambles? Bird watching?

If O'Grady mercifully relented for a day or two in his persecution of those lonely men in the park, he poisoned my lunch with demeaning comments directed to the boys he was paid to teach. We all sat in the faculty lunchroom up a short flight of stairs from the cafeteria. Each day I would hear the hush announcing O'Grady's entrance into the student cafeteria. For a moment the boys would stare silently into their plates, waiting for him to pass on his way upstairs. Without pausing even to check out Mrs. Gabriola's menu— the man seldom ate, O'Grady asked of the gathered faculty, "Who'll I punch today? Pick out someone once a day. Knock him around. Keeps the little jerk-offs in line." He would be greeted by good-natured guffaws emitted between gulps of over-cooked spaghetti and dry yellow cake iced with thick pink frosting.

He never punched Majestic de Angelo, however, or Principe Mangora. He wouldn't want to mar their pretty faces. (Personally, I thought their looks too Greek.) Primo de Popalano, with his bold Sicilian features, O'Grady punched at will.

I suppose it was the boy de Angelo who told O'Grady of my condom lecture, or Principe Mangora, one of his spies.

The day following my condom lecture, O'Grady and I were alone in the faculty lunch room.

"I hear you're teaching birth control in your classes, Virgil," O'Grady began. "How did you fit that into the history curriculum?"

"When I mention birth control at all," I replied, "it's as the guiding principle of a movement. Questions on Margaret Sanger are included on eight out of ten Regent Exams."

I returned to reading the *Times,* waiting for lunch to be sent in.

"Let me give you a piece of advice, Virgil. You're new here." O'Grady's tone was civil, if condescending: I was the student, he the teacher. "Coogan is a little wiseass, and there are a lot more like him in this school. When they pull shit like that, slap 'em down. You'll be doing yourself and the rest of us a favor."

"I never expected teaching to be easy, Gerald." The gall of the man! Presuming to give me lessons on student control. "Besides," I added, "I abhor violence, especially when perpetrated on the young."

O'Grady's expression switched from condescending smile to threatening sneer. "You guys fresh down from Fordham—think you can turn it all around, set up paradise on earth."

"Thank you for the compliment, Gerald, that I appear to be of college age. Correct diet, plenty of sleep.... Actually, I am a recent graduate, but not as young as you—and so many others—imagine. Before enrolling at Fordham, I spent several years...well, exploring other lives."

For a moment I toyed with the thought of letting O'Grady in on the secret of those other lives, if only to shock him into silence.

When O'Grady next spoke, his voice turned threatening. I had scorned his advice.

"Other lives. Like learning the art of blackboard pornography."

"I don't consider lessons on the human anatomy pornographic."

"When has the human anatomy—illustrated—become part of the history curriculum?"

"The history of man is a comprehensive subject."

O'Grady was obviously out to get me. I folded the *Times*. I would leave the bitter man to himself. But where to go? The classrooms were all in use. Murphy would be teaching in the library this hour. To escape O'Grady, I would have to leave the school, spend what remained of my free period at Tina's, sure to be jammed at this hour of the day.

O'Grady tightened the screws.

"You're wasting your time on birth control lessons, Virgil. Pills and condoms will soon be obsolete. Too many faggots. If it gets much worse, we'll be force-feeding women fertility drugs."

Was the man suggesting that I was part of the problem? I glanced up from my paper. Impossible to tell. The same insinuating sneer. That was O'Grady's power, the reckless use to which he put his skill at instilling fear through innuendo. In a school of adolescent boys unsure of their masculinity and a faculty of men only one of whom was married, everyone walked in fear of being labeled. I chose a rational response drawn from history.

"When the population of Ireland reached nine million souls—three times what the island could support—half the men ceased to marry. To compensate these harbingers of ZPG..."—O'Grady frowned in ignorance of the acronym—"of zero population growth, God in His Justice and Mercy provided alternative consolation."

"They joined the priesthood," O'Grady warned me.

"Or chose to teach in boys' schools."

O'Grady turned livid. "And what do you mean by that?"

O'Grady's voice had dropped to a harsh whisper. He stood up. He was very tall. He gripped the back of the folding chair with his large hands turning white at the knuckles. He would not attack me physically, would he? Oh, the scandal: One teacher, the big one, beating up on the slighter.

I wished to say, "You're approaching forty, Mr. O'Grady. Why haven't you married?" I said nothing. There was something so intimidating about the man, his great size, the suddenness with which he slipped into violent temper, and worst of all, the malice of his smile. Even if he did not assault me physically, if I dared to defend those men in the park whom O'Grady attacked with such venom, would he step up his defamation of me? If Kevin O'Connor was right, it was O'Grady who first matched me to the Virgin Queen, a byname meant to ridicule my natural attributes of beauty, brains and breeding. He had stopped at joking insinuation then only because he was convinced of my harmlessness. I posed no threat to his debased domination of faculty lunchroom entertainment as long as I kept my humble place. In the past I had listened to his and Brother Adolph's crude allusions to the boys' burgeoning sexuality without objection. What further rumors might he plant if he discovered that I was not the effete pushover he believed me to be?

"I meant that men who do not marry, who lack sons of their own, might seek to satisfy their paternal instincts in alternative roles. Some go into the priesthood. Others teach the young. Some try to fuse the roles of father and lover, and fall by the wayside. Others—"

I broke off, hearing the cock crow thrice.

My shameful capitulation ignited an anger in me I was careful to conceal but determined to nourish. I returned to the *Times* and reflected on what I knew of the man. I was ticking off indications of possible vulnerability when Francis X. McDougal, who the students referred to as Brother Adolph, entered the room where I sat alone with O'Grady. Brother was no longer a Little Brother of Divine Grace. Not anymore. He had been released from his vows by special dispensation of Pope John XXIII for reasons known only to the provincial of his order. He had requested and been granted the permission to continue on as a teacher of English literature. Today he wore a natty three-piece suit in houndstooth check. I barely nodded when he entered, and buried my face the *Times*.

"That little bastard Muldoon," Brother Adolph began before he had so much as washed the chalk from his hands. "I caught him in the john again, beating-off."

I looked up from my paper to announce that tens of thousands of people had descended on Washington to protest our involvement in the war raging in Vietnam. Neither Brother Adolph nor O'Grady took note of the interruption.

"How did you do it, Francis?" O'Grady asked. "He's too fast for me. By the time I find him he's finished and got his pants up."

"I saw him bug down the stairs between second and third periods, so I told the class if they opened their mouths, they'd find them too painful to chew. By the time I could get to the can, Muldoon'd locked himself in the crapper, so I took off my shoes so he couldn't hear me coming and…"

Again I folded up the Times, opened my briefcase and slipped the paper between The Pageant of History and The American Republic. I considered retreating to the park, it was a dry day, but by now it was too late to walk over to Union Square and return in time for lunch. So I locked myself in the faculty bathroom and did not come out until I heard the babble of new voices as more teachers entered the room. While I lunched on Mrs. Gabriola's canned ravioli, I was forced to listen to Brother Adolph's retelling of his nasty little story, egged on by the prurient Greek O'Grady. I spent the remaining three periods of the school day feeding my anger until I had worked myself into such a state of nerves that a stop at the County Cork became a therapeutic necessity.

After a shot and a beer, my anger subsided. I could think again. My thoughts returned to O'Grady, searching for flaws in the fabric of his respectability. What was his hold, for example, over the boys de Angelo and Mangora? Discover that and I might be able to use either the information or the boys themselves to get rid of the man.

Somewhat later that afternoon—perhaps it was evening; the bar had filled and emptied and was filling again—I found the courage to swear that it was either me or the Greek, that St. Lucy's wasn't big enough for the two of us. Not only O'Grady. Belloli, Brother Adolph, maybe even Mother Murphy if I couldn't get him to lay off the Jews. They all had to go. I downed a final shot in celebration of my new resolve, tipped Sean the bartender more than my budget allowed, and left the bar. Passing the church of St. Lucy, I went in to tell the saint of my exciting discovery, how alcohol, properly used, can turn negative vacillation into positive intent. If she smelled the bourbon on my breath, which I doubt she did, her olfactory nerves were so deadened by the scent of incense, she would not chastise me. Lucy's final request, before those pagan men of Sicily plucked out her eyes, is one of the few documented facts surrounding her life on earth. She asked for and received the ancient equivalent of a liter of stout Sicilian red to speed her soul's journey up to heaven.[1]

IT WAS LATE, nearly midnight when I turned the corner onto Avenue B and home. Spring was in the air and the walk across town through the balmy night had cleared my head. The shot and beer—well, perhaps more than one; I made a few stops along the way—had left me wonderfully relaxed and ready for a good night's sleep. I neared the stoop. Nothing between

---

1 *Saints for Our Time,* Sister Philomena Hallihan, SMBR, Pacem in Terris Press, 1953

me and bed now but five flights of stairs. Hang onto the rail, Virgil. You've made it to the top on worse nights than this—

"HELLO, MR. QUINN."

Startled, I turned to look behind me. No one on the street. I peered into the dark well beneath the stoop.

"It's me, Mr. Quinn. Kevin."

"Kevin?" I knew no one by that name likely to be waiting beneath my doorstep at such an hour.

"Kevin O'Connor. It's Kevin O'Connor."

I bent over the rail and peered down into the gloom. "Why Kevin. It's you. I couldn't make you out in the dark."

The boy remained seated on a garbage can and I descended the three steps to his level where I took a seat on the fourth can in the row. In the dim light of the street lamp, the boy's red hair appeared black, his skin florescent white.

"Whatever are you doing down here at this time of night."

I listened as I spoke for slurred vowels. I heard none. No cause for alarm.

"Had a rough night, Mr. Quinn?"

"An opening uptown. An emerging artist, startling vision… But what are you doing here?"

"Waiting for you."

"For me? What for."

"Oh, I don't know. Thought you might like some company."

"How long have you been here?"

"Two hours, I guess."

Two hours! But then the very young have so much time left they pay scant attention to its passing. How long had it been since I had waited two hours for anyone? A very long time. The thought saddened me.

"I want to… I want to talk to you," the boy said. "Can I come up?"

I panicked. If anyone were to see me conduct a student into my building, especially a boy of Kevin's reputation…

"Oh, no, Kevin. Not tonight. It's far too late. And we both have school tomorrow." I was still sitting on the garbage can. I stood up. "Perhaps some other time. Now I think we should both get some sleep."

"I really need—I really want to talk to you."

Kevin looked at me, pleading, his long vigil wasted.

"Well, perhaps," I relented. "Let's walk down to the coffee shop on the corner. It's open late. We can talk there. And I need a cup. How about you?"

Kevin ordered coffee light. I ordered two poached eggs, a half cup of cottage cheese, one toasted English (dry), four stewed prunes with lots of juice, and coffee black. All those shots and beers had left me ravenous. I would fast tomorrow.

"We order by numbers here," the waitress replied. "One, two, three or four. Take your pick."

"Just fill my order, please," I replied politely. I never argue with waitresses.

"One, two, three or four."

I excused myself to Kevin, walked back to the kitchen and spoke to the chef. The man and I shared a nodding acquaintance. We both enjoyed the old-fashioned sport of taking late night strolls on the Avenue. He filled my order.

Poached eggs cool quickly. I finished my midnight breakfast before asking Kevin what it was he wished to talk about.

"I've got to leave home." Kevin spoke without emotion, as if the decision was already made and there was nothing more to do other than work out the details.

There are black Irish and red Irish. I'm a classic example of the former, Kevin the latter. A shock of tousled red
hair curled about the boy's ears and fell over his wide intelligent brow. His lips were full, his skin thin as shell, almost
translucent.

"I need your help, Mr. Quinn."

"You've just turned sixteen, Kevin. Far too young to leave
home."

"Age has nothing to do with it," the boy insisted.

"Have you had a spat with your parents?"

Kevin combed his rumpled hair with slender fingers and
sighed in resignation. "Not a spat. Not the way you mean it
anyway. We fight all the time. Nothing I do is right."

Like so many St. Lucy students, Kevin's parents were
immigrants, once-removed. The paternal grandparents worked
hard to provide their oldest son, Kevin's father, with the leisure to get a high school education. Having leisure, he took
to drink. In some families, notably Celtic families, an over-
fondness for drink is like the propensity of its women to bear
twins—it occurs every other generation. Of the many gifts
God has granted me, I count my falling into the off-genera-
tion as the one for which I am most thankful.

I once met Mr. O'Connor at PTA. He stood in humble, stoned support as Mrs. O'Connor berated the older son,
Kevin, for lacking the manly virtues so conspicuous in the
younger, then asked for my advice on how to turn the boy
around. Recalling this embarrassing scene, I decided that little good could come from my making a personal visit to the
O'Connor home in Middle Village, Queens.

"They just don't want me around," Kevin continued.
"They disapprove. At least my father does, and she goes
along with him."

She. To talk of one's mother like that. A bad sign. I asked for particulars.

"My father calls me a commie-queer, among other things. And she does nothing to shut him up."

"Why that's absurd, Kevin! Doesn't the man know the two camps are bitterly opposed? A Cuban friend of mine began the revolution in that ill-used country selling bonds for Castro and was repaid by being dressed in black pajamas and forced to plant tomatoes under an armed guard of revolutionary cadre. All Communist regimes are puritanical. Doesn't your father read the papers?"

"Just the *Daily News*."

"And you read the *Times*. I see."

Was it necessary to quiz the boy further concerning his problems with his father? Hardly. The man had fathered a son who already far outstripped him intellectually, and instead of taking pride in his accomplishment—or at least his genes—the father felt threatened. Kevin had betrayed both his father and his class.

"As I told you the last time we had a little talk, Kevin, courageous men make a lot of enemies. You were recently struck by a teacher, I believe, for indulging in a bit of adolescent whimsy."

"Oh. I don't mind the Bull so much. At least he doesn't discriminate. Everyone gets hit sooner or later. But when your own father... And he isn't the only one. You must know what O'Grady calls me; *and* Brother Adolph, *and...*"

"Yes, Kevin, I do. And you must know what they call me. You are beginning to discover how vicious our detractors can be. A valuable lesson, one that I learned at a very young age, younger even than yourself. A lesson that takes me back to Omaha..."

To reassure the boy, I repeated the words used by Sister Philomena to console me so many years ago when a vengeful student accused me of stealing his candy. Sister called me in after school to get to the bottom of the affair.

"Do not weep, Virgil," Sister crooned as she wiped tears from my eyes with a man-sized handkerchief she withdrew from one of the many secret pockets nuns have hidden beneath their bibs. The fine linen square, lavishly embroidered with a gothic "P" surrounded by a crown of thorns, smelled of lavender. "Remember that Christ's enemies, before they crucified Him, accused Him falsely. If He had not been accused, He would not have died, and we would not be saved. Knowing this, He forgave His enemies their sin."

Since the ambiguities of my own nature remained to be clarified, the relevance of Sister Philomena's comparison of my ordeal to Christ's passion eluded me. Christ, being divine, could afford to forgive his enemies, especially since He had no choice in the matter: It was all part of God the Father's Eternal Plan. I did not tell Sister then, and I saw no reason to tell Kevin now, how I dealt with snitches and detractors. My record, when revealed, will speak for itself. Instead I reworded the moral of Sister's story to make it serve both men and gods. "The extent to which a man is persecuted, Kevin, measures the degree to which he shares in Christ's divinity."

"I have not been falsely accused, Mr. Quinn," Kevin continued. He raised his eyes to meet mine. They were the purest shade of blue. "The paper I wrote for you, *The Capitalist Mire*, have you read it? I didn't write it just because you assigned the subject."

The paper Kevin referred to ran to thirty-four pages, well beyond the two or three I expected from his classmates.

Half-way through, I realized that the boy had gone rather deeper into his denunciation of capitalism than I was prepared to follow. I passed it on to a recent acquaintance of mine, a professor of political science at NYU, met while making a late-night sortie into one of the less well known quarters of the city, the old meat packing district that occupies a strip of land near the West Side docks only a stone's throw from St. Lucy's. After darkness falls and the streets empty of workers, the district takes on a character unique to the city not to be missed by anyone truly interested in the urban environment and the frenzy of underground night life such a district provides. Leon advised me to submit Kevin's manuscript to the East-West Review. I never got around to it at the time, and I feel guilty now for neglecting the professor's suggestion.

"And as for the rest of my father's hyphenated definition of my character," Kevin said as he puddled his cup of coffee with a spoon, "well, Mr. Quinn, you must know that—"

"Sticks and stones may break my bones..."

As a sophisticated man, what Kevin wished to tell me did not alarm me so much as that he should want to tell me at all. We were friends, foremost. Our being here, student and teacher drinking coffee in a late night café, attested to that. As his friend, I was of course the first to know. As his teacher, I should be the last told. Our difference in position demanded at least the pretense of distance.

"Virgil—" Kevin hesitated.

I looked at Kevin with the suggestion of a frown. Using my given name was a liberty I permitted no student, not even Primo de Popalano. Adolescent boys are changelings. If intimacy breeds contempt, as Sister Philomena insisted, then familiarity with a student is an invitation to blackmail. On the other hand, for Kevin discretion was as much a part of his nature as was his precocious intelligence. Should I allow an exception?

"Mr. Quinn—" Again he hesitated, unsure now how to address me. My smile told him he had made the right choice. "I don't know how to put it. It's just that I need to tell—"

"You know, Kevin, it just came to me. It probably wasn't O'Grady who came up with my nickname—or yours. It was more likely Mr. Murphy. Yes, I actually believe he was the man. We've had some bitter confrontations in the past year, bitter indeed. He simply will not let up on the Jews. And his position is so irrational. Of all the men I know, Mother—ah, Mr. Murphy—has the least reason to complain against the cards fate dealt him. Why, he never ever tried! So of course he's a failure. When I asked him what..."

I rambled on, watching the need to tell fade from eyes blue as a Nebraska sky in May. Now, recalling that moment so long ago, I wonder what part it—and I— played in Kevin's tragic end. Of course, I had no way of knowing then that the boy had no one else to turn to, no one to talk to. I didn't know, for example, that Kevin had abandoned priests at the age of fourteen when the last one he confessed to, a Franciscan monk, accused him of playing into the hands of the Communist conspiracy by indulging in adolescent sexual experiments. My ignorance, not knowing how alone the boy was in his confusion, is my justification for shutting him out. Yet sometimes I think if only as one man to another—But what *could* I do? As much as both of us might have wished it, I could not allow Kevin into my life nor could I enter more closely into his. I could not take the boy in, give him refuge. That would have led to unacceptable complications. I could not even become his mentor in a matter as intimate as a boy's emotional needs. My survival depended on my silence.

When my ramblings had run their course, Kevin laughed, a careless bitter laugh that echoes to me still. It bore no relationship to the comment that followed.

"Mother Murphy? Don't be paranoid, Virgil. The man's as harmless as a Union Square crazy. The guys think he's a joke."

The confessional moment had passed and Kevin fell back into the cynical humor that had until now preserved him.

We sat for a moment longer, sipping coffee that had grown cold.

"I will do what I can, Kevin, to find you a place to stay. I have a friend who works for Family and Children Service. Maybe he can help. I'll call him tomorrow."

I did so.

"Is he being abused?" was the first question Norton put to me. "Physically? Sexually?"

"Well, no. I mean yes, but not the way you say, at least not that I know. His father calls him derogatory names, demeans him."

"There are no statutes governing the language parents can use with their children. But if he gets into trouble, then we can help him. We have shelters for boys waiting for a hearing or just back from reformatories. Other than that, there's not much he can do but wait it out, put in his time."

But Kevin was running out of time. The conversation I had with him that night at the coffee shop was one of the last times I would talk to him outside the classroom. I have related what I have to demonstrate how little even a teacher as sensitive to the problems of youth as I could do to help a boy in trouble. I listened—to as much as I could afford to hear. I had been expelled from my first career and decency forbade me to return to my second. To have done more to help Kevin now would have put my third career, teaching the young, in jeopardy, and if a man must choose between work and the heart, he would fall below the expectations of his gender to choose the latter.

7

S EAN, THE BARTENDER AND philosopher in residence at
the County Cork, was telling me that fate had replaced
the social environment as the causal principle explaining the
lives of tragic men.

I had just come from a conversation with Primo de Popalano during which I had extracted from the boy the shocking
means Kevin had used to resolve his dilemma. After hearing the news, I found myself heading for the County Cork
more for Sean's advice than for whatever solace a shot and a
beer might bring.

I arrived during the afternoon lull, and Sean was filling
his brief respite from thirsty customers by organizing the bar.
Using a small tin funnel he poured nearly empty bottles of
bar bourbon into one labeled Wild Turkey, a practice certainly illegal but not likely to be reported because I was the
only witness to Sean's deception. When he finished with the
bourbon, he began on the Scotch. As he poured he went on
with his discourse.

"I wouldn't let this seeming denial of absolutes disturb me, Virgil," Sean said, elaborating on his take on tragic men. "Revisionist theories are as common to philosophy as they are to history. Confronted by the bizarre, the horrendous, the gratuitously cruel, man shifts from mythology to science and finally to the stars in his attempt to interpret the unacceptable.

"Not that things were always so," Sean added. "When I wrote my dissertation at the University of Chicago, I held that a child's environment, at least if the child was poor, determined his future. Born to poverty, blighted for life. Criminal child, look to the slums. That was the mantra when I was young. I suppose we all read too much back then, both students and teachers. All those novels of the Forties and Fifties with their naïve assignments of cause and effect. Now, with the kids from every class ignoring common sense—born in Westchester County, popping pills at ten—we invoke fate, or random chance, to explain it all: Some in all societies will seek out self-destruction. Spin the genetic wheel and hope it passes your number by. So much for Marx and his bunch."

Before Sean was called away to serve the first wave of the five o'clock rush, he poured me a shot from the bourbon blend he had just prepared. Not bad, actually, not for the price.

As I sipped, I searched my own experience for proof or refutation of what Sean had said. I recalled Monica, my lady friend who fell into a state of morbid guilt accompanied by crippling depression when her teenage daughter chose, for the third time, to return to the bondage of the pimp who had first debauched her. Monica sought the help of her priest-therapist. "Why is she doing this?" she asked of her daughter. In the opinion of the therapist, the pimp offered the daughter a security Monica had failed to provide. Monica's guilt deepened.

When the daughter's behavior did not change, despite her mother's efforts to make her feel secure, Monica returned to the priest-therapist for advice. Father Doherty, an intelligent and articulate man when Monica first sought his counsel several years previous, had in the intervening years been born again.

"Since your daughter is obviously in the clutches of Satan," Father Doherty insisted, "there's nothing to do but pray."

The priest then commanded Monica to kneel with him as he broke into a highly emotional plea for direct intervention on the part of God in All His Forms and Powers. They beseeched the heavens for a month like that, the two of them. When prayer did not prove efficacious, Monica sunk into deep depression.

I didn't see Monica for some months. When she next called, it was to invite me over for Sunday brunch. Her mood had lifted; she was her old optimistic self. I inquired, discretely, whether her daughter had resolved her problems.

"Oh, not at all. Worse than ever," Monica replied with a contradictory smile. "She'll never change. She's wanton, you know."

I repressed my doubts concerning the adequacy of her summing up and joined Monica with a smile that matched her joyful approbation of life.

Some thought Kevin O'Connor wanton. Brother Principal was of that opinion, although he did not use the word. Some weeks after my late night talk with Kevin in the coffee shop, Brother had called me in for a scheduled conference dealing with problem students during which Kevin's name came up. Brother spoke of the boy's 'rebellious nature,' and warned that his 'willful rejection of the Faith would lead to his destruction.'

Brother Principal was never strong in logic. I unraveled this flaw in his education by pointing out that a man's nature is, by definition, a given. "If it is Kevin's nature to rebel, then it follows that his rejection of the Faith, if indeed he has rejected it, can hardly be willful. The latter would, it seems, follow necessarily from the former. Such a logical progression leads us deep into the heresy of predestination and—"

"Let me suggest," Brother cut me off, "that you make an appointment with Father McGraw, Monsignor Delaney's new assistant. He's fresh out of the seminary and should be able to treat the subject better than I."

I did not talk with the young assistant; I could not accept Brother Principal's medieval analysis of Kevin's behavior; Monica's resolution of her problem seemed therapeutically wise but hardly served to explain Kevin's tragic end; and I wished to get the opinion of science before assuming that my own analysis of the event was the correct one. For all these reasons I called on Mr. Stanley O'Fallon, teacher of biology at Mother Help of Christians and the only scientist in my acquaintance. (Bull Belloli, biology teacher at St. Lucy's, was an impostor.)

Stanley was a *Mischling*. His mother was Jewish and his father Irish, facts he had revealed to me one evening during after-school drinks at the County Cork. I mention Stanley's Jewish mother because of the assurance I derived from his disclosure. One could rely on a Jewish biologist to give a rational opinion. Jews, even half-Jews like Stanley, can ill afford the dark luxury of superstition.

"Kevin's behavior," Stanley told me, "was programmed from birth. Certain genetic combinations render the recipient incapable of dealing with his environment and the threats it contains." Trying further to console me, Stanley began a long dissertation on the mysteries of recombinant DNA. I nodded at what I presumed to be appropriate moments while understanding not a word he said. I could not tell the man that the study of biology to the Sisters of Mercy of Baton Rouge, who taught me all I know of the subject, consisted mostly of the pleasurable exercise of fixing autumn leaves to the thick pages of one's personal scrapbook. DNA was yet to de discovered. Sister Mary Beatrix, under whom I studied the subject, was reputed to be eighty years old and speaking of retirement. When she studied biology, genetics had not yet probed much beyond Mendel and his peas. I ordered another round for Stanley and me and finished my shot and a beer about the same time that Stanley concluded his lecture.

"Can science determine," I asked, " the genetic combinations likely to produce doomed creatures?"

"Such a possibility does exist," Stanley assured me, 'but to do it we must first decode the human genome, and that will take centuries.'

So it was fated. Whether marked by the curse of Cain or skewered by a faulty helix, the causes behind our behavior seemed determined by forces beyond our control.

I retreated to history in search of answers, or rather into literature, history's richest repository. There is, however, little time in a reformer's schedule for reading works other than his own, and I turned to my only published work, the historical epic, *Philomena of the Plains*.[1] In *Philomena* I dealt at length—the poem runs to 432 lines—with innocence and early death. I was barely sixteen and despondent when I wrote the poem, and my attempt to reconcile God's Will with the

---

1   See Vol. 1, No. 1, p. 3 ff of the *Omahahan Review*. The *Omahahan* ceased publication after its initial issue.

reality of Sister Philomena's sudden death at so young an age
was not entirely successful. I had fallen back on what I had
been taught, that 'God works in mysterious ways,' a conclusion that both begged the question and lessened the dramatic
impact of my work.

Was God again at work?

I didn't ask this question idly. How much easier it would
have been to accept Monica's interpretation of her daughter's
fall, or that Kevin had been programmed by God or science—they both come to the same thing, don't they? Either
explanation would exempt all of us—Kevin's parents, friends
and teachers—from any moral responsibility in the affair.
Conclusions that ignore history are best left to the intellectually lazy and the morally weak. I could not forget Kevin's
painful years at St. Lucy's, nor cease to reflect on what part
I might have played in making them so. If I had been bolder,
could I have found a way to protect the boy?

Yet I had done what I could, I tell myself that. Knowing the boys taunted Kevin for carrying around the operatic
recordings he was so fond of, I had purposely asked him in
class to pick me up a ticket the next time he camped out at
the Met waiting for the discount tickets to go on sale. Later I
set aside an entire period to discuss twentieth-century sopra-
nos, culminating in my own interpretation, sung a cappella
and entirely in falsetto, of the mad scene from *Lucia de Lam-
mermoor*. I would like to have played a recording of Joan
Sutherland's rendition of the extended aria if only to give
the students a more balanced impression of the soprano's art,
but the school possessed but one phonograph and it was not
in repair. So I did what I could with the scene, which was a
great deal indeed. I had heard—and more important seen—
Joan perform the role some years earlier. I remembered her

dramatics well. It was the only opera I'd ever found time to attend, a fact that made my recollections of it vivid indeed.[1]

Following my operatic debut, I heightened my reputation as a patron of the arts, and indirectly lent support to Kevin's cultural aspirations, by inviting a boy or two upon occasion to the ballet, paying for the tickets out of my already pathetic salary. Word got around. Mother Murphy, in one of the few issues of the school newspaper to reach the press, gave me a nice write-up on that. His portrayal of me as the 'harbinger of culture at St. Lucy's' was particularly apt and went some distance in shielding Mother from the worst of my wrath when I began cleaning house at the school.

The task I had set for myself would be an uphill struggle. For an educational statistics class that I later took at City College, I did a study on the socioeconomic achievements of Irish and Italian working class boys who attended parochial schools. For case studies I plucked names of graduating seniors from old issues of the *Lucian*, the school yearbook. My research revealed that in later life, graduates of St. Lucy's tended to mirror the unbridled greed of the secular establishment while rarely pursuing its cultural pretensions. Long after the ex-Lucian substituted a salary for the hourly wage, he preferred the Mets to the Metropolitan.

But I'm no alchemist, and if I failed to change peasants into aristocrats in a single generation, I at least did what I could.

---

[1] A principle, by the way, that applies to all the arts. To read *all* of Shakespeare, or listen to *all* of Beethoven is comparable to visiting *all* the cathedrals of France: in recollection one can't recall what spire rises from what nave.

During the weeks preceding Kevin's disappearance from school, his teachers and classmates had escalated their insistence on conformity from smirks and giggles to direct attacks on the boy's masculinity. Kevin sometimes indulged in the adolescent pretense of adding his mother's surname to that of his father's, signing his name Kevin Kelly-O'Connor. Crude sketches began to appear on blackboards and desks. Vulgar graffiti from the streets coupled with his name, or rather a variation of it, Kelly Girl, made the intended victim unmistakable. Kevin's persecutors did not show much ingenuity in their choice of epithets. They had lifted it from the billboard that sat atop the building across the street from St. Lucy's school advertising the secretarial agency of the same name.

In spite of such torment, for two months or so, all through March and April, Kevin never missed a day of school. In this way he avoided detection. For some time now he had not been living at home. No one knew, not even I, certainly not the office. Brother Principal would have discovered Kevin's break with home had he missed so much as a day. At St. Lucy's, if the boy was not in by nine, Mrs. Mulcaney, Brother's part-time secretary, began making calls.

And neither did the parents call the school with news of their missing boy. Perhaps they wished to hide their shame from Brother Principal. They intended, evidently, to let events take their course. Perhaps the school would never learn of the boy's absence from home, and for the time being at least they were rid of the impertinent child who criticized them and ridiculed the culture from which he came. If one of Kevin's eccentric friends from the city took him in, all the better; the parents might be shed of him for good.

Kevin was the school's best student. Now his grades began to slip. I didn't overreact to this. At some point during puberty most boys' grades suffer. According to his age—Kevin was six-teen—he should have already passed through the more jolting period of sexual awakening. Judging from our late night talk at the coffee shop some months previous, I believed he had. But he was slight and terribly underweight now. Perhaps poor health had slowed his development. Whatever the cause, and I knew I could be wrong about the puberty theory, I meant to get to the bottom of Kevin's scholastic troubles. It was late in the school year. If the boy was to score well on his final exams, I must get to him soon, and during seventh period, my last for the day, I asked him to meet me after school.

All classrooms at St. Lucy's were bugged, even the con-ference room. Brother Principal called it his 'public address system,' a euphemism to conceal the fact that the speakers receive as well as transmit. With a flip of a toggle switch, Brother Principal could pick up word of rebellion among stu-dents and teachers alike. For this reason I invited Kevin to meet me for tea at Tina's, the intimate café where I did some of my best extracurricular counseling.

Kevin first refused my offer to pay. When I insisted, he greedily downed one prune and two cheese Danish. The boy must not have eaten in days. For myself, I ordered dry toast and tea with lemon.

"You know, Kevin," I began, after the boy had blunted the edge of his hunger, "your grades have fallen off the past few weeks. I wouldn't like to see it continue. I expect you to win the Monsignor Corby Memorial Scholarship." Monsi-gnor Corby, the previous pastor of St.Lucy's Church, had died leaving a large sum of money to be used for the education of a Lucian at a Catholic college of his choice. Not at Fordham, however, my alma mater. The Monsignor would do nothing to support the Jesuits. Cultists, he called them.

"If I go to college," Kevin answered indifferently. He picked at the crumbs on his plate, avoiding my eyes.

I must have let slip a murmur of alarm, for he looked up and said, "I'm sorry, Mr. Quinn." His wide mouth trembled. His voice was barely audible.

Teachers live on hope. We forego wealth and fame hoping that our students, students like Kevin O'Connor, will achieve it in our stead. When Kevin published the first revolutionary analysis of the Western world since *Das Capital*, I would be immortalized in its dedication. 'I owe it all,' Kevin would admit, 'to my high school history teacher, Mr. Virgil Quinn.'

"What will you do then, when you leave St. Lucy's, if you don't go on to college."

"Oh, I don't know. Work, I guess."

"At your job, or some other like it I suppose? How much do clerks in card shops earn nowadays? Two or three dollars an hour?" I tried to repress the note of sarcasm that crept into my voice, but pretense has never come easy to me.

"No," Kevin replied, "the job I have in mind pays three hundred a week."

"Why Kevin! That's impossible," I stammered. "Why, I hardly make half so much. True, we're terribly underpaid, but—"

"You're not a prostitute, Mr. Quinn. You're a teacher."

My first impulse was to anger. Was I to take his words ironically? No, Kevin couldn't be so cruel. Persecuted himself, he would never stoop to insult.

"What do you mean by that, Kevin?"

"I mean that will be my new job, working in a house for boys."

"A *whorehouse*, Kevin?"

"That's a rather old-fashioned term. The place where I'm going to work is called the Relax-a-Lounge Health Club. It has a portable sauna and a set of weights."

"But Kevin, you're so young, so—"

"You have to be young, Mr. Quinn. Under sixteen, or look as if you are. It's for old men with juvenile tastes." Kevin spoke without rancor, just as if he were enumerating the qualifications for a position selling insurance.

"But Kevin, you're so clever! Accept a small gift now and then to get by, perhaps, but to *fraternize...* " I couldn't speak the words 'on a *commercial* basis'—"I don't see how you could bring yourself to do it."

"That will be a liability, my cleverness, as you put it. The others—I've met two of the guys who work there; they told me about the joint—nice guys, but they don't have that problem."

"Then *why*, Kevin?"

"Because it's big money, plus room and board. That's how the place is run, like a boarding house. And if I've found out anything since splitting from home, this city is an expensive place to live."

I didn't take Kevin seriously although he gave me every reason for doing so. Talk about it, yes, for the shock effect. Youth loves to shock, especially those in authority. Or for the thrill derived from vicarious exploits. But never would Kevin O'Connor sell his body like a common hustler.

But he did. And much sooner than he had led me to suspect. Some weeks later, again over tea at Tina's, he told me that he had spent nearly a month in the Relax-a-Lounge.

"It doesn't appear to have harmed you, physically," I said. I didn't mean to sound sarcastic—Kevin had been through quite enough without being lectured by me. I honestly meant what I said. The boy wasn't nearly so thin. His color was good. He had a set to his mouth, however, that hadn't been there the last time we talked.

"Lobster Newburg, prime rib, French pastry, all I can eat."

"Boarding house fare?"

"Oh, no. Served in the best restaurants. I left the Relax-a-Lounge a long time ago. For the last month I've been living with my lover. Lover? No, loved one. I'm sure he doesn't share my feelings."

Kevin continued to stare out the window at the passers-by, not bothering to check by so much as a glance whether or not I understood the manner in which he used his terms. Presumptuous of him. At the beginning of the school year, when first we met, he would not have used the terms at all.

"An older man?"

"Older, but not old. Your age, I suppose. Perhaps a little older. He's thirty-something."

What a perceptive boy Kevin was! I was only a month short of my—well, age is not important, but with my good skin, clear black eyes and superbly trim figure, few suspect I'm more than twenty-eight.

"I thought your...place of employment catered to an older clientele."

"It did. But occasionally a younger john dropped in. Afraid of being seen in the bars, fear of raids, fear of blackmail, fear of entrapment, various fears. Some just like buying it. The sporting life, you know. Anyway, that's how I met my...that's how I met Michael Lowenthal."

Kevin explained that he hadn't moved directly from the boarding house brothel to the penthouse apartment of his wealthy lover. As I had predicted, he was spiritually unprepared for the numbing sleaze of the Relax-a-Lounge. Less than a month after he signed on, he promptly quit, an act that probably said more about Kevin's disdain for life than any other aspect of his recent behavior. The thugs who ran the place, hired to do the work by shadowy entrepreneurs whom Kevin never saw and certainly never met, promised to 'break your legs and mess up your pretty face' (repeating dialogue, I supposed, from some cheap *noir* movie) if Kevin, or any of their recruits, dared go back to the streets.

For the next week or two Kevin shifted from bed to bed, not all of them male. He had met several young women, runaways like himself. Street people, especially very young ones, form more intimate friendships in a month than their parents do in a lifetime of church socials. Some nights he stayed with his new friends, with whichever one of them had found a place to crash. Two or three times a week he spent the night with Michael. How he continued going to school under such conditions I can't imagine.

Nonetheless, he did, and on a more or less regular basis, even though this must have been his most insecure period, the weeks between his escape from the boarding house and the move to the apartment of his friend. Only a boy like Kevin, so young in body and old in mind, could have done it. I certainly didn't have the stamina, not even then, to be up all night and teach the next day. But then it took me thirty years of study to develop a philosophy that permits me to express my variable nature—usually on weekends—and still pursue my life's work, teaching the young.

Suddenly, without any trailing-off of attendance, Kevin ceased to come to school at all. One day his desk was empty. I could not ask Brother Principal for an explanation for fear of exposing Kevin. Brother had certainly called the O'Connor home, that was the rule. The parents had to be covering for their wayward child, out of shame, I suppose, for their failure as parents. Which meant Brother knew nothing of the boy's actual situation. A month passed. I didn't know it yet, but I would never see Kevin again. Our conversation at Tina's, the day he told me that he had graduated from prostitute to kept boy, would be the last time we talked.

I finally spoke to Primo. Afraid that I might be violating Kevin's confidence—I didn't know how much even Primo knew—I made it clear to Primo that anything he might tell me would not come as a surprise and would not be repeated.

"I don't know nothin'," Primo replied. "We don't see each other anymore."

"That's not true, Primo. I know you saw him as recently as a month ago," I lied.

"How do you know that?"

"I know. I make it a point to know." I gave Primo my omniscient look that told him I could read boys' minds and I had certainly read his. "Now tell me what's happened to Kevin."

And so he did. Primo, after swearing me to secrecy, told me what little I know about Kevin's last days with the lover who took him in, delighted in what innocence Kevin still possessed (his romantic notion that only if he loved enough, his love would be returned—pity the young), and then turned to other interests when his ardor cooled. Primo spoke shyly of such things. Perhaps he knew even less than he implied, or understood less than his words implied, although this is unlikely: Any boy Primo's age growing up in New York City knows these things. Whatever the explanation, the details remain hidden from me even now. I can only put together the rapid slide from brightest boy to doomed vagrant—our late night talk at the coffee shop, his running away from home, starvation driving him to that sordid brothel followed by a brief and disappointing respite with the man who took him in. Then silence.

Only the manner of Kevin's death is clear. The boy leaped from the penthouse parapet of a Beekman Place address. His family buried him in a private—clandestine might be a better word—ceremony in Mount Olivet Cemetery. Nothing was said at school. No memorial was held. Brother Principal did not mention the funeral over the public address system. Among the faculty, only the school's consulting psychologist was told of the boy's death. Months later, after a few—too many?—drinks at the County Cork, the psychologist told me of his slight involvement in the affair. Monsignor Delaney had pressured him, he said, to declare Kevin mentally ill in order to avoid the scandal of burying the boy in unconsecrated ground.

The newspapers reported neither death nor funeral. At that time, boys like Kevin did not exist. Now it appears the press has come full circle. Note the sensational coverage given my heterogeneous past in recent weeks. Ah, well, the times are fickle.

> When hustlers fall no one cares to make a scene.
> The *Daily News* itself reports the fall of queens.[1]

> *Julia Caesar,*
> Act III, Sc.I

---

1 Allan Causey, *Julia Caesar.* Chapbook. Privately printed. 1968.

8

NOT SO LONG AGO newspaper people employed the word 'articles' when referring to the blocks of print they use to flush out their pages of advertising. Now they call them 'stories,' as well they might. If language is to remain meaningful, it must reflect reality.

Those of you who read the sympathetic account of my years at St. Lucy's in last week's *Village Voice* perhaps made note of the story's fictional style:

> 'Despondent over the meaningless death of his young friend and determined to rectify the abuse of authority he believed had caused it, Virgil Quinn picked up a gun and joined the revolution.'

SHAPE A STORY, tell a lie.

First this matter of guns. Symbolism and metaphors have no place in journalism unless clearly labeled as such. Then

too, when I returned to my classroom in the fall of '69, my
change of tactics took place over months, not days, and show
a gradual rather than a sudden escalation. I had not yet made
the connection between the mandate I had been given to
clean up St. Lucy's and the part Kevin O'Connor's tragic
end would play in bringing this about. I was keenly aware of
my own cowardly role in Kevin's death and wished to lessen
my pain (and mark Kevin's passing) by rectifying the evils
that had caused it. The intent was there, but I still lacked the
courage to launch a full frontal attack. A semester would pass
before I whipped up the courage to challenge the insidious
Greek O'Grady or the apparently invulnerable Bull Belloli.
Or to demonstrate to Brother Principal that students—and
teachers—were not the powerless minions he believed us to
be, that his notion of school administration was more suitable to Old World institutions of the previous century. Until
then, I continued to attempt reform from within the system.

The skilled revolutionary, to hasten destruction of the
old regime, accepts support from all factions regardless of
ideology. Just as the totalitarian Lenin made use of the par-
liamentarian Kerinsky, early in my second year at St. Lucy's,
I formed an alliance with Brother Bob, or Brother Lib as
the more conservative students called the monk because
of the passion with which he took to the liberal reforms in
the Church initiated by John XXIII and Vatican II. Working
together, Brother and I launched our 'Do Your Ethnic Thing
Day' and completely revamped the annual religious retreat
from three days of enforced silence and prayer into a period
of 'investigation of self in light of social change.' Boys from
Queens scribbled racist graffiti on our 'Black Peoples of the
World' display, and reactionary teachers complained to the
Monsignor that Brother Bob and I were turning old-time

religion into half-baked social psychology. Brother Principal banned our mimeographed pamphlet 'Notes on Masturbation' from the classroom, but not before we got several copies into circulation. These passed from hand to hand until they were lost, stolen, or fell into dog-eared shreds.

By reminding Brother Principal that the court order to integrate America's schools was now nearly two decades old and we still could not boast a single student of color, unless one put the dark Sicilian Figliano into the count, we increased the black enrollment three hundred percent. This figure represented three boys six foot four or taller. Here we must give Bull Belloli his due. He personally traveled into deepest Harlem to recruit these 'talented and representative members of their race,' and it must have been no mean task for the Bull to find three such boys willing to transfer, even on scholarship, to St. Lucy's, a school that drew blank stares when coupled with either academic or athletic achievement. But he found them and persuaded them to enroll. Or rather persuaded their parents to enroll them. All three boys had been in trouble with the police, and Bull promised the parents that St. Lucy's approach to discipline would turn the boys around. That season Bull drove the St. Lucian green and gold into the archdiocesan semi-finals.

I had long been disturbed by the position of women at St. Lucy's. We had only three, two cooks and Brother Principal's part-time secretary, Mrs. Mulcaney. Such staffing practices did nothing to elevate the role of women in the eyes of the boys: Men taught, women served. I urged Brother Principal to fill the next faculty vacancy with a woman. Brother put me off by saying he foresaw no vacancies. Therefore, until I could see to it that a vacancy did in fact occur, which required more time, I arranged to bring Mary Ellen McKay, a teacher

at Transfiguration for Girls, to St. Lucy's. Under a temporary exchange agreement, I would replace Mary Ellen at
Transfiguration.

I had three reasons for selecting Mary Ellen from the
several women who volunteered to come. She was eager,
she was over thirty, and she was plain. Perhaps I also had
a premonition of what role she might play in my future
struggle with the Cardinal, but if I did, I was not conscious
of it at the time.

"The way they *stare*, Virgil! And where they fix their eyes!"

"I was afraid of that," I sympathized. "But what can you
expect? You are probably the only mature woman other than
a near relative they've been in the same room with for any
length of time. You provide them with fantasies their history
text cannot."

In my classes of girls at Transfiguration I avoided Mary
Ellen's problem. I had learned as a post-adolescent in my first
career, and only a few years older in my second, how the
cut of one's dress can be used to conceal what one would
rather not be seen. Before entering Transfiguration for Girls, I
draped myself in a jacket and baggy trousers expressly tailored
by Mrs. Goldberg, my Orchard Street haberdasher, to conceal my provocative figure. I thought that Mary Ellen, lacking
my allure, would have no need for camouflage. In doing so
I underestimated the novelty that any mature woman, other
than a mother or an aunt, presented to the boys. Nonetheless, Mary Ellen had the courage to match her egalitarian
principals. She was not to be intimidated and would have
persisted in her experiment as the first woman to teach at St.
Lucy's if Brother Principal had not put an abrupt end to our
experiment. His reason for doing so became, as my reforms
progressed, a too often heard refrain: "It's too soon, Virgil.

The boys aren't ready yet, and it's best not to rush into these things."

I was working on it but I had not yet discovered a means of speeding up Brother's itinerary for change.

The results of my collaboration with Brother Bob and Mary Ellen McKay were not among my flashier accomplishments during this period of political evolution. I made my biggest hit in a series of lectures I delivered on a subject some would say I knew nothing about. Virgil Quinn? Neither spouse nor parent, and showing little inclination to either? Presumptuous of him to say the least.

They would be wrong.

In retrospect, I can see that Mrs. Doran, my sex-ed teacher in tenth grade, influenced me more than I might have once wished to believe. Take the matter of credentials; they played no great part in our appointments to mold the sexual mores of our respective generations. Money, and our willingness to forego it, was the more decisive factor. Historians handicapped by an obsession with economic necessity will greet this admission with I-told-you-so smirks. In their rush to promote a single causality explaining all human behavior, these academics place themselves where they rightfully belong, within the ranks of propagandists and ideologues. First reduce history to a few easy principles, as the Marxists did, then reverse those principles and man's redemption is at hand. Simplistic. As if man would ever willingly give up the stimulating intrigue of Byzantium for the honest boredom of Utopia.

All this aside, the careers of both Mrs. Doran and I advanced as the economics of our institutions declined because we agreed to work without pay. Mrs. Doran made it repeatedly clear during the fifteen sessions of her sex-ed course that she worked for higher motives. As the mother of three priests—'I gave *all* my sons to God'—it was her duty, she said, to teach still more boys that sexual pleasure was synonymous with perdition. And, if we giggled when we should have been sadly contemplating our souls all besmirched with the sin of masturbation, she would first regale our senses with the consequences of this evil: "I can always pick out a boy who does it," she would say. "His eyes tell me, lusterless eyes withdrawn and ringed with shadow. The smell too. Scrub as they might, boys who do it will never rid their hands of the taint of semen."

We glanced furtively at our classmates, looking for eyes sunk in shadow, sniffed for telltale whiffs of what none of us yet produced much of. And if her purple prose failed to sober us, she tried guilt. "I do this without taking payment of any kind. It is my gift to you, your parents, the Sisters of Mercy of Baton Rouge and Holy Mother Church."

This usually did the trick. Not because Mrs. Doran managed to dredge up residual guilt, but because we were sincerely afraid that if we didn't shape up, Mrs. Doran might throw in the towel, abandon us to the boredom of nun or priest. Mrs. Doran was, you see, at that conservative time and place, our only source of pornographic entertainment.

I learned a great deal about lecturing from Mrs. Doran. Just the touch of prurience needed, for example, to keep the boys awake. And her stories. I would use many of them. Given the right spin, they nearly always achieved the effect I desired. But most important, Mrs. Doran taught me the rewards of volunteer service. If not for her, the chance to mold the sexosociopsyches of ninety-nine boys would have gone to Bull Belloli. At the height of the struggle, the words of Mrs. Doran's refrain, "I do this without payment of any kind," came back to inspire me and I plucked that plum of an assignment for myself.

My meeting with Brother Principal that resulted in victory began with defeat. Six weeks into the new school year, I had begun, ever so gingerly, to confront the brutality I too often witnessed in hall and classroom. I had got so far as to report each incident as it occurred to Brother Principal.

"But Brother," I pleaded, "how can we look aside when a man the size of O'Grady strikes a boy half his weight who is not even allowed to defend himself?"

Brother took his customary gradualist line. "We can't hope to change in a year what it took generations to entrench. Besides," he continued, stripping his do-nothing attitude of whatever legitimacy it might have warranted, "Primo probably deserved it."

"I have taught Primo for three semesters and I have never found cause to strike him."

"Primo has an impudent swagger."

"Primo is a fifteen-year-old boy who is discovering his remarkable virility. You would agree, wouldn't you, Brother, that a boy with Primo's…leopardian prowess,"—I couldn't find a better term to describe Primo's jungle manner of holding every muscle of his feline body in taut readiness for flight or fight—"that Primo will cause wonder in whatever world he chooses to move."

Brother pulled nervously at the thick lobe of his right ear. He seemed disinclined to discuss Primo de Popalano's electric presence.

"Primo's physical attributes, whatever they might be, are a God-given gift that, in my opinion, he is exploiting to the risk of his own soul. If it were not for our discipline, judiciously, if sometimes harshly administered, who knows what would become of the boy?"

I had a ready reply to such claptrap. "If God chose to create so lavishly as He has in Primo's instance, who is Mr. O'Grady to destroy that perfection? I speak of Primo's split lip."

And then I did a cowardly thing. Afraid that I had gone too far in questioning Brother Principal's moral authority, I backed off. "But you must decide these things, Brother. Far be it from me..." and I mumbled apologies I later chose to forget.

Brother Principal was not a vindictive man. What manager of a business constantly on the brink of bankruptcy can afford to be?

"You must not take these things so much to heart, Virgil." Brother's tone was sweet, conciliatory. "We will succeed in God's own time to change what we can and to learn to accept those things that we cannot...change," he added, destroying the pompous rhythm of his reply. "And now I would like to let you in on a little secret, Virgil. No, a big secret, and one you must promise not to tell anyone, not even your fellow teachers." I nodded in assent. I love a confidence as much as any man. "The time isn't ripe yet. Next year, however,"—and Brother leaned over to whisper—"next year I intend to petition the most prestigious organization of private schools on the Eastern Seaboard, The Hudson Valley Academic Association, for *full* accreditation. As you may be aware, now we only have provisional accreditation. But there's a hitch. HVAA requires courses in the arts and the humanities for full approval, and we have neither the space nor the budget to implement additional courses. All our rooms are filled, seven periods a day. Our faculty is teaching the maximum load allowed of assigned courses. I think, though, that I've struck on a way around this dilemma."

St. Lucy's had long before reached the limits of its expansion. The school when I arrived consisted of a quaint stone building built in 1892 and still used for the purpose it was built—to educate the children of immigrants. As need arose, the school had incorporated the two townhouses to either side and now consisted of five attached buildings whose floors lay each on a different level, requiring a great many short, up-and-down stairs to move from one building to the next. My homeroom, with its low ceiling sloping to either side, was housed on the topmost floor of one of these townhouses and had no doubt once been used to sleep the maids.

Thus constricted, Brother intended to expand St. Lucy's curriculum beyond the traditional three R's by coercing his teachers to conduct a program he called 'Cultural Enrichment.' To encourage volunteers, he would pay a stipend of two hundred dollars for each one-semester course, to meet just once a week, and he handed me a list of possible assignments.

I was perplexed. Music Through the Ages, Renaissance Painters, The Art of the Orient? Who on his faculty, other than myself, did Brother have in mind when he drew up the list? During a year of communal lunches, I had yet to hear a conversation concerning art. To my fellow teachers, the city's great museums and concert halls were like the stock exchange and the diamond market, places they had all heard about but saw no reason to visit.

"This will be tough on the teachers," I replied, after glancing through the list, to underline my solidarity with the faculty. "Especially so, coming as it does on top of the new state requirements."

Directives from Albany had recently ordered us, if we wished to remain accredited by the state, to add a course in Marriage and the Family and another to teach students how to handle Citizen Stress. From the moment word of this requirement leaked out, I set my eye on Marriage and the Family. So did Bull Belloli, who needed the six-hundred-dollar stipend that went with the course not only to help feed the brood of kids that he added to every second year with incontinent abandon, but to support the pack of dogs the boys told me he kept on his tenement roof. As a presumed celibate—one's intimate life is one's own affair—and with neither children nor dogs to feed, I was not in a strong competitive position. Such things count in institutions grounded in primitive ideologies.

"And tough on the budget," I added. "Where are you going to get the money to cover all these stipends?"

"God will provide," was the only collateral Brother came up with.

The germ of an idea took root in my subconscious. Somewhere in all this there was something for me, something owed in compensation for my surrender over the O'Grady issue. I pretended to study the list, waiting for the sprout to blossom. Through Brother's office window, which was open to the street, I heard the rumble of a food cart and the sound of its tinkling bell. The bell fell silent to be replaced by a woman's voice. *"We must not let these boys fall into the hands of another Mrs. Doran."* I immediately recognized the voice as that of Sister Philomena whispering to me from the recesses of Brother Principal's open filing cabinet. *"I do this without payment of any kind."* Sister Philomena quoting Mrs. Doran. Of course. Money. A trade-off.

"Brilliantly conceived," I murmured to Brother as I handed back his list of arts courses gleaned from the chapter headings of *Pageant of History,* the same text I used in my second-year World History courses. "Properly implemented, I can't imagine the HVAA turning us down for lack of artistic enrichment. You can count on me, Brother, to do my part. Probably something in the visual arts. Over the years, I've developed considerable innate talent in that line. A friend of mine who works at the Whitney tells me that my landscapes—but we can talk about that at a later date when I bring in my portfolio. I would like to mention now, though, that I've given a great deal of thought to the new course, Marriage and the Family. For many years I've followed the latest thought in family studies, ever since my grade school days. The Sisters of Mercy of Baton Rouge were, you know, the first teaching order of nuns to throw out Health Habits and make Marriage and the Family a requirement, K through 12. The public system picked it up from them."

"Amazing!" Brother sighed. "Nuns capable of innovation. I had no idea."

Nor had I until moments before. In face of Belloli's unfair and unearned competitive lead, I had to improvise.

"But I had Mr. Belloli in mind for that particular course, Virgil. As the only married man on the faculty and father of six, it seems only right—"

"Is he academically qualified? How many hours does he have in family psychology?" I felt an aggressive rush of testosterone.

"Well, I'm not quite sure," Brother responded breathlessly. "I'll have to check."

"Go right ahead," I said and glanced to the open file cabinet from which Sister Philomena had whispered her directive to me. "I'm free for the remainder of the period." I had no intention of allowing Brother to search the records at his leisure and then fabricate for Bull a minor in sociology.

"Even without a *formal* preparation for teaching the course," Brother continued, "I still think Mr. Belloli can rest on his *practical* experience as a family man."

"If practical experience rather than formal training was the best teaching credential, Brother, why then does our system require at least a bachelor's degree to teach in the classroom?"

Obviously, Brother did not intend to make the assignment on the basis of qualifications.

"Of course, Brother, I would teach both the Enrichment course *and* Marriage and the Family without pay.'

While waiting for Brother to calculate what this sum equaled in boxes of chalk and frogs in formaldehyde, I fiddled with the zipper on my satchel. zzziiPPP, ZZZiipp, zzziiPPP, ZZZiipp. Like a boy's mind, I mused, clutching the bag in my lap. Waiting to be filled with the crude fantasies of a monogamous middle-aged coach or the rich experience of a gourmand who had feasted at some of the better set tables of life. To reach the mind of a single boy...

Marriage and the Family would provide me with the platform for reaching ninety-nine boys in ways that I could never hope to with my present schedule of classes. So many areas of thought on which I had so much to say could not be covered in history courses, not even by someone who looked upon history as comprehensively as I. Archaic sexual mores in need of updating; the status of women, barely touched upon in my lectures on the Suffragette Movement; the need for tolerance and empathy when confronted by the variability of man's nature. I could not treat any of these subjects in the depth they deserved without leaving myself open to accusations of wandering afield, a fault common to so many teachers and one I'd been careful to avoid.

"Very generous of you to give of your time, Virgil," Brother Principal replied after giving my proposition a moment's thought.

"I am a teacher," I replied. "To give generously of one's time is the soul of the craft."

"I wish we had the funds to properly reward your service. You have undertaken so much."

"There are rewards greater than money." My response contained more truth than its pious phrasing might imply.

"You should have joined us, Virgil, taken vows."

"God works in mysterious ways," was my ambiguous response, declining to reveal the vows I had taken—and broken—in the past.

BULL BELLOLI, WHEN he learned that I had beat him out of the competition to shape the marital minds of the entire junior class, began mouthing it about that "the Virgin Queen is sure some choice for a marriage counselor."

I didn't let this attempt to undermine my credibility disturb me. I was accustomed by now to facing hostile audiences of boys turned against me by an envious faculty, and I always researched my group before beginning a class. Knowing a student's previous teachers helped me determine the nature of his indoctrination and I shaped my introductory lectures accordingly.

"Experience," I began to my class of restless sixteen-year-old boys, "is something none of you have much of. Just as well. Your lack of sexual know-how will not be a handicap in this class. Neither will the fact that I'm single. Experience is the best teacher only if the subject has taken the time to reflect upon his condition, which few have.

"People who marry with the intent to bear children—and fortunate for the world there are some of us who do not—most often do so at a very young age. All these men and women, all that is except the very rich, claim to have married for love. A better term for love at twenty is lust. The consequence of lust is over-population. Raising too many children on too small an income does not permit either parent the time to reflect upon his condition until he has failed, grown old, and attempts in retrospect to give meaning to his confused existence by pointing to his lumpish children as justification for his life's work. Men and women who have lived a married life must, therefore, be categorically forbidden the opportunity to indoctrinate the following generation with their own willful delusions concerning the sacred state of matrimony.

"If you followed the concise logic of my analysis of modern marriage, any doubts you may have harbored concerning my qualifications will have now been put to sea.

"When I was your age, no one, certainly no Sister of Mercy of Baton Rouge, thought it necessary to set aside valuable class time to lecture us on marriage and the family."

"Neither do we," someone shouted. Mangora? De Angelo? Someone from the cluster of jocks huddled in the back corner.

"Time taken up by interruptions will, of course, only extend the class beyond the scheduled hour, and since this is the last hour of the day, we will be forced to continue on *your* time.

"As I was saying before that cowardly boy who prefers to remain anonymous interrupted me...when I was your age, we didn't study marriage and the family. Most married, and failed; some of us did not and we've had time to study modern marriage and discover its shortcomings. We also serve as a counterweight for those of you who will undoubtedly over-breed. There are people in this provincial city, including the late, over-rated senior columnist of the *New York Times,* who believe that America consists largely of empty space. These men and women, after one brief excursion west when young, henceforth flock eastwards to the countries of Western Europe. Europhiles all, they return from abroad convinced that the densely populated countries of the Old World should serve as the bench mark for acceptable population here at home. These men and women are insensitive to most species of life other than human. Although they live in New York City, an environment that can barely support a tree, they've never learned, or do not care, that where man and his cattle dwell all else must perish.

"In Omaha where I attended my first twelve years of school, we were subjected in our sophomore year to three weeks of sex education. And who should be chosen to teach it? Certainly not a man like myself who married his work and dedicated his life to social research, keen observation and rational deduction. No, day after day we sat there, fifty-three pubescent boys, listening to the lurid tales of a middle-aged and middle-class matron whose knowledge of sex was circumscribed by twice-weekly monogamous copulations performed in the missionary position.

"You are giggling, Andrew Coogan. Do you find Mrs. Doran's position in life amusing? I'm sure she didn't. And I expect you, if you should marry, to look beyond your own too hurried gratification and show more imagination in satisfying the needs of your wife. I will show you, as we penetrate deeper into this series of lectures, how that goal can be accomplished.

"If I had to rely on what I learned in Mrs. Doran's classes, I would be able to teach you very little. She spent her time—and ours—telling stories. There's nothing wrong with using

stories to convey knowledge. It's a method as old as teaching. But Mrs. Doran's stories—well, perhaps I should give
you an example.

"'The boy and girl I am going to tell you about,' Mrs.
Doran began, 'were about the ages of you boys, perhaps a
year older. They had been going steady for several months,
and that, I dare say, is where the trouble began. They were too
young, as you boys are, for keeping steady company. Intimacy
breeds contempt and should be saved for marriage.'

"'For some months before it happened,' Mrs. Doran went
on, 'the young couple had fallen into the dangerous habit
of leaving the dance or the game to drive to secluded places.
We can't prove just what they did while parked, but judging
from their sad end, we can presume they engaged in heavy
petting. Heavy petting, boys, is a mortal sin, just as is sexual intercourse out of marriage. This does not mean that
because you went *part* of the way you might as well go *all* the
way. That would be playing games with God's law as handed
down through Holy Mother Church. No, it only means that
you don't have to go through with the sexual act to incur the
wrath of God.'

"'It was the night of the Senior Prom. When it was time
to leave the dance, Bill and Darlene, the unfortunate couple
of our story, said goodbye to their friends. Little did anyone
know that it would be their last goodbye. For they did not go
directly home as they should have, but drove to what is gen-
erally referred to as a lover's lane. This was no lane, however.
Lookout Mount was a deserted spot some miles out of town
atop the river bluffs from whose precipitous edge the lovers
could look back upon the lights of Omaha.

"'I will not go into the details of what took place inside
their car that night. Just let it be said that when the two young

people were found the following day, it was at the bottom of the cliff, imprisoned in the crushed body of Bill's vintage 1939 Nash Lafayette, a sedan with fold-down seats. The police were called and, with the aid of acetylene torches, the car that had become Bill and Darlene's coffin was cut apart. When the last piece of twisted metal was wrenched aside, Darlene and Bill were discovered clasped in each other's arms and locked in copulation.'"

I paused as Mrs. Doran had paused when telling her story to let the nature of Bill and Darlene's death work its prurient course. Mrs. Doran had the narrative style of a Sarah Bernhardt and we thought she had finished.

But she was not quite finished.

"'Bill and Darlene died like that, in a state of mortal sin,' Mrs. Doran concluded her horrid little tale in a whisper that terrified her audience, 'and because of it will spend eternity in hell.'"

I broke the silence that had settled over the class after Mrs. Doran leveled her judgment on poor Bill and Darlene.

"I've only bothered repeating this ridiculous story—however true it might be—to demonstrate how a class such as ours should not be conducted. Can anyone tell me what's wrong with Mrs. Doran's method? No? No hands? Well, it's getting late, the hour has nearly passed, so I will do the work for you—this time. To begin with, Mrs. Doran's story contains not one shred of useful information. Does she ever tell us why Bill and Darlene began going steady? Were they surrounded by adults like Mrs. Doran who did not understand their needs? Were they children of parents who were seldom home and were therefore simply lonely? Were they over-sexed? Or did they finally consummate their love in hopes of discovering why the movies they saw always stopped short of doing so. We'll never know. Is there a single aspect of this story that might show any of us how to conduct our own sexual encounters? Not one. For Mrs. Doran is careful never to define her terms. Heavy petting? Does she mean that Bill played with Darlene's breasts and Darlene fondled Bill to ejaculation? We'll never know. And that mysterious elision from parked car to death by crushing. What happened? Was the night so cold that they left the car running? Did the two young people in their passionate flailing about knock the car into gear, hit the gas and go shooting over the cliff so suddenly that Bill did not have time to withdraw? Mrs. Doran, for all her talent in winding up a story, gives us little of the action leading up to the climax.

"There is perhaps a single lesson, boys, to be learned from Mrs. Doran's story. You do not, living as you do in New York City, own a car. And even if you did you could not find a secluded place to park it. So you must make do with what privacy your environment provides. Like the generations of novice womanizers who have preceded you, you will do it on the roof. And therein lies the only possible moral of this holy woman's tale: If you fuck on the roof, stay clear of the edge.

"And now I see that it's time to part. Until next Wednesday then?" I snapped shut my briefcase, flicked a speck of chalk dust from my narrow lapel, spun on a heel and left the room.

9

For decades following the McCarthyite Terror of the Early Fifties, when no one but the radical right was safe from the senator's accusations of treason, liberals controlled the educational institutions of this country. But the rules of history are harsh. Factions too long in power go to fat. At the time of my separation from St. Lucy's, rhetoric was all that differentiated liberalism from its opposition.

At no time in its hundred-year history could St. Lucy's have been called a liberal institution. Surface thaws do occur, however, even in tundra wastes. The fissures that appeared for a decade or so in St. Lucy's glacial opposition to change resulted from the mercurial rise of the Boston Dynasty and ended with the Christmas Bombing of Hanoi just ten years later. To lend credence to the new president's claim that his allegiance to Rome in no way impinged upon his sworn duty to serve the ideals of the republic, even the Cardinal of New York became more reticent in his condemnation of dissent. The Cardinal made no mention of the equally compelling reason for opening the Church to the doubtful winds of change. His schools were strapped for cash and Albany had stood firm: Either bring your schools into the twentieth century or we do not allocate a single dollar for textbook purchases. That the Cardinal had no abiding interest in reform needs hardly be dwelt upon. The evidence is everywhere around us. One need look no further than his inquisition that intends to burn me, slated for Friday next, which is, by the way, the feast of St. Lucy of Palermo.

If St. Lucy's can be considered the polar cap of American education and the Kennedy era the beginning of the thaw, then I arrived when the ice had withdrawn to its narrowest limits, which coincided, more or less, with the Pagan Ascendancy of the late Sixties and early Seventies. If I had only arrived a few years earlier, or the thaw had persisted a little longer... The blame for a tardy start lies elsewhere. I did not choose, I was chosen. Those who decided the time and the place must bear the responsibility for the outcome.

When I arrived at St. Lucy's, Brother Principal was having a difficult time recruiting teachers who would both work for six thousand a year and be tough enough to survive relentless persecution by working class boys. Only the profoundly dedicated and the grossly incompetent could be enticed to teach at St. Lucy's. Belonging to the first-mentioned group, I was almost alone.

Toward the end of my first year at the school, Brother Principal had held his moistened finger to the wind and prophesied a turbulent era for the parochial schools. Revolts at the universities had for some time now left students and administrators divided into hostile camps. It would only be a matter of time, Brother believed, before ripples of dissent reached schools as insular and inconspicuous as St. Lucy's. (As indeed it would. I was already there.) Rebellious students and those bothersome progressives on every faculty would make demands. As principal, he believed it his duty to direct this energy into multiple channels, whereby diversion and obstruction of the torrent could be tamed. But how? Dealing with radical change had not been part of his training at Our Lady Help of Angels, the elementary school where he had interned. Where else to turn for enlightenment other than God? If Brother did indeed pray for some clear sign from heaven indicating what course he should follow, none was forthcoming, and at the end of the school year, after the last student had been passed or failed, the last sorrowful parent mollified, he had hurried up to Columbia Teachers' College, the local seat of secular humanism, and enrolled in a seminar for administrators in need of direction.

It's unlikely that Brother learned much from Columbia's doctors of education. They themselves had no very clear idea of what to do with students who said no. Brother's teachers no doubt advised him to do what they were doing: Ignore dissent, it will pass; all things do. Your job is management, and management is the same regardless of the product your plant is designed to produce. The key to success is efficient use of manpower. Never do yourself what can be delegated to others.

For a month of his time and a large fee, Brother returned with a blueprint for implementing the committee system. Appointing committees, he had been advised, allowed the principal to delegate unwanted work to underlings while simultaneously enhancing his democratic image. Brother Principal was not, however, a man to move quickly, and it was not until our first faculty meeting following the Christmas recess that Brother announced his plan for reform. It had taken him six months, but by that time Brother Principal was prepared for change. So was I.

"Committees," Brother began, "seem to me the more democratic method of conducting business among professional men. Ad hoc task forces staffed by those who know the problems best—you, the teachers—would seem to be the more rational approach to problem-solving." As he talked, Brother pulled meditatively at his right earlobe, a habit that had left the appendage abnormally distended.

"It has occurred to me that our rules and regulations have not been revised for several years. Certain chapters are no longer an adequate reference when dealing with student queries. In order to create a handbook that reflects the views of the entire faculty,"—Brother no longer used the word administrator; he was no different than any other faculty member, only had a special job to do—"I suggest we divide up the task of revision by establishing separate committees to do in-depth studies of each area needing updating. If you will turn to the index of the handbook before you, we can check off those chapters to begin work on."

Most men are lazy and concern themselves with nothing much other than comfort and pleasure. Aware of this most fundamental aspect of the human condition, the Communist Party gained control of such diverse groups as the Association in Search of Truth of Eau Claire, Wisconsin and the Mine, Mill and Smelter Workers of the Western World. Nearly a semester had passed since Kevin leaped to his fate. In all that time I had done far too little to avenge his death. It was time to make my move. Opportunity was at hand and I grasped it.

I volunteered to work on Chapter IV: Discipline, and Chapter VII: Dress. I offered to chair both committees but Bull Belloli, in a rare instance where his fear of change overcame his distaste for work, pulled seniority and won control of discipline. Who would chair the dress code committee was never in doubt; as the best-dressed man on the faculty, naturally I was appointed. I insisted as well upon a seat in Bull's group. If I could not control, I would at least obstruct.

I scheduled my first meeting for the coming Tuesday.

"Read if you will, Brother Bob, the passages outlining the code we are presumably dressing under, to clothe, so to speak, our memories in fact."

I returned the small smile Brother tossed my way to indicate he had caught the pun. Bull missed it entirely, demonstrating the lack of sophistication I had to contend with in so urbane a matter as student fashion.

Brother began to read.

"Here at St. Lucy's we look upon our students as gentlemen and expect them to be so dressed at all times. You are being prepared to take your place in the outside world in the vocation of your choice. Good grooming, whatever your choice of careers, is absolutely essential to success in the world of business.

> Boys without class
> Will always be last.
> Men on the rise
> Always wear ties.

"AT THE BEGINNING of each school day, each boy will be dressed in tie and jacket, white shirt, dress pants and suitable foot gear. Ties will be of conventional design, width and length, and tied about the neck in a Windsor knot. Jackets *must* have lapels not less than two and one-half inches or more than three and one-half inches at the spread. The jacket *must* reach to the apex of the curve of the buttocks but *must not* extend below the point where buttocks join the back of the leg as such. Shirts must be white with white buttons, tailored for a tie, and be devoid of all ornamentation.

"Pants must be belted with a leather belt passing through loops of the same fabric as the pants. We will not spell out the types of allowable fabrics; the burst of new technology in the textile industry makes this impossible. We suggest, however, that your trousers be of gabardine or gabardine-like material. *No* denims of any color, shade or cut will be tolerated. Reporting to class in denims of *any* design will result in immediate suspension. All trousers must be cut in a traditional manner. No exotic-type pants will be permitted, regardless of the current fashion. The following test will be used to determine which pants cut is allowable and which is not: A ping-pong ball will be inserted beneath the front waistband of the pants in question. When released *the ball must drop freely from upper groin to cuff. If the ball lodges between the body and the pants at any point on its downward fall, the pants will be considered exotic-type and therefore impermissible.* Infractions of this regulation will be dealt with accordingly."

Brother Bob looked up from the page. "This last part seems to have been written a long time ago, Virgil. Pants loose enough in the crotch to pass the ping-pong test have been out for years. Did they have zoot suits in mind?"

"Sounds like late Forties early Fifties to me," I agreed. "Well, we'll bring it up to date. Before I give my recommendations, does anyone have suggestions?"

Dionisio 'Eyes' Panuccio, our teacher of freshman English, as well as several other subjects, squinted through his thick telescopic lenses, desperately trying to pull me into focus. "I think we could simplify these regulations, don't you, Virgil? I mean, I'm not going to drop ping-pong balls down any guy's pants." As he spoke, Eyes squirmed in embarrassed discomfort. "It's not my job. I'm a teacher."

Ah, such innocence. I mentally chalked up one for support of reform.

"I'm sure most of us here share your distaste for such intimate inspections, Dionisio." I looked pointedly at Mother Murphy.

"Yes, Orfeo? Do you have something to add?"

"Een Arhainteena, all was more seemplay. The boys weer ooniforms—blue blazeers and gray pons. No problemas."

Brother Principal thought Orfeo Animan—Orphan Annie to the boys—his find of the year. "A real native Hispanic, Virgil. He should not only provide the boys with a valuable language experience, but a unique cultural exchange as well."

That Orfeo could not speak English and not one of his students understood Spanish, including the Puerto Rican, Angel Hernandez, was an obstacle to teaching apparently overlooked when Brother hired the Argentine.

"We appreciate your opinion, Orfeo, but in one of our few reforms of the past century, St. Lucy's did away with uniforms in 1954. Uniforms are, of course, still worn by some societies, both East and West. China, for example, wears uniforms to symbolize the birth of an egalitarian order, and history tells us uniforms are worn in your country to preserve order of any kind. We, however, live in America, and so it must be the purpose of this committee to bring the school's dress policy into alignment with our tradition of individual choice, at least in regards to costume. Yes, Mr. Belloli?"

"I don't see any sense in this talking about clothes. If the laws we got now aren't any good, forget 'em. We all know what kind of clothes we don't like. If the freak's dressed like a fag, throw him out. No sense shitting around with rules."

"Mr. Belloli, your disregard for law and the judicial process is well known to this committee. But rules—law—wisely formulated, properly propagated and justly administered protect the weak from the strong. You might, for instance, observe the rules of social discourse. If you wish to imply that a correlation exists between modes of dress and sexual preference, then I suggest you use the term 'homosexual' or 'gay,' the designation preferred by the oppressed minority of whom you speak. You might also use correct grammar and refrain from gross vulgarities."

"You calling me ignorant, Quinn?"

"Mr. Quinn or Virgil, not Quinn. We are not yet governed solely by the Pentagon. I'm suggesting, Mr. Belloli, that your choice of language falls short of your station in life. As teachers we should—"

"Don't preach at me, Quinn!"

"If you like, Mr. Belloli, I'll adjourn this meeting. I'll have to explain the reasons why to Brother Principal, of course. 'Unprofessional behavior on the part of—'"

Brother Liberal interrupted. "Okay, Virgil. Enough. It's nearly four o'clock and we haven't torn into the real work yet. Now I suggest we keep the preamble part about gentlemen, etc., and the tie and jacket rule. Just knock out the ping-pong clause. Tapered pants are gone for good anyway. It's all bells now, and worn so tight no ball is going to fall to the floor."

"So what's new?" Mother Murphy asked. "The bells they wear are just as tight as pegged were, just in different places. The way bells grip the crotch is scandalous."

Mother thought the too-tight rule should be retained and enforced, but not by the falling ball method.

"The new clause should read something like this..." and he read from a 3x5 index card. "Unless the inspecting teacher is able to grasp at least two inches of fabric in his hand at any point from waist to knee, the pants will be considered unallowable."

Brother Liberal guffawed and grabbed Mother Murphy by the butt.

"Oh, oh, oh!" Mother screeched, and leaped to his feet. "Brother Robert! I'm shocked! And you a religious!"

"Please, men, *please!*" I shouted. "Quiet down! Brother, would you *please* stop laughing."

"I can't help it, Virgil. I mean, can't you just see it? Mother—Mr. Murphy, beg your pardon—grabbing a boy by the—"

"Enough, Brother Robert. We've come to reform, not ribaldize. Now please quiet down so we can continue."

I waited a moment for Brother Bob to get control of himself—at times he acted no older than the boys he taught—and then continued.

"Now, for my recommendations. I suggest we do away with these bothersome regulations altogether and clearly state as much—" I glanced at Bull Belloli—"in the school handbook. The tie and jacket rules were designed by an immigrant clergy intent on pushing working class boys into the lower middle class. In lieu of a well-educated alumni, which the Church could not afford to produce, the clergy offered the corporations and municipal bureaucracies an army of submissive clerks accustomed to the bourgeois uniform of jacket and tie. The young men, most of them at least, knew how to spell and do their sums. Those who didn't were sent to the fire and police departments. The bosses rewarded their docile employees with pension plans and the social approval of having made it. They were told they were now truly middle class.

"All that is changing now. Tomorrow's world belongs to classless youth. Observe the nonchalance with which young people in all parts of the world discard the costumes of the past. As professional educators, we must prepare our boys for an internationalist tomorrow, not a parochial yesterday. And so I say, Off with the ties! Off with the jackets! Let us flaunt the body electric!"

A brief silence swallowed up the emphatic crack of my open hand striking the oak table top. We all listened to the echo. No one, I'm sure, noticed me wince as arthritic pain shot through diseased knuckle joints and swollen wrist.

Mother Murphy was the first to break the silence.

"You would have them *naked*, Virgil?"

"You're a pagan, Quinn," said Bull Belloli.

"I believe my Christian credentials are equal to yours, Mr. Belloli," and I rapidly ticked off the sacramental anointments and the degrees from sectarian institutions preparing me for this moment.

"I'm not sure," Eyes Panuccio murmured. "It might get out of hand."

"The world is out of hand, Dionisio. Only the other day while walking home from school at six-thirty in the evening"—I paused to let the length of my workday sink in—"I saw a young man coming towards me on Second Avenue. He was dressed in tight dungarees, like sailors wear. An embroidered bumblebee, so positioned to appear to be sucking nectar, sat on the head of his either large and flaccid or semi-erect penis. The bulge was just that noticeable. I recognized the young man, Dionisio. He was a recent graduate of this school, the valedictorian for his class, in conspicuous and total rebellion against a dress code that had not allowed him youth's prerogative to exhibit its physical charms. And not one block further on, I stopped at a newsstand to check the photos on the front page of the afternoon tabloid—I never read the rag. And whom should I see? The senator who chairs the Armed Services Committee leaving St. Veronica's Hospital where he had recently undergone a facelift and neck tuck. With our leaders going to such painful extremes to recapture their youth, can we deny our boys the right to flaunt theirs?"

Brother Liberal was the next to comment.

"Virgil, I know where you're coming from and I hear a lot of what you're saying. But don't you think we're moving too fast? I mean by doing away with all dress codes. Sudden changes cause resentment. I suggest a simple modification of the rules. Let the kids wear flared pants, lightweight boots and whatever jacket and shirt they think decent. During the warm months, June and September, we could even do without the tie."

"Brother Bob, the rules and regulations we are here today to bury were a liberal compromise with the code that preceded them—uniforms. The world today is changing much too fast for compromise. The modern mode is scarcely in when a more startling fashion deems yesterday's fad passé. My authority as a spokesperson on fashion is derived from experience we do not have time to elaborate upon at this time other than to say my work exposed me to the shallow heart of that flamboyant profession. But I can predict with certainty that today's bells will be succeeded by styles reminiscent of the early Forties—loose bags and drapes—altered by exotic nips and tucks yet to be conceived. Are we to return to this trivial matter of dress every semester? What will be the relevance of the ping-pong test when pants are absurdly loose? What criteria then?

I should think we have more important work to do than to try to keep up with Seventh Avenue."

Brother Liberal folded. By playing on Orphan Annie's immigrant status and Eyes Panuccio's incipient naïveté, as well as his wish to be respected for his maturity and intelligence, I got the votes I needed. Mother Murphy proved a bitch. Bull Belloli had voted No before we started.

I wrote up the committee's decisions and presented them to Brother Principal.

"Hmmmmmmmmm, Ummmmmmmmm, Hmmmmmm-mmmmm." Brother moaned and reached for his earlobe. "Interesting, Virgil, interesting. Put a lot of effort into this, I can see that. Hmmm. Excellent work. Thank you for your recommendations, Virgil. We will bring this matter up at a future faculty meeting. Until then, I want to thank you again for your sincere efforts in this regard."

10

MILITANTS ARE MADE NOT on the barricades but in committee rooms. At some point every dedicated reformer realizes the futility of heading one more task force or formulating yet another study group. Postponing the day of reckoning becomes reprehensible in itself; patience is not a virtue we should expect from the oppressed. Putting off the inevitable not only attenuates the pain of the downtrodden, it allows those in power to shore up their defenses by weeding out the opposition.

When Brother Principal returned in September, bubbling with enthusiasms after a month under Columbia's doctors of education, we had been led to believe that the recommendations of our several committees would be put to a vote of the faculty. A week passed. He had ample time by then to have studied my simple presentation—in essence, a paragraph doing away with dress codes, followed by a six-page essay demonstrating why codes ran counter to both the principals of the republic and the direction the Church was taking under the reformist pope, John XXIII. His reply, when it came, appeared in our mailboxes, a slip of paper no bigger than a bookmark. It was more a statement of Brother Principal's commitment to thrift in all things than it was a reply to weeks of tortuous committee work.

"The office has decided that dress regulations will, for the present time, remain unchanged."

Read for 'the present time' the natural life of Eyes Panuccio, the youngest member of the faculty; for the 'office has decided,' an abrupt dismissal of St.Lucy's first attempt at democratic centralism.

More than a year had passed since I heard St. Lucy's call to abandon the second of my careers and take up social reconstruction. During this time Brother Principal and I had developed a cautious appreciation of each other's work. If we didn't often agree on policy, neither did we publicly voice anything but admiration for the other's dedication to his job. This was largely romanticism on my part. Although I had precious little to go on, I had wanted to see Brother Principal and me as a team, the enlightened director and dedicated activist collaborating to move St. Lucy's into the twentieth century. (I foresaw that when the time came for Brother to be transferred to the chancery, promoted because of our success at St. Lucy's, his position would fall to me.) His curt betrayal of my dream left me disillusioned. I felt abandoned, like a lover might feel after the sudden dissolution of a relationship expected to last a lifetime. My work suffered. My lectures on American history shrunk to little more than a superficial exegesis of the text, those on marriage and the family to dry homilies dull enough to cause my teachers—Kinsey, Masters and Johnson, Havelock Ellis—to sneer in sharp derision. When the last bell sounded for the day, I crept home to my unkempt apartment and fell onto my narrow cot to mope. Deeper and deeper I slipped into the darkest depression of my life, that pit of loneliness and rejection St. John of the Cross called 'the black night of the soul.'

A single week passed. And then, on the seventh day, appalled by my indulgence when all around me men and women suffered real oppression, I leaped from the bed to find myself more fit for the struggle than ever I had been during my youthful innocence. For it would be war now, and fought with all the weapons at my disposal—the experience of a richly varied past, my persuasive charm, my remarkable oratorical gifts, and most important of all, the will to win, the product of close mentoring by my idol, my queen, my Sister Philomena.

But whose tactics to follow? Prussia's greatest strategist, Alfred von Schlieffen, made the single-front offensive his cardinal principal of war. With his paper plan he expected to conquer all of France in a single month. Napoleon Bonaparte, the Great Liberator, moved real armies on several fronts and conquered all of Europe. Von Schlieffen's legions never crossed the Marne. Napoleon, for all his conquests, died in exile. I never thought Elba would be my fate. Did Bonaparte? History is perplexing.

It was at this time, the midpoint of my second year at St. Lucy's, that Brother Principal's true ambition struck me. He wished to rule. Not this minute principality on West Sixteenth Street, but the entire kingdom. St. Lucy's was but a stepping stone to the throne. Provincial Head of his order perhaps? Brother General of all the Little Brothers of Divine Grace? Men going places cross the gulf of anonymity on a bridge of ships, all tightly run. Rock one boat and their entire career might flounder.

If I was to drag St. Lucy's into the New Order, I must eventually divest Brother Principal of his power. Until that time I would neutralize his authority with the constant fear of revolt.

Brother had the habit of suddenly breaking into classes by calling over the loudspeaker, "Everyone over to the church." It had taken me a week to type out the hundred questions of my World History mid-term exam, only to see my work destroyed. Exam half completed, ample time now in the going over and the bored sitting through some archaic Lenten exercise for the boys to arrive by consensus at the answers to my trickiest questions.

Brother's command to move occurred on a Friday afternoon. Following orders sent down by Monsignor Delaney, he drafted us to insure a packed house for the Stations of the Cross, a medieval religious exercise commemorating the Via Dolorosa of Jesus Christ. We marched the boys over two-by-two to take their places in unpadded pews. After the Monsignor had stood us, sat us and knelt us to the irritating clack of his clacker through fourteen Stations, he led the nodding boys through an hour of sorrowful hymns, dirges of no artistic merit groaned slowly into the microphone turned to peak volume.

Great leaders perceive the subtle shifts in power sooner than the men about them. Lapel buttons bearing the slogan 'God is Dead' had barely appeared on the street when I concluded, correctly, that if He was truly dead to man, then power must pass to the people. Nature abhors anarchy. The Chancery and its appointees—the Brother Principals and Sister Superiors, God's hierarchy—would soon be superseded by a student-teacher coalition, and I would mold the bloc.

Tactics alter to fit circumstance; integrity demands strategy remain unchanged. Reform was my objective. *They* were many, I but one. Just as Napoleon used end runs to demolish his foe, I would use the boys to accomplish what I could not achieve alone.

Boys hate regimentation as much as they enjoy singing; both are as natural to their age as rebellion. They would need little encouragement to rebel against the Monsignor's travesty of art and religion. Doubtless this refuse heap of stale tradition would have ignited in time by spontaneous combustion. I merely provided the spark that hastened the moment of conflagration.

On the following Thursday, the eve of the next Lenten service, I designed my lectures to include a little homily on modes of worship through the ages.

"The posture we choose to assume in church should result, *I* think, from the churchgoer himself deciding what position he prays best in. Certainly an incessant clacking of clackers is ill suited to the inducement of a prayerful attitude. Standing, sitting, kneeling? Is this important to the Crucified Christ we worship in Lenten exercises? Of course not. Does He care whether we sing or not? And if we sing, our choice of song? I shouldn't think so. The Gospels would indicate by omission that Christ Himself was tone deaf and never sang at all."

In this way I reached six classes, 283 boys in all. I spoke with greater frankness to Primo and his friends, stretching the truth a bit to achieve the objective I had in mind.

"What do you think, Mr. Quinn? I mean personally, about what we should do about these Lenten exercises." We were having an after-school snack at Tina's Coffee Shop. Ten or twelve other boys whom I had no reason to distrust gathered around us in a huddle.

"Well, boys, we're not in the classroom now so I suppose I can speak my mind. Personally—and I say again, this is strictly my opinion—I think religious worship should be left to the individual in all rituals not specifically programmed by the pope. I myself stand when I wish, sit when I wish. Sometimes I sing, sometimes I don't. Occasionally I choose to hum a tune, discretely of course, different from the hymn selected. Variety. Spontaneity. I think both add zest to religious ritual, just as they do to the circus."

The boys took it from there. Friday arrived and, right on schedule, right in the middle of fifth period, we heard the screech of the loudspeaker, the heavy breathing of Brother Principal as he adjusted himself to the mike. Then the order: "Everyone over to the church."

Spontaneity rare to Catholic religious rituals marked each Station of the Cross. Some boys up, some down, all in time to the clack of the clacker. Singing, humming. Christmas carols interspersed with Stabat Maters. The old Monsignor's face turned as purple as his Lenten vestments. Brother Principal's face blanched white with anger and I thought just a little fear. Dissent, held at bay for centuries, had cracked the unity of the American Church.

Brother punished the boys severely. Trained to fortitude, he succeeded in sitting out the healthy chaos of those Friday Stations of the Cross, then marched the entire student body to the gym, packed them in. There he held them, standing at attention and in absolute silence, the slightest quiver or tiniest whisper grounds for immediate dismissal, until six that evening.

The boys had fought brilliantly and I did not desert them during this bitter showdown. The gym had two doors, one at either end. On pretext of passing through the gym to the faculty room beyond, I repeatedly reviewed the ranks of silent boys, lending support with resolute nods of my head,

demonstrating to each of them that I, Virgil Quinn, was prepared to stay and suffer as long as they.

I passed through for the last time at five-fifty. Shortly
thereafter Brother dismissed them. (Mrs. Condé, the brothers' excellent cook, served dinner promptly at half-past six
and for some time now the aroma of corned beef and cabbage
had been seeping through the adjoining buildings from the
brothers' townhouse three doors down.) Not a boy cracked
beneath the strain to beg for quarter or reveal the names of
the provocateurs.

But I did. Not snitch on those responsible for civil disobe-
dience, of course, but nearly cracked beneath the strain of
waiting for some frightened and exhausted boy to step forth
and finger the instigator of the rebellion. I felt too disturbed
to talk with students that evening and fled the school premises minutes before they were dismissed. I can't say I didn't
know where I was going. *He found himself standing at the bar
of a neighborhood tavern, downing a boilermaker, unaware of
how he got there.* Such flights from anxiety had occurred often
enough in the past for me to know I was headed straight for
the County Cork, that I would bury myself among the protective bodies of the working class men who filled the place
from five to seven, and have a boilermaker or two.

Someone put me in a cab later on. Someone else—I believe
he came out of Stuyvesant Square where the cabby mistakenly dropped me off—walked me home and helped me up
the stairs to my apartment, a good turn I would never have
allowed if I'd been sober. When we reached the door, I must
have passed out because I don't remember a thing after that.

11

For weeks the halls of St. Lucy's rumbled with gusty recapitulations of the Lenten Revolt. My sporadic calls for help from Primo and his friends had evolved by now into bi-weekly strategy sessions. The boys were impatient to tighten the screws on Brother Principal. If I had given them the least encouragement, they would have brought St. Lucy's academic life to a standstill.

Struggles of this sort, however, did not fit into my plans. A point to be considered by those who now accuse me of 'revolutionary intent.' If I had wished to substitute anarchy for fascism, the boys' enthusiasm certainly gave me the opportunity. I did not do so because I believed greater good could be achieved at less cost by other means. Then too, the boys' timing was off. We must first see to the proper positioning of the forces of good and evil before electing the course of Armageddonian conflict.

In reply to the boys' call for greater disruptions, I urged magnanimity as the better part of victory. Primo did not agree.

"When you got the principal by the balls," he said, "press your advantage."

My advice to Primo ignored whatever political wisdom his words contained and emphasized instead the boy's personal development.

"If you wish to rise in the world, Primo, you must learn to express yourself in more tasteful metaphors."

Brother Principal presumed correctly that students acting alone had not precipitated the Lenten Revolt. But what could he do beyond a harsh questioning of conspicuous instigators—Primo de Popalano preeminent among them—and a petty enforcement of the unpopular dress code? This was no time for an ugly purge of faculty and students, what with the Cardinal running up to Albany once a month, bargaining with his political chums for as much school aid as the Supreme Court would allow, sending his couriers to the far corners of the vast diocese to spread the Word, all to present a progressive image. Time enough for housecleaning after the funds are allocated. And of even greater importance to Brother, he had to present an image pleasing to the Hudson Valley Accreditation Association. His drive to make St. Lucy's the first parish school so honored must not fall victim to reckless sackings. His reputation—that is, his future—hung on the association's decision. Student dismissals were perhaps acceptable, if it came to that; an additional expulsion or two might go unnoticed. If teachers were sent packing, however, the people from HVAA were sure to ask why.

I had a year to accomplish reform, perhaps two if Albany balked at funding the schools educating one-third of the state's students. No time to dally. The Cardinal and Brother Principal might be content with image. I was not. I expected the parochial school system of the diocese of New York, larger than the public system of Omaha, Nebraska, to live up to its responsibilities. Isn't that why I was sent?

THE YEAR OF the Lenten Revolt I spent Easter recess as a houseguest of a recently met friend on the island of Bimini. Axel took up sudden residence on that dot on the map of the Caribbean within days of the IRS opening an investigation into his household appliance empire. If the appliances Axel sold were in fact of untraceable origin, I wouldn't know. In Bimini we enjoyed a wonderfully primitive ten days in a grass hut without so much as a refrigerator. Such an enjoyable holiday, at no expense to me, rated Axel an entry in my Black Books, highlighted with a big red star.

Perhaps the long nights alone with Axel, listening to tales of his entrepreneurial coups in places as far flung as Allahabad and Zamboanga, caused me to realize upon my return to St. Lucy's, that if I was ever to influence life beyond my classroom, I must find a larger platform. Years of indoctrination had displaced intelligence in the boys I taught. Untangling these snarled threads of prejudice was a noble occupation in itself, and a less ambitious teacher might have been content to make such a task his life's work. I had loftier goals.

It was my habit then, and is now, to scan the city newspapers, all of them, everyday. During the month preceding my annual spring conference with Brother Principal, I followed the course of seven coups d'etat running concurrently in as many Third World countries. In each of these revolts, the insurgents moved first against the media. When the tanks left the barracks, they headed straight for the television stations and the newsrooms.

We didn't have closed-circuit television at St. Lucy's, not
even a set tuned to receive news of the outside world. No
parochial school did. We were forbidden access to those marvelous coffers of the state which, regardless of how deeply and
how often public school administrators dip in, are miracu-
lously refilled to overflowing. St. Lucy's did, however, boast
a fee-supported print media, and its control became my next
objective. How to spread the message of reform without it?

When Brother Principal and I sat down that spring to
hammer out my next year's contract, I hinted that if I was
not appointed moderator of the yearbook, I just might look
elsewhere for employment. Was Brother's look of response to
my veiled threat one of alarm or relief? Ambiguous, for sure,
the look of a man who would like to be rid of an agitator, but
not yet. No way could he afford to lose his hardest working
teacher in the middle of an accreditation process.

"I was just reviewing your credentials, Virgil," Brother
replied. "You are by far the most qualified teacher on our
faculty in this regard. You are even, as you note in your *curriculum vitae,* the author of a published work, *Philomena of
the Plains.*"

As indeed I was. My experience went well beyond Philomena. At the age of ten, I was apprenticed to my Uncle
Isaac, who ran a print shop in Omaha. Although our business was limited to the printing of broadsides advertising
bargains featured by local merchants (and a single run of
Philomena), I saw no reason to mention this on the résumé
that Brother had directed us to work up in anticipation of a
visit by the HVAA.

"But there's the matter of seniority," Brother continued. He
cocked his head to one side, stared into space, then inserted
the long nail of his little finger into his ear and plucked out

a troublesome chunk of wax. "Mr. O'Grady has been at St. Lucy's for many years."

"As a criterion for advancement, Brother, seniority insures mediocrity."

"But the faculty expects it."

"Mediocrity? You would promote a fellow teacher solely because he had served more time?"

"Seniority, Virgil! Seniority. We—the religious—work for a higher motive."

Catching and holding the gaze of his small black eyes with my own, I permitted myself just the hint of a condescending smile. "I'm sure you do, Brother. We are alike in that."

Brother Principal did not reveal his thoughts with a look of disbelief.

"You are a dedicated teacher, Virgil. You work hard. But you already moderate the Forensics Club. You have Marriage and the Family."

"What's another ten or twenty hours a week when the reputation of St. Lucy's is at stake?"

Greek O'Grady had published the yearbook for five years. His most recent product, just off the press and noteworthy only for its shocking lack of taste, lay closed on the corner of Brother Principal's desk. I reached for the book and flipped it open. Immediately following the book's dedication (to Private Pino Chiano, a recent graduate, now a casualty of the war raging in Vietnam), a full page had been given over to a four-color reproduction of Zuccaro's famous portrait of Elizabeth I. The detail was sharp, the color good. Oh, vile man! I could gouge out his eyes! O'Grady had cleverly cut out the face of the Virgin Queen and replaced it with a black and white photo of me. A vicious trick perpetrated by the Greek and one for which he would dearly pay.

"That," I said, "is grounds for libel."

Brother tried to hide his little smile of delight behind a quick look of feigned disapproval.

"This yearbook is a scandal," I continued. "Bad layout, worse graphics, a book whose only theme is ridicule." I flipped to a page of candid snapshots and placed the book in front of the principal. With a manicured nail I pointed to the photo picturing Brother with his finger in his ear. "*I* would use the yearbook as a vehicle for learning. The boys selected to work on it would get a thorough grounding in journalistic responsibility."

Recalling the importance money had played in my winning Marriage and the Family, I suggested that the moderator's fee was much too high.

"I will take the job for a mere honorarium. We can spend what we've saved on a new set of world maps. The ones we're using predate World War I, and the boys are confused by a world dominated by British imperial pink."

Brother quietly closed the book and set it aside. Then he rose from his chair to indicate our conference was drawing to a close.

"I will consider your offer, Virgil. I'll announce my decision on all extracurriculars at the final faculty meeting before summer vacation."

I had no doubt what Brother's decision would be. But I didn't revel in my success. There was still too much to do. As I left the office, I had already begun to speculate on what turn of events would provide me with the opportunity to wrest control of the school newspaper from that potentially dangerous bigot, Mother Murphy.

12

EVERY GREAT GENERAL IS an opportunist at heart. This principle is so basic to the study of military history as to need no further demonstration. Recall the conquests of Alexander the Great. The fabled Macedonian would bring whole armies to a halt, then suddenly wheel his forces to strike at some distant and unsuspecting foe foolish enough to expose his flank.

I managed much the same feat when Flash Fagan, the man occupying the chair that should have been mine, presented me with a windfall opportunity the gossips of St. Lucy's would later refer to as 'Under the T's.' Taking my cue from Alexander, I instantly suspended my dream to monopolize the printed word and struck for the certain victory of a departmental chair.

No one holding down as many jobs as Flash could do them all well. Nonetheless, anyone electing to teach should bring at least the rudiments of learning to all tasks assigned.

I was teaching my first period class when I stumbled upon Fagan's most recent blunder and just the evidence I needed to dislodge the man from the only position he held that I coveted. Chairman of the History Department. Although I could hardly believe my good fortune, I did not gloat. Good fortune is not of our making. The form our fortune takes is dependent upon the whim of God. He determines these things and should, therefore, receive the credit for whatever gifts fortune delivers into our hands. However, since some of us expend a great deal more effort than others detecting the rise of opportunity, we should be rewarded accordingly.

Such incompetence! Would anyone believe me? I busied the boys with a homework assignment, then hurried next door to tell all to Mother Murphy.

"All under the *T's*. Would you believe it? For this he's paid five hundred a year."

"You're pulling my leg, Virgil. No one's that dumb." Mother Murphy smiled demurely, deepening the dimples in his chubby cheeks.

"I'm not lying to you, Charles. I sent the McCabe boy down to fetch a copy of *The Saints of Yore*. I wanted to acquaint the boys with the life of St. Philomena. She was the first, you know, to be struck from the cannon."

Mother clucked in sympathy. "Keep her memory alive, Virgil. When we get rid of this reformist pope, we'll all go back to the old ways."

"I was speaking of Philomena, Charles, not counter- revolution.

"Anyway," I continued, "McCabe went first to the boys' room to smoke a cigarette, as I expected him to, then to the library where he checked the card catalogue.

"'The book ain't down there,' he said.

"'You've been smoking,' said I.

"'No I haven't,' he lied.

"'You reek of smoke, McCabe.'

"'I ain't been smoking in the can,' the boy swore.

"They lie nowadays without blinking an eye. TV taught them, Madison Avenue. Washington, DC. No shame."

"Virgil, you're such a leftist," Mother Murphy giggled.

"'What did you look under, McCabe? In the card catalogue.'

"'*S* for Saints.'

"'Good boy. Shows you've learned something even if not what destroys your health. But why didn't you find it then? I know it's down there. I saw it on the shelves only a week ago.'"

We had few books in our little library then, mostly religious works and donated volumes of nineteenth-century classics like Dickens and Longfellow.

"'It ain't down there.' McCabe was firm.

"In truth, Charles, I didn't believe the boy. I suspected him of spending the entire time in the john, so I went down myself. The book was not under the *S*'s.

"Rather than delay my lesson longer, I decided to read from *Tales of Christians*. It's good on the early saints. I went to the *T* drawer. Charles, there were three! Would you believe it? Three drawers of *T*'s in a library the size of ours, a good one-third of the entire stack of files?

"I pulled out the first drawer and began to thumb through. No, I thought. There's been some mistake. No one could be so ill-informed. Fagan had catalogued all the titles beginning with *The* under the *T*'s."

Mother looked aghast.

"Well, I marched right over to Fagan's room, called him to the door and asked where in the name of Jesus he had learned to catalogue books."

"'It's how they do it at the Library of Congress,' he said, showed me the shiny seat of his threadbare trousers, and closed the door on his dozing classroom."

Mother Murphy was St. Lucy's most avid gossip. By last bell every teacher in the school had heard Mother's version of 'Under the *T's*.'

I was fairly certain Brother Principal had heard the story as well. Not much escaped the cupped ear of his two-way intercom. Yet a week passed without word of a visit by Mr. Fagan to the office for a refresher course in the art of filing. I decided then to ask Brother for an appointment.

Brother wished to appear puzzled over the reason why I came. I was in no mood for games, and paused only long enough for anger to raise my voice to the pitch of outrage. "I simply can't continue working under a man who never mastered third grade study skills."

"An amusing instance of absent-mindedness." Brother chuckled. "Something we administrators have learned to expect from history professors—no offense intended, Virgil."

"This was not just one or two titles, Brother, but every *the* title in our collection. Drawers and drawers full, all methodically filed. *The Age of the Anti-Christ, The Bread of Life, The Catacombs of Katmandu.* How did the man ever get through college? How did he ever find a book? Or were students not required to read at whatever school he attended. No, I simply cannot, will not continue to serve under such a man. I have my academic reputation to consider. Can you imagine the reflection on the department when this story gets out?"

"Your reputation is secure, Virgil." Brother did not say so, but judging from the note of irony I caught, I'm sure he would like to have added, "for good or for ill."

"This incident will blow over, Virgil," Brother replied in resignation. "All scandals do."

So the man intended to do nothing. This came as a surprise, even from him. Would nothing move the man to action? The managerial mind. Insist that the employee gets to work, more or less on time, and at least appear to be occupied. There your obligation ends. Change is futile. The next one you hire will be no better than the one fired. Brother should have gone into civil service.

My mind raced, searching for ammunition. Should I again threaten to resign? He knows he will never get another teacher quite like me. No, keep that weapon in reserve for bigger game than Fagan. Hint—ever so obliquely—that if he does not comply, he may face a repetition of the Lenten Revolt? No, too risky. Either he does not suspect my part in the affair or prefers that the instigator remain anonymous. So do I. Brother pulled at his earlobe, a sign of growing impatience. I had to decide. The HVAA. Faculty competence was certain to be on the association's list of qualifications. Who would accredit a school where a department chairman was such a stranger to books he never learned the trick of filing?

"It would be very difficult," I began, "to conceal something like this from HVAA. Everyone in the school knows, and every teacher has an enemy or two among the students. It would be so easy a matter for one of the clever boys—and it is they who most detest Mr. Fagan—to drop this bombshell in the ear of a member of the accrediting committee." I paused to allow my own shell to reach its target. It did. Brother shuddered under the impact, then began pulling at his ear. "Risky, don't you think, Brother? And there's no reason why Mr. Fagan need know why he's being transferred to a new position. There's no one, for example, doing anything to prepare the boys for domestic life."

Mr. Fagan and his parents, with whom he had lived for all of his thirty-eight years, had recently put a down payment on a semi-detached bungalow in further Queens. Home ownership had encouraged him to improve upon his single specialty, a profound knowledge of home economy. Rarely a lunch period passed without his giving us yet another lesson on the intricacies of computing household heating units, or when and where to buy garden hose on sale, experience that would serve him well in his new job.

I continued to press my case. "The addition of such a course to our Enrichment Program would set very well with the accreditation committee, I should think. Very progressive. Few boys' schools can boast a course in home economics.

"Use the stipend attached to the chair," I offered, "to pay Mr. Fagan for his duties. I'm sure he needs it to meet his mortgage payments. As for me, the opportunity to improve St. Lucy's reputation for academic excellence is all the payment I require."

Brother Principal appeared sincerely relieved. And why shouldn't he? I had done all the work for him. He now had a department head eminently qualified for the job *and* a teacher of home economics, both at no added cost.

Victories are rarely won without losses. At the faculty meeting held the following Friday, the last meeting of the term, Brother Principal announced the extracurricular appointments for the following year.

"We have decided that Mr. Fagan is uniquely suited and will better serve the needs of St. Lucy's by designing, implementing and in every way directing an Enrichment course in domestic arts than he did as his department chairman. His stipend will, of course, remain the same."

In describing the content of the course I had outlined for Flash, Brother avoided the term I had used, 'home economics,' and substituted in its stead 'domestic arts.'

"Brother Bob will continue his efforts to develop a greater sense of ethnic pride within the student body. As an adjunct to this activity, Brother also hopes to develop a higher level of ethnic tolerance—among the faculty as well as the students.

"Mr. McDougal has requested that he be relieved of the duties he shares with Mr. Fagan, the post of co-librarian. Francis wishes to dedicate his time exclusively to the formation of a new extracurricular here at St. Lucy's, The Law and Order Society, with Mr. Belloli assisting him in an advisory capacity. In light of the deteriorating social climate of our city, I have agreed."

Brother Bob and I exchanged shocked looks. No one had leaked a word of Brother Adolph's new activity. How had he managed it? At St. Lucy's? Where the stuff of gossip was unearthed with all the tenacity of a hungry ferret set loose in a rabbit warren? He must have imposed the confessional seal before revealing his plan to Brother Principal.

"Mr. Murphy will continue to moderate the school newspaper and its sister publication, the literary quarterly. We hope that a bit more progress can be made next year in getting both publications off the ground and onto the presses.

"Virgil will continue his superb work with the Forensics Club as well as assume the chair to be vacated by Mr. Fagan. In regards to his class Marriage and the Family, which, by the way, Mr. Quinn teaches without remuneration, we hope that he is giving as much attention to the sacramental nature of marriage as he is to…it's procreative function."

Brother paused to shuffle his papers. I waited for him to continue. I wondered what words he had chosen to break the news of O'Grady's shift from the yearbook to some less sensitive assignment.

"And Mr. O'Grady will continue, as he has for so any years, to moderate the yearbook. We would like to suggest, however, that next year, Gerald, you exercise more control and better judgment in the selection of candid photographs to be printed in a publication with such a long shelf life."

The man droned on but I had ceased to listen. Everything of importance had been said. Brother had betrayed me—for the second time. First his refusal to abide by the decisions of my dress code committee, now this. My case against the Greek's continuing in his position was watertight. The man was not only reckless and tasteless; he also knew nothing about the graphic arts. Only cowardice could explain Brother's failure to grant me O'Grady's post. The Greek's talent for intimidation had won the day. Brother, it appeared, was simply afraid of the hole O'Grady would leave in the faculty if he quit. Good math teachers are hard to find; and men schooled in Greek as well as Latin even harder. It was an obvious sellout, and for that Brother Principal must pay. If he was afraid to attack the Greek, I was not.

TERRENCE X. CALLAHAN has publicly accused me of 'seeking Mr. O'Grady's dismissal in order that his offices might fall [to me].' I mean really! But who's to believe the man? A gossip columnist, no less, the least respected of a disrespectful lot. And for whom? The *Brooklyn Scroll*, the Church's contribution to yellow journalism.

As if I needed a motivation for getting Greek O'Grady beyond the crimes the man so blatantly committed—brutalizing boys and then bragging about it. No reason to look for Quinnian machinations behind Greek O'Grady's fall. When chance presented me with an opportune piece of scandal-tainted evidence, of course I used it.

13

CONTRARY TO WHAT EXPERIENCE had taught me to expect, Axel and I continued to keep in touch after my return from Bimini. Axel was one of those men who liked to make things over, everything from defective refrigerators to house guests suspected of frigidity. I had met men like Axel before and believed I could handle whatever problems might arise. Therefore, when he invited me to spend July and August at his summer place on Lake Namekagon, one of the larger lakes of Northern Wisconsin, I did not refuse.

I'm not sure why men as rich as Axel make primitive retreats to grass huts and log cabins. Perhaps it's a macho derivative of the Pygmalion complex. Whatever the explanation, Axel was determined to make me over. He dressed me, entirely at his expense, in plaid shirts, Levis and high lace-up boots like lumberjacks wear. He taught me how to catch walleyes and muskellunge using repulsive black leeches for bait. He transformed my Apollonian figure into a physique rippling with useless muscle by ordering me to chop wood to stoke the antique range on which he cooked our flapjack breakfasts. All this I allowed him. Indeed, I allowed him more than a less generous man could have hoped for. To show my gratitude for the expensive baubles he had given me—an 18 K money clip holding more large bills than I had the opportunity to spend, a silver and turquoise vintage Navajo belt buckle to cinch my Levis, an artifact of great value to a collector—I agreed to pose atop a granite boulder, my arms uplifted, worshipping the rising sun while dressed in nothing but a revealing loin cloth, a war bonnet, and a quiver full of arrows. While I posed, Axel spied on me from behind a clump of willows, doing, I suppose, what he had to do.

But Axel wanted more. Don't they all? When his demands for a consummation of the good life could no longer be denied—'It's as necessary to health as a good night's sleep,' Axel was fond of saying to justify his lust—I borrowed one of Axle's several credit cards, hitched a ride to Ladysmith, and chartered a small plane to fly me back to civilization.

For making demands he had no right to expect, I scratched Axel's name from Black Book v.

The importance Axel placed upon giving expression to the libido in the maintenance of good health proved to be exaggerated, at least in my instance. Denial, as is so often the case with people of high principal, tends to increase my energy, not diminish it, and I returned to St. Lucy's more committed than ever to the early banishment of Greek O'Grady.

He had to go. I began by lodging complaints against O'Grady at one- or two-week intervals, hoping to wear Brother Principal down and force him to admit to the habitual nature of O'Grady's brutality. Each time I walked into the principal's office, Brother assured me he would urge Mr. O'Grady to control his temper. I had made my sixth complaint and was convinced nothing I said would incite Brother Principal to action, when I discovered O'Grady's penchant for Sapphic verse.

As we've already seen, I put a lot of time into cultivating my reputation as a man of culture. Such foresight led William Prentice, a sophomore and the only truly middle-class boy at St. Lucy's, to come to me first, believing I read Greek, with the puzzling inscription on his paper.

"Can you translate this for me, Mr. Quinn? Mr. O'Grady wrote it, but when I asked him what it meant, he just smiled and wouldn't tell me."

I glanced at the line penned in red ink beneath the last equation of the boy's midterm geometry exam. The word *Eros* jumped from the confusion of Greek letters.

"A few archaic verb forms still give me trouble, William. Could I borrow this for the evening? I'll translate it at home and return the paper to you tomorrow."

That afternoon I found a very helpful young man up at Central Library kind enough to translate the Greek phrase and identify its source. When he had finished, he smiled and gave me a look suggesting further inquiries of a more intimate nature would be answered with equal generosity.

"I'm off at four," he ventured.

"I have a little more research to do—coffee then?"

Such a kind young man. It's always reassuring to find one's taxes going for purposes more elevating than war.

Coffee, an early dinner, drinks at Philo's while I listened to him expound in Greek on the sexual mores of ancient Athenians. After our second bottle of retsina I couldn't understand a word he said. After the third—I can't remember a thing after that, but when I awoke in the morning I was in Philo's bed.

No one moves from the obscurity of Omaha, Nebraska to the front page of the New York *Daily News* by missing opportunities. In the O'Grady campaign, I knew what I had. Vacillating principals might ignore charges of brutality leveled by a teacher, but they dance to a different tune when faced by outraged parents bearing evidence of carnal misbehavior in the classroom.

I first swore the Prentice boy to secrecy, then suggested he show the examination paper to his father, a product of the Jesuits like myself, but of an earlier vintage. I hoped Mr. Prentice had retained more Greek than I.

He had. Within twenty-four hours the irate father burst in on Brother Principal, waving William's geometry exam. "What is this?" he demanded to know. "Could you please explain for me the relevance of Greek erotic poetry to the study of geometry?" He dropped the paper on Brother's desk and pointed to the inscription with his right forefinger.

Brother Principal, who read Greek no better than I, stared dumbly at the words and had no way of knowing they were Sappho's lovely, although embellished line, 'Eros burn me.'

The father did, and for the next several minutes and in a voice loud enough to reach the corridor where I had paused to listen, he not only translated the line for Brother but used the most disparaging terms to label the great poetess from the island of Lesbos who inspired it.

Brother Bob pressured me to join him in coming to O'Grady's defense.

"It's a matter of academic freedom, Virgil. If we let this pass, they'll be muzzling us all."

"Clumsy innuendo. Handwritten at that."

"I expected more support from you, Virgil."

"The man's a brute. *And* his endless ranting against those men who haunt the Rambles in search of love... it's his hypocrisy that makes him so detestable."

Brother Bob pleaded for time. "When reforms are in place, it won't be necessary for men like the Greek to hide behind violence."

The day before Brother Principal intended to announce O'Grady's resignation to the faculty, he called me to the office.

"I hope, Virgil, that you'll say nothing to the others concerning our little talks over the past few months. Some of the faculty might think Mr. O'Grady's sudden resignation results from his methods of discipline. We must guard against any impairment of our esprit de corps"—and he waved his pale thin hand with its bitten nails in a little clerical flourish of denial—"for which our faculty is famous." Then, frowning, "Neither would we want our Cultural Enrichment program to be in any way obstructed by this incident. The program depends on faculty cooperation, especially since it requires after-school hours. If it were mistakenly assumed that either of us played a part in Gerald's resignation, the faculty might rightfully wonder whether the office still supported it in matters of discipline, and in consequence withdraw its cooperation. This might well result in a bold rejection of school regulations, and nothing, Virgil, is to be more feared in a boys' school than anarchy."

Brother leaned back into his swivel chair and continued in his managerial tone.

"You and I know, and of course cannot reveal, that parental disapproval is solely responsible for Mr. O'Grady's decision. He told me that under the circumstances he thought it best to sever his relationship with St. Lucy's. 'It is too difficult to work with the young,' Gerald told me yesterday, 'when

parents disagree with one's educational philosophy.' I com-
mended him for his integrity and assured him any future
request for a recommendation will be forthcoming and will
in no way suggest his services were anything but satisfactory.
More a matter of differing pedagogical approach, I should
think. What do you think, Virgil?"

"O'Grady is a vicious pervert. He should be banned from
teaching."

"I see. But don't you think"—and Brother Principal rose
to put his hand on my shoulder—"that your denunciation
of Mr. O'Grady might be just a bit harsh? In a different setting, say in some small town away from inner-city pressures,
he might do very well for himself?"

"I'm sure he will, in whatever school that's reckless enough
to hire him."

Brother left my side to pace a lap around the room before
returning to the matter of who would be told what concerning O'Grady's dismissal. He walked with a weary step.

"Discretion, Virgil, is a virtue difficult to sustain. This is
especially true in a school as small as St. Lucy's where common civility requires so few to converse so often about so little.
Nevertheless, the future of the school depends upon our cautious silence, and I would like to encourage your efforts in
this regard by asking you, now that Mr. O'Grady is no longer with us, to assume his old responsibility as moderator of
the yearbook. Your great interest in the project, demonstrated
in past conversations, your great talent and experience in the
field of publications..."

14

I HAVE GIVEN MUCH ATTENTION to the study of time, how great men use it and lesser men waste it. All men who have made their mark in life did so by reducing recreation to habits that require the minimum amount of time to achieve the optimum degree of pleasure.

Perhaps my greatest pleasure consists of reading the morning papers while enjoying a coffee light. In the days before taking leave of St. Lucy's, I invariably stopped at the corner candy store, picked up the *Times,* a container of coffee and an unbuttered hard roll, no seeds. For the thirty minutes or so preceding my first period class, I read, sipped and nibbled, carried by the whirl of the day's political revelations into a world distant from my own, where men like myself carried the banners of righteousness. When the bell rang calling me to my first class, my head was clear, my purpose fixed, and I went on to achieve the goals I had set for the day.

Habits die hard. Now that I no longer teach at St. Lucy's, I still arise each day at six, bathe and shave, dress in suit and

tie, and pick up the *Times* and a *caffe latte,* double espresso,
before returning to my fifth-floor walk-up to drink and read
alone. The day's events fire me with the same determination,
inspire goals more ambitious than yesterday's, but now no bell
calls me to my audience of waiting boys. Most days I shoulder
my sandwich boards and march uptown to call attention to
the Cardinal's sins. Other days, when I am unable to endure
the humiliations of the crowd, I sit back, relive the old days
and watch my victories pass in review.

FOLLOWING MY SUCCESSFUL campaign against the noxious
Greek O'Grady, I slipped into a period of unexpected calm.
Much had been done, so much still left to do. Kevin was
dead, hardly remembered it seemed by anyone but myself. I
mourned him still. The monument I meant to erect to mark
his passing lay far from finished, yet I could not arouse myself
to get on with the work. Instead I busied myself with six periods a day of classroom instruction. I continued my lectures
on Marriage and the Family. I conducted my weekly session
in studio painting, doing my part to support Brother Principal's Cultural Enrichment program which, although now in
its second year, had not convinced the HVAA that St. Lucy's
was ready for appraisal. My art classes were an immense success. I began with an introductory course designed to expose
the boys to the female form and drew upon colleagues from
my second career to pose, not nude of course, but as scant-
ily clad models. From here we went on to twelve sessions
of landscape painting during which I left the boys to work
pretty much on their own. The twelve impressionist paint-
ings I completed before the end of the term would, if I had
chosen to exhibit them, place me somewhere between Gaugin

and Claude Monet. That's what my friend who worked at the Whitney said, although his position as a security guard didn't give him the leverage necessary to get me hung.

Eight classes in four disciplines, plus the Forensics Club and yearbook, both award-winning activities if the Diocesan Awards Committee had not been hopelessly biased against unorthodox treatments of any kind. Added to all this I had to see to my duties as Chairman of the History Department, which included teaching Flash Fagan the intricacies of alphabetical filing. As much as I wished to bring every aspect of instruction at St. Lucy's into conformity with my standards, I could not take on anything more. At least not without help. And since my revolutionary breakthrough, that I need not struggle alone, was yet to come, I tossed about in search of a new opponent whose defenses might prove vulnerable to a well-placed charge.

Where to strike next? Not an easy decision to make when presented with so many fronts. Bull Belloli was the most compelling choice. Now that O'Grady was gone, Bull's brutal treatment of the boys moved him up to number one from the number two slot on my list, the position I had assigned him when he coined the epithet now inseparably joined to my name by the unbreakable chain of schoolboy tradition: Virgil Quinn, the Virgin Queen. Oh, he most certainly had to go. He would, however, be hard to get. Married with six kids, Brother Principal held up Bull as the model of Catholic manhood.

St. Lucy's, like most small schools, could not afford a full-time coach, not someone assigned to the gym seven periods a day to put pudgy boys through their exercises. And so Bull Belloli was allowed to teach. Working-class boys, whose economic survival depended upon at least a passing acquaintance with biological principles as basic as genetics and photosynthesis, fulfilled Belloli's course requirements by sitting in the dark, day after day, watching bees hive and birds nest on a movie screen, while the coach sat at his desk plotting game plans by the light of a tiny sensor lamp.

I could have overlooked the man's professional incompetence; to have 'cleared St. Lucy's academic grove of dead wood,' as the writer in last week's *Voice* so imaginatively put it, would have left me camped in a desert, teacher of all subjects and sole prophet to four hundred boys. Such a fantasy never occurred to me.

Bull Belloli had to go but not, like the ill-starred Fagan, because he was incompetent or held some position it was mine to assume; I had to pursue him because he persisted in living up to the implications of his nickname, The Brooklyn Hitter.

It was Primo de Popalano who first used the name and made it stick. That it was a student and not I who first matched man to vice in so apt a sobriquet should be sufficient proof that Bull's abuse of authority and not his lack of intellectual refinement first set me against him. I return to this point because my detractors have suggested my distaste for the man originated in a personality conflict. This is absurd. I have never let feelings of repulsion or attraction influence my reformist mission. Remember Greek O'Grady. He was a man with whom I shared an interest or two in common— the culture of the ancient Greeks, for example—yet he was number one on my hit list.

The problem remained: How to get rid of a man whom my colleagues chose to discount as an innocuous buffoon?

Everyone expects coaches to be gruff; it goes with the territory. "His bark is worse than his bite," Brother Principal assured me. I knew better. Bull used bellicose expression to screen his more serious problem of child abuse. And in this he was largely successful. Even the boys rolled with Bull's punches. When I spoke to Brother Bob, expecting him to support me, he fell back on easy humor. "Oh, the Bull's all right," Brother joked. "He's just seen *Back to Bataan* too often on the late show."

"Amusing," I replied. "Tell that to the de Popalano boy. No, better not. It's painful to laugh with a split lip."

In their impatience, people whose calling it is to right social wrongs sometimes indulge in caustic remarks. Watching Brother Bob slink sheepishly down the hall, I chastised myself for wounding a man who meant me no harm. Sarcasm, the sin of the intellectually gifted and the spiritually deprived. I promised to make amends—at a later date. Right now I had to seek redress for sins greater than my own and that meant a talk with Brother Principal.

"He must go, Brother. He can't control his anger. Again he's struck Primo de Popalano."

"A temporary fall from grace, Virgil. Aren't we all subject to unfortunate behavior when caught in the grip of temper? Forgive Remo. True—and I say this in confidence—Mr. Belloli is not the most...well, astute member of our faculty, and I know you grow impatient at times with his shortcomings. But Remo serves a necessary function, one we can hardly do without, and gracefully accepts the hardship of inadequate equipment. Only today I had to turn down his request for a half-dozen new basketballs. At $9.95 each—well, the budget just can't absorb such an expense. And I think we should all keep in mind that he's a family man, married with six children in the Church and another on the way."

I was furious. Six children and the wife pregnant again. On his salary!

"I fail to see a compensatory relationship between indiscriminate breeding and child abuse. Better we have fewer children and value them more."

Brother Principal rose to my anger. "If the future of the Church depended on the offspring of *most* members of our faculty here, the pews of St. Lucy's would be empty in a generation."

The implications of Brother's response caught me at a rare loss for words.

"The Little Brothers of Divine Grace have chosen a life of celibacy," I ventured.

Brother spiked his reply with innuendo. "And out of nine lay faculty members with an average age of thirty-four, one is married. The rest do not even bother to bring a woman companion to the annual Christmas dinner,"

"Celibacy cannot be deemed the sole prerogative of clerics."

We were skirting dangerous ground. Both of us knew it and transmitted the thought in a furtive meeting of eyes. Sadness pulled at the corners of Brother Principal's thin lips, dimmed the usual glitter of his small black eyes. For a moment, I was overwhelmed by a wave of sharp nostalgia, remembering the days when we often shared moments of concern for the future and reputation of the school we both loved. Now we pulled back. Brother was the first to offer conciliation and a new tack. "Remo has his following, Virgil, just as you do."

This was true. Remo Belloli had his coterie of admirers just as Fagan did, just as Greek O'Grady did, when he was still with us. But a teacher's worth cannot be gauged by the existence of a following. No teacher, regardless of his lack of conspicuous suitability for his job, is without one. Insecure adolescent boys will gravitate towards any adult male who shows them attention. What Brother Principal failed to include in his insistence that all teachers have their place was the means men like Belloli and O'Grady used to hold a following. The finger of blame still pointed to Belloli as the man who dubbed me the Virgin Queen; it was Greek O'Grady who immortalized the insult (yearbooks are forever), by imposing my classic Irish features on the head of that notorious English whore, Elizabeth I.

I could not look to Brother for support. How then to protect the boys from Belloli's violent outbursts? He would certainly never provide me with the easy evidence of O'Grady's poetic proposition. There was, in fact, no reason to believe Remo's macho slappings of boys' asses to be anything more than the reenactment of timeless locker room ritual. I doubt he had the imagination to perceive those rich variables inherent to human sexuality. And though it is true that no man is without fault, some are remarkably skilled in concealing those faults known to be publicly reprehensible. To bring Bull down, I needed scandal.

As I sometimes had in the past, I turned to Primo de Popalano. Young men, I've found, especially street-wise boys from Manhattan, often come up with solutions to which my more sheltered upbringing in Omaha did not expose me.

Because of the sensitivity of the matter to be discussed, I waited until after my Saturday yoga class to speak with Primo. As those of you who read the tabloids know by now, I began my Saturday morning elective class in hatha yoga during my second year at St. Lucy's. Terrence X. Callahan of the *Scroll*, in an especially titillating bit of innuendo, suggests my choice of location for these classes was 'at the least, self-serving.' Whatever could he mean? For one thing, reporters of his ilk never say the least, always more than they know to be fact.

What is it he wishes to imply? It was either allow the boys into my home or hold no classes at all. Using the school gym was out of the question. Even if Monsignor Delaney had not banned yoga from the school as a cleverly concealed expression of pagan religious ritual, the boys and I could hardly have donned our white cotton loincloths to do serious meditation while snickering bystanders lingered at the doors. Renting a private studio was out of the question. On my salary? Why, I could barely avoid eviction from my rent-controlled, fifth-floor walk-up tenement apartment! So I had no option other than to turn the twelve-by-twenty-foot floor of my bed-sitting room, covered for the occasion with grass mats, into the Avenue B Meditation Center.

On the Saturday following my conversation with Brother Principal concerning Belloli's most recent loss of control, I asked Primo to stay after yoga class. I was distracted for a moment by the classic image of the boy as he stood there, one arm outstretched, one powerful leg bent in supplication to the Infinite, clad—well, clad in nothing but a scrap of imported Indian cotton knotted about his narrow waist in the fashion prescribed by Rama Nagarajan, the Hindu guru I had invited in when I first set up the class for the purpose of purifying our admittedly amateurish attempts to penetrate the wisdom of the East.

"Put this on, Primo." I handed him my robe, a vintage piece of slick maroon satin.

"I haven't done the cobra position yet," Primo protested.

"Primo!" I sharpened my voice, releasing the awful power familiar to every student who passed through my classes. "Clothe thyself. I have a serious problem to discuss with you, one which might require a harsh solution. I've found it wise, when emerging from the calm world of interior travel, to mark the shift into reality with a change of dress. There,"—and I draped the robe over his shoulders—"now we can get on to more important matters."

"What's on your mind, Mr. Quinn?"

I touched a finger to my lip, indicating where a small white scar creased Primo's upper lip. "This, Primo. The scar and what it represents."

"You mean where Bull—I mean Mr. Belloli—punched me?"

"Yes, Primo. That scar marring your otherwise—" No. No sense in calling attention to this flaw in Primo's features. The boy had so little vanity that such a tiny mark could be of no importance to him.

"Aw, it's nothing, Mr. Quinn. I've been knocked around by the best of them." Boys take pride in any type of courage. "That Sister Stanislavia back in sixth grade, did *she* ever pack a whollop! I'd like to see her strong-arm the coach. He wouldn't have a chance."

Primo smirked in delight at the thought of nun versus coach, their arms locked in combat.

"This violence, Primo, must stop. We must put an end to this brutality. This is twentieth-century America, not nineteenth-century England."

"Teachers are always in the right," Primo answered flatly while running one long forefinger beneath the band of his loincloth, nonchalantly tickling his lower abdomen, then drawing in his stomach, leaving a shocking gap between cloth and privates.

"Don't *do* that, Primo. It's unseemly. Cinch yourself. Now, the question is how, not if."

"What? I don't getcha."

"I'll tell you this in confidence, Primo. You mustn't tell a soul." I waved my forefinger as a warning to silence. "Mr.

O'Grady is no longer with us at St. Lucy's. Do you know why?"

"They said he got a better job, taking people on trips to Greece and Rome."

"That's true, I did get him that job. A travel agent friend of mine—but teachers don't quit in midterm to take better paying jobs. Teachers who do that become unemployable. He left, Primo, because I had him fired."

"Really, Mr. Quinn? I thought only Brother Principal could fire a teacher."

"Brother okayed the dismissal, of course, but I insisted he get rid of the man." I avoided mentioning the role played by the Prentice boy and his father in O'Grady's fall. To do that, I would have had to quote Sappho's impassioned line as well as give Primo a literal interpretation of it. Repeated to the wrong person, such an incident could have been used to denounce me.

"Why did you do that?" Primo asked. "I mean, get some guy fired you work with."

Primo's question was not an accusation. I would have been surprised if it had been. Primo's ethical system reflected influences other than the truisms so hypocritically fostered by his teachers. I made note of this and determined to discover just what those influences were.

"He had to go. For the same reasons Mr. Belloli should seek employment in some field better suited to violent men."

Primo's brow wrinkled in uncommon concentration. With considerable effort he searched for the trait shared by two men so apparently dissimilar.

"Ahh, I got it. O'Grady was a thumper."

Primo's hard-won conclusion justified my years of teaching boys the tools of logical deduction.

"And Mr. Belloli must never be allowed to strike another child."

"I ain't no kid, Mr. Quinn." Primo threw open his robe and inflated his hairless chest, casting his maturing pectoral muscles into bold relief.

"Indeed you are not. I was speaking figuratively. Now, how do we get him?"

"Get him?"

"Tenured teachers can't be fired without grave cause, Primo. Mr. Belloli may be crude, but semi-literacy is not sufficient cause for dismissal, not in our time. And in our place, this city inhabited by immigrant parents who themselves fled tyranny, neither is beating children into submission. These parents have decided, all said and done, that they prefer draconian order to democratic anarchy. No, we must discover Mr. Belloli's Achilles' heel, Primo."

Primo lifted his left leg and inspected his own heel for enlightenment.

"His *moral disorder*, Primo. Some habit or characteristic that, rightly publicized as moral turpitude, the blanket clause used from time immemorial to sack teachers of every persuasion who fall into disfavor, will force Brother Principal to ask for Belloli's resignation."

"You mean, if he's a drunk or something?

"Something like that, although in the coach's instance, I suspect we will have to dip deeper than drink. He's of Italian descent. Italians don't drink to excess. A nation's incidence of alcoholism is inversely proportionate to its exposure to civilization—and booze. Jews, for example, are never alcoholics; Italians rarely so. Both nations have been exposed to the fermented grape for at least 15,000 years. Men prone to over-indulgence in alcohol often avoid the responsibilities of

rearing a family. The urge to drink supplants the urge to cop-
ulate. For these reasons, inebriate men breed fewer children,
and natural selection has left Mediterranean gene pools largely
free from alcoholic potential. The Irish, on the other hand,
like many of the Nordic peoples, were introduced to drink
by soldiers of the last marauding Roman legions, a scant two
millennia ago. Natural selection is a slow process and there
has not been time to—

"Now if Belloli was descended from Northern rather than
Southern stock, we could begin our search by looking for
the bottle."

"Do you hit the bottle, Mr. Quinn?"

"I do not 'hit the bottle,' Primo. I am a disciplined drinker
who uses alcohol—in moderation—as one component of my
stress management program. The Greeks established moderation as their seminal moral principal. It is mine as well. To
the Greeks, excess was the only sin, that and the violation of
tradition. Take Plato's famous symposium on…"

Boredom began to dim the light of Primo's black and
slightly protuberant eyes.

"But to return to the crimes of Mr. Belloli…" I drew the
boy closer with a gesture and dropped my voice to a whisper.
I outlined the plan.

"Surveillance, Primo. Careful, sustained surveillance."

"Gotcha, Mr. Quinn. Leave it to me and my friends."

15

I PUT BULL BELLOLI's FATE in the hands of a student, knowing that if the job could be done, Primo would do it. Certainty came from my knowing that Primo had a much better grasp of the job to be done than Primo himself suspected.

Primo had supported me in nearly every crusade I launched, at times from the sidelines, at others as an active participant. In the Lenten Revolt he had led the resistance. Whereas I despise unenlightened authority, Primo despised all authority. He was, I suppose, an anarchist, although he would never have used the term and insisted on giving lip service to authority. In a quiz on which a definition and historical application of anarchy constituted forty percent of the score, Primo turned in a blank sheet of paper with the single line, 'I don't know nothing about anarkie,' scrawled across the page. This was not entirely true. If he had traced his own political bias to its peculiarly Sicilian-American origins, I would have passed him with a ninety-eight.

When I succeeded to the position of moderator of St.
Lucy's yearbook, I prepared myself by studying every edition of the publication dating back to 1904. I was surprised to
learn that de Popalanos figured prominently in nearly every
book I opened. Male members from three generations of the
family, several as photogenic as Primo, had graduated from
the school. Primo's grandfather had only attended through
the eighth grade. In those days that was the final year at St.
Lucy's. Senior high school was not added to the curriculum
until the late Thirties. In anticipation of war and the lucrative
orders for goods it would generate, corporations were anxious
to install automated devices in their factories. They coerced
the states to enforce compulsory education laws already on
the books in order to keep young men out of the labor market
and, statistically at least, off the unemployment roles. Added
to the already massive number of unemployed, the weight
of these idle men might well have tipped the scales toward
revolution. To adjust to these corporate demands, St. Lucy's
did away with its elementary school to make room for the
older boys.

There are those who do not agree with my theories on the
origin of compulsory high school education and suggest that
altruism rather than corporate greed and fear accounted for
this progressive change in law enforcement. These scholars
belong to the Pollyanna school of history.

While familiarizing myself with the high school careers of
Primo's ancestors, I uncovered several de Popalanos who had
done quite well at St. Lucy's. One of them, probably an uncle
of Primo's, delivered the valedictory address to the class of
'41. Another won a National Science Foundation scholarship.
(Had St. Lucy's known a golden age?) Where, I wondered,

were they now, these de Popalano achievers. And why, with ancestors such as these, was Primo such a wretched scholar?

Finding ways to motivate students to do their best is as much a teacher's responsibility as insuring him an unbiased education. What better way to encourage Primo to do better than to hold up members of his own clan as role models? But to do this, I would first have to better acquaint myself with their lives. It wouldn't do to point out a de Popalano for Primo to emulate only to learn from Primo himself that the man was now selling hot dogs from a cart on Forty-second Street.

Where to begin? With the telephone book, of course. If historians of an earlier age had had access to this tool, they could have saved themselves a lot of legwork. Knowing your subject's address permits several valuable deductions: His approximate wealth, for example, and how long he has had it; his standing in the community; even a good guess at his politics. I turned to the listing of de Popalanos, checking the directories for all five boroughs. The result was discouraging. Even if I limited my investigation to the Primos, Principes, Caesares and Majestics, names favored by the de Popalano alumni of St. Lucy's, I came up with the unwieldy number of 1, 653.

Only a research historian of my tenacity (and with my connections) could have accomplished the task I set for myself. For Primo's sake I determined to sift through every name on the list until I found a de Popalano who had attained if not wealth and position, then at least respectability.

I could not, of course, go traipsing about the city appraising the living standards of all those Popalanos. I did not have the time. And the cost! Why it would take a king's ransom in subway tokens. For both these reasons I resorted to a research technique peculiarly my own.

I have always been a curious, even gregarious man, who makes a lot of friends. In the course of three careers I have come to know hundreds of people. I never forget a name, a talent I reinforce by recording the names of those I meet, if the person is at all memorable, in black books identical to those used by teachers to record grades. After each name, address and telephone number, I make note of the enrollee's occupation and other useful data in case I might, at some future date, have need of a friend's expertise. My Black Books tend to fill up rather quickly and I now have seven of them dating back as many years.

What I needed now to facilitate my investigation of the de Popalanos was a taxman, someone in the Internal Revenue Service, and I soon found him in Black Book III. I met Milford during a period, sometime before I came to St. Lucy's, when he was enjoying flush times and I lean. Milford was older than I by many years, and in return for the pleasure of my company—Milford's demands were not excessive; I had only to pose in loden green kneesocks and hiking boots, in *Lederhosen* open at the flap, and with a haversack slung over my naked shoulder while he, poor man, did what he had to do. He insisted each time we parted on giving me a little something to help out with the rent. I don't drop old friends. When Milford fell on bad times—he lost his position with the IRS due to budget cutbacks—I still continued to accept his calls. Unfortunately, I was too busy after he lost his job to actually visit Milford, but I always found time for an intimate chat with him on the phone and, a day or two later, sure as I'm Virgil Quinn, a check signed by Milford came in the mail.

Where was Milford now? Layoffs from the federal bureaucracy are rarely permanent I told myself as I dialed Milford's number.

"Milford? Milford Sholtey? Guess-who-this-is!"

"Virgil. I haven't heard from you for years." No one who has heard my voice ever forgets it. "Why now?" Milford asked.

"Oh, just a friendly call, Milford. I was wondering how you're getting along. Back at the IRS, I suppose?"

"Have been for years," Milford replied. Was it a note of wariness I heard in Milford's voice? Or one of doubtful anticipation?

"Well, Milford, that's good news, an event worth celebrating."

In the past Milford had been quick to jump at my first hint of availability with an invitation to dinner. Too often he chose restaurants he couldn't afford, requiring him to dip into savings best kept for a rainy day. Now he did not respond at all, forcing me to be more direct than I cared to be.

"It's been so very long since we went out for a good dinner, Milford. Do you remember that little German place on East Eighty-sixth Street? That charming Gaststätte with the beer garden? I'll never forget their *Kassler Rippchen*... and the hours we spent there together..."

Judging from Milford's silence, he was either economizing or not in the mood for either German food or nostalgia, and I was forced to invite him to dinner at my place.

"Just good homemade food, Milford, nothing fancy. Saturday at eight then? Fine? Bring a good appetite."

Since I rarely serve the same dinner guest twice, I usually prepare my gourmet specialty, Filet of Sole, Bonne Femme. Monica, a woman friend of mine, once said that it was perhaps the best meal—but I may have already mentioned the acclaim my fish has received. Unfortunately for Milford, the price of Dover sole had skyrocketed over the years. Gourmet meals were still a reasonably inexpensive means of impressing young men with unsophisticated palates, but I had to become more selective in what I served to whom. Would a man Milford's age require such a steep investment? I thought not. Milford would be content with simpler fare. It was, after all, my company he sought, not French sauces far too rich for a man suffering from chronic heartburn.

I decided on hamburger hotdish, a nutritionally balanced, one-dish meal very popular in Omaha. Mother had taught me how to make it and revealed to me the secret ingredients that made her hotdish the envy of the parish: a half cup of dark molasses and a pinch, no more, of ginger.

How easy it is to satisfy a man. Much later that Saturday night, after a jug of hearty California burgundy and an hour of... intimate conversation, Milford agreed to do the research required on the de Popalano case. He would comb the IRS files for de Popalanos and make note of those with declared incomes of $100,000 or more. I thought the figure too high and explained how a de Popalano worth half that would serve my purpose. Milford, however, claimed more experience than I in matters of income, and held to the figure of a hundred grand as the watershed between the rich and the inconsequential. Before leaving for the night, he extracted a promise from me for a date in the future. I agreed, hinting that the length of our next meeting would hinge on the quality of his research.

THE INFORMATION MILFORD gave me in return for my hospitality consisted of a list of names, all de Popalanos, and the addresses at which they resided. He made the added effort of checking the real estate taxes paid by each and discovered, quite by chance, that a C. de Popalano, the resident owner of an unpretentious building on Mulberry Street, paid the taxes as well on an immense chunk of commercial property in the Lower Manhattan neighborhood popularly known as Little Italy. That Primo lived on Mulberry Street, the main thoroughfare of the district, was probably, I told myself, mere coincidence. Several of the Italian boys attending St. Lucy's lived on or near the street. Historians, however, like detectives, do not presume evidence to be coincidental unless proven to be so. In this case it was an issue easily resolved: The answer could be found in the school records.

When I discovered that Primo did in fact live at the same address as the Caesare (and Magdalena) de Popalano discovered by Milford in his search of the tax records, the thrust of my investigation took quite a different direction.

Such wealth! How in the world... I had met Mr. de Popalano on more than one occasion. I admired the man. He didn't send Mrs. De Popalano to pick up his son's report card, as so many fathers did; he came himself to take his place behind charwomen and waitresses with swollen feet to stand for up to three hours in the line unwinding before my desk to hear my exhaustive progress report that conscientious teachers deliver along with the card.

Caesare spoke with a decided accent missing from Primo's speech.

"Ah, Mr. Quinn, my boy Primo speaks only the good things about you. You must have great pride in your profession."

The usual spiel from parents trying to accomplish with flattery what their sons had so miserably failed to achieve in the classroom.

"And what is your line of work, Mr. de Popalano?"

"A very humble job compared to yours. Just a little shop the wife and I built up from nothing. Italian specialties—candies, delicatessen, a small line of imported kitchen wares from the old country. You like pasta, Mr. Quinn? I just got in the pasta machine to beat all pasta machines, nickel plated, very high quality. I would be happy that you have it. Primo could..."

From this mom and pop shop to a real estate empire worth millions? The explanations for such an entrepreneurial feat was not likely to be discovered in records open to the public, and certainly not to those of the IRS. This time I needed someone with access to the most confidential information a state can accumulate, someone on the inside, a Byzantine eunuch who knew his way around the labyrinth of city hall; a man who, if he proved too timid to pry, could be encouraged to do so by reminders of favors granted in the past.

I consulted my Black Books, running my finger down the columns of names, stopping to ponder only those marked with a blue circle or a red square—blue for small favors owed, red for large.

I chose a lawyer friend of mine who worked as a clerk in the office of the attorney general and who rated a decidedly bold red star. I had saved the man from certain dismissal by swearing in court that the scandalous state in which the arresting officer claimed to have discovered my friend while checking out the men's room of the Spring Street subway station must have been a case of impersonation backed up with stolen identity cards. It could not, in any case, have been my lawyer friend because he was, I testified, spending the night with me. To further muddy the waters, I confessed that he had moved in with me to escape the harassment of one of his numerous lady friends who could not accept the affair she and my friend were having for the playful romp it had always been and that he insisted it remain.

My lawyer friend—I dare not mention his name; the falsity of an accusation has nothing to do with the effect it has upon one's reputation: Look what's happened to me. My lawyer friend—the name Channing is appropriate—had expensive tastes. His salary was never adequate to his needs and he lived always in the upper reaches of credit card debt; when the judge balked at my testimony, we had some trouble coming up with the money to change the court's mind and…

But that is a tale I'll leave to serious muckrakers of the city's legal system. Here it's best told briefly: I used my jewelry collection, gifts I had received over the years, as pawn to borrow the money necessary to have our testimony accepted by the judge and the charge itself erased from the record.

These, now, were better times. Channing retained his position in the courts and went on to become a prosecuting attorney himself and, if incapable of bringing his social behavior more in line with the accepted norms of the society he was paid to defend, he became at least a good deal more careful. In recent years he has not, to my knowledge, been charged with a crime other than disorderly conduct (Channing drank rather too much), a misdemeanor which, if it constituted grounds for dismissal, would lead to mass unemployment in his profession.

I once thought Channing to be a gracious man who, if he had been born with conventional desires, would have lived an honest life. It was these traits that first endeared him to me, that and his frequent invitations to accompany him and his friends on skiing weekends in Vermont. Although I don't ski—there are no mountains in Nebraska—ski wear becomes me, and since both the clothes and the lodging were gifts from Channing, I rather enjoyed those apres ski get-togethers, posed one arm on the bar, sipping hot buttered rum and basking in the admiring glances of bona fide skiers of both sexes.

"Do you still, hmm, ski? With your group?" I asked Channing when he picked up the phone.

"Only when my wife is out of town."

"You're *married*, Channing?"

"Yes. I thought it best, given my ambitions."

Channing's bitterly direct response left me aghast. Had he bought so deeply into the system? Lost whatever integrity he once possessed? Gracious men are sensitive to the needs of others. I've always believed that if a man finds himself incapable of showing a woman the extraordinary tenderness women require, he should at least inform the chosen mate of such before marrying her. Obviously many men do not agree with my notion of fair play.

When I called Channing, I had thought a simple request for his help would be sufficient—a favor in exchange for mine in the past. This was not to be the case. This new, now sadly callous Channing obliged me to toughen up my tactics. But even then I chose discretion, and it took no more than the subtlest reference to past indiscretions for Channing to ask, "What do you want, Virgil?"

I told him of the research project I had set for myself, unearthing the roots of a typical Italian-American family and how my efforts had dead-ended in vast real estate holdings. Channing hesitated, mumbled something about the sins of youth coming back to haunt him, then agreed to search the files. "And, Virgil, if you ever so much as hint to anyone where you obtained your information, I will personally see to it that you are charged and convicted, on evidence planted by me, of crimes so foul you'll be sent up for life."

"Channing! How thoughtless of you to believe me capable of such imprudence. You of all people should know it is because I'd die before revealing my sources that I've become so well informed."

A week later Channing called me, from a pay phone, to tell me the attorney general had been working for years to prove Caesare de Popalano of Mulberry Street to be the link between a number of shady businesses and the Mafia family to which he was related.

I was not shocked. It had long been rumored that the sons of the Mafia were in attendance at St. Lucy's. Where else were the dons to send their sons but to the teaching brothers, their daughters to the nuns? Certainly not to the effete private schools run by and for WASPs. The Little Brothers of Divine Grace would properly discipline their sons and the nuns would teach their daughters submission. Beyond the three R's, those were the only lessons needed.

The news of Primo's ties to a powerful family elated me. Who could be better qualified to get the goods on Bull Belloli than the son and ostensible heir of one of the city's underworld kingpins? Where better for the boy to begin than with the smaller world of St. Lucy's? Primo could start by checking out my premonition that a man like Remo Belloli would not remain content with abusing boys, and must, at times and places unknown, indulge in lustier sports unbecoming a teacher.

I joined Primo in the hall and closed the door to the bugged classroom behind us.

"Any news, Primo? Concerning our project?"

But Primo would tell me nothing and teased me with an impish grin. "All things come," he said, "to those who wait."

That note of ambiguity, just like the tone I used to use when flirting with Sister Philomena! Ah, if I were sixteen again… an unholy thought that set off a cacophony of bells ringing in my head, a fierce clanging heralding that I knew by now and feared, a message of reproach direct from heaven.

"But you are not sixteen, Virgil Quinn." A female voice, the voice of Sister Philomena, but speaking now in the harsh tones of the Avenging Angel. *"You are, if the truth were told, a good deal older than the twenty-nine you sometimes admit to being. You have taken vows. Vows to me, vows to St. Lucy, vows—You're merely passing through a phase. A middle-aged identity crisis, trying to recapture the youth we stole from you. Now back to work!"*

As usual, Sister had gotten it all wrong, just as she had the youthful indiscretion that resulted in my broken nose. In my desire to be young again, it was Sister Philomena I longed for, not Primo de Popalano.

Back to work, she said. There was not, however, much to do at the time except wait for Primo's disclosures. Nothing, that is, but continue to teach my courses, deliver my lectures and see to my extracurriculars. Scarcely enough to do to rid my mind of thoughts Sister Philomena called a betrayal of my vows to her and unworthy of the vocation she had dedicated her life to nurture. I was spending far too many evenings at the County Cork. Even the well-meaning naïf, Eyes Panuccio, handicapped as he was by his occluded vision, asked one Monday morning if I had been ill that weekend.

"You look a little puffy around the eyes, Virgil. And your nose is red. Maybe you ought to take a sick day."

The shame! Hangovers I could deal with. But puffy eyes? At my age? Destroy the effect of my aristocratic features, heightened by the slight break in the bridge of my nose, by superimposing on such a face the veined bulbous nose of the heavy drinker? Never! And that very afternoon I took the tunnel over to the church and beseeched St. Lucy for help in overcoming my growing addiction to booze. I prayed. I wept. I did not see the saint, as I sometimes do, but she sent in her place Sister Philomena clothed still in her forbidding black and starched white bib, but different than I remembered her, glorious now as she descended with an arpeggio of chiming bells, surrounded by an aurora of blinding light, the sign of those who have been admitted into His Awful Presence.

It must be true what they say, that before we are admitted into God's presence, we are restored to the time when we looked our best. Philomena had scarcely aged at all. She appeared to me now much as she had all those years she stood before me in the classroom. And the smile she gave me—Oh, Blessed Woman! Love of My Life!—rekindled memories of our years together and, overwhelmed by emotion, I begged her to give me a sign that she had forgiven me my sinful thoughts, that she still loved me.

Years before, on the occasion of my single pilgrimage to Rome, I spent most of the free time Father O'Hern, our tour director, allowed us, contemplating Bernini's electrifying Ecstasy of Saint Theresa that occupies a side chapel inside Maria... Maria—Oh, there are far too many churches named for the Virgin to remember them all. Day after day I returned to marvel at the saint, begging her to allow me to experience just once in my life what she had, and just as Theresa in her ecstasy defied gravity to rise from her cot to embrace the Holy Presence—the moment perfectly immortalized by Bernini—so did I begin to rise now from the floor of St. Lucy's Church, arms outstretched, head thrown back, staring with bulging eyes at the face of Sister Philomena, a woman who had known the Beatific Vision.

For how long I hung suspended in ecstasy I do not know, but when Philomena parted her petal lips to speak, she delivered a single line: *"Hear me Virgil: An idle mind is the devil's workshop."* And with that she let me drop. My head striking the cold marble floor of the church awoke me. I rose to my knees, searching the chapel for the sainted nun. She was not there. Philomena, fickle woman, had deserted me again.

I had levitated. It was the first time I had been permitted to enter the ecstatic state. Such an event could not go unrecorded, and to keep my mind occupied, as Philomena had ordered me to do, that very day I began to write up a paper analyzing the phenomenon of levitation and submitted it to the *Brooklyn Scroll*. The *Scroll*, I thought, was the only local publication likely to be much interested in my ecstatic experience. How wrong I was! Today the tabloid press seems interested in little else and presents my levitation as evidence of my deteriorating mental state.

I began the article with a straightforward account of my experience, wondering why I was the only man, to my knowledge, in the great litany of saints, to have been so honored. Could the predominance of female levitators be explained, I asked, by the principle of flotation? Women, as we all know, are better floaters on water than men. All the great Channel swimmers have been women. Just as women are buoyed up in water by layers of subcutaneous fat, I argued, so this same principle might enable them to float about in air more successfully than their male companions in ecstasy.

The logical extension of my argument led directly to androgyny. My attempt to investigate the puzzling questions raised by the androgynous condition floundered on my ignorance of the subject—What could I, Virgil Quinn, know about androgyny, a state so foreign to my character?—and I cut the passage from the final draft.

Efforts to explain my own ecstatic levitation, a unique exception to the women-only rule, suffered the same fate. I toyed with, then rejected going into my long and complex involvement with Sister Philomena. I did not want to imply that the laws of gravity could be reversed by hysteria rising from sexual repression (my unrequited lust for the beautiful nun), for this would have been a surrender to secular values.

I underestimated the *Scroll's* disdain for fresh thought. Without offering a shred of scientific evidence to refute my thesis of flotation, the editors of that dull and seldom read weekly rejected my essay. This did not depress me. Writers, like all artists, learn to accept rejection by people less talented than themselves as the price they must sometimes pay for the right to practice their craft.

Now might be as good a time as any to set down a brief résumé of my published writings. I have already mentioned my first published work, the somewhat autobiographical *Philomena of the Plains*. *Philomena* depicts the tragic struggles of a beautiful and virginal woman desirous of one man but betrothed to Another. The heroic nun tries first to forget the young man she loves (one of her students, modeled on myself), then to deny her vows as a Bride of Christ. She learns that she can do neither, falls into despair and ends her young and virtuous life by leaping from the Missouri River bluffs and plunging to her death in the turbulent waters below. I wrote *Philomena* during a single summer at the age of sixteen. Poetry, however, was not to be my—

I simply can't go on. My fingers are too stiff. It has become too painful to strike the keys.

16

NOT LONG AFTER MY flight with Philomena through the groined spaces of St. Lucy's church, I began to notice that the fingers of my right hand had grown steadily stiffer. By midterm it had become difficult to write.

As the pain increased, I was asked by friends better paid than I why I didn't go to a doctor. They stared in disbelief when I reminded them that their fringe benefits equaled a quarter of their inflated salaries while Monsignor Delaney, who ultimately controlled St. Lucy's budget, looked upon group health insurance as an unwarranted expense. Brother Principal, much to his credit, had tried to get us coverage. The Monsignor's reply was not unlike the advice Marie Antoinette gave the workers of her day: "Hire younger teachers."

I doubt I would have gone to a doctor, prepaid or not. Like all who were raised poor in the days before Medicaid, going to doctors led to indentured servitude. And so I had turned to folk medicine which, if seldom effective, was at least cheap.

Mother, when she was afflicted, used to lean back in her rocker while soaking her swollen knuckles in a hot bath of Epsom salts. I began this treatment, using a chipped enamel basin I retrieved from a pile of castoff house wares on the Avenue.

Mother Murphy thought I should make a pilgrimage to Lourdes to seek a miraculous cure for my degenerating joints. When I asked if, through prayer, the Virgin might grant me an advance for airfare, Mother thought no, that the BVM, if she subsidized her petitioners, would leave herself open to charges of conflict of interest. Bull Belloli, in an unexpected show of sympathy that in no way caused me to indulge in second thoughts concerning his planned demise, fell back upon his faith in sports and recommended physical therapy. His advice seemed more within my reach than Mother Murphy's, and I began to cast around for some hobby involving digital exercise.

Again my thoughts turned to my mother. How many hours had I watched those strong stubby fingers of hers manipulating a silver hook through what must have been miles of cotton thread. Why of course! I almost knew the stitches myself, just from watching. I stopped at Woolworth's that very afternoon and bought a size H crochet hook and several skeins of yarn. Mother had worked small, lace doilies mostly, exquisitely done. I thought four ply wool yarn and a larger hook would be more appropriate for a man.

Three lessons from Mrs. Podchek, the Ukrainian super's wife, and I was on my own. I chose a granny afghan pattern for my first project. As a beginner, I would stick with flat work, and all the little squares, each a finished piece, would fit my cramped schedule.

After crocheting my first few squares, I learned I could easily knock out a motif with border between my last essay correction and bedtime. An ample afghan, however, would require hundreds of squares. The ochre, brown and green I selected to work in, earth colors suitable to a bachelor apartment, harmonized so well I became perhaps too anxious to finish.

The short homeroom period of each school day proved just long enough to finish one motif. I explained to the boys of 3C the therapeutic purpose behind my needlework and arranged for a class outing to visit the Whitney Museum, whose current show featured American folk art, specifically, the patchwork quilt. Quoting extensively from Mr. John Canaday's commentaries on nineteenth-century American crafts, I delivered a lecture on the emerging Counterculture and its interest in reviving American cottage industries.

Their teacher's interest in a handicraft really seemed to fascinate the boys. For an entire week they sat watching the crochet hook fly, and during all that time I can't recall reprimanding a single student.

Then the snickering began. Giggles faded into smirks when I entered the room. The derogatory comments always emanated from a group of five boys I had tried but been unable to reach. Three were long-time members of Bull Belloli's bunch; the other two, once followers of the deposed Greek O'Grady, had now drifted into Fagan's scruffy following. Belloli and Fagan were, of course, at the boys every chance they could get, twisting therapy into caricature, a unique educational experience into cheap gossip for the amusement of the lunchroom crowd.

Given the leaders they had chosen to follow, the behavior of these boys didn't surprise me. Due to the uncommon nature of my therapy, when practiced by a male, I expected to see a certain number of raised eyebrows. But I was not prepared for the conversation I overheard while working behind the closed door of the mimeograph room.

"He's taken up knitting now. Does it right in class—purl one, knit two."

"I can't believe it. I mean, rumors so widespread already, his (the word was muffled) relationship with that kid who did himself in—what was his name? You'd think the Virgin Queen would have the sense to be more careful."

"It'll be Sweden next, for the operation." Followed by crude guffaws.

That bitch Murphy! Dealing in spite and lies just as if he hadn't greeted me in the hall an hour earlier, all smiles and charm, inquiring into my poor gnarled hands. No mistake. Even through the mahogany door, I identified the giggling Murphy as one of the gossips. Okay, Mother. If it's war you want, the Virgin Queen will hit you with an armada big enough to blow every sniggling little bigot off the island of Manhattan!

I flipped the mimeograph machine off and on a few times to let them know someone was in the room. Better to lull one's enemies into a false sense of security by making them think you haven't heard. I shut down the machine, opened the door and greeted both teachers with a warm smile.

"Charles, Mr. Fagan. I didn't know you were free this period."

The two of them shuffled about with fixed sheepish grins.

"Well, we aren't, Virgil. But we're both testing this period, so we stepped outside for a breath of fresh air."

I looked at Fagan and smiled knowingly. The one-time head of my department, since deposed, winced in fear. "The

testing students no doubt appreciate your absence, Mr. Fagan."
I ignored Murphy.

As I walked away I took out my grade book and scribbled
a bit, then looked over my shoulder and gave Fagan another
crocodile smile. Flash hunched his narrow shoulders into his
baggy flannel jacket and marched haughtily into his classroom. I had made a note of the date, the time and incident.
Behavior involving dereliction of duty would come in handy
if the man ever became foolish enough to attack me openly.

"Why are such teachers tolerated?" Kevin O'Connor once
asked me in that accusatory tone youth uses when questioning the behavior of adults in authority. At that time I believed
teachers must stick together at all costs. I moralized: "Tenure,
Kevin, is sacred to teachers. We must have job protection if
we are to be free to teach what we believe is true. Mr. Fagan
is a tenured teacher," my homily ran, although I had no idea
how tenure was defined at St. Lucy's. "If Mr. Fagan hadn't
proved himself a competent instructor, he wouldn't be here."

"Bullshit," Kevin replied with the apt succinctness of the
young.

"Kevin, vulgarity offends me. Especially from you. It
reflects a background I hoped you had left behind. With a
vocabulary the size of yours, you need hardly stoop to the
language of the gutter."

This sort of drivel to a boy on the verge of despair.

If Mother Murphy had held his tongue, controlled his
addiction to gossip and his habit of racial slurs, he might
have earned a respite from my wrath. It was not my intention
to bring him down, not with my campaign against Belloli
still unresolved. Eventually something would have to be
done about his diatribes against the city's largest minority. I
had suffered the WASP's sting too often as a boy to stand by

now and listen to this caricature of a man rail against the
Jews. Perhaps I drew strength from the accident of place. In
Omaha, Methodists, Baptists and assorted Non-Denomina-
tionals excluded Catholic dissenters from public life. I grew
up beneath the cruel paw of minority oppression. I came east
to find my own kind filling positions from mayor to Mafia
boss. As a member of the ruling elite for the first time in my
life, I could afford to be magnanimous.

But my majority status, I had begun to realize, only par-
tially explained my newfound courage. We hesitate to admit
that it is far easier to come to the defense of those whose
loathed tag we do not share. How much more difficult to
rise in defense of the man whose detested brand marks us as
well, or leaves us open to the same accusations and therefore
the same persecution. After all, with my porcelain skin, for-
get-me-not-eyes and straight black hair, no one would assign
Virgil Quinn to the ranks of the Israelite.

"It will be Sweden next…" Oh, the bitch. The nasty spiteful bitch!

And so with Kevin's death still fresh in my memory even
after so long a time; still fearful that at any moment, as I
roamed the forests of Central Park on a quiet autumn afternoon, a vengeful Greek O'Grady might leap from behind a
tree to beat me unconscious as he hinted he had done to others; still anxious over the Belloli campaign, whose successful
outcome was by no means certain; still wrestling with the
devils who drove me to the County Cork, I now had to take
on the Jewish Problem.

Single-handedly too. I could expect little help from the
others. Brother Liberal would come up with some mumbo-
jumbo about Murphy's problem being historical and leave
it at that. Eyes Panuccio and Orphan Annie would keep to

their customary silence on all controversial matters. The rest of my colleagues were men who came directly down from their religion classes to bait Mother into fits of anti-Semitism.

"Listen to this, Murph. It says here,"—and Brother Adolph waved the *Daily News* like a red flag—"all the public schools have off today and tomorrow because of Passover."

Mother Murphy jumped to the bait. "Of course they do. The schools are run by Jews, just like everything else in this city. But they don't close the schools on Holy Days of Obligation. Oh, no. *That* would be too fair, and who ever heard of a Jew being fair? Let up on the pogroms and they take over the city, squeeze everybody out."

He ran on like this for the better part of the lunch period. His fury grew in proportion to the distance he drifted from his initial complaint. If he lagged, one of the teachers fed him a line. They laughed. He ranted. He raved. The village idiot incited by the crowd.

Mother Murphy was not entirely a fool; he was more like a neon cross with dead spots—in places he sparkled. He was literate, at least within the Lucian definition of that term. He taught French and, unlike so many teachers of a foreign language in American schools, he was fluent in both English and the language he taught. At times he could be amusing. He told hilarious anecdotes of his life with the seven aunts who raised him. To escape their oppressive mothering, he fled to a seminary. There he developed most of the skills and at least some of the peculiarities that characterized him in later life. He perfected his French and, in a long overdue plan to upgrade clerical publications, he was sent to Boston University to study journalism. Unfortunately, upon winning the starring role in a seminary dramatic production, Murphy became star struck. He developed a passion for the theater.

He became convinced that his true vocation lay not at the altar, but on the stage.

Like myself, Mother was not a native New Yorker. But where I had come to the city in search of anonymity and had fame thrust upon me, Mother came down from Boston looking for fame and found himself relegated to obscurity.

Mother had aspirations. Since arriving in the city, he had attended every Broadway opening during the cut-rate previews. In the mind of a fantasist, it is but a small step from attending the theater to creating the play. He convinced Brother Principal of such, and in a package deal including the school newspaper, the literary journal and the Drama Club, Brother appointed him moderator of all three with a stipend of a thousand a year.

This was a terrible blunder on Brother's part, but one that we must excuse. Torrence O'Day, St. Lucy's impresario before being pushed aside by Mother Murphy, appeared well qualified for his job. He taught English literature and drama, directed the school choir and composed oratorios in praise of the Virgin Mary. (Torrence, too, was an ex-seminarian. Not all that unusual at St. Lucy's; most of the faculty were ex-something or other, including myself.) He promised us a theatrical season studded with such Broadway hits as *The Royal Hunt of the Sun* (Primo would have made the perfect Inca), to be followed by an expurgated and shorn version of *Hair*. Following each announcement, Greek O'Grady dutifully arranged with Torrence for pre-rehearsal photographs meant to fill those pages of the yearbook allocated to the drama club, an organization that seldom met. When the yearbook was released seven months later, boys draped in costumes and posed in dramatic gestures recalled plays that were never staged.

Mother Murphy, with fewer qualifications, was more ambitious still. In early October he used the first of the two or three issues of the school paper we would see that year to announce his plans to produce a season of original works, all to be written and directed by himself. *Boys Will Be Boys*, Mother's first production, would have its 'out-of-town opening at St. Lucy's and then move to an off-Broadway house.' Mother asked me for pre-rehearsal photos to be published in the yearbook just as his predecessor had done. I was not the gullible Greek, however. I pleaded a shortage of film, 'just enough to shoot the actual production.' There would be no photos until opening night.

After six weeks of scheduled rehearsals, few of which were actually held, Mother's contemporary drama actually had a performance. Just one. The huge cast, most of the senior class of ninety boys and nearly as many girls from Transfiguration, had only the vaguest notion of what they were to do once on stage.

The entire student body of St. Lucy's Boys and Transfiguration Girls sprawled on the cafeteria floor, cleared for the occasion of tables and chairs. Pressure from behind encouraged those in front to inch forward with each change of position. By the beginning of the two-act spectacle, the stage area, delineated only by cheap muslin hanging at either side wall, had been largely occupied by the audience. For the duration of act one, position alone distinguished audience from performer. Those lying down and sitting were audience; those standing, actors. But trips to the water fountain at one side of the stage, to the bathrooms at the other, and the general debut exhaustion of the actors, mixed audience with performers. A kind of living theater was thus achieved, spontaneously generated and totally unrecognized by Mother Murphy, who when asked during the following weeks, never responded to comments concerning his directorial debut.

I could not allow the boys to carry so warped a notion of the theater into adult life. For many of them the drama as performed at St. Lucy's would be the only live theatrical experience they would ever know. To justify man's ageless fascination with lights and grease paint, when professionally applied, I decided to stage a production of my own.

Aware that Brother Principal and the Monsignor might take alarm at my moving in on another teacher's turf, I designed a pageant that they could not easily refuse, a performance without compromising their mission to inculcate Christian ideals.

Christmas was barely a month away. On the eve of Christmas vacation I suggested we should commemorate the great feast and our school's patron saint with our own 'Santa Lucia Festival of Lights.' No one knew, and I saw no reason to detract from my growing reputation for originality, that just such a pageant occurred every year at this time in Scandinavian settlements across the Midwest. As a boy, I had seen it often in the town of Pinch Horn, Nebraska, an hour's drive from Omaha. In reply to Brother Principal and the Monsignor's request for a script, I composed a simple tale with a few stage directions and called it an old Nordic (pre-Lutheran) Christian celebration.

Properly staged, the Santa Lucia pageant requires a large cast of blond virgins. Eyebrows were raised when word got around that I was casting young men in the role of Nordic maidens. To squash such criticism, I threatened Mother Murphy with a visit from the Civil Liberties Union if he did not print the article I wrote for the school paper defending the pageant. In it I waved the flag of Church tradition. "The

cultural source of our pageant," I wrote, "will be ancient
Christian ritual. Need I remind you that in the early days of
the Church, all roles were performed by men and boys since
women were banned from the stage?"

The play went on.

The pageant, as I saw it enacted in Pinch Horn, was an
unpretentious musicale. Twenty or thirty girls, as many as
the churches could muster that year from town and surrounding farms, were robed in white and marched up to the
choir loft of the Lutheran church. When the audience had
filed in and settled themselves, the church lights were extin-
guished. Everyone sat in darkened silence for a few minutes to
heighten the drama. As the first notes of 'Santa Lucia,' sung
in Swedish, floated down from the rafters, all heads turned
to catch their first look at that year's Lucia. The nubile saint
led her caroling attendants up the aisle in slow procession.
St. Lucy was a natural blond, as were all the girls. No wigs
were needed in Pinch Horn. Blond locks intertwined with
household philodendron—laurel does not survive the harsh
Nebraska winters—formed wreathes topped with a crown of
candles, in olden days genuine beeswax, now electric facsim-
iles cleverly powered by batteries concealed in the maidens'
bosoms. The girls continued their march up the center aisle,
took their places in a semi-circle in front of the altar and sang
some more Swedish songs.

That's all there was to it. In thirty minutes everyone hurried down to the church cafeteria to gorge themselves on
sandbakkels, krumkaker and aebleskiever washed down with
cup after cup of thin black coffee.

Authentic ritual often survives in cultural outposts like
Pinch Horn long after it has been corrupted in the mother
country. Decades ago Swedish journalists began hyping the

Santa Lucia pageant until today it has degenerated into little more than a beauty contest. Since no one, however, other
than myself, knew what the pageant should include, I could
see no harm in borrowing a trick or two from the Swedes'
corrupted version to generate interest in my own.

I gave the boys a week to announce their nominees for
the lead role and conduct their campaigns. For five days the
bleak halls of St. Lucy's looked like the office of a theatrical
booking agent. Huge blowups of the school's more androgynous boys filled all available wall space.

At Friday's general assembly the winners were announced,
and to no one's surprise, the comely William Prentice won
the role of Santa Lucia. William, the boy who moved the tortured Greek to cry, "Eros burn me!" and got the sack, had the
advantage of being the school's only natural blond.

"AN INSPIRING PERFORMANCE," the Monsignor commented
to me during the after-theater party he threw in his recently
renovated luxurious flat adjacent to the church. "I was *most*
impressed. Show business could learn a lot about uplifting
spectacle from an artist like yourself."

I smiled graciously and reached for another glass of champagne which some young cleric, drafted into service for the
night, was carrying around the room on a silver butler's tray.

"Nothing but a Christmas drag show," the spiteful Mother
Murphy interjected, but no one paid him any mind. Mother
Murphy, quite drunk by now, had just spilled champagne on
the Monsignor's new inch-thick Karistan carpet and then got
sick in the Monsignor's spectacular bathroom. I went in to
help Charles but was too stunned by the room's lavish beauty
to come immediately to his aid. The bathroom was half the

size of my one-room walk-up apartment. Egyptian blue tiles covered walls, floor and ceiling. The black porcelain bathtub was sunk deep into the floor. The black toilet bowl over which Mother Murphy now crouched was, judging from its elegant lines, an Italian import. Next to the commode stood a matching douche! Skillful plumbers had fitted the shower stall into a black marble column extending from floor to ceiling. When I touched the shower's curved glass door, it moved effortlessly aside. I took a thick towel the color of blood from its heated rack and, dampening one end, cleaned up Mother, then the toilet bowl, and threw the soiled towel into the shower stall. Next I took the pearl-handled douche gun from its hook and flushed the evidence of Mother Murphy's gaucherie down the drain. If Mother was asked to resign, it would have to be for reasons more germane to his job than befouling the Monsignor's Cleopatrian bath.

Mother repaid my kindness by panning my pageant in the school press.

Perhaps it was the huge success of the Santa Lucia Festival that finally drove Mother Murphy over the edge. Certainly he had never ranted for such a very long time or worked himself into such an anti-Semitic lather as he did that day in the lunchroom. As I tried to shut out the vulgar, repetitious raving of the man, I sifted through the names of boys loyal to my ideology for likely recruits with which to staff the school newspaper and literary quarterly, publications soon to be mine. Chris Delmonico—he has a flair for words. And William Prentice, the only boy left at St. Lucy's, now that Kevin was gone, capable of speaking the king's English. But can he write? I'll put Primo on sports, an assignment where his vernacular will—

But I simply could not go on.

"If it weren't for Jewish domination of the theater, I'd be directing on Broadway. Every producer, every director, Jews, Jews, Jews..."

"Shut your fucking mouth!"

My words shocked me as much as they did my fellow teachers. They lowered forks of overcooked spaghetti and stared with open mouths, at me, not Mother. I stared back, unblinking, numb. I had always prided myself in having risen above my class by breaking the habit of vulgar usage. After leaving Omaha I began mixing with many upper-middle and truly upper-class people. From them I learned to silence and condemn with a mere lowering of the *Times*, a slow sweep of the hand to even the fold, a piercing look directed at the offender of civilized behavior. Nothing in my public image had informed my fellow teachers of this moment; neither was there anything in the image I had of myself to inform me.

Mother Murphy blanched. His mouth fell slack. His hand shook. He looked suddenly very old. Then anger rushed to fill the void and a gush of words and spittle punctuated the stunned silence.

"I will not be silenced! I will not be silenced! These filthy liberals! I have a right to speak! I have the right! I will not be silenced!"

He wasn't. He said more, shouted meaningless phrases. But no one listened. He had lost the moment to me. Flushed with hate, trembling and dancing about the room, he waved his arms in impotent fury. They, the other teachers, studied their plates of cold spaghetti in embarrassment.

Early that evening—the bells of St. Lucy's were striking six as I left the school—I had worked out the broad outline of my attack. I had the witnesses, and this time they would not get off the hook. I would go to Brother Principal with the charges. I would compel them to testify, regardless of the means I might have to employ to ensure that they did so. And this time if Brother Principal should drag his feet, I would seek out someone with the power or influence to make him act. Did my Black Books contain such a name? I was not sure, but with my record of resourcefulness, I was confident I could come up with my man.

17

For his indulgences in public bigotry, Mother Murphy had to go. Not out, forced to resign as Greek O'Grady had been and Bull Belloli would be if Primo's assignment bore fruit. No, Mother could stay if he wished, but he must be put under quarantine and discouraged from spreading his unwholesome racial attitudes (and disrupting my lunch). He could continue to lead boys through grueling conjugations of French verbs; someone had to shoulder this unrewarding task if the foreign language requirement of state and accreditation boards were to be met. Bigot he might be, but he was not a brute. For these reasons I chose not to pack Mother out the door. He belonged to that group of men as old as Christianity, failed men who see every name in lights, if that name is not their own, as recognition that should have gone to them. Most of the faculty had witnessed Mother Murphy's outburst. But would they swear to it in front of Brother Principal? I discounted Flash Fagan, Brother Adolph and Bull Belloli; none of these would come forth. Eyes Panuccio had heard it; so

had Brother Liberal and Orphan Annie. But would they say
so? Since it was Brother Bob's chosen responsibility to further positive attitudes to ethnic diversity, I was sure he could
be brought to testify. To bring Panuccio and Animan around
would require persuasion of a different sort. I began looking
for tender spots to probe and found Orphan Annie's in an
amazing disclosure of Chris Delmonico.

I had drawn up a chart for Marriage and the Family demonstrating how power in the family had shifted
through the centuries from the maternal to the paternal
line, where it had remained with disastrous consequences,
most notable being the development of capitalism. I needed
forty copies for my lecture that day on 'Marriage and
Materialism: How to Avoid the Playboy Pitfall." When I
stopped at the mimeograph room to run off the chart, I
found the door ajar and the machine running. Who could
be using the machine during an hour when every teacher
other than myself should have been in a classroom? I
pushed open the door to find a student, Chris Delmonico, running off pages of Spanish notes. On the table
to his left were several completed pages arranged in neat
stacks awaiting collation into packets. For security reasons
school regulations forbid students to be in the mimeograph
room—they had been known to lift test questions from
impressions left on the drum—and I asked the boy what
his purpose was in being there.

"Oh, I do it for Mr. Animan," Chris answered innocently.
"For every completed packet, I get ten percent of the take."

"The *take*, Chris?"

"Mr. Animan charges a dollar for every packet of learning
aids. This one is vocabulary, from *Don Quixote*. Here, take
a look. Nice work, don't you think? I used to have trouble

with ink smears, but I'm getting the hang of it. If you hold your hand here on this plate and press hard—"

"I'm familiar with the machine's idiosyncracies. Very interesting, these pages. And it is nice copy, Chris. How many packets would you say you've completed this semester?"

"Oh, I don't know. I've lost track. Probably ten or twelve."

Numbers ran through my head. We did not use office calculators at St. Lucy's. Brother thought them a needless expense, which in a sense they were. After a few years of grading three hundred students six times a year, any teacher with a brain could add and average a column of figures in the flash of a brain wave.

"Four hundred and eight dollars. Ten percent of that—you're doing quite well it would seem, Chris. Now if you're finished with Mr. Animan's commercial enterprise, perhaps I could use the machine to run off my own material for which I do not charge my students a penny. Here, let me help you collate these. We'll finish sooner."

As we worked, I chatted with the boy. "Now that I've taken over the yearbook—and who knows, perhaps the newspaper as well, but you must keep the news strictly confidential, Chris; it's not yet official—I could certainly use your talents. I've always thought you might make journalism your career."

The boy, to be sure, had no idea what he meant to do after graduation—working class boys seldom do—but he was sufficiently distracted by my show of interest in his future to enable me to drop a copy of Mr. Animan's publication-for-profit into my open brief case without it being noticed.

When we were finished, I asked the boy, "Would you please, Chris, be kind enough to ask Mr. Animan to drop by Room 13 after his last class? There's a small matter I want to talk to him about."

As I ran off my charts, I tried formulating the precise phrases I would use when Orfeo and I met later in the day. In light of Orphan Annie's nationality, my thoughts turned for inspiration to Eva Peron, his country's foremost exponent of slippery politics. How would Eva have proceeded? A touch of fear, I supposed, coupled with a bit of charity from lady bountiful.

Perhaps Orfeo had counted his vocabulary packets and discovered one missing, heard I wanted to see him, put two and two together and concluded the game was up. Certainly his diffident, almost crestfallen entrance into Room 13 made gaining his support possible without resorting to pitiless methods. After we had agreed upon the need for teaching aids developed with our teaching methods in mind, and that the preparation of such routine materials might better be left to assistants that we did without at St. Lucy's, I began tightening the screws.

"The sale of such material is not traditional in America, Orfeo. Now I may know that your unfamiliarity with the American way accounts for this unfortunate incident. But we have other teachers here who, although American by birth, are equally ignorant of the American way. Isn't it your intention, Orfeo, to apply for resident status in this country? If this is the case, it would be better if the authorities concerned were not to hear of this business of selling students material for which their tuition has already entitled them. You should know as well that I've led more than one Third World refugee from oppression through the mazes of the Department of Immigration and that I'm prepared to do the same for you. It would make my task a good deal easier if, considering your country of origin, you demonstrated strong disapproval of bigotry by supporting the other teachers who intend to have Mr. Murphy up for reprimand."

I can make some claims to cosmopolitan exposure, and if I could barely discern the meaning behind the sounds Orfeo uttered in response to my suggestion, conceive, if you will, the confusion he created in the minds of his students.

"Awwthers?" Orfeo asked. "Iee deedunt eer dee awwther teachers saee nawtheeng."

"Oh, there are others who were as outraged as I, Orfeo, although it would be better not to mention their names at this time. However, if you agree Mr. Murphy's diatribes are indeed regretful outbursts, and agree as well to admit your outrage to Brother Principal, I would be willing to forget I ever heard of this little matter of compelling students to purchase materials it is your job to furnish free. No one could expect you to repay the several hundred dollars you have already extracted from them. It would be wiser, however, to shut down your presses before someone less tolerant than I discovers your ingenious enterprise."

Orfeo folded, as I thought he would. Children spawned by elitist oligarchic societies are no match for survivors of the American adversarial system where every bone won has been snatched from the jaws of a competing citizen.

It was my intention, because of Brother Principal's distaste for change, to get at least three dependable witnesses to testify where mine alone should have been sufficient. I had Brother Bob and Orfeo in the bag. But Dio? How could I bring Eyes Panuccio around?

I stand in awe of innocence, and Dio's sweet demeanor forbade me to use hardball tactics against such a man. This, his true innocence, and the speculation that regardless of how intensely I might peer behind those thick green lenses clouding liquid eyes the color of molten chocolate, I would discover no evil deed committed, not even, I believed, what Sister Philomena referred to under the euphemism, 'lively thoughts.' I mulled over this problem, as I often did, and returned to a rereading of Machiavelli. Well, not an actual rereading of *The Prince*, I didn't have time for that—only a half hour's reflection upon the body of oral tradition associated with Machiavellian thought. How did the Great Manipulator persuade the innocent to bear witness? Torture was out, and neither could I make much use of his less brutal methods. Like so many politicians, Machiavelli no doubt built on the premise that every man has his price. Those who can't be bought can be compromised. But I am not a ruthless man; for me, the end only justifies the means if those to be ruined have already forfeited their right to better treatment.

I reviewed what I knew about Eyes Panuccio, which was not much more than I could see. A head of thick brown curls capped a well shaped head in proper proportion to a young man who stood no taller than his average freshman student. He was sweet, demure, ingratiating, not unlike a younger and more diminutive version of Brother Bob. But unlike The Lib, who had publicly defined himself and must therefore, to protect his integrity, act accordingly, Dio's image of himself was as blurred as the world he saw through the thick lenses of his tortoise shell glasses. He presented no side of himself to appeal to. He was as smooth, cute and ungraspable as a baby hippo.

I would invite Dionisio for a beer at the County Cork. A cold drink after a hard day might lead to inspiration.

After sixth period, I paused just long enough to excuse my absence to the group of junior boys gathered to hear my next lecture on Marriage and the Family.

"A young man," I explained, "has asked me for counseling concerning his decision to marry. This will be his last chance to reconsider before he abandons the uncertain delights of promiscuity for the secure monotony of matrimony, so I must talk to him. On Monday we continue with our discussion, 'The Celibate Marriage: Frustration as an Alternative to Ennui.' Peace," I called in salutation, and threw the boys the sign in a quick little gesture of camaraderie.

Dio was on his first beer when I arrived. After allowing him to buy the first round, I insisted upon paying for the more expensive whiskeys with beer chasers. We were sitting on adjoining barstools. As the afternoon wore on, working men pushed in from either side, forcing us to turn towards each other, our legs dovetailed.

"Tell me, Dio"—and I bent even closer, trying to make contact with eyes staring in unfocused lines to either side of my head—"how have you enjoyed your first year at St. Lucy's?"

"It's tough, real tough. The hardest job I've ever had. I really like teaching, I like the boys. They're good kids, we have a lot of fun. But sometimes I don't know if I'm going to make it. If only they knew when to stop."

It was difficult, looking into Dio's classroom, to distinguish teacher from students. All were behaving in much the same manner, laughing, joking, wisecracking. When Dio arrived at St. Lucy's, he had tried to establish order. His daily confrontations with the students, while sorely distressing Dio, only incited the boys to worse behavior until Dio gave up and joined what he could not change.

"Yes, I know what you mean," I sympathized. It's too bad teachers are not given more on-the-job-training to master the techniques of classroom control. I'm sure that in your case, all you need is more time, the chance to get a year or two of hard experience under your belt."

Dio struggled to bring his eyes to focus on mine. "But I might not get that time, Virgil. Brother Principal implied that if I don't get my classes under control he might have to let me go."

"Oh, Dio, I can't believe that. The boys love you."

"I try, Virgil! I really do. They just won't settle down. And I won't use physical punishment. I couldn't do that."

"To your credit, Dio. As you said, the boys are a good bunch basically, just a little rough at times. I only wish all of our faculty thought as you do."

"Aw, they're not so bad," Dio said of his fellow teachers.

"I've never heard you use disparaging words of anyone, Dio. Bigotry is a form of violence, too, you know. I'm thinking of Murphy's disgusting outburst at lunch on Wednesday. It came as such a shock to me. I mean it wasn't the first time, but never so virulent. I've always rather liked the man—until that day."

"You mean what he said about the Jews?" Dio lowered his voice and looked about him. No one turned a head. The County Cork had remained ethnically pure long after neighboring bars began to reflect the city's racial rainbow. Among the pink-skinned clientele of the County Cork, even Dio stood out as a dark foreigner. And he was. We were served promptly only because of my own conspicuous ethnic credentials; that, and because every bartender in the place knew me by sight. "Don't take Murphy serious," Dio went on. "He doesn't mean half of what he says. Just rants on out of habit."

"We can't have an open bigot in charge of the school publications, Dio. Think of the potential danger. What if he begins to use the newspaper as a tool to warp the minds of the students? Spoken bigotry is one thing; words are lost to ears beyond the walls. The printed word is carried into the streets."

Dio failed to see the threat. In fact, he laughed. "The paper is a joke. No one reads it."

"Just one issue. That's all it would take to destroy St. Lucy's reputation for racial and religious tolerance."

Dio lowered his eyes in recognition of my altruistic call to defend the school's reputation.

"Well, maybe it isn't the best idea having the Murph in such a position, but—"

I rushed into the opening Dio provided more quickly than I might have if we had not been on our third—or was it our fourth?—boilermaker. I have always been good at holding my liquor, an accomplishment entirely of my own doing and mastered in spite of troublesome genes on my father's side. At the age of fourteen I learned the humiliating effect liquor can have on one's behavior when I woke up in a bed not my own and had no idea of how I got there. I swore then that I would never again allow myself to behave in such an undignified manner. Years of discipline worked its intended effect. Now, my only behavioral change was sharply clipped diction and a certain rigidity of bearing, an over-compensation for what I feared might become the slurred speech of a falling down drunk, crying in his beer or soaring on flights of empty rhetoric, behavior all too common to my race.

"If you will support me, Dio, when I talk to Brother Principal next week, I think we will see Mr. Murphy silenced. Just admit that you were present when he—"

"No, I can't do it," Dio insisted. "Anyway, it's not my concern. Not anymore. If I'm to be fired... " Dio stared dejectedly into his beer.

"Dismissals do look bad on one's record. And you're just starting out in life. Who knows what positions you might apply for in the future, or when you might need a good reference?"

Dio sunk lower on his stool.

"There is, however, just possibly, a way for you to regain control and persuade Brother Principal to change his mind."

"No way, Virgil. I've tried everything."

"Yes, *you* have," I replied. "But *I* have yet to try at all."

"Oh, no, Virgil. I couldn't let you step in. It wouldn't be fair."

"Fair?" I asked, sincerely puzzled. "To whom? What does fairness have to do with it? Are the boys being fair to you? It's a hundred to one, their favor. Besides, you have no choice. Continue as you are and you will be replaced, probably by someone who'll be far harder on the boys than you've been—or ever will be. Look upon it that way. You'll be saving the innocents from a worse fate. Rely on me and I can promise you if not a model teaching atmosphere, then at least one that will appear acceptable when observed through the window of your classroom door or listened to over Brother's intercom."

So I got the promise of support I needed, and I did not have to stoop to undignified means. Only an exchange of services anyone could appreciate.

I asked Dio to draw up a list of the ringleaders in each of his five freshman classes. Several of the worst trouble-makers appeared on more than one list. Then I called in each boy separately for a chat. Separately, because I wished the boy to feel hopeless and isolated when confronted by the legendary Mr. Quinn, who brooked no quarter, took no hostages. My warning to each was the same: "Either cut out the rough stuff or you will face years of the most excruciating torture when you matriculate into my history classes, classes that you cannot avoid because all of them are required and I'm sure to get you sooner or later."

18

I HAD SECURED MY WITNESSES. Three would be sufficient if Brother Principal judged the issue of Murphy's bigotry on its just desserts. But I did not trust our principal. If he tried to wiggle out, as he had in the O'Grady debacle, then I would need powerful forces in reserve to see the attack brought to a successful conclusion. But where to gather them? Organized student support was out of the question. Young people habitually call each other names unfit to print and must be excused for failing to take alarm when adults refer to minorities in deprecating terms.

It's odd how so many of our pivotal decisions are brought about not by choice but by necessity. This was certainly the case in my decision to approach the Anti-Defamation League of B'nai B'rith, the city's most vocal opponent of bigotry. Where else to turn? Still I hesitated. Until now I hadn't gone beyond the walls, unless it was into my Black Books to ask the advice of a friend, for the support needed to implement reform. I had worked alone. I was not an organization man.

I had contacted no outside group. If I did so now, I would not only be seeking the help of organizations accustomed to media limelight, but I would find myself, some way down the road, the head of a resistance movement made up largely of non-Lucians.

Such is the behavior of great leaders and martyrs: One unfree act determining another until we find ourselves nailed to a cross on Calvary.

How to gain the ear of an organization as powerful as B'nai B'rith? Would the organization listen to a complaint emanating from one of the city's smallest schools? When I telephoned, B'nai B'rith brushed me off as a disgruntled quack, someone out to disrupt the organization's uneasy armistice with the Church, one of its oldest oppressors. Humiliating. What I needed was an influential advocate.

I began by combing my Black Books for Jews, and despite their discreet history, I found a Jewish name or two. Neither appeared to be of much help. My occupational notes accompanying each name placed one in wholesale yarn and the other in frozen fish. I turned to Black Book VII, the last of the books with pages yet to fill. Halfway down the first page I came upon the name of Michael Lowenthal, a man I had never met but should have. He was certainly just the man for the job. But how to meet him, the man Kevin was so fond of and the man with whom he had been living when he died? With Kevin gone, the only person I knew who knew Lowenthal at all was Primo de Popalano.

In light of Primo's family connections, I would rather not speculate on the nature of the methods he used to persuade Michael to meet with me. A degree of coercion was no doubt involved. Michael's behavior following Kevin's death made it quite clear he wished to disassociate himself from the event itself and everyone who knew of his ill-fated liaison. He did not attend the funeral; he did not send flowers. And when Primo went to his apartment to pick up Kevin's few possessions—his operatic recordings, his schoolbooks—the man did not answer the door himself but sent the cleaning woman. He had Kevin's belongings in boxes, packed and ready, stacked inside the foyer door.

"He'll meet you," Primo informed me the following week, "at the Horn and Hardart, the one at Forty-second and Third, tomorrow at four."

"How did he respond when you talked to him?" I asked.

Primo stared out the classroom windows, shuffled about, finally coming to rest closer to where I sat than was proper for a student. He propped himself on the edge of my desk, his long legs crossed, his eyes on the flag which hung in the corner of the room. Primo was becoming a poser. He focused on the flag not out of love for the symbol of the republic, but to present his features in profile, his best angle.

Primo chose to be stingy with details. He would tell me nothing more, only repeat in tones heavy with implications that Michael Lowenthal had "come around." I thanked Primo for his help and then changed the subject from one he obviously did not wish to talk about to one I hoped he did.

"You've told me nothing about your inquiries into the Belloli case. It's been weeks, Primo. Haven't you discovered anything that might help us in ending his violent reign? Everybody's talking about Tuesday's incident in his homeroom. Scandalous. Another case of disciplinary excess."

Primo shifted his position, twisting his torso about until his eyes met mine. He permitted himself a small, satisfied smile.

"I was meaning to tell you—on Friday."

"Now, Primo!"

"Do you read the papers?" Primo asked, knowing that I did.

"*All* the papers, everyday."

"I only see you reading the *Times*. Too high-class. Read the *News.*"

"I *scan* the *News* daily. A history teacher must be familiar with what the papers are passing off as current events."

"Then you'll find your answer. Sometime next week. Probably Sunday."

And with that he picked up his green and gold athletic bag, the kind used by St. Lucy students to transport books to and from school, but in Primo's case was too light to contain much more than a jock strap. He strutted to the door, stopped to smile and salute, obviously enjoying his game of wait and see, and disappeared into the hall.

For a few minutes after he left, I sat at my desk speculating on what incriminating discoveries Primo might have made that would guarantee Belloli's exposure to the press. An outrageous stag party? Dealing in numbers? No, nothing so tame would make a New York paper, would never, in fact, get beyond the police precinct walls. What could Belloli be doing then that was newsworthy *and* fell within the limits of his imagination?

My thoughts were broken off by the bells of St. Lucy's striking the hour. Four! I had completely forgot my yearbook staff, working to refurbish our new quarters. I raced down six flights of stairs and into the tunnel leading to the church.

I was needlessly anxious. I had chosen my staff well. Each boy was selected for his ability to work without undo supervision, or if this was beyond his abilities, to have formed a friendship with a boy who could work independently. When I arrived, the boys were all busily at it. The old coal room, which hadn't been used for decades, not since the church's conversion to gas heat, had been swept and scrubbed and made ready for its new use. This would be the darkroom. The large adjoining storage space, crammed to the ceiling with papier-mâché vases, rickety prie-dieux and plaster statues of saints no longer in vogue (including a garish image of St. Philomena, the saint most recently relegated to the dust bin of hagiology), would become our layout room. The light was poor and damp oozed from the ancient granite walls; however, it was either use these rooms or continue to work in classrooms where nothing could be left set up overnight. The school buildings proper could not spare us more than a closet for storage. St. Lucy's had been built to hold two hundred and twenty, maximum; the enrollment had now reached four hundred plus. As teaching religious who worked for room and board became harder to get, the Monsignor had kept the budget in balance by compelling the Little Brothers of Divine Grace to take in more paying students to increase the income. And there was no place for the school to expand. Beyond my homeroom—3c, housed in what had once been the maids' quarters of an adjoining brownstone—was real estate worth millions. With each article in the *Times* reporting the consequences of over-crowding in the state prisons, I trembled to think what might someday happen at St. Lucy's. Would our claustrophobic environment result in another Attica Prison Riot? Would the boys someday rise up to butcher the lot of us, then burn the school to the ground? Until such martyrdom occurred, the diocese, apparently, intended to do nothing.

The following day I left the boys with instructions to dump the peeling saints and junk bric-a-brac on the street, and when they had finished for the day, to turn off the lights and lock up. "I'm sorry I can't stay to help you, but I have an appointment with a Mr. Lowenthal that promises to be of far greater consequence to St. Lucy's than mothering boys quite capable of managing on their own."

I left through the church itself and paused for a moment before the statue of St. Lucy. "Give me strength," I prayed, "to transcend my humble origins, to confront this man of wealth, to ignore the fact that while I must buy my clothes from Mrs. Goldberg, he buys his from—" Try as I might I could not formulate an image of Michael Lowenthal, and Kevin had been far too discreet to give me a physical description. Pierre Cardin? Custom tailors? Suave, urbane? Oh, most decidedly so, and gifted with the devastating intelligence typical of his race.

I had taken particular care with my own dress and grooming the day I was to meet with Michael. That year I typically dressed in black. Surprisingly, no one ever took me for a cleric. No doubt the Italian cut of my jacket and the close fit of my trousers told everyone, at least those with an eye for fashion, that Milanese couturiers and not some clothes mill serving the religious trade designed my wardrobe. What they don't know is that everything I wear comes from Mrs. Goldberg's shop on Orchard Street. She knows my preference and haunts the best Italian haberdasheries, picking up ends of lines and window samples.

"Black, Virgil. You must always wear black. Black sharkskin in fall and spring, blue-black wool worsted in winter. I have just the thing." Mrs. Goldberg rummaged about in huge piles of menswear thrown all in a heap and drew out a dark suit. "Feel the softness, Virgil." She rubbed the luxurious fabric between thumb and forefinger. "Made for a gangster, that I'm sure of." She held up pants large enough to encircle my waist twice around. "I got it from Arnie Schulman who got from Giovanni's of Flatbush Avenue who made it for a gangster who died and couldn't pick it up. With your complexion, what can I say?" Mrs. Goldberg held the collar of the blue-black worsted jacket to my cheek and described the stunning contrast of dark wool against creamy skin touched with just a blush of pink. "Looks like yours, Virgil, are best served with the inky colors."

Mrs. Goldberg was a magician with needle and thread and for the suit of clothes, now a perfect fit, and her services as fashion consultant, she charged me ten cents on the dollar.

I bought the three-piece ink-blue worsted from Mrs. Goldberg while recuperating from an awful bout of mononucleosis that left me six and half pounds lighter than my usual 147 well placed pounds. I've never worn loose fitting clothes, not even back when respectable men draped themselves in gray flannel sacks designed to hide the male body. But neither did I go over to the current craze, men publicly exhibiting bulges and dangling appendages. Except for a party outfit or two, I never went in for crotch-hugging bells. My major field of study accounts for my freedom from fads. As a historian I'm too well acquainted with the fleeting dictates of fashion that has caused men to flaunt themselves in everything from the all-concealing robes of ancient Rome to the shocking padded codpieces worn by Renaissance man. By and large I have ignored the trends, and I guide Mrs. Goldberg's nimble fingers to take a tuck here, a pinch there, relying on subtle definition, not coarse revelation, to further my deductive purposes.

I slipped into Mrs. Goldberg's creation, adjusted the pouch of my bikini, took a deep breath and fastened the hasp of my beltless trousers. Standing before the full length mirror fastened to the bathroom door, I threw back the flap of my jacket, stood hand on hip, and studied the effect. Elegant, with just the hint of lewdness men like Michael Lowenthal found irresistible.

Michael Lowenthal, when he arrived twenty minutes late for our appointment, was dressed in faded blue jeans and beef-roll penny loafers. A gold stud set with a tiny red stone pierced his left earlobe. He was pushing forty, squarely built, and stood three inches shorter than my five foot ten and a half. He scanned the room, then walked directly to where I sat at a window table.

"How did you know," I asked, "that I am Virgil Quinn?"

"Your young friend, the Italian kid, gave me a description. He said you'd be dressed like a—no, I better not get the boy in trouble. That, his description, and the chalk dust on your sleeve. *And* that bag."

I glanced down at my briefcase setting on the terrazzo floor. I blushed. Perhaps it was time to get rid of it, exchange it for one of those sleek, hard edge attaché cases all business-men carried nowadays. My bag was the satchel type with two handles. I found it nearly new in a thrift shop three years before, the day I went to work at St. Lucy's. To give it that just-purchased look, I had my initials, v.q., stamped in gold leaf to either side.

"Nice kids you're turning out down there," Michael offered. "Tough. Forceful. What are you training them for, the Mafia?"

The accuracy of Michael's opening thrust jolted me. What had Primo done to get Michael to come here? I chose to be sententious in my reply. "Remember, Mr. Lowenthal—"

"Please, call me Michael."

"Our boys come from the working class. They haven't had your—or my—advantages." It was best to establish from the outset that I considered Michael my social equal.

"No, I would never have learned his skills in my family." Michael took a packet of sugar from the rack on the table, emptied it into his cup, stirred once, and drank. "So what is it you want of me? The young hood wouldn't tell me."

"He didn't know," I replied. I was prepared to go into the historical causes of bigotry at St. Lucy's and Mother Murphy's in particular. Michael's restlessness, however, told me he was a man in a hurry. So I threw away my notes and jumped directly into the matter.

"We are having problems with a certain teacher at St. Lucy's. He's beneath our standard. I may not need your help in what I intend to do, but then again I might. Principals are not always predictable when proper moral decisions come in conflict with their desire to avoid disruptive staff changes." I paused, preparing to go on. If Michael was to understand the political morass of St. Lucy's, I had to go into considerable detail.

"You're saying you want to get someone sacked."

A disagreeably direct man if ever I met one.

"Not exactly. Dismissal, in this case, may not be necessary. Silencing the man is."

"Kevin spoke of you as a champion of academic freedom."

"And he was right," I replied, both pleased by this reminder of Kevin's regard for me and surprised at Michael's bringing Kevin into the conversation at all. "But this is not a matter of academic freedom. The man I refer to is an anti-Semitic bigot."

"Ah," Michael sighed, and smiled the tired smile of a man who has never suffered from an evil he knows to be prevalent and that he is now being asked to combat.

"The world, Mr. Quinn, is full of bigots. Why single out this one?"

"Because he is of *my* world, Mr. Lowenthal. To do noth-ing would make me personally responsible."

"But why come to me, of all people. Do you expect me to silence him?"

"Not personally. You are, however, a member of an influen-tial family, one that is, judging from what I read in the papers, active in matters of this sort. I believe David Lowenthal, past president of B'nai B'rith, is your uncle?"

"David and I don't talk. He considers me a scandal."

"I'm sorry to hear that," I replied politely. "If I can avoid bringing you into this matter, I will do so. For Kevin's sake." At my mention of Kevin's name, Michael winced. "But by next Thursday, the day I have chosen to rid our school of bigotry forever, I will need your assurance that if Brother Principal refuses to act on this clear-cut case of anti-Semi-tism, you will see to it that B'nai B'rith greases the wheels of whatever machinery it employs to see justice done."

"My, my, Virgil—may I call you that? Kevin always did, to me."

"Feel free."

"You *are* a crusader, aren't you?"

"I prefer to see myself as a man of integrity."

"Which in our time comes to the same thing."

"I will need you to speak to your uncle."

"As I said, we don't speak."

"Then perhaps this is the time to mend family fences." I allowed the urgent tone I used to have its affect. "Perhaps its time to put aside family quarrels to achieve a greater good. You might," I added, "consider your intervention as a sort of memorial to Kevin O'Connor. We certainly have little enough to remember him by."

The busboy who had been roaming the mostly empty dining room collecting dishes and trays stopped his cart at my
shoulder, mumbled something, and when he wasn't responded
to, rudely asked me to remove my bag from the floor. "Do you
want to kill someone, trip em up? People who don't know no
better than to leave their stuff in the middle of the floor..."

Disconcerting, a busboy presuming to speak to a patron
in such a tone. Back in Omaha...

When I returned to Michael Lowenthal to hear his answer,
he had turned aside and was gazing out the window at the
five o'clock crowds on Forty-second Street.

"You will give me your help then?"

Michael remained silent.

"I had hoped," I told Michael, "that it would not be necessary to go into the consequences of your refusing to help."

"You wouldn't do that!"

"I would rather not. If compelled to do so it would only
be done to achieve a greater good. Halting rampant anti-
Semitism takes precedence, I should think, over whatever
comfortable arrangements we've made to avoid embarrassment in our private lives."

"And you, Virgil? What arrangements have you made?"

I've become deaf to innuendo of this sort. Michael
continued.

"Why don't you go to my uncle yourself if you're so hot on
getting rid of this bigot guy?"

"I tried to avoid coming to you, Mr. Lowenthal. I called
B'nai B'rith and they gave me the brush off. I have no reason
to doubt your uncle would do the same. If you simply talk
to him and get his provisional approval, I'll have all the clout
I need. I doubt that I'll even have to use the organization's

help, at least if Brother Principal is as cautious this time as his behavior in the past has led me to believe."

"You walk a narrow line, Virgil Quinn."

"What man of integrity does not?" I reached for my brief-case, pushed well under the table. As I did so I noticed Michael's leg twitching nervously. I gave him time to compose himself and then continued. "Michael, the last thing I wish to do is damage the family ties of a man as close to Kevin as you were. All I need is your uncle's assurance to bring in B'nai B'rith if needed, make inquiries, telephone the Cardinal, do whatever they've found effective in matters of this sort."

I toyed with my spoon. Michael said nothing. The tension was more than I could bear. I reached for a packet of sugar, tore off a corner and emptied the contents into the spoon. Allowing just the tip of the spoon to touch the tea in my cup, I watched the sugar turn brown, creeping from tip to handle. I raised the spoon to my mouth, inverted its load, and in a bold violation of my vow to Sister Philomena to forego sweets, raked the spoon clean with my tongue. A nasty habit of my father, Barney Quinn, which, if I slipped into it myself, would in a few years time destroy my figure and harden my arteries, resulting, as it did with my father, in a fatal coronary seizure at the age of fifty-eight. Michael watched. I ignored his look of disapproval, noting that his own ethnic group had a weakness for cheesecake and choc-olate eclairs. The Irish simply preferred their sweets neat, I told myself, as we did our whiskey.

"Please give me a call after you've talked to your uncle. Here's my card."

"Nice," he said, holding the gilt-edged card between thumb and forefinger while running the pad of the other over the raised Gothic lettering, "When did high school teachers begin carrying business cards? Embossed, no less."

"About the same time third-generation Jewish immigrants forgot their ancestors' reasons for coming to this country. On second thought, it's better you didn't call me at school. Try me at home. The number is not on the card, but I'm in the book. There's only one Virgil Quinn."

"To be sure," Michael murmured.

I reached for my black bag. I gathered up my black trench coat and fold-up umbrella in its sleek black leather case. "I had always wished, Michael, to have met you under better circumstances, while Kevin was alive. I was not invited. Now I have the feeling we may never meet again."

Michael, when he raised his dark melancholy eyes to meet mine, seemed relieved to hear that.

19

JUDGING FROM PRIMO'S INCREASING indiscretions, he was nearing the end of the Belloli assignment. As he closed in on our quarry, his behavior towards the coach became openly contemptuous, and his liberties with me alarmingly conspiratorial. The casual smile with which he usually greeted me changed to cool, cloak and dagger jerks and twitches. When these turned to jivy winks and smirks, I hoped he would soon bring his clandestine work to a speedy conclusion. On Wednesday afternoon of the week following my talk with Michael Lowenthal, he dropped by my attic classroom to tell me I could make my move at any time. He had the goods on Bull Belloli.

'Tell me, Primo, how did you do it?"

"Well, Mr. Quinn, to be successful at this kind of work, you got to have two things going for you. You've got to be patient and you got to know the right people."

"And how did you go about it, you and your friends?"

213

"Oh, we just staked out the coach's building. Not every night, just on weekends. He stayed pretty close to home on school nights. We broke the weekend into shifts, two hours on, the rest of the night off, from six in the evening to two in the morning."

"Still a lot of waiting, Primo, standing in the cold for four weekends—or has it been five?"

"Five. We could've nailed him sooner, but he had a car and we didn't. Couldn't tail him."

I waited for Primo to tell how he had solved this problem. When he didn't offer to do so, I asked.

"We... borrowed a car. Different car every night so the Bull's neighbors wouldn't become suspicious, seeing the same car, and tip off the coach he was being tailed. The third weekend we began to get a picture of what he was up to. The fourth we knew for sure, and the fifth we called the guys over at the *News*. The rest is history, as you'd say, or will be when Sunday's papers hit the stands."

IT WAS THE unusual nature of the bust, I suppose, that accounted for Bull Belloli making the front page of Sunday's *Daily News*. He was not alone. The photograph covered one-half of a tabloid page, everything above the fold. Several other men and one woman were grouped around him, all caught by the camera with fists raised clenching wads of paper money and mouths open, apparently cheering something going on in the foreground. The photographer had focused on the spectators, not the action, and the object of all this excitement was unclear, just two small black blobs in the center of a circular pit. Behind them, making up the blurred background, a cluster of people sat hunched forward on raised benches.

Above the photo ran the headline set in three inch type: 78 NABBED IN DOG FIGHT BUST.

Stories covering the incident took up much of page three. No wonder. There had not been a raid on organized dog fighting in the city for thirty years. In the following days, several of the more reflective weeklies picked up on the incident. Jim Malone, an old classmate of mine from Fordham and now on the staff of *Commonweal*, tied in the resurrection of dogfighting to the resurgence of the Ku Klux Klan, the new prominence of fundamental Protestant preachers, and the angry response to Roe vs Wade. Amazing. And the week after? Would some journalist, equally imaginative, argue that Belloli was just a working-class entrepreneur promoting a sport no worse than prizefighting? I decided not to leave Bull's fate in the hands of a fickle press and that very day I skipped lunch and used the time to visit the offices of the Association for the Prevention of Cruelty to Animals.

Miss Trish, of the ASPCA, stood behind her desk feeding bits of rotisserie baked chicken to her pug-nosed Pekinese. The dog sat upright, forepaws raised, in anticipation of each choice morsel.

"Yes, Mr. Quinn," she replied to my question, "I did read the *News* articles on the resurgence of dogfighting. That people are still amused by such barbarous games came as no surprise to us here. Our files contain many incidents equally lurid." Miss Trish pulled a tissue from the dispenser on her desk and wiped the mouth of the Pekinese. "But why have you come to us about Mr. Belloli? It would seem that his case at least has ended up where all such instances of cruelty to animals belong—in the courts."

"Not all of the people in this city consider dogfighting the abominable crime you and I believe it to be."

"Is there any doubt the man will be arraigned? It's my understanding, and that of our lawyers, Mr. Belloli will be charged with a felony, plea bargain and get a suspended sentence with two years probation."

"That may be true, Miss Trish. I came to you because I need your help in making certain the matter doesn't stop there. Mr. Belloli is a school teacher. What he does to dogs, I can assure you, he does to boys."

"I have no doubt you're right, Mr. Quinn. But cruelty to children does not fall within our area of concern. Many years ago when I joined the ASPCA, I realized I could not save every defenseless creature in this city. Just as you've dedicated your life to saving boys, my colleagues and I have dedicated ours to saving dogs. It's a matter of economics, you see, both financial and emotional. We only have so much money, so many active supporters, so much love to give. We cannot right every wrong in a city with more than its share."

The Pekinese had by this time devoured both chicken breasts and was now nibbling strips of dark meat that Miss Trish carefully deskinned before presenting to the dog.

"There are other organizations," Miss Trish continued, wiping her fingers on a tissue, "whose major concern is the protection of children. I suggest you go to them."

"None come to mind," I replied.

"Try the child welfare department. Perhaps they can do something."

I gave Miss Trish a condescending smile. Was she really so naïve as to believe the city's social agencies protected children with the same zeal as her organization did cats and dogs?

"Miss Trish, let me tell you—" But I didn't tell her of my efforts to find alternative living arrangements for Kevin

O'Connor, a boy whose life was made miserable by parents who demeaned him. Was there any reason to believe the state would intervene now in a situation that had persisted unchecked at St. Lucy's for decades?

Miss Trish's refusal to use her organization on my behalf left me dejected and more than a little apprehensive. What recourse would I have if Brother Principal ignored the ramifications of Belloli's rude amusements and kept him on the job? When the dogfight furor blew over, I would have nothing to force Brother's hand—

'Forcing someone's hand.' What was the source of that strange expression. Was it first used in cards? Hands, cards, poker, bluff, mission pennies, Sister Philomena. My mind raced through free associations. The day Sister Philomena taught me how to play poker came back in a flash—cold, clear and instructive.

"For all of us, Virgil, life is a gamble, and your life, I'm afraid, will be riskier than most." Sister and I sat to either side of her desk in the empty third-grade classroom. It was the dead of winter. A whiteout blizzard was roaring across the Nebraska prairie, and Sister Superior had sent home the few students to come to school that day. I had stayed behind, hoping to spend the day alone with Sister Philomena. "If you hope to survive," Sister Philomena continued, "you must master the dual skills of the gambler's art—figuring the odds and sustaining the bluff. There's no better game for teaching these skills than five card stud."

With that Sister reached for the mission bank that always occupied the left corner of her desk. This was the same bank she had made for me to carry on my rounds during mission week. Our donations that year were earmarked for the 'starving babies of China,' and Sister created a curious Chinese figure to inspire greater giving. From an orange she sculpted a bald head with slant eyes and a flat nose and a wide slit of a mouth to receive our coins. She disembodied the Chinaman now by pulling on his orange-husk head, dried to a dark yellowish brown, to which she had attached embroidered robes at the neck. The pint jar beneath was nearly full of pennies.

Sister dumped the pennies onto her desk all in a pile. She pushed half the pile to my side and kept half for herself.

The game began.

Two hours later so many of the pennies had crept over to Sister's side I could no longer match her bets.

"I have won all your pennies, Virgil, because you can neither figure the odds nor sustain a bluff. Either you bet the same amount on every hand, banking on my having nothing in the hole, or you instantly fold when I bump you five."

Sister turned to look out the window where the blizzard continued to obscure the city. It had begun to grow dark.

"Enough for today, Virgil. But we'll play again from time to time until you acquire my skills."

I thanked Sister for her help.

"Why should you thank me, my child? I have been given a mandate to teach, and so I teach whatever it is that needs to be learned."

Who needed Miss Trish? With Sister Philomena's help, I had learned to turn poor cards into a winning hand.

AN OMINOUS LULL followed the publication of Belloli's fondness for dogfighting. The faculty responded to Bull's page-one spread with strained jokes and forced guffaws. The only teacher other than myself to express disapproval was Brother

Bob. He greeted the man responsible for cruelty to animals with a haughty silence meant to convey moral outrage.

I made an appointment to see Brother Principal. I would allow a week to pass. If in that time Brother was not moved by taste and decency to sack the Bull, I would force the issue.

Days passed and Bull continued his classes of slide shows and game plans. Finally, on the following Monday, I asked Brother for an explanation.

"Another crisis?" Brother asked jauntily when I entered the office. "What's it this time?"

To have answered, "As if you don't know," would have been unnecessarily provocative. "I'm ashamed," I said, "to be part of a faculty that allows a man like Mr. Belloli to remain on the job."

"We must all be permitted our own forms of recreation, Virgil."

"*His* form has been illegal in this state for over fifty years. He was arrested by the police. He—"

"Mr. Belloli has been accused. His guilt has yet to be proven in court."

"Proven? Does anyone deny it? Even Remo?"

"Remo says it was nothing but a dog show. That fits the facts as I know them. He has bred dogs for years, you know, on the roof of his building in Brooklyn."

"A dog show catering to the bizarre delights of degenerate connoisseurs."

"Strong words, Virgil."

"And appropriate. There was a single breed of dog at that pit. The police confiscated eight pit bull terriers, dogs bred almost exclusively for fighting."

"We can't make judgments based on circumstantial evidence."

"The condition the police found those dogs in can hardly be called circumstantial evidence. They were dripping blood, ears torn, eyes gouged from their skulls."

Brother winced. "If that's true, I'm sure it will all come out in court."

Brother Principal rose to announce that, for him, the interview had ended. I rose with him. We stood eye to eye. Mine did not waiver. I had learned the Philomena bluff.

"I think you should know, Brother, this unfortunate incident has gone beyond the courts. An acquaintance of mine, a Miss Trish, heads the local branch of the ASPCA." For a moment Brother stared at me with a look of incomprehension. I didn't define the anagram but allowed him time to work it out himself.

"You mean the group that picks up animals off the street?" Brother asked.

"No, dog catchers do that. The ASPCA *cares* for unwanted animals. They also support a powerful political wing. My friend belongs to that group. She is a lobbyist for the organization."

"Yes?" Brother asked suspiciously.

"Miss Trish and I are, by chance, both members of an environmental protection group, The Izaak Walton League. We ran into each other last Friday." According to circumstances, some schools of moral thought justify white lies. "It was at the 'Mexican Jaguar Survival Benefit' held at the Museum of Natural History. She mentioned during the course of the evening that her group had no intention of letting this dog-fight bust be swept under the rug."

"And what," Brother asked, "do they intend to do about it?"

I dropped the corners of my mouth in a sad acceptance of the power wielded by irate dog lovers. "She mentioned applying pressure through the *Times*—letters to the editor, that sort of thing."

Brother sighed in relief. No one he knew—certainly not the parents of the boys at St. Lucy's—read the *Times*. The editorial position of the newspaper had no more influence on the daily working of the Church than did the opinions of the *Daily Worker*. What the *Daily News* had to say, that was something else again. The *News* broke the story because it made good copy, especially with that spectacular photo of Bull Belloli, mouth agape, fist raised, screaming his dog on to victory. The paper had promptly let the matter drop, allowing the usual big city mayhem to usurp the space needed to pursue developments in the case.

"Miss Trish also mentioned demonstrations."

"Demonstrations? What kind of demonstrations!" Brother Principal was now visibly alarmed.

"She didn't say. But animal rights groups are notorious for using all the tactics of the anti-abortionists and then some. They will begin, I predict, with marchers carrying placards on the street in front of the home of the accused, then escalate if necessary to his place of business. Harassment is often effective, both groups have found, when the courts are not. Have you ever seen dog lovers demonstrate, Brother?"

"No, I can't say that I have. I never cared for dogs myself."

I let the narrow provincialism of his reply go unnoted. "Animal lovers are a special breed of people. I have never owned a pet myself. I have so many friends, I meet so many new and interesting people, I've never felt an over-powering need for companionship that must motivate people of this city to share their space, often hardly larger than a rabbit hutch, with animals other than human. But I have a keen interest in the behavior of all people, even those whose needs

I do not share. For this reason I attended the meeting held at Riverside Church last month to discuss the pros and cons of letting dogs run loose in the neighboring park. I was simply appalled, Brother, at the fury dog owners directed at anyone who suggested that dog excrement in the parks posed a hazard to children, not to mention everyone's footgear. One speaker in favor of stronger leash laws was physically attacked, right there on the stage of the auditorium, and had to be rescued from the enraged mob of dog lovers by armed police officers.

"If such a group appeared here in front of St. Lucy's, it would be difficult, I think, to guarantee Mr. Belloli's safety, or the safety of the school that gives him refuge. If those people are aroused to violence over a matter as relatively unimportant as dog shit, then just think what they might do if confronted by a man caught maiming and killing dogs for pleasure. The dogs do fight to the death, Brother. And to teach them to ignore their instinct to survival, the trainers often kidnap cats and small dogs that are then tossed into the pits to feed the bull terrier's blood lust."

A green pallor replaced the more typical ashen gray of Brother Principal's cheeks. It was as I expected. Brother was no better informed than most when it came to the gory details of dog fighting.

"The newspaper stories said nothing about that, Virgil."

"Perhaps out of deference to their readers' taste for violent sports, like prizefighting. The ASPCA has no such qualms. Their library contains ample documentation of the brutal sport.

"On the other hand," I continued, intending to give the subject fair treatment, "the organization's literature, not surprisingly, is scant when it comes to the behavior of those who love animals to excess. If they do show up here, I would expect no less than smashed windows and graffiti scrawled walls."

Brother Principal slumped down into his leather recliner, closed his eyes and rested his outstretched hands on his oak desk. With the fingers of his right hand he began to drum a sad tattoo for his decaying faculty.

20

B ULL BELLOLI WAS THE first teacher in the history of St. Lucy's to be offered severance pay when asked to resign. The Monsignor arranged it. In a moving statement not at all typical of the man, the Monsignor recognized the true cause of lawless and anti-social behavior and hoped to spare the Belloli family the consequences of poverty.

"It is my responsibility," the Monsignor announced to the assembled faculty, "to see that the souls of those six dear children of Mr. and Mrs. Belloli, all baptized in the Church, are not lost to the pressures of poverty and crime. The Church in her mercy does not throw faithful servants to the dogs, and so we have decided to grant Mr. Belloli a month's severance pay to tide him over until some suitable employment can be found for him."

The Monsignor no doubt had a position in mind like janitor or caretaker. I could certainly do better than that. I searched my Black Books for someone with the power to hire a man with Remo's qualifications and found him in the

person of Jarvis B., Personnel Director for Corrections, whose
facilities had incarcerated more than one of my past acquaintances. I placed a call to Jarvis in which I praised the Bull's
disciplinary techniques that were, if sometimes harsh, effective and probably just what Jarvis was looking for over at his
Rikers Island site. I mentioned Bull's superb work with St.
Lucy's Law and Order Society (which, with Bull gone, I correctly expected to wither on the vine).

I am not a vengeful man. Like O'Grady before him, I
had no wish to see Belloli hounded to desperation; I just
wanted him out of St. Lucy's. Even now, when I myself am
struggling to keep a roof over my head and hardrolls on
the table, I do not begrudge the Monsignor's discrimina-
tory largesse in granting Bull severance pay while offering
me not a cent. The Monsignor felt no compunction over
my being thrown to the wolves, and when the Cardinal
made offers to me, he attached strings that made his money
little more than a bribe. Recalling how little my years of
service to the Church has meant to all concerned, I sometimes weaken and harbor vengeful thoughts. At those
times I repeat the words printed on the placard that hung
above the blackboard of my third-grade classroom: "The
good men do lives after them, the evil is interred with their
bones," a pragmatic guide to behavior brushed in India ink
on glossy white poster board by that skilled calligrapher,
Sister Philomena. It was Sister's advice that motivated me
to find O'Grady and Belloli better paying work than they
knew at St. Lucy's in positions they were not qualified to
fill. Reassured, I take comfort knowing that in time the
means I used will be forgotten while the objectives attained
will be remembered. My head in three-quarters profile will
stand in bas relief on a silver plaque, there on the corridor

wall bearing the portraits of past principals of St. Lucy's. Each boy, as he leaves the principal's office, shaken if not repentant, will glance at my memorial and draw strength from the heroic features of the martyred man he sees there.

I HAD MET with Michael Lowenthal on Thursday of the previous week. Mother Murphy's anti-Semitic outburst had occurred two weeks before that. The longer I allowed Mother to go unchallenged, the lesser were my chances of getting him silenced. "Why did you wait so long, Virgil? If you had only said something sooner..." Brother would use my dalliance as an excuse for his vacillation.

Brother Principal did not come to the door of his office to meet me as he had in the past, but left it to Mrs. Mulcaney to announce, "Brother will see you now."

He sat in his darkened office. He hadn't bothered to turn on his desk lamp or the overhead lights. A dim bulb burned in a small lamp on a table in the corner of the room. When he spoke, I heard the voice of a beaten man resigned to more bad news.

It was one forty-five in the afternoon. I had spent my free period whipping up a sense of righteous outrage towards the man for whom my feelings had always been ambivalent. For thirty minutes I had meditated on the plight of the Jew in history. I retold myself every nasty Jew joke and repeated every hateful epithet I could recall from my Nebraska boyhood. By the time I walked into Brother Principal's office to keep our appointment, I was ready to feed Mother Murphy to Bull Belloli's dogs.

"What is it this time?" Brother asked in a dry and bitter rasp. "Which member of the faculty is no longer fit to serve?

No, you don't need to answer that. I already know, have for some time that Charles would be the next to go."

"Then you've heard?" I glanced involuntarily at the intercom system installed behind his desk.

"Not by intent. I don't—not as a rule—eavesdrop on our faculty. I left the speakers on by mistake, and when I returned to my office, I heard, well, nothing worse than I've heard before."

So I wouldn't need the three faculty witnesses to whom I had—needlessly it seemed now—indebted myself. Ah, well, I would keep my part of the bargains nonetheless if only to demonstrate I was a man of integrity who upheld his end of the deal.

"Yes, I suppose that if Mr. Murphy kept the ranting of a disappointed man within these walls,"—I made a gesture of insignificance—"no harm could be done. The boys hear as bad or worse at home. Although I've always believed we should expect more of a teacher than we do of a parent. We are, or should be, *trained* for our job."

Brother had not asked if I wished to sit down. I had been on my feet for five periods. I rested one hand on the back of the chair and eyed it longingly. When he still did not respond, I asked if I could sit. "As you may have noticed while monitoring the halls, I rarely sit while teaching. A seated droning teacher induces sleep in the most motivated student; a teacher on the move keeps even a dunce awake."

Brother nodded for me to be seated.

"What is it you want me to do?" Brother asked flatly.

"I don't really think we have much choice, Brother. A friend of mine in the theater, a young man who—I've heard Mr. Murphy has allowed his racial animosity to reach far beyond the walls of St. Lucy's. My friend—his name is

Michael Lowenthal; do you know the name?—Mr. Lowenthal is acquainted with Charles, both dabble in the theater, and he was alarmed to discover that in his day job Charles is a teacher. In Mr. Lowenthal's eyes, Mr. Murphy is a terrorist, or rather as Michael put it, 'a trainer of terrorists who may become a direct threat to my survival.' An extreme reading, Brother, knowing Charles as you and I do, but I'm sure you can understand why Jews put a graver interpretation on such matters than do you and I."

"Mr. Murphy is a master of the French language and a good teacher. We should be thankful we have him."

Just as Greek O'Grady was proficient in classical languages, I wanted to add, but his learning did not make him fit to teach the young.

"I'm sure," I replied, "that Lucifer could do quite a respectable job teaching Scripture."

Brother raised tired eyes to mine and for a moment I thought there might be a struggle. But his heart wasn't in it. When he spoke it was to say, "Why not let this be, Virgil? I'll talk to Mr. Murphy, ask him to keep his views to himself."

"I'm afraid it's too late for that, Brother. Charles is pushing forty. In his eyes he's a failed man. He never made it. His hate runs deep. If you effectively muzzle him in the classroom and the faculty lunchroom, his frustration will be only that much the greater. At some point—who knows when? after another disappointing audition?—he may choose to launch a grand if suicidal attack using the only tools he has at hand."

"Tools at hand? Grand Attack? Whatever are you talking about, Virgil."

I paused. I stared deep into the man's tiny black eyes, implying by my delay and searching look that he knew the answer to his question but chose to ignore the fact that

Mother Murphy controlled St. Lucy's two most potentially influential publications.

"Mr. Murphy moderates the newspaper and the literary journal. He controls the press. Try to imagine the damage he could do to St. Lucy's—no, the entire American Church—if one day he should turn out a particularly scurrilous issue attacking the Jews, make a run of thousands of copies and spread them on the streets? This is New York City, Brother, not Omaha, Nebraska."

Brother Principal, for the first time since our conversation began, straightened his back. A bit of the old fire flashed in his eyes, "Mr. Murphy would never do such a thing. He's a devout man, a daily communicant, perhaps the only lay member of our faculty who is." Brother delivered his last line almost as an aside, "He would never bring scandal upon the Church."

"He already has. Mike—Mr. Lowenthal—mentioned to me in a confidence I hesitate to disclose, that he is seriously considering taking up Mr. Murphy's anti-Semitism with B'nai B'rith. You see—I suppose I should have mentioned this earlier—Mr. Lowenthal is the nephew of the current president of the Anti-Defamation League."

David Lowenthal? Morris Greenburg? Michael Lowenthal? So and so's nephew? Did it make any difference who heard what when? Murphy repeatedly indulged in anti-Semitic rants and the goal was to silence him. No one denied his bigotry and that, when all was said and done, was all that mattered. If I was forced to talk to Michael again, and B'nai B'rith actually called on the Cardinal, who said what to whom would be forgotten in the fracas to follow.

"In the past year we have lost two senior teachers. Now another. How... " But Brother did not complete his thought.

I presumed his thoughts had turned to the HVAA's requirements for accreditation, number of faculty, length of service.
"I don't see how…" and again he faltered.

I offered him a supporting arm.

"I don't think it would be necessary to go so far as to ask
for Charles' *resignation,* Brother. If I could take back some
proof to Mr. Lowenthal demonstrating the incident was just
that—an incident—and would never be repeated, I think
I could bring the man around, quiet his justifiable outrage.
Michael is not an unreasonable man."

"What action do you suggest I take?"

"Well, I think a public apology to the assembled faculty
might be in order. Public confession discourages recidivism.
Then, and most important—" Oh, I didn't want to go into
this. My days were already far too long—"Charles must be
stripped of the means of broadcasting his bigotry. I would
suggest you remove him from the school newspaper and the
literary journal."

"And who do I have to replace him, the only teacher here
with courses in journalism?" When I moved to speak, he cut
me off. "No, don't tell me. You, of course, will find the time
and the talent somehow to do the job. And probably do it better than Charles." The yearbook, my first edition, stood on
Brother's desk alongside a dozen or so others from previous
years. Where all the others were done up in green and gold
padded leatherette, the school colors, with each book indis-
tinguishable from its predecessors, mine stood out clean and
sharp, its hard, streamlined covers bound in elegant puce and
gray linen. The book's graphics, like its cover, demonstrated
a boldness of concept and a tasteful rejection of convention.
Brother's more progressive administrative colleagues thought
it most impressive and had told him so.

"I will find the time," I promised. "My lectures on Marriage and the Family are coming to a close. I usually work until six or so. If I extend my day a couple of hours—Besides, Brother, what choice do we have? We can't allow the school publications to fold entirely. When St.Lucy's produces its first great writer, we will want him to say he first broke into print on the pages of *La Luciana,* the name my staff and I have chosen for the literary journal."

I accepted my usual fee, half the stipend of my predecessor. Tainted money? A just end achieved by dubious means blurs the distinctions between good and evil: For the good achieved, I accepted half the usual stipend; for any evil done, I gave up half in reparation. Nevertheless, as whores and gamblers know, the danger of residual guilt is such that earnings from questionable endeavors should not be kept long in hand, and heeding their advice, I hurried down to Orchard Street.

Mrs. Goldberg convinced me it was time to change my fashion silhouette. Wasp-waisted jackets and flared pants would soon become passé, she advised, just as had the tapered leg they had replaced. She wasn't sure just what the Uptown shops might send her way tomorrow, but she was banking on a more conservative line.

"No, Mrs. Goldberg. I simply will not go back to those pajama suits of the Fifties."

"You think I'd do that to you? You don't know Mrs.Goldberg yet? No, Mr. Quinn, what I have in mind is an all-new wardrobe, stuff way ahead of its time, clothes to put you into the twenty-first century."

I spent the entire afternoon with Mrs. Goldberg as she rummaged through her piles of not new but never worn clothes searching for basic resources to create the classic outfits she had in mind—a straighter leg, a longer, fuller sleeve.

I posed before her tri-paneled mirror until I was dizzy from all the turning and giddy from studying the triptych of my reflected figure. She chalked, pinned, tucked and gathered. Before I left, Mrs. Goldberg instructed me to return in one week's time to "pick up the new you" and I arranged to pay a bill that would eat up all of the stipend to be paid for moderating the extracurriculars that would have still been Mother Murphy's if only the daily communicant had learned to rise above prejudice.

THE SUMMER FOLLOWING my year of coups would be the most carefree I had known since my boyhood days in Omaha. Bitter fratricidal struggles were behind me. Thanks to me, Greek O'Grady had gone into work where he could do no harm, and I sincerely hoped he would find himself in Greece and Rome. I had won my rightful place as Chairman of the History Department, and Fagan appeared to be bringing no less imagination to his new duties as teacher of Domestic Arts than he had to his old. Again thanks to me, Bull Belloli was gainfully employed at Rikers Island for a salary well above what he made at St. Lucy's, guaranteeing that his children would be fed without the father having to indulge in dehumanizing sports more fitting to Diocletian Rome than a modern American city. With Bull gone, I had defanged the Law and Order Society by engineering the appointment of Brother Bob as the group's advisor, a move that promised to firm up the anti-fascist front at St. Lucy's. In somewhat the same spirit of obedience as a priest who is forbidden to hear confession but allowed to continue to say Mass, Mother Murphy, once humbled, accepted the muzzle placed upon him. Before resigning as moderator of the newspaper and literary journal, he had

persuaded the entire staff of both publications to quit in protest, a vengeful parting shot that missed its mark because I
had, of course, already recruited my own people.

It seemed to me then, three years after my arrival at St.
Lucy's, that I had completed my mission, and when I returned
in the fall, there would be nothing to do but teach. My lack
of enthusiasm at such a prospect prompted me to extract what
pleasure I could from the summer months.

For vacation ideas I turned to my Black Books, searching
for acquaintances who lived in cool scenic places and could be
encouraged to take me in for the months of July and August.

I selected Rodney from the several possibilities because the
conditions of his inheritance required him to spend much of
the year at his place in Nangaweenuk, a tiny fishing village
on the coast of Maine, a hundred miles east of Portland. As
a rule I've found a guest can expect a more generous recep-
tion from hosts cut off from society than from those in the
city who have grown jaded from too much companionship.
Since it was late June and Rodney would have been alone in
Nangaweenuk since early April, I believed him ready for a
collect call.

"Rodney? Is that you, Rodney? Guess-who-this-is!"

Rodney invited me up for the summer on one condition:
I must agree to spend at least four nights a week at his home.
Rodney complained that on previous visits I used his place
like a motel, a room to return to after days in Portsmouth
and Bangor. I thought his change in arrangements uncalled
for, but agreed to his conditions nonetheless. I so love Maine!

I read a lot that summer, broadening my adequate but not
particularly extensive knowledge of the American labor movement. I completed a book a week, Monday through Thursday.
Weekends I was off to Portland where I hired out as a tour

guide. I thanked Rodney for his offer of an allowance if I would remain the entire weekend at home, but explained that I needed to feel independent. I saw no reason to tell him that my clientele consisted largely of foreign sailors looking for entrée into Portland's flourishing underground which, due to the small size of the city, is by necessity both discreet and difficult to penetrate.

Out of consideration for Rodney's hospitality, I always made it home in time for Sunday dinner. Afterwards we would play a hand or two of rummy, and then to bed, Rodney to his, I to mine. I needed my evenings free for study, a necessity that became more urgent as the summer wore on. For the deeper I read into the history of labor, the closer I came to answering the question that had brought me to Maine in the first place: What will you do with yourself, Virgil, now that your work at St. Lucy's is done?

21

I F MY FATHER WERE to see the list of organizations to which I now belong, he would lump me in with that group of people—nearly everyone he knew—whom he referred to as 'joiners.'

Barney Quinn belonged to nothing and no one. Even his allegiance to the Church was conditional and depended on the degree to which the current pastor resisted convention. He detested the tendency of the Irish race to organize their lives around stodgy institutions. "You will *not*," he warned me, "join the fire or police departments. You will *not* go into the civil service. And you will *not* take out membership in the Order of Ancient Hibernians and spend the rest of your life anticipating next year's St. Patrick's Day Parade." If I were to break any of these commandments, he made it clear, we would no longer be father and son.

Father wanted me to fulfill his own dreams by becoming a lawyer. He used my tenth birthday party and many thereafter to tell me so. "You're a chip off the old block, Son," he told me. "You're going to be in the courts one way or the other, so you might as well be on the right side of the bench."

Father had lived his life beyond the pale and presumed, particularly since he forbade me all conventional pursuits, that I would live mine there as well. I don't know with what blasphemies he would have greeted my decision to answer the call to teach because he didn't live to see the day. Mother and I waked him some years before, not long after I was expelled from my first career. No one, not even the doctors, suggested a causal relationship between my disgrace and father's coronary occlusion.

How could they? It was not as if I had donned the habit of a holy woman surreptitiously or even voluntarily. I had been led to that convent gate by a power stronger than my will to resist. And once inside I did what any talented soul would have done—I aimed for the top.

"Your scrupulous devotion to duty," Mother Superior said to me, "is remarkable. You have been given a great gift, my child, one you must cultivate and we must nurture. For this reason, despite the short time you've been with us, I am creating a new position, Mistress, Inférieur, of Discipline, with you in mind. Mére Angélique, our Director of Novices, is swamped. She is also far too wimpy for the job at hand. We have never had such an undisciplined group of girls as this year's crop. You are the answer to my prayers. God has sent you. You are the lash we will use to whip the girls into line."

Humility, that's what the girls lacked, and scrubbing floors was just the means to teach it. In keeping with my new position, I was no longer required to scrub, but how better to teach the girls the true meaning of humility than for those raised high to stoop low?

One novice gave me particular trouble. This stunningly handsome creature would stand some way down the cloister, leaning against a pillar with a smirk on her face, eyeing me as if she knew what was hidden beneath my habit and would exploit it at a time of her choice. It was while teaching this young thing how to properly scrub a stone stairs that I had my accident that resulted in my sudden dismissal. Did Barney learn of my disgrace before his death? I think not, for in my shame I avoided my family home and fled instead to lose myself among the throngs of New York City.

My father might not have found much to alarm him in the earliest stage of my political development that began shortly after his death and some years before I joined the faculty of St. Lucy's. I don't think he would have been particularly upset over my participation in demonstrations that began with the First March on Washington and climaxed with the infamous Scout Pool Love-in in the fall of '69. Although a chaste man, Barney was not a prude. If he had seen me gamboling about, naked except for the large Stop the War button taped to my pubic hair, he probably would have applauded my audacity in joining those beautiful children, naked as I, splashing their way toward the Lincoln Memorial in the nation's first great celebration of paganism. Barney had, after all, planted the seed that matured into a body so exceptional that the crowd chose me, in spite of my age and over so much competition, to be lifted onto the strong backs of a dozen brothers in protest, carried the length of the pool, and laid in the cool marble lap of the Great Liberator. Father would only have insisted, because he had no experience in guerrilla politics, that if I continued to participate in mass movements, I do so as an individual and remain apart from the herd by refusing formal membership in any group or organization. He would not have understood that when arrested—as indeed I was and was intended to be, the sacrificial lamb of the peace movement—and penned up with common criminals, I would have rotted in jail and suffered God knows what violations if not for my newfound friends. Unlike other young men arrested with me that day, I was not repeatedly raped. I suffered, in fact, nothing more than verbal abuse spit out by cops and inmates ignorant of the battle we were fighting. It was partisans outside the prison wall who organized a campaign to spring me, and I left the nation's capital with my virginity intact, a phenomenon I credit entirely to the band of loyal supporters who surrounded me in jail, protecting me with a cordon of bodies, much as bees do their queen.

By reflecting on the failures of Barney's generation, I learned a lot, not least of all the value of organization. For the first twenty-nine years of my life, I held membership in a single organization, the Church of which I am still a member, albeit in near danger of excommunication. The rules that were part and parcel of my first career forbade me to join any outside group, and my second career, which knew very few rules indeed other than starve yourself, groom yourself, required me to belong to only one, the agency that saw to it that I remained one of the world's most photographed creations.

And so, taking my father as a model, I stood alone—until I was gassed, jailed and saw my chastity threatened.

Barney might have just tolerated my anti-war activities, but he would have taken pride in my work at St. Lucy's. The anti-authoritarian aspects of the Lenten Revolt would have appealed to him, as would the grass roots momentum that carried it through to success. He would have justified my moves against Greek O'Grady and Bull Belloli by ignoring the fratricidal struggle necessary to dislodge them and focused instead on the arbitrary nature of their violence. And certainly he would not have objected to my muzzling Mother Murphy.

As much as he deplored violence, he detested irrational pho-
bias more specific than his own hatred of *they*, a force he never
defined and habitually enjoined. But Father was not a cynic.
He lived his life in lonely opposition—loud, incessant, unre-
mitting, shouting into an impotent void until silenced by an
early death. He spent life's limited energy denouncing everything and anything, unaware that in his awful anger he had
burned hope to a cinder.

In all the instances of my doing battle with the devil, my
father would have been proudest in knowing I had worked
largely alone. Now, I belong to more organizations than I can
easily enumerate. Only yesterday, years after I promised to do
so, I sent off a two-dollar check to the Save the Whales Society, making me a lifetime member—a member, that is, until
my own death or the death of the last whale.

Joining outside groups became, in time, a natural corollary
to my reform work at St. Lucy's. So many of the problems I
encountered in the school were local manifestations of the
national dilemma. Racism, minority oppression, bigotry—
oh yes, St. Lucy's knew them all with the single exception of
the struggle to save the environment from over-consumption.
Catholic schools are so poor that conservation of resources
is absolutely necessary to survival. If a homework assignment filled one side of a sheet of loose-leaf paper, the teachers
returned the corrected page to the student to be utilized in
full. Contrary to popular belief, thrift, not chastity, is the
virtue to which parochial school children are first indoctri-
nated. A church made up of free love advocates is conceivable;
a church with a spendthrift following too poor to fill the collection plate is not.

I pondered St. Lucy's relationship to society at large each
evening when I sat down to work on my afghan of a thousand

squares. As the stacks of tiny motifs filled the cardboard boxes I used for storage, a gradual change took place in my style of living. I went out less. I stopped attending first the theater and then the ballet. Invitations to parties from old Black Book friends went unanswered. I hadn't been to the Metropolitan Museum of Art—once my favorite Saturday afternoon haunt—since I filled the first box of a hundred floral motifs.[1] And the last to go, I no longer made my late night promenades of the Avenue, or at least not so often as I once had.

I now look back upon those weeks between my reform of St. Lucy's and the launching of my next, much grander crusade as one of those periods of reflection activists too rarely find time for. Our dedication drives us on relentlessly. Reformers must see to it that the people get what they neither knew nor cared to know they wanted.

My thoughts turned to the past, to the family life I knew for so brief a time, to my father, gone these many years, to Mother still struggling back in Omaha to develop new recipes from too few ingredients with hands stiffened by arthritis. Mother's disease had continued unabated, and by now had consumed the cushioning cartilage in every joint of her hands. Would Mother's fate be my own? To prevent or at least forestall this eventuality, I continued to crochet my granny squares and soak my feet—the disease had metastasized to the joints of my toes. I would sit for hours on my white brocade loveseat, balls of yarn to my right, tape recorder to the left, putting hook to yarn and listening to tapes unravel the

---

1　Which coincided in an interestingly trivial way with the tenth anniversary of the Cardinal's disingenuous pronouncement, shamelessly plagiarized from a policy speech by Chairman Mao, that the time had come to 'let a Hundred Flowers Bloom.'

hectic days of this century's most tumultuous decade. Milford—or was it Rodney?—had given me the recorder years
before as a parting gift, or perhaps in expectation of favors
sought but not received. I can't recall. I used it though to
tape political speeches for later study. Initially, I meant to use
the tapes to sharpen my own political awareness, and later,
when I heard the call to teach, I saw them as possible classroom aids. I was not the confident public speaker then that I
came to be in later years, and I longed to match the persuasive power of H. Rap Brown and Stokely Carmichael. When
I finally surrendered to the call and joined the faculty of St.
Lucy's, I discovered I had no need for source material other
than myself. Nonetheless, I had kept the tapes in a shoebox
protected from dust and roaches, and took to listening to
them now as I wound my way down memory lane.

I imagined that my purpose in playing the tapes, inasmuch
as this nostalgic pilgrimage to old shrines knew a purpose,
was to discover in the past a direction for my immediate
future. Increasingly I'd heard the bells until there was an
interminable ringing in my ears. Through the infernal static
I identified the voice of St. Lucy on several occasions, but she
was speaking in Sicilian dialect and I couldn't make out what
she was urging me to do. I had carried out the saint's mandate to civilize her school. What did she want of me now?

Ear doctors advise those suffering from ringing in the head
to turn on the radio. Background noise often serves as a less
stressful distraction. I did that now, raising the volume of
my recorder to drown out the ringing of the bells. I listened
again to the fiery sermons of Bobby Seale and Huey New-
ton. They demanded I support the Panthers, and back then I
had. I could not, of course, hawk the *Panther* on the streets.
I wanted to, but Kiril forbid it, and with a patron such as

Kiril, you did as you were told. Kiril was not opposed to my
politics, not on principle; he still retained a vestigial sympathy for the anti-capitalist system under which he had lived
much of his life.

"But your face is far too well known," he told me. "You
can't be hustling outfits to women with more money than
sense one day and be out on the street the next hawking
the journal of anti-capitalist revolutionaries. If Lyle were to
know..."

Lyle was the best known designer of his day and, inciden-
tally, my boss. He had reached the peak of his long career
and no way was he going to jeopardize his position by having his top mannequin snatched from the runway by a covey
of undercover agents sent by the FBI.

Nonetheless, and unbeknownst to Kiril or Lyle, I continued to accept my allotment of the *Panther* each week. Large
handbags were in fashion that season. I stashed the papers in
my Gucci and surreptitiously scattered them about the offices
of the rich and powerful to which I had easy access. I paid for
the papers myself, a donation that made no dent at all in my
extravagant salary. Besides dispensing propaganda, I listened
as Nanette Rainone defined women's oppression in the high
school, but since the only women I associated with were some
of the highest paid people in the world, I could do little to
help Nanette in her struggle and filed her thoughts away for
possible use at a later date. When I couldn't make it to Washington demonstrations in person, which was too often the
case due to my crowded schedule, I marched on radio waves
with Dave Dellinger and Rennie Davis and recorded it all for
posterity. At the bequest of the Christian Leadership Conference, I transferred my savings, $54, 438.53—Yes, I've known
wealth as well as fame—from First National City Bank to

Dime Savings and Loan. Dime Savings played it both ways. While publicly denouncing progressive attacks on the policies of its sister banks, Dime did continue to advertise that it held no investments in South Africa. When I heard of the alleged plot to kidnap Henry Kissinger, I did a quick analysis based on what I knew and taped my commentary: The kidnapping was not a plot hatched by nuns, as Washington sources 'who wish to remain anonymous' claimed, but emanated from the bizarre precincts of the CIA, whose agents concocted the story to embarrass certain Catholic revolutionaries (whose names I could not then and cannot now divulge). Although I never became privy to the inner working of the Black Panther Party, I listened then and listened again now to that once powerful organization crumble and traced its disintegration to unparalleled police pressure and intramural scrabbling.

I had recorded it all.

Crocheting my afghan squares and listening to those voices from the past on my tapes, some shrill, some coarse, others simply exhausted from too many years pleading too many causes, a single theme seemed to dominate all their partisan appeals: Join us in our fight... A powerful union of all the people... Unite to crush... In each instance the speaker's message could be reduced to a single plea: Organize. If you mean to be effective, organize. And the idea dozing in my subconscious awoke with a jolt. Bringing down Greek O'Grady, Bull Belloli and Mother Murphy was like shooting squirrels in a corncrib, as they say back in Omaha. Even if you hit your mark there was always another varmint to take its place.

What the parochial schools needed was a union, radical in concept and bold in its determination to correct abuse. Not just a gathering of those few teachers I knew at scattered schools who cared or could be persuaded to care, but a union of all teachers of integrity in whatever school they taught. Whether Transfiguration for Girls or Christ Crucified for Boys; Mary Magdalen High or Our Lady of the Angels Elementary; from Chinatown to Harlem, from St. Stephen's on the East to St. Lucy's on the West, the movement for reform would spread from Manhattan to the Bronx and Brooklyn, from the Irish ghettos of Queens to the pagan sanctuaries of Westchester County. In all the vast fiefdoms ruled by His Eminence, The Cardinal Archbishop of the Diocese of New York, second in wealth and power only to the pope himself, I would search out every teacher of merit, whether religious or lay, male or female, young or old, and bring them all together in a movement so powerful that our assault on the episcopal mansion on Madison Avenue would go down in the annals of revolution alongside the battle of Bunker Hill. Each school might be small, no larger than St. Lucy's and equally impotent. But together we comprised a force larger than the public school systems of all but a handful of American cities.

Oh, where are you now, Bobby Seale? Did you then, so many years ago, know what tardy forces you might unleash?

I had done all I could acting alone. Somewhere out there in those four hundred parochial schools there must be others who believed as I did, teachers who, while continuing to teach in such a system as the Cardinal's, made us guilty by association. And if they were not aware of the moral implications of collaborating with malfeasance, I would instruct them. They must be brought together, persuaded to Join! Federate! Associate! Unite! Weathermen, Panthers, Birchites, NOW, GLF, VFPF, WLF, SDS. As I listened to the tapes it came to me. Parochial Educators of New York. PEONY! Buttons the size of saucers. A large pink flower on a field of green—in Church rubrics, the symbol of hope—the acronym in black Gothic script.

Four hundred schools, ten or twelve teachers to a school. Five thousand teachers, more than half of them laymen. Thousands of potential union members. Some of these new religious, very radical. The Berrigan brothers, nuns who threw themselves in front of tanks. Many of the religious would go out in sympathy, given a just cause. And who would lead them? Who else? 'Virgil Quinn, now there's a leader I can follow. He's president of PEONY, you know, the lay teachers' union. When that man speaks... Oh!'—and the young woman shudders in anticipation—'I could tear down my school brick by brick!'

I dropped my crochet hook and half-completed motif, dried my feet and moved to my desk, an executive-sized model that served in my studio apartment the additional functions of room divider and kitchen table. With the diocesan directory open before me, I made lists of every school, primary and secondary, where I knew at least one teacher. When I had finished for the evening, I had a list of forty-three schools where I had a contact. Less than one-eighth of the total, but a start.

I felt a tiny prick of fear. What of my past? Was it wise to go beyond the relative anonymity of St. Lucy's and show myself to the larger world? If my past was to become known, what effect might it have on my future? Would I *have* a future?

For advice I sought out Sean, my counselor of many years and the bartender at the County Cork. Sean would understand. His past, while less exotic than my own, had taken a detour or two before he found his calling behind the bar.

Sean began with a parable, as was his custom.

"Yesterday I visited my old pal Lucinda who recently moved to Fort Apache. When I asked her why she chose to live in the roughest neighborhood in the Bronx, she said, 'I didn't choose to live here. I made mistakes in my life that I've now got to pay for, and these were the only rooms I could find that were affordable.' I then asked how she dealt with her neighbors. 'At first I was terrified and rarely left the building. I prayed for a reprieve and it came in the form of an epiphany in which I saw my present neighbors—mostly crooks, dope addicts, pimps and the desperately poor—as no different from the frauds and scoundrels I used to meet daily on East Eighty-first Street. I pretend I still live in my Upper East Side townhouse that I shared with George until he became demented and handed over our money to a broker who invested it in start-up companies of no discernable value. The ability of the human mind to alter reality is an amazing gift, and I've now been accepted by my new neighbors as one of their own, although obviously with a different pedigree.'"

I ordered another drink and asked Sean how his friend's experience was relevant to me.

"Fear," Sean replied. "We can't live with fear. Do what Lucinda did and create a new reality. Forget the past. Become in mind what you are in fact today—a teacher of adolescent boys determined to right the world's wrongs."

Thirsty customers called Sean away, and as I nursed my drink, I thought of the boy who had shaped my purpose and launched me on my quest. Kevin had every reason to be afraid, but he did not live in fear. When his world became untenable, he reached out to shape another. First to me, and when I let him down, to others. In his determination to find a life that fit his needs, Kevin took risks. He failed. Despite his keen intellect, he was not emotionally up to the task. He was not a survivor. I was, and I would use my wits to build a living monument to Kevin that would work to protect all the Kevins to follow—the young, the vulnerable—and I would call it PEONY.

THE ORGANIZATIONAL STRUCTURE of the Church has remained essentially the same for five hundred years. It is highly centralized in doctrinal affairs, largely decentralized in finance and administration. Within a single diocese, schools might be administered and funded in any number of ways— by the diocese, the parish, an order of nuns or monks, or a combination of the three. The need for a single union strategy emerged. If PEONY was to win, it must force the Chancery to capitulate. If the mansion fell, the Cardinal would have to devise some method of bringing all the schools to a single bargaining table.

I leaned back into my wing-backed chair, massaging my arthritic knuckles. I dozed, I dreamed. Great numbers of teachers shouting in righteous anger poured out of the side streets and massed before the high, fenced courtyard and shuttered windows of the Cardinal's mansion. A thousand placards jutted into the air, their irreverent slogans and pleas for reform turned toward the Cardinal's glinty eye focused on the leader of the rebellious flock through a crack in a second-story shutter of his fortress. I would raise the PEONY banner, and with a deafening cry we—

Bells, bells. The sound of bells that I tried unsuccessfully to muffle by covering my ears with my hands.

"Enough! Here you sit with nothing but a paper army of fifty men and women, and you've already stormed the Bastille. Dreamer. No different than the rest of your race."

I snapped awake. Sister Philomena, when she used that
tone of voice, reminded me of my father, Barney Quinn, the
great deflater.

I was not, however, as impetuous as Sister might think. I
had done my homework by rereading von Clausewitz's *On
War*. The brilliant Prussian military theoretician believed victory could be won in three ways—by destroying the enemy's
army, by seizing his capital, or by occupying his territory.
Obviously, the first two were not options open to me. How
could I sweep aside the Cardinal's army of principals and
monsignori? Neither was I prepared to seize the Chancery, at
least not yet. But I could occupy the territory of the Cardinal's
schools by recruiting into PEONY the teachers who manned
the trenches. And that is what I set out to do.

What I needed was an issue. Not some altruistic message like an anti-brutality crusade or a campaign against
Mother Murphy's brand of bigotry. Too many prospective
union members might themselves be compromised by those
transgressions. I recalled what I could of my reading on the
labor movement during my Nangaweenuk summer. The labor
movement in America, as I understood it, began with Samuel Gompers reading from inspiring literary works to his
union brothers and sisters as they rolled cigars, and ended
with John L. Lewis closing the coal mines, for the last time,
until they were made safe to dig in. After that, Lewis and
all subsequent labor leaders made money, a bigger cut of the
pie, the only issue worth their continued attention. The labor
movement came to reflect the narrow materialism of big business, the enemy unions were created to defeat. I would have
no choice, arriving as I did so late on the scene, but to go
for more money if I expected to draw a crowd. The workers
had already been corrupted. Once I had them inside the hall

with doors locked, time then to lecture them on professional-ism, humanism, and the necessity for restructuring the lines of school authority.

With the problem of issues settled, I moved on to organi-zation. Who was qualified to assist me in building a union? I am an idea man myself. I lack both the patience and dogged persistence necessary for building infrastructure. I needed someone bright enough to attend to complex detail, diligent enough to see it through, efficient enough to complete the work with minimum assistance, and finally humble enough to give me her unreserved assistance. I never considered a man for the job. At some point, the most unimaginative man will invariably allow ego to interfere with good sense and insist on sharing the limelight, even to the detriment of the cause.

I had nearly despaired of finding the right assistant and was considering doing the job alone when I struck on the woman I needed, Mary Ellen McKay, the teacher from Trans-figuration for Girls and my old friend from my infant days of educational reform.

22

ADMIRERS OFTEN ASKED ME how I managed to organize a union as large as PEONY in so short a time. My answer has been, "I was born to rule." Although this may well be true, it hardly says it all. I have known since my first sortie in Transfiguration for Girls that Mary Ellen McKay was in large part responsible for PEONY's remarkable success. But it was necessary to hold to the concept of a single leader if I was to put together an organization so powerful that it would force the Cardinal, after a lapse of over a hundred years, not since the bloody Irish Riots of 1863, to again use what the city engineers call the 'Chancery Tunnel' on his comings and goings from St. Patrick's Cathedral to the episcopal mansion.

Keeping Mary Ellen in mind, I targeted Mary Refuge of Sinners, however, not Transfiguration, for my first organizational drive. This was a mistake. I chose the school because of a promising contact I had there. I had met Joe on one of my late night strolls along the seaside Promenade over in Brooklyn Heights. Raised in Omaha, an inland city, I'm

enchanted by fog and the haunting bellow of the horns sailors use to navigate it. On such a night I bumped into a young
man dressed in a polo shirt with broad horizontal stripes and
snug navy bells. Startling! The fog, the melancholy horns, a
young man dressed like a castaway from a vessel sailing out
of the last century. A romantic delusion. Joe was in his last
year at St. John's University, a school that lay some distance
to the east. He had walked so far that foggy night because, he
said, his landlady would no longer accept promises in lieu of
rent for his room with kitchen privileges. Where better for a
young man in search of a place to sleep than the Promenade?
I took Joe in—a homeless man; common charity demanded
as much—until he could make other arrangements.

In exchange for my favor, I would ask one of Joe, his signature on the union sign-up form I had run off on St. Lucy's
mimeograph machine. Joe, during our short acquaintance,
had shown little interest in reform movements of any kind.
Still, I felt confident he would sign. Paranoia, it came with a
territory both of us shared: Though Joe and I might see his
short stay at my apartment as a simple trade-off of shelter
for companionship, as teachers we lived in fear of what ears
cocked for smut might come up with. Fear is as much a bond
between oppressed people as is resentment.

Joe signed, the only member of that all-male faculty to do
so. The rest agreed with an English teacher dressed in rags—
Should I send him over to Mrs. Goldberg?—who spoke in
proverbs. "A bird in the hand is worth two in the bush," he
replied to my impassioned call to solidarity, which, when
translated into Refuge of Sinner terms, meant a decision to
continue working for poverty-scale wages rather than face
the wrath of the pastor by joining a union.

I wore my dove-gray suit the afternoon of my first visit on union business to Transfiguration for Girls. Mrs. Goldberg had persuaded me, when she made up my spring outfits, that we lighten up my wardrobe of basic black. I gave her a tentative yes, and when I looked in the mirror and saw how the soft, lightweight woolen fabric clung to my hips, I agreed with her that it was indeed time for a change.

Arriving at Transfiguration I asked for Mary Ellen McKay. Why Mary Ellen? She was, as far as I knew, no more of an activist than any of the several other women I knew at our sister school, and I made my choice almost at random. Or so I thought then. I know now she was chosen by design, that I was directed by a Hand more powerful than my own.

"Why, Virgil Quinn! What brings you way up here? I haven't seen you for months."

I smiled and let my eyes rest for a moment on Mary Ellen's flat chest concealed beneath a prim white cotton blouse buttoned to the neck. "Is there someplace we could speak, in private?" I asked, allowing my voice to suggest any number of motives.

"There's no private place at Transfiguration. Every room is bugged. But we can go to my homeroom and talk in whispers." Mary Ellen dropped her voice to a whisper and gave me an intriguing smile implying possible adventure. When she smiled like that she didn't appear at all to be the plain thirty-two-year-old spinster I knew her to be.

Mary Ellen took the chair behind her desk. I took up position on the corner of the desk, to her right, unbuttoned my jacket to expose a tightly vested waist, raised one leg and let it rest along the edge of the desk—very businessman like, very male. My left knee reached to within inches of Mary Ellen's small right breast. Each time she lowered her eyes, her gaze fell to thigh or hips bound in soft gray worsted.

"Do you know, Mary Ellen, that the faculty here at Transfiguration earns a thousand less a year than does ours at St. Lucy's?"

"Maybe yours is a richer parish." Mary Ellen was defensive.

"Even if it were, would that justify paying women considerably less for doing the same job as men?"

"What are you getting at, Virgil?"

"That sexual discrimination is common to parochial schools and would shock teachers if they were made aware of it. Oh, there are cases more pathetic than yours, more unjust. Do you know the school in Harlem called Black Catholic? A woman I know there, a Bahamian immigrant with thirty-three years teaching experience, makes just half of what you do here. If the diocese shared the bounty..."

"But I don't understand, Virgil. Why are you telling *me* all this?"

I dropped my hand and let it rest gently where it fell, on my inner thigh. Mary Ellen's eyes followed the falling hand, stopped when it stopped, focusing on it or a point just behind it. I did not disturb her fantasy. A moment passed and, to avoid embarrassment, I murmured, "You are admiring my ring. Fordham, '66."

Mary Ellen jerked up her eyes to meet mine. "You didn't come way up here to tell me about wages in Harlem."

"Well, no. Not entirely. I've meant to visit you for months, but I've been so busy with extracurriculars—"

"I have a phone."

"We should go out to dinner sometime."

"Anytime, Virgil."

"I know a little place."

"I would have to go home and change."

"Where do you live? You've never said."

"Middle Village, Queens."

I tried to imagine what enticement it would take to lure me to distant Queens. None came to mind.

"For the place I have in mind, it's better to dress down."

"My coat's in the faculty room."

The ten or twelve young women gathered in the faculty room fell silent when we entered; seen together in the unflattering setting of the faculty lunchroom, their uniform drabness impressed me anew. Most had Mary Ellen's coloring, hair neither brown nor blond, blue eyes no one would call remarkable, and skin that, if exposed to the cold North Atlantic winds that had whipped the cheeks of their ancestors, might have taken on a blush of pink. All wore the Transfiguration faculty uniform, a modest blue or white blouse tucked into a dark straight skirt. In an age of faith, such women would have taken the veil.

These women had, however, rejected the nunnery. I acknowledged their choice by showering them with a series of looks meant to convince each that she had the sex appeal of Mary Magdalen. In return I was bombarded with attention.

"Virgil! You here?" Mary Katherine asked.

"We thought the subways only ran one way," Mary Martha added, "for all we see of St. Lucy's men."

"We should start the teacher exchange program again, Virgil," Mary Anne suggested, not half in jest. "Mix things up a bit."

"Good to see a man," Mary Clare stated bluntly. "How did you get in?"

Such is the source of revelation. A dozen young women eager for a mate.

And so it was that I came to know how I would succeed in melding the forces of four hundred autonomous schools into the most powerful dissident force ever created within the American Church. Starting from nothing but a short list of contacts in a fraction of the schools, without funds or staff, not even an office, I would erect a school system benign in intent and humanistic in method that would be held up as a model by the civilized world. First New York, then Boston, rippling out from the urban centers of the coast until every town, every village where nuns drilled the catechism into children's heads using whatever methods the times allowed, schools would rise to proclaim the victory of persuasion over violent coercion. I would succeed because I had charisma. No, not charisma. That was for an age of belief. I had more. I had what every great leader in the television-saturated, Post-Hollywoodian Age has possessed to excess. I had sex appeal.

Mary Ellen was a bit surprised when I told her that the place I had in mind for our first dinner date was on the corner of Seventh Street and Avenue A.

"But that's in the East Village."

"You'll love it, Mary Ellen. It's a charming little ethnic restaurant called the Polskyrama. Nothing fancy, just good honest food."

"OK, then. We can catch a cab at the corner."

A cab? All the way to the Lower East Side? Then dinner? Way beyond my budget, and I could hardly ask Mary Ellen to share, not on our first date, without losing stature a union president could not do without. The subway? Too depressing. No way to sign up my first important contact.

"Oh, let's just walk, Mary Ellen. It will do us good."

"But, Virgil, it must be miles."

"It's not so far. We're at Eighty-third and Amsterdam. If we cut across the park—it's such a lovely day—we'll be there in no time."

Better than most men I understand why women persist in shodding themselves in crippling shoes. Mary Ellen propped herself up on three-inch heels to lend artificial line to legs lacking fashionable definition. We had crossed the park and reached Fifth Avenue when Mary Ellen began to complain that she simply could not go on. I gave into her protestations and we hopped a bus for the ride downtown. For the long walk from Fifth over to Avenue A, Mary Ellen dropped all pretension to style, slipped off her shoes, and walked the rest of the way in stocking feet. She felt conspicuous in heels, I suppose, when all around us were working women wearing flats and sandals.

We took a booth near the front with windows facing Seventh Street. A stout woman with ruddy cheeks brought us menus and dropped them without a word onto the bare Formica table.

"You order, Virgil. I can't read Polish."

Neither did I, but I knew from previous visits when the English menu could not be found that the fourth item on the list was meatloaf. I had been struck each time I ordered by the size of the portions and wondered how any restaurant could remain in business that served so much food for so little money.

Although Mary Ellen finished everything on her plate, if she was impressed with the meal she did little enough to show it. I have frequently found this true of women. So often their expectations soar above any reasonable hope of fulfillment. I drew Mary Ellen's attention to the mashed potatoes. "They're real, you know, not boxed. This is one of the few affordable restaurants in town that still prepares potatoes from scratch."

"They are good," she agreed.

We spent the first hour of our first date wrestling over topics of conversation. Mary Ellen talked about her several sisters, all happily married, she said, to policemen, firemen and plumbers. She had no brothers. I smiled at each anecdote of family life she related, waiting for the proper moment to address the subject I had walked miles to broach.

"Mary Beth is moving to the Island next month," Mary Ellen said of a sister. "She and Jack just bought a new house out there. With two kids and one on the way, they thought it was time to spread out."

"Jack must make good money."

"Oh, he does. Very good. He's a welder."

"Union?"

"Of course."

"*Union* welders must make twice what we do."

"I caught that, Virgil. I'm not *against* unions, you know. My whole family is union. I would never cross a picket line."

"And if there was a picket line in front of Transfiguration, would you observe it?"

"Of course I would! My father would turn me out of the house if I didn't."

Mary Ellen McKay was living up to my hopes for her. "Easy to say. But you'll never be tested, not teaching at Transfiguration or any other parochial school." And then to demonstrate how each of us had a personal stake in unionizing, I mentioned the marital statistics of men who taught in parochial schools. "Do you realize that less than five percent of us are married? And why? Even if one of our teachers wished to pop the question, he would hesitate to do so. Who could decently support children on our salary? Which gives the admonition of St. Paul, that it's better to marry than to burn, a special irony when applied to us. If we wish to pursue our vocation to teach the young, then we must remain celibate, and if not celibate, well"—and Mary Ellen blushed—"we burn."

"Oh, I wouldn't want that!" Mary shuddered as she took her first spoonful of vanilla pudding. "There must be a way to prevent that."

"There is, there is." I reached across the table to take Mary Ellen's free hand in mine. When I felt the reassuring pressure I presumed I should be felt under such circumstances from the romantic novels I had read, I made my pitch. "And this is what we must do…"

23

MARY FLAHERTY MCKAY—FOR THAT is how Mary Ellen began signing her name when she became vice-president of PEONY—plunged into union organizing with a zeal equal to my own. Within a week she had signed up every lay teacher on her own faculty and induced three nuns to sign affidavits of support. She beat down the objections of her conservative colleagues with a battery of weapons ranging from accusations of betrayal of their heritage to blandishments of the creature comforts an increase in salary might buy.

"How many outfits do you own other than the one you have on, Mary Theresa? What effect does your showing up in the same old skirt and the same white blouse and the same black shoes have on your students? They have to look at you everyday. Don't you think they deserve a change of outfit?"

"The nuns don't change," Mary Theresa retorted.

"That's just the point, don't you see? You are not a nun, and your students know it. You are—or should be—a role model for all those girls who don't intend to take vows. And you should dress accordingly."

Mary Ellen was not above threats.

"PEONY will prevail, you can be certain of that. My talent for organizing coupled with Virgil's inspired leadership will ensure that it does. Holdouts don't last long in union shops. And why should they? Parasites living off the gains others have fought for?"

Mary Ellen at thirty-two enjoyed a freedom from social distractions that is the reward of celibacy. She lived with her parents in their semi-detached house in Middle Village, Queens. Eager suitors did not plague Mary Ellen with telephone calls. She had a lot of time to spare and had for years, unconsciously I'm sure, been seeking some worthy cause to free her from the burden of weekly novenas, meetings of the Altar and Rosary Society, Friday night bingo with her mother.

No one could, of course, not even a woman with the leisure and new-found energy of Mary Flaherty McKay, organize over four hundred schools scattered over the vast Archdiocese of New York City stretching from Battery Park and Staten Island into the foothills of the Catskill Mountains. At our next strategy meeting I pointed out to Mary Ellen the need to encourage new members of PEONY to join in active recruiting. After an hour's meditation in the lotus position, I had come up with the slogan to make her work all that much easier. "Each one signs one," became the vow made by each new recruit. Mary Ellen harassed those who pledged but did not pay with the persistence of a pack of wolves determined to bring down a kill to feed its young. She directed each of her recruiters to submit weekly lists of backsliding union members. Working from these lists, Mary Ellen telephoned the proscribed teachers at times when she thought them most vulnerable—at seven in the morning or at the end of a long day. If this did not bring them around, she paid them unexpected visits at their schools, timing her appearance to coincide with lunch period, when she could expect to find the apathetic recruit in the company of her colleagues. After a public denunciation, the lazy unionist began to hustle.

As the movement spread and Mary Ellen could no longer keep in direct contact with its burgeoning membership, I delegated to her the power to select business agents from her most trusted sisters.

Mary Ellen chose her sergeants well but they were not Mary Ellen. Mary Ellen had begun by organizing the girls' schools because she wanted to build up union membership, and a union treasury, as quickly as possible. She also had nothing to fear there. No Sister Superior could intimidate Mary Ellen. Not so with her agents who, Mary Ellen said, lacked attitude. The women were too often ignored, sometimes ridiculed, and in some instances, warned off the premises.

"We must give our organizers some protection," Mary Ellen insisted, expecting me to provide it for them.

"What we need is a good labor lawyer," I said and mentally scanned my Black Books for a lawyer familiar with labor law who could be persuaded to advise us pro bono, or failing to get advice without a fee, would accept my escort services as payment in kind for services rendered. No such advocate came to mind.

"We can't afford labor lawyers, Virgil. We can barely afford subway tokens for the organizers. Anyway, I don't see why we need one. If every union had needed a lawyer to get started, the labor movement would never have got off the ground. There must be laws governing what employers can and cannot do, and laws to be just must be promulgated." Mary Ellen's

exaggerated faith in the law surpassed my own. "Which
means we have to do some research."

"Of course. The Fair Labor Standards Act, the—"

"Wagner Act, the—"

"Taft-Hartley Act, the—"

"Landrum-Griffen Act."

Two American History teachers, we knew our acts, but
neither of us had a very clear idea of what they contained.
No matter. Mary Ellen would see to it, and I would continue
without interruption my work of formulating PEONY policy.

Three days later Mary Ellen appeared at St. Lucy's with
an attaché case bulging with pamphlets from the National
Labor Relations Board and a legal pad filled with notes written in her neat, minuscule script. Her notes concluded with
a reduction of pertinent labor law running a scant four pages.

"Admirable, Mary Ellen. Such economy." I thought but
did not say that without scholars like Mary Ellen, capable of
condensing reams of close print into readable digests, my education would not be as complete as it has become.

I scanned the outline of organizational procedure
Mary Ellen had drawn up, noting in particular the rights
of workers to organize 'among the employees of your
employer.' Great. But who *was* our employer, the school in
which we taught or the diocese of which each school was
a part? The answer, I knew, lay at the heart of the struggle. And it was still unclear whether the National Labor
Relations Board even had jurisdiction over parochial school
systems. But at the time Mary Ellen and I were putting
together PEONY, the NLRB *asserted* jurisdiction, and that
was all we needed. It would be years before the courts
handed down their decision, and by then the fate of PEONY
would have been decided, yea or nay.

Mary Ellen took a bundle of pamphlets from her brief-case. "These, Virgil, are duplicates of those." And she pointed to the pamphlets spread out on my desk. "It might be a good idea to send a batch over to the Cardinal. Just in case he's not well informed."

"Smart, Mary Ellen. Even if he doesn't read them, he can't fail to grasp the political implications of our gesture. I don't think I would send over a copy of your synopsis, though. He might just read it and assume it's our plan of procedure. Let's keep him guessing."

"Now," Mary Ellen said, "we must assemble the girls I've chosen as union agents for a little pep talk from their president." I agreed, and the following Saturday we met in the composition rooms the boys and I had renovated in the basement of the Church of St. Lucy, the only school space I had access to that was not bugged.

I began with a simplified version of the rules as laid down by NLRB.

"Consider *all* the schools," I told the women, "even those staffed entirely by men, as fair game. Just march right in and do your job. Don't be afraid. Tell the principal and whomever else you run into that as a union official you have every right to be there. Wave one of these NLRB pamphlets in the face of anyone ill-informed enough to challenge you. We *do* have the right to organize. *Where* we do has yet to be determined because ours is the first attempt to unionize diocesan schools—anywhere in the country.

"We're making history, girls! We're plowing new ground for the labor movement, and we will make the law as we proceed. And never fear that the Cardinal will get a court order to keep us out of the schools. The issue is far too volatile. New York is a union town. The vast majority of the Church's congregation consists of blue-collar workers. To expel union organizers would look bad. It would put the Cardinal on record as a hypocrite, a supporter of labor when it's to his advantage—prosperous workers give more to the Church—and an enemy of unions when they appear in his own house. When the Cardinal chooses to reveal his true anti-union bias, as I believe he will, he will do so in a more equivocal manner.

"But whatever way the Cardinal goes, we stick to our plan. He either deals with us collectively, or we refuse to bargain at all. When PEONY has the backing of the majority of lay teachers, we will have other means of persuasion at our disposal.

"So, girls, think of your opportunities. Remember who you are, the junior execs of a growing corporation. You're headed for the top." And then I advised them to do what I had already seen to personally in Mary Ellen's case. "Go out and buy yourself some decent clothes. Nothing flashy, now," I admonished them, "but nothing dumpy, either. If you don't know the difference between flash and class, walk uptown and stand in front of the Time-Life Building. Observe, select your type, and plan your wardrobe accordingly."

For the occasion of my little talk, Mary Ellen wore her new saffron silk shirtdress belted at the waist. It was I who advised her how to dress to best show off her better features—in the case of the silk dress, her plump derriere—and I wish the critics who now denounce me as having coerced Mary Ellen to play worker bee to my queen would remember that.

"But, Virgil," a fiscally conservative young woman pleaded. "We may have a union, but we haven't got a raise yet. How can we buy new clothes?"

"Spend your savings. Borrow. Forget about those hope chests you've been filling. They hold nothing but the chains of chattel women. A couple of good outfits are a far better investment in your future than bed linen and frilly nightgowns."

Before the beginning of the Christmas break, Mary Ellen's agents had signed up a majority of the faculty of the girls' schools of Manhattan, Bronx and Queens, and she had placed an agent in most of the girls' schools in distant Richmond and further Ulster County. But I was not content. A contented man, I've invariably found, is a man who has abandoned his ambitions—half the schools still remained in enemy hands: St. Peter in Chains, Christ in Thorns, Five Wounds, Sebastian Slain.

The litany of schools yet to be organized filled pages of my grade book. All had one thing in common: All were staffed with all-male faculties. I immersed myself in thought. We did not as yet have payroll check-off, of course, that would come at the bargaining table, but money from hundreds of union members flowed in. PEONY rented its first office, an 8' x 10' space located on the ninth floor of the Roanoke Building and, previous to our tenancy, used for storage of janitorial supplies. I spent my time now over at the Roanoke, a one-man think tank feeding ideas to Mary Ellen's recruiters. The union had reached a point where it either broke the seamless front of the boys' schools or became a rump movement scorned by the misogynists who ruled the Chancery.

Where to turn? Was I making adequate use of my resources? Or was I trying to do too much with too few skilled organizers? Was it time to ask for help from my brothers and sisters in existing unions who had already put their shops in order?

Those raised in sectarian circles hesitate to venture out into the secular world in search of advice or assistance. Always in the past I looked no further than B'nai B'rith and the ASPCA, organizations almost spiritual in nature. Both pursued their goals with a religious fervor that made me feel one with them in purpose and method. Were we not all, each in our own way, working to convert the heathen? This could hardly be said of the unions capable of helping me now.

Seeking the assistance of organizations with goals as narrowly materialistic as the American Federation of Labor, or its affiliate, the American Federation of Teachers, seemed potentially corrupting. Nonetheless, on the afternoon of January 25, the feast of the Conversion of St. Paul, I found myself in the office of Walter Lueken, strategist for the AF of L.

Mr. Lueken rose to greet me as I entered. He was tall and thin and somberly dressed and, as he stood there, marking the page of the book he had been reading with the long forefinger of a gnarled hand, I imagined him a modern day Abraham Lincoln. Curious to know what labor leaders were reading nowadays, I cocked my head to one side, the better to see the book's title. I was expecting a work by one of the apostles of socialism—Louis Blanc, Engels, or even Thorstein Veblen. I was disappointed to discover *Process Flow Analysis in the Corporate Workplace.*

"We are, of course, entirely in sympathy with your cause," Mr. Lueken replied to my request for assistance, "and sensitive to the difficulties you are encountering. But I wonder if our joining your struggle with the Cardinal might not create more problems than it solves—for both of us."

"Oh, I wouldn't want ours to be an *intimate* association, Mr. Lueken," I hastened to add. "Our philosophies of labor are too dissimilar for that. I was thinking more in the line of training for PEONY organizers, use of your office personnel, that sort of thing."

"And what is your philosophy of labor, Mr. Quinn?"

I did not respond immediately. I needed first to ascertain if the sardonic smile I thought I saw lurking behind Mr. Lueken's sad expression was, in fact, a projection of my own distrust of the secular establishment.

"We wish, sir, to ennoble the worker."

"A goal with which I'm in complete agreement," Mr. Lueken added, "and best achieved, I should think, by increasing his pay."

"Higher pay without spiritual guidance leaves the worker prey to the ravages of materialism. Samuel Gompers—"

"An evangelical response to an essentially secular endeavor, Mr. Quinn. The economics of organized labor does not rightfully allow for moral exegesis. The worker has a product to sell—his labor. We ask management to pay whatever we think we can get."

"My ambitions for PEONY are more expansive."

"I am not surprised," Mr. Lueken replied. "If a man of your qualifications *chooses* to work under the conditions you do and for the salary you earn, you must be highly dedicated to your work. You probably insist as well upon introducing moral purpose into everything you do. We in organized labor do not encourage dedication to one's job. Too often dedicated workers end up either collaborating with management or muddling clear-cut bread and butter issues with notions of spiritual reward. Working for payment in the hereafter is only a step away. Organized labor avoids moral issues. If we bring them up at all, it is usually in a patriotic context and meant to rally public support for a difficult struggle of questionable merit. At the bargaining table we limit ourselves to the finite issue—wages and benefits."

"Necessary but insufficient," I interjected.

"We are acquainted with the leadership of movements such as PEONY," Mr. Lueken assured me. "It is because you are rarely content with the traditional objectives of organized labor that we have not offered our assistance in the past and hesitate to do so now."

"We are all workers, Mr. Lueken. We have that much at least in common, and reason enough to pull together."

"But not—and I'm sure you would agree, Mr. Quinn—if to do so put to risk what labor has so far achieved in this city." Mr. Lueken paused, assuming, apparently, that his words needed no further explanation.

"I do not understand," I replied.

"It's a matter of public opinion, Mr. Quinn. Teachers who are actually working in the parochial schools attempting to organize themselves, that the public might accept. But for it to appear that organized labor is laying siege to nonprofit religious schools, that would never do. Freedom of religion, you know. The union movement is only as strong as its public support. I am speaking, of course, of boycotts, the observance of picket lines, stronger protective legislation."

"The workers are not hypocrites, Mr. Lueken. They will not deny us what they took for themselves by means similar to those we expect to employ."

"You may be right. I hope so. But regardless of how the people go, there's still the matter of the Cardinal. You are at war with a powerful opponent, Mr.Quinn, one who wields far more influence than his position entails. Opposed by such a man, you might very well lose."

"I will win, Mr. Lueken. I can assure you of that. And when I do, I'll bring three thousand souls into the union flock."

"Win or lose, if organized labor supports you, we incur the wrath of the Cardinal, a man whose cooperative silence, if not public support, we have enjoyed in the recent past. Your offer of 'three thousand souls' is inadequate compensation for the loss of such an ally."

Mr. Lueken fiddled with the book he was holding, anxious to get on with his reading.

"To ignore political realities, Mr. Quinn, would be for me neither wise nor just. You might, however, pay a visit to Albert Shanker of the AFT. As a fellow professional, he may have experience helpful to you."

Careful to conceal my disappointment behind a parting smile, I turned to leave. I had my hand on the door when Mr. Lueken spoke for the last time.

"You've got spunk and daring, Virgil, traits that may get you into difficulties with the Cardinal. If you should ever need my personal assistance, let me know. I'm a lawyer, and a damned good one."

I took Mr. Lueken's advice, and on the following Wednesday afternoon I called upon the offices of the American Federation of Teachers. Mr. Shanker was out of town attending, I was told, a conference of Third World teachers in Molepolole, Botswana. I was received in his stead by Benny Kaufman, Shanker's second in command. Mr. Kaufman was wearing what I supposed to be the sagging jacket of one suit to top the pants from another—not the best testimonial, I thought, for a union that made teacher affluence its major attraction to new members.

"You're a hot potato, Virgil," Benny told me after I outlined my problems. "Al thinks so, I think so, every labor leader in the city thinks so."

Benny went on to tell me why he thought so, and his reasons closely paralleled those of Walter Lueken in content if not in eloquence of expression.

I reached for my trench coat and umbrella, preparing to leave mainstream labor to union politicians. Benny stopped me with a word of advice.

"Hang in there, Virgil. Bust those boys' schools. To get the men to sign up, though, you've got to offer them something they can't do without. And what's a union got to offer but money?"

Give them what they can't do without.

I can't say that my scheme to win over the male faculties came to me at that very moment, but Benny's words stuck with me, and through careful reflection and calling upon all that I had learned in my two earlier (and more exotic) careers, I turned Benny's advice into a set of tactics that in their novelty stunned the world of organized labor.

24

WHEN I CALLED MARY Ellen to set the date for our next strategy meeting, I decided not to tell her of my meetings with the city's big time labor organizers. The decision to seek their support had been mine alone, and I did not want to make known the high regard in which Lueken and Shanker, men of much experience and wide reputation, held the Cardinal's power. If Mary Ellen and her agents were to learn of my failure to win organized labor's support, it might cause the women to doubt the Cardinal's vulnerability.

We agreed to meet, as we had so often in the past, at the Polskyrama. Mary Ellen and I, although we saw each other several times a week, were nearly always surrounded by union workers. Opportunities for small talk rarely occurred. With my wider social life, I felt no particular need for chitchat, and would have preferred to get right down to business. To assume that Mary Ellen felt the same would have ignored the very different conditions under which we lived.

"And how did you spend your weekend, Mary Ellen? Fully booked, I hope?"

Her laughter carried a bitter note. "My weekends are never 'fully booked' as you put it, at least not in the way you mean. I was busy, though. Mother was ill again."

"Ill? What's wrong?"

"Mother has been ill for a long time and there's little hope for improvement." Mary Ellen went on to explain in a dispassionate tone that Mrs. McKay suffered from a vaguely diagnosed nervous ailment that left her incapacitated more days than not. "So this weekend I did the laundry, prepared my father's meals, did the shopping, cleaned house. On Saturday night friends and I, women I've known since grade school, met at the Shamrock Village for a beer, music, dancing—all the staples of a fun-filled night on the town."

Like the note of bitterness I heard when speaking of her mother, the ironic tone I heard now was not typical of Mary Ellen.

"It's a disco, the Shamrock Village?" I had difficulty picturing Mary Ellen shaking her booty to the rhythm of the new jungle beat that was just beginning to take over the airwaves.

"Hardly a disco, Virgil. The Shamrock's a place for men and women my age who missed the Cultural Revolution. There are a lot of us in Middle Village. So that's how I spent my weekend, Virgil. Now let's get down to work."

This wouldn't do. Successful men and women do not realize their ambitions by harboring sentiments of personal failure. PEONY was very much in need of Mary Ellen, and if she was to do her best work, she must think well of herself. To compensate her for the social backwaters into which she had apparently drifted, I called attention to her unquestionable success as a union organizer.

"You really have done a marvelous job, Mary Ellen. We already have a sound basis of support to build on, and our campaign has hardly begun. Are you sure you haven't had experience in this sort of thing that you're hiding from me? Another life perhaps?"

We both smiled and Mary Ellen shook her head,

"Nope. No secret résumé. Just inspiration that has until now never come my way." Mary Ellen gave me a pointed look, nothing forward, before continuing. "If I'm good at what I do, it's because of dormant talents recently awakened." And then she said quickly, "Of course, a more courageous woman would have sought out situations to test her abilities long before this. But I'm not the adventurous type. If you hadn't persuaded me to try, I'm sure I'd still be doing nothing more exciting than teaching American history to eleventh-year students. That, and going out once a week with the girls."

It is comments such as this, coming from people as admirable as Mary Ellen McKay, that make each of us content to be the person we are.

I wondered how a woman as dependent upon a supportive partner as Mary Ellen had never married. But if you ask a question like that you've got to be prepared for the consequences.

"I was raised without expectations, Virgil, or rather the expectations my father—and yes, even my mother when she could still attend to matters as practical as my well-being—had for me were not those I had for myself. Not that I had defined very clearly what I *did* expect of myself. It is only since—well, since we began building PEONY, that I've come to realize why I don't want the life my sisters are living."

"And what might those reasons be?"

"Scope. Their lives lack it and will never have it and I've decided I want it."

"That doesn't sound like the answer of a timid woman."

Mary Ellen smiled. "I guess I'm the one who likes going along on the hunt but am not resourceful enough to launch the safari. You are."

I turned from Mary Ellen and fixed my eyes on some infinite point. "The expectations under which I labor are, I sometimes think, more than I can bear."

"Family?" Mary Ellen asked sympathetically.

"In a sense," I replied, although Barney's aspirations for me were an easy burden compared to the expectations of the saints who controlled me and who in recent weeks, far more than in the past, kept up their incessant chatter inside my head. Voices, voices, first the bells and then the voices…. It was a burden made heavier knowing I could not tell Mary Ellen of the role the saints played in my life, at least not until I knew the extent of her loyalty to me and the depth of her faith in the agents of God.

Mary Ellen disrupted my thoughts on burden and how to bear up by announcing it was time to discuss the problems at hand.

"The union is in trouble, Virgil, and we've—you—have to get us out of it. We've hit an impasse. We haven't signed up a new member in a month, and I've run out of ideas."

"I've told you before, it's time to move in on the all-male faculties."

"Not good enough, Virgil. My girls are simply terrified of entering their faculty rooms. I've pointed out over and over again that we've accomplished nothing until we sign up a majority of every faculty—male and female—but they just won't budge. Endless excuses for staying home, or making another foray into Mary Help of Christians, ground we've worked to death already. You simply must come up with a *new* idea, Virgil. Something I can use to rekindle their old enthusiasm."

Unfortunately, nothing came immediately to mind, no catchy slogans like 'Each one signs one.' And yet I had to come up with something. We had only three months left in the school year. If we didn't crack the male front soon, summer vacation would be upon us. We would lose a year at best, at worst allow the Chancery to regroup for a fatal assault on the union.

"Mary Ellen, could you leave me alone for a moment?"

"Of course."

Mary Ellen wasn't put out by asking her to leave the table. Her behavior at critical junctures, when she knew I was under pressure, justified my choice of a woman, and Mary Ellen in particular, to assist me. A man would have chosen just this moment to assert himself and destroy the peace of mind I needed to concentrate. Mary Ellen had her own unshakable center. She did not allow obscure requests to diminish her newfound sense of worth, she just took her cup of coffee and moved to a stool at the end of the counter, well out of range of my gaze now fixed upon a fly ascending the white enameled wall in front of me. I watched the fly's slow progress toward the spot on the wall—a splash of gravy?—and I determined that when it was reached, an inspiration would come. Just as the fly reached the spot, I heard the tinkle of the cook's bell calling the waitress to pick up her order.

"Hold up to them the promise at least of what no man can do without."

Sister Philomena, of course, quoting Benny Kaufman and speaking now through the guise of a common housefly.

"Mary Ellen," I called over the hubbub of shouted orders and the clank of heavy china striking Formica counter tops. "You can come back now." Sister Philomena had come through again!

"Can you arrange for your parents to be out of the house this Saturday from one to four?"

"I don't know—well, I suppose so. But why? What should I tell them?"

"Just say you're having some teacher friends over to tea and would like the house to yourself for a few hours, something like that."

"Why my house? Middle Village is an hour's ride for some of the girls. Wouldn't your apartment be more convenient?"

"Much too small. And I'll need an interior staircase."

"Should I prepare anything special?" Mary Ellen asked. "I mean, should I really prepare a tea?"

"No, this will be a work session, not a social gathering. And I want the women to be at their slimmest. In fact, ask them to fast that day. Fasting, I've found, adds an ethereal grace to movement."

"Will you need anything to work with, Virgil? Union records, charts?"

"No, just a hall, a staircase and a room with a door, preferably a large room, one that takes several steps to cross. I know now, Mary, why our girls have hit an impasse. It came to me in a flash. I've neglected an important aspect of their training. The women lack confidence. Men intimidate them. And no wonder. Most of them were raised and educated by women in the company of women. They were discouraged from exploiting the very talents they were born with. I told the girls what to do, but I didn't show them how to do it. I'll correct that oversight this Saturday afternoon. Oh, by the way, Mary, instruct each girl to wear one of her new outfits, something she feels she looks her best in."

"NOW GIRLS, LET's begin with posture. No man is going to pay attention to an organizer who slumps. Mary Martha, throw back those lovely shoulders of yours, raise that bust line. When you face the all-male world you've got to do it with knockers up! Mary Katherine, cinch that delicious jersey knit you're wearing tighter around your waist. A girl with your measurements should show what she's got to best advantage.

"We'll start at the beginning. When you approach a school, your first obstacle to grace and confidence will be a flight of stairs. Look at those stairs as an opportunity, not an awkward invention to get from one level to another while showing your backside to those below. Remember, you never know who might be ascending in your wake. He could be your first male recruit, become your loyal contact in some dreaded Jesuit stronghold of male sovereignty. He could be the man... no, too soon to be thinking of *that*. Remember too, the men you will encounter have had as little intimate exposure to women as you have to men. Like you, they were raised in same-sex environments from the age of puberty. Turn this curious anthropological fact to your advantage. To this male you will be, when I've finished with you today, the nascent Eve entering what has been until your arrival an all-male Garden of Eden. The median age of the male lay teacher in the parochial school system of New York City is twenty-seven—men older than that drift off into jobs that pay a living wage. Mary Fla-herty McKay, who has compiled this and many other statistics you'll find useful in your work, assures me this is true. You can be certain, therefore, that most of the lay males you meet inside the school will be at or near the apex of their virility. Biology will do the rest. A few men will not respond as you hoped they might, perhaps more than a few in some of the more notorious schools. Don't be alarmed, don't be discouraged. Just make note of the names of those men who turn a disinterested eye. I'll contact them personally at a later date.

"So first the stairs. This is the way a man with sex appeal climbs a stairs. Would you take my jacket, Mary Ellen? Thank you." I ascended the stairs, head up, back straight, touching each tread with a sure light step reducing hip sway to a minimum. It was the walk of a confidant man, a man who knows he'll reach the top, and when he does, it will be with the eyes of those below him firmly riveted to the sharp curve of a hard bum.

I reached the second-floor landing leading, I presumed, to the McKay family bedrooms. I paused, one foot on the last tread, one on the landing above it, the seat of my dove-gray trousers stretched taut over a butt that's turned the head of legions. I turned to face the girls.

"That," I announced, "is *not* the way a woman who wishes to be noticed ascends a stairs."

Employing a joyful, all-American-boy gait, I tripped lightly down the stairs to stand before the circle of girls eager to learn the techniques of a master.

"I bring considerable professional expertise to what I am about to show you. I haven't spent all my life teaching boys the truth of their cultural past. In both my first and second careers—teaching was the third, revitalizing the labor movement is my fourth—I associated with many women. During the course of my second career, I knew some very elegant women indeed, women who made as much for a few hours work as you—or I, now—earn in a year." I heard a collective gasp. "I observed these women carefully and memorized every movement they made as if my survival depended on it, as indeed it did. And if I learned anything from these women it was this: Graceful movement, provocative charm, and seductive allure, all those qualities we associate with predatory femininity, depend not on the body God gave us, but on how we choose to use it."

The girls stood spellbound.

"Okay, union maids, enough storytelling. Now let's get back to work. I'll show you once, then I expect every woman here to mimic, as far as her physical attributes allow, the exact technique I employ in ascending these stairs."

It had been so long. Could I do it? I closed my eyes and concentrated on all that I had learned. Again I watched from below as Sister Philomena ascended the stairs of Band of Angels School. I listened to her repeat the instructions she gave me as she prepared me for my first assignment, one that led to so much misunderstanding, so much shame.

"Exhale, Virgil. Let the full weight of your torso settle into your hips. There, that's better. Now, without displacing the center of gravity you've achieved, inflate your chest, Expand those hips, drop those shoulders. With your build, you'll have to exaggerate a bit if you mean to be really convincing. Now do your breathing exercise. In, out, in, out. Relax, Virgil, but hold it all together."

Ascending the stairs, I put it all in motion. *"A figure eight, Virgil,"* Philomena coached me. *"The buttocks roll in a figure eight. First the right bun—feel it roll, up, up over and around. Glide smoothly into the left ascendant. Up, up, over and around, pull in the small of your back, accent the derriere. Marvelous, Virgil, marvelous."*

When I reached the top of the stairs of Mary Ellen's house I turned to the girls to receive their acclamation.

"That's lewd, Virgil." Mary Theresa spoke up from the far end of the semi-circle of novices at the bottom of the stairs.

When I replied to Mary Theresa's accusation, it was in a gentle voice.

"Mary Theresa, when your namesake, Mary the Mother of God, found herself unexpectedly with child, she didn't hang back until it was too late. She picked her man, the carpenter Joseph, a man with a trade highly respected and decently paid even in Biblical times, the best Mary could hope for given her class and condition. Then she pinched her dusky cheeks, slipped into her most seductive shift, picked up her water jar and headed for the well. She hoped to bump into Joseph on the way. She did, and the rest is history. How old are you, Mary Theresa? Go on, you can speak up. Consider me one of the girls. Twenty-eight? Twenty-nine? If I were in your shoes, Mary Theresa, I'd forget about what does or does not constitute a lewd walk and do what Mary did, learn what I have to teach you and then get out there and get your man." Mary Theresa was crestfallen. To lighten the mood I added, "And when you get him, Mary Theresa, be sure to get him into PEONY *before* you take him to the altar."

The girls all laughed at that, lifting the heavy mood that threatened to destroy the carefree ambiance so important to the day's work.

After each young woman had done her best to bring a little play into hips constricted by the disapproving culture in which they had been reared, I suggested we next work on the feminine approach to entering a room. For this exercise we moved across the hall and into the McKay family living room with its contemporary sofa in aqua brocade shot with silver threads and protected from wear by a clear vinyl fitted cover.

"Now, girls, imagine this room filled with twenty horny young male teachers. They are there, seated on either side of the dining room table, reading the Daily News, correcting papers, smoking cigarettes. In fact, the air is blue with smoke. Styrofoam cups of cooling coffee litter the table. Here, some of you girls sit at the table. Good. Now bow your heads, bury them in whatever work or distraction fits a teacher on his lunch hour or free period. You will be out there, girls, in the hall. The task confronting you is how to get through that door with your charm intact, your position of union organizer apparent in every movement of your body, in every word you speak. You have thirty seconds to rivet their attention and strip the men of their defenses. No easy task, I can assure you. It took me years to master the technique, but I can promise you that once learned, you will never again know loneliness."

The lesson that followed was a plagiarized performance. I gleaned it in its entirety while watching reruns of the *Loretta Young Show* with a past client of mine old enough to have delighted in the first-run originals. Norman was a fan of the woman who in the Fifties transformed the simple act of opening a door and entering a room into one of the few flamboyant gestures in an otherwise insipid era. None of my class of girls that Saturday afternoon seemed aware of the derivative nature of my style.

"Mary Anne, give it a try. Imagine yourself dressed in calf-length chiffon rather than the fetching frock you're wearing that clings oh so becomingly to your hips."

Mary Anne made her entrance, marvelous to behold, her right arm outstretched behind her, her hand resting on the door knob, breasts up, head thrown back, her face a smiling, condescending mask.

"Perfect, Mary Anne. Perfect. But *say* something.! Don't just stand there, a frozen smile on your pretty face."

"I don't know what to say," Mary Anne moaned and dropped her head, destroying in an instant the confident image it was my purpose to instill.

"Try, 'So here you all are! I thought I'd find you men off by yourselves, sharing nothing more exciting than the stale smoke of each other's cigarettes.' Something just a little bit demeaning, but holding out the promise of something more. Throw in a phrase that reminds the men you are offering an alternative to the frustration of doing without."

After each woman had practiced her entrance, we broke up into smaller groups to work on entrance remarks appropriate to a variety of situations. For gym scenes, where the men had gathered to play a little ball at the end of a hard day, each girl promised to practice her shot. Bursting in on the men suited up in their satin shorts, she would call out sharply, "Put it here, Butch," catch the ball and drop a clean shot from the centerline.

I spent thirty minutes teaching the girls the only effective method of crossing an empty space to take a standing position at the open end of a table lined with men. For this exercise, I borrowed a Mexican bean pot used by Mrs. McKay to hold an arrangement of plastic pussywillows and daffodils. After dumping the hideous fake flowers on the floor, I lifted the vase to my head and, balancing the pot with one upraised hand, crossed the floor.

"It was carrying an urn such as this and walking in just this manner that Mary Magdalen approached the well and won by her grace and bearing the promise of eternal salvation."

We worked on several smaller points of movement, the well-crossed leg, the use of a free hand to dawdle with a bauble dangling between the breasts—but I was just too exhausted to go on! I took out my handkerchief (mono-grammed, I noticed with a little shudder, with initials not my own), wiped my brow and collapsed onto the vinyl-encased sofa. The girls were solicitous. One prepared tea, another fixed a sandwich.

"There's so much to learn, girls," I whispered, "so much to learn. I simply can't go on. But there will be other days, brushup courses after you've put what you've learned to work in the field. Until then—ah, thank you, Mary Beth. Yes, liverwurst will be fine. I've always been fond of liverwurst. Did you put on lots of mayonnaise? No? I like my liverwurst with a thick spread of mayonnaise, on both sides of the roll, please."

"Sugar in your tea, Virgil? Milk?"

"Both, Mary Margaret. Three spoons of sugar—I know I shouldn't but I need the pick up—and just a drop of milk."

I sipped my tea, nibbled my liverwurst sandwich, then set both on the coffee table before giving my last advice of the day.

"Remember, girls, when you enter those faculty rooms, hit 'em hard, hit 'em where it hurts, and don't let up until you've pinned them with a PEONY."

MARY ELLEN WAS sitting alone in a corner of her mother's living room on a chair that matched the sofa. At some point in our busy afternoon, I had lost her, and what I saw now—a fleeting look of suspicion? Of fear?—caused me a moment's alarm. Had I overplayed the part? Had I disclosed too much of my past? Oh, but the fun of it! I hadn't enjoyed myself so much in years.

"And now, Mary Ellen, if you'd show me to the door?"

Mr. and Mrs. McKay were opening the gate of the chain link fence when Mary Ellen and I stepped onto the stoop covered with grass green carpet. Mary Ellen introduced me to the couple and I mumbled how much I had enjoyed the opportunity of seeing their lovely home "in such a well-kept neighborhood."

"We like it," they replied in unison, from long practice, and added how thankful they were to live "a bus fare beyond the subways."

Again that arcane expression. I had learned its meaning from students who lived in Middle Village. Commuters using public transit to come and go from work had to pay two fares, one on the subway, one for the bus. The added expense discouraged the darker, and poorer, people of the city from moving here and left neighborhoods like the McKay's nearly as white as those they had been born in but then abandoned to the blacks and Puerto Ricans. Another cause, another struggle. Oh, so much to do, so little time! Hurry, Virgil, hurry!

Mrs. McKay, all smiles and showing no signs of the chronic aliments Mary Ellen spoke of, jolted me out of my demographic ruminations.

"Mary Ellen has told us so much about you, Mr. Quinn. I hope you will be back soon for dinner? Mary Ellen is a wonderful cook, you know. I hardly ever prepare a thing. A thrifty shopper, too," the mother added. "She saves us more than her board in bargains."

Mr. McKay moved even faster: "There's a fine house for sale, Mr. Quinn, just three streets over, something you might be interested in, as an investment, of course. When you come out for dinner, we'll drive around and have a look. Hardwood floors, new plumbing and wiring, storm windows all around. One could do worse…" Mr. McKay trailed off as if to suggest such deals in housing were not to be found everyday.

"Certainly, Mr. McKay. I'd love to."

"Sunday then?" Mrs. McKay asked hopefully. "Mary Ellen does a nice roast beef and Yorkshire pudding. You could use a little meat on those ribs, Virgil. Can I call you Virgil?" Mrs. McKay laughed and bent closer to hear my reply.

While Mrs. McKay baited her hook, I glanced to Mary Ellen. She stood well back and to the side with a fixed smile of embarrassment, but she did not come to my support.

"Sunday I'm tied up," I said as I backed down the sidewalk and nearer to the bus stop. "Novena of St. Jude? You're a follower? No? He's the patron saint of impossible cases, a favorite of mine—"

Mrs. McKay persisted. "Easter Sunday then? We'd love to have you."

By then I was out of easy earshot and did not reply. I've always been dismayed by parents who allow desperation to stampede them into matching up their offspring with improbable mates.

As the bus made its way to the subway terminal, I reflected on my day's work. I was sufficiently schooled in sexual politics to take little pride in what I had accomplished. To teach young women how to exploit their gender in ways so heavily abused by the media was not the kind of activity expected of an auxiliary member of the Women's Liberation Front. On the other hand, Mary Ellen's recruiters were women who had lost their instinct to power. Attributes associated with male leadership—knowhow, self-confidence, aggression, the ability to defend one's turf—had in these women atrophied through generations

of disuse. They did not even know how to make use of
the most important weapon remaining to them as a subject people—how to render themselves desirable and make
men, those in power, dependent upon their desirability. Sex
appeal. Was it realistic to expect women to succeed in a
male world without it? I thought not and, putting theo-
retical considerations aside, I concentrated on the struggle.
The boys' schools must be won over, and quickly. Argument, debate, consensus, ennobling as such a political
process might be, would require years to produce a majority. PEONY had less than a year to prove itself. Time enough
when PEONY women were in positions of power to introduce means of control more appropriate to an egalitarian
order.

THE DRINKS WERE cheap at the bar opposite the subway station in Outermost Queens, a quarter cheaper than Midtown
bars, and rather than pass up a bargain, I ordered a double
Irish Mist second time around. I had spent the entire afternoon surrounded by people, Mary Ellen's union agents, yet
I felt a dreadful loneliness descend upon me as I sat sipping
my drink. I was on my third, fourth at most, when a young
man took the empty stool beside me.

"Buy the man a drink," I called to the bartender, "and have
one yourself. I'm celebrating," I said to the man on my left.
"Today's my birthday." Which was not the case, of course, but
one had to have some reason for offering a young man a drink
in a bar like Slugger Joe's.

Fog was rolling in off the East River when I entered
the subway station. I boarded an express, changed at
Grand Central and caught a local. Thirty-third Street,

Twenty-eighth Street, Twenty-third Street, Fourteenth Street, Astor Place. The doors of the empty car in which I rode opened onto the deserted platform of my stop. I rose to go, procrastinated until the doors banged shut, then rode the train to Brooklyn Heights. After a day in Middle Village—and yes, one too many Irish Mists—a walk the length of the Promenade would do me good. I passed an aging man sitting on a bench who looked as lonely as I. I joined him. We did not talk but sat there side by side, our hands joined in a desperate grip. He lifted his arm and dropped it around my shoulders, pulled me to him. Ah, poor man. I rose, thanked him but no, and walked away shrouded in fog and loneliness. A strip of pale light appeared on the far horizon. Exhausted, I found an empty bench, lay full length, pulled my trench coat tight around me, and nodded off to the sound of distant church bells calling the faithful to Sunday morning mass.

Bells, first the bells and then the voices…

"We simply cannot allow this kind of behavior to continue," St. Lucy was insisting. She held a triangle of toast in her right hand and used it now to emphasize her words.

"What's bothering you at this early hour?" Sister Philomena asked. She spoke in a bored tone, not bothering to lift her eyes from the *Omaha World-Herald*, the newspaper she was reading.

The women sat at a small wrought iron table on what appeared to be the balcony of a heavenly mansion. Pink clouds formed a canopy overhead and the rising sun gilded the marble balustrade a rosy gold.

St. Lucy tapped the shell of her boiled egg with a pearl-handled knife and deftly removed the cap.

"Crashing on park benches, dragging home at this hour of the day. Scandalous!"

"*What's so scandalous about a young man keeping late hours?*" Philomena asked.

"*The boy is jeopardizing his eternal salvation. Any catechist worth the name knows that.*"

"*Just one moment, Lucy!*" Philomena slapped her paper on the table, causing her coffee to spill. "*Aren't you forgetting I was Virgil's teacher? By impugning his moral judgment, you censure mine. And even without the eyeglasses you vainly refuse to wear, you can see that I'm sitting here in this heavenly palace just as you are. Apparently, He Who Judges who's to be saved, who to burn, does not agree with your catchall definition of sin. It's comments such as yours that make me think you've gone over to the Mrs. Doran School of Sexual Morality.*"

"*Don't act as if you don't know what's going on, Phil.*"

"*So he let an old man stroke his thigh. A more generous mind than yours might call that an act of charity.*"

"*He collaborates in sin.*"

"*He provides a service, what's called an escort service, I believe. He does no more than he has to do to get by and selects his patrons accordingly.*"

"*Clients, not patrons. Posing naked on a rock—*"

"*He was wearing a loin cloth.*"

"*Near naked, while that horrid Axel did—*" Lucy turned her head aside in a show of modesty.

"*Quid pro quo alters the nature of the act. It's not as if Virgil gives of himself freely.*"

"*His clients are only the half of it. What about those young men he's always bumping into. Like that young Greek who picked him up at the library.*"

"*So they spent the night together. It isn't as if Virgil consented to a consummating act, Lucy.*"

"*You don't believe that!*"

"*Permits. Maybe he permits them to, oh, do a little something. But he does not give full consent, at least not when he's sober.*"

"*He drinks to avoid owning up to it.*"

"*For an act to be a sin it must be willful.*"

"*He's in denial, Phil. He refuses to admit to his behavior.*"

"*But not out of shame. Virgil is not your standard closet case. What are his options? If he admits to his behavior*—"

"*—Comes out.*" Lucy appeared to take smug delight in her misuse of hip idiom.

"*Then he must leave the Church.*"

"*He could just say no.*"

"*Like you did.*"

"*And won this.*" Lucy raised a fine-boned hand to touch the gold tiara worn by all virgin martyrs.

"*And lost your humanity.*"

"*Love the sinner, hate the sin, Phil. That's Church teaching.*"

"*Code for repression. Hasn't the boy had enough of that? We created Virgil, Virgil did not create himself. We've left him no out. Damned if he does, doomed if he doesn't. His Church—one might say all of Christendom—tells him that if he makes love he can't be saved. We've exiled him from the world of respectability. So he's created his own world with rules he can live by, shaped his own path to salvation. He's become a perfectionist whose standard will be forever beyond his reach, a utopian idealist condemned to create heaven on earth—or die trying. He denies the act and compensates by trying to save the world. I shudder to think of Virgil's future...*"

EDEN, APPARENTLY, LIES some distance to the east of New York City, for the rays of the rising sun that had warmed Lucy and Philomena some moments before did not begin to play upon the gothic arches and graceful cables of the Brooklyn Bridge until I had entered the nave of those cathedral spaces. I paused at the crest of the span to marvel at its design, and left Lucy and Philomena to argue my fate before the throne of God while I reflected upon the glories of man.

25

I F IT'S TRUE THAT a man is only as strong as the woman who stands behind him, then imagine if you will the power of a man backed by as many women as I was. I had only to pick up the phone, make a call, and Mary Flaherty McKay would carry the ball from there—"Virgil says it's time"—and two hundred women, Mary Ellen's agents, would hit the streets bent on reducing the Chancery to a pile of rubble.

Once the girls perfected their tactics, the solid fronts of the all-male faculties cracked beneath their collective pressure. With contact made and the sign-up of a teacher or two in each school, we intensified our recruitment. I spent nearly all my time now planning and producing social events. For the first big blowout, I spent the union treasury down to its last dollar. Food, a great deal of wine and beer, and decent rooms centrally located, rented because no union member had an apartment large enough for throwing parties. Arrangements made, Mary sent out the invitations to the fifty-three men who had chosen PEONY as their bargaining agent.

Forty-seven men showed up for our first attempt at adapting corporate business practices to union organizing. Forty-seven men and hundreds of women. It was my responsibility as union president to show the men that when PEONY did anything, even throw a party, we did it right. I assigned four women to every man who entered the door.

"John Reilly. So good of you to come. This is Mary Beth, this is Mary Katherine, this is Mary Anne and this is Mary Margaret, also a Reilly but not related, so have no fear of incest. Now all of you just move right over there to the sofa and make yourselves comfortable. Mary Ellen will be by momentarily with a little something to lower your inhibitions.

"Silvio Santopietro, I believe? From Christ Crucified? I've heard no one brings *Julius Caesar* to life in a classroom of sophomore boys like you do! Do you still teach it in a toga? Tell me your preference—Italian or Irish girls? Something more exotic? We have one Chinese, but I don't know where Velma Lee Ling is at the moment."

There were a few men who politely, but quickly, dropped the women I had assigned to gather by themselves in a corner. I had fitted out the alcove for just such a probability. It's amazing what you can get for a few dollars on Fourteenth Street. I covered the floor of the room with cozy heaps of velveteen pillows and placed a couple of very low tables in convenient places. These were of mock Oriental design like the six-paneled screen I set up to conceal the room from the revelers on the other side, exotic furnishings I thought men with curious tastes might enjoy.

Once everyone had settled in and switched companions to everyone's satisfaction, I, like the good host I was, gathered the men who preferred the companionship of their own kind and led them behind the screen into the 'Gentleman's

Club.' Men are all boys at heart. They never lose their need for a clubhouse, and we spent the rest of the evening as men are prone to do, making man talk.

THE AUTHOR OF a letter recently printed in the *Times* has stated that I used 'frivolous methods of recruitment' during my tenure as president of PEONY. Give such innuendo no more weight than a handful of dust thrown up by some ambitious Chancery cleric ordered by the Cardinal to come up with real dirt. I don't know in what precise manner he used the term frivolous, but if he is suggesting I was anything but serious about means used to show potential members what PEONY had to offer, he's dead wrong. Each event required hours of hard work that paid off in a flurry of sign-up sheets. The members and guests attending our first party returned to their schools with tales rivaling those of the Decameron,[1] and union membership exploded.

All successful movements have one factor in common. They are not, as too many uninformed historians insist, tied to 'an idea whose time has come.' Neither is a movement's success or failure dependent on the soundness of its goals. Few of the zealots who constitute a movement's strength are capable of defining its objectives. In the case of PEONY, only Mary Ellen and I and a handful of true believers knew that PEONY constituted a revolutionary movement with goals that went well beyond the usual demands for higher wages. If they had, they might not have joined. Leaders are important, of

---

1 Teachers at St. Lucy's could make reference to Boccaccio's racy anthology of ancient tales but were forbidden to teach the classic in their literature and history classrooms.

course—PEONY would not have got off the ground without
me—but that is putting the cart before the horse. I became
the first man in the world to successfully organize parochial
school teachers because I knew what they wanted, correctly
ranked the priorities of their needs, and knew how to orches-
trate those priorities into a deafening crescendo of revolt.

Right now the teachers wanted parties. So I gave them
parties, week after week after week until the social lives of
three-fourths of the lay teachers of the diocese were as dependent on PEONY parties as addicts are upon their drug. Guest
lists grew to the point that I had to rent the entire third floor
of the Dolly Madison Hotel (which one reporter has been
so callous as to label 'a flophouse for the homeless') to enter-
tain them all.

PEONY's parties were not the result of random scheduling.
We had long since signed up the thirty percent of the lay faculty required by the NLRB and could now legally petition the
Board for elections. But I did not want to hold an election.
Preparing for elections is a lengthy process and would set back
my timetable for winning a contract. Before the semester drew
to a close, I intended to sign up such a large number of the
teachers that the results of an election would be predictable
and therefore irrelevant. Anxious as I was to reach my goal,
I suspended all partying for the duration of Lent, then held
blowouts on the two following weekends and wound up the
season with a smashing eighty-three percent of the faculty of
all schools (diocesan, parish and those run by religious orders)
committed to the union.

In a letter dated May 1, the feast of St. Joseph the Worker, I
informed the Cardinal of what we had accomplished. According to Mary Ellen's digest of labor law, the Cardinal could
choose one of three responses: Voluntarily admit to the

obvious, that PEONY represented the vast majority of the lay teachers and was henceforth their 'exclusive bargaining representative'; insist upon a neutral 'third party check,' probably by someone from the NLRB, and then agree that our sign-up cards were indeed legitimate; or question the validity of PEONY's roster of members and demand a certification election held under the auspices of NLRB.

What course would the Cardinal take? The politics involved in unionizing Church schools are not the same as those in the industrial world. Unless he intended to use the intervening months to go into the schools and proselytize against the union—a futile endeavor considering our eighty-three percent sign-up—the Cardinal had nothing to gain by demanding elections. He had much to lose. By questioning faculty signatures, he would heighten the level of confrontation. The Cardinal also knew that union elections held in the schools would raise student awareness. If he had to recognize a union, any union within his organization, the Cardinal would want to keep its formation as quiet, and ineffective, as possible.

In a gracious letter to the State Mediation Board (and a copy to PEONY), the Cardinal 'voluntarily recognized PEONY as the chosen representative of the lay faculty of the diocese' and went on to say that 'each and every school administrator looks forward to a long and fruitful association with the union.'

Each and every. A slippery man and well advised. The Cardinal had relinquished his rights to call for elections because he knew he would lose. Now, if I read him right, he meant to compel PEONY to bargain with each school separately. If he succeeded, the peculiar organization of his schools, a system without districts or boards and therefore unique to labor law, meant that he could delay meaningful negotiations indefinitely, long enough, at least, until union membership drained away.

The school year was drawing to a close, however, and little more could be done at the time. Summer vacation was a month away. Every teacher in the system was busy in the mimeograph rooms running off page after page of multiple choice questions gleaned from commercial tests. There was no time for parties. Just as well. The summer lull would give the teachers time to return to their old lives and learn again the loneliness of the corner bar. Come fall and the beginning of the school year, they would be ready for whatever I had planned, and I had plenty.

Just one more little task to see to then, before putting aside union organizing for a month of coaching students on how to pass a history exam. In my last piece of union business for the year, I sent a letter to His Eminence informing him that I had seen through his scheme and that I expected him to whip his four hundred schools into a single bargaining unit before school resumed in the fall. I suggested that he direct the schools in the diocese to elect a board empowered to negotiate with PEONY. I informed him as well of the consequences if he failed to heed my advice: on All Soul's Day every school would be closed; none would reopen until all agreed to join the bargaining unit. If he wished to take PEONY to court for violation of fair labor practices, he would do so at the expense of empty classrooms. Then I retired from politics and got down to the less exhilarating task of preparing boys for final exams.

Certain I had assigned the Cardinal enough work to keep him in the city through the hottest months, I arranged to spend a quiet summer on Fire Island, cooled by sea breezes and gin and tonics. A friend of mine—the older gentleman I met on the Promenade the night I returned from Middle Village had unbeknownst to me slipped his card into my trench coat pocket—had taken a house on Fire Island for the season. Harry owned a chain of laundromats stretching from Far Rockaway to Pelham Bay. His Georgian townhouse overlooked the Brooklyn docks and commanded a spectacular view of the Lower Manhattan skyline. When Henry pulled open the drapes to show me the twinkling lights of the massive city across the bay, I told him that, despite my youth, I was the president of one of the city's most powerful unions. Harry took immediate interest in my work.

"What you need," Harry said, after I reviewed my work of the past year and gave him a précis of what was to come, "is time to recuperate, time to plan your fall campaign. And I have just the place."

I outlined my needs—a room with a door that locked; a charge account at the nearest good bookstore; a diet of fresh fruits and vegetables and nuts in the shell; a wardrobe—nothing lavish—suitable for a Fire Island summer; and a large beach umbrella to shade me from the sun.

"I'll fly in papayas from Guatemala and books from the Vatican Library, if that's what you want," Harry promised.

My Fire Island summer burned to a close watching Harry's extravagant promises turn to thin-skinned oranges and salted peanuts in a can when he asked for but did not get what—heaven forbid—I could not give him.

26

I RETURNED TO THE CITY alone. As the train pulled out of the station, I looked back to see Harry standing on the platform waving a last goodbye. I waved in return and gave him my warmest smile. I thought of Harry until the train reached the next town. Then matters bearing more directly upon my future drove Harry from my mind. What was the Cardinal up to? Throughout the summer Mary Ellen continued to forward to me weekly packets of PEONY mail. They contained not a word from the Cardinal concerning my ultimatum. Had he brought his schools together? Worked out a method of financing the salary demands he knew would be forthcoming? Mary Ellen thought he had, but confessed she had nothing to go on other than union rumors.

Mary Ellen and I met at the Polskyrama for our first working dinner since the previous spring. Mary wore an organdy frock a shade of violet blue to match her eyes, which she had accented with a delicate eye shadow and just the quickest brush of mascara. Was I correct in thinking she had done a little something to elevate her bust line? Mary Ellen might never be a ravishing woman, but she looked better that night than I had ever seen her.

For a starter I ordered a plate of piroshki, expecting to share them with Mary Ellen, but she refused.

"I've put on weight, Virgil. You must have noticed."

Which I hadn't, other than her rather appealing increase in breast size, and wondered if Mary Ellen was becoming overly aware of her less attractive features. She might be disappointed with her somewhat heavy thighs, but I wasn't. I grew up surrounded by large-thighed women. Mother had large thighs. She said they ran in her family, that 'all the Brady women have the legs of an Irish bog trotter.' Even Sister Philomena, judging from the outline of her legs pressing against the heavy black wool of her habit, had substantial thighs.

Mary Ellen confessed she had been coming to the Polskyrama frequently throughout the summer, unable after our weekly dinners of the year before to stay away for long. She gave me a sentimental smile and I knew what she meant.

I finished the plate of piroshki and ordered dinner. Mary Ellen ordered a small glass of tomato juice and an egg salad on rye. She refused to join me for pudding. I finished one plate of beef and cabbage and ordered another. All summer I had kept to my diet of fruits, nuts and vegetables. I was as lean as a whippet. On my evening walks along the beach, suited up in one the new leisure outfits, all in shades of blue, that Harry had bought for me in town, I got many an admiring glance. No mean feat in the highly competitive crush of Fire Island.

"And how was your summer, Mary Ellen? Oh, I forgot. *You* went to school. Were your courses stimulating?"

"Yes and no. The one on sensitivity development was, well, disturbing. Dr. Snyder used the confrontation method. Each day he would ask one of us to stand in front of the class, introduce ourselves, and describe our cultural background. Then he would ridicule our ethnic and religious attitudes for the remainder of the period."

I thought of my tolerant if somewhat exotic neighbors on Fire Island. Had Dr. Snyder spent a summer there himself, been impressed by his broad-minded fellow islanders, and believed he could introduce the social process that had nurtured tolerance in those men, subjected as they had been to a lifetime of abuse, into his classroom?

"Infuriating, isn't it?" I said to Mary Ellen. "The facile educator's knack for coming up with teaching methods that require no particular preparation other than a close reading of bathroom walls."

"I've missed you, Virgil," Mary Ellen told me matter of factly. "The city is dull with you gone."

"You should have got out of the city yourself," I admonished her. "Teachers of the young can't afford to begin the new school year exhausted from the old."

"But where would I go? I couldn't just pick up and go to Fire Island or some other vacation spot like you do. I don't know anyone who goes to such places and they are too expensive to go to alone. You have to share a house, things like that."

"Yes," I replied, "you do have to share. There's no way for people of our class to enjoy the better things of life without sharing." I wanted to add 'ourselves,' but such practical advice would have presumed a degree of compromise for which Mary Ellen's secure and sheltered life had not prepared her. How would she react, I wondered, if she learned of the compromises fate had demanded of me? Of the lives I had lived, the careers I had pursued, and the scandalous interpretations to which they could be put by enemies?

"But I can see," I added quickly, "that for a woman like yourself, sharing can be a good deal more problematic. And how is your mother?" I asked, to change the subject. "She seemed well the day we used the house for our lesson in deportment."

"The more I'm home, the more frequently Mother is ill," Mary Ellen replied. "A state of affairs I've been aware of for some time now and am as much to blame for as she is. If I had left home years ago, after college... But I didn't."

"Your family is fortunate having you there to look after things."

"That may be true, but it's not for them I stay. Each time I think about getting an apartment of my own, I tell myself that as long as I'm single, I've no justifiable reason for leaving."

Single? Leaving home? Again the conversation had taken an unexpected turn that I was not prepared to pursue. Didn't Mary Ellen have a confidante with whom she could go into these matters more fully? A sister perhaps? I was of a mind to assume that role for myself, then rejected it as impolitic (a public perception of sexual tension between the president and vice president of PEONY by both the supporters and detractors of the union lent interest to our profile), and I redirected the conversation to the business at hand.

"No word yet from the Cardinal? Anything on the bargaining issue?"

Mary Ellen reached into her bag, a practical canvas tote, and handed me a packet of mail bound with a thick rubber band. I thumbed through the stack. Mostly unpaid bills from last year's union parties.

"We must raise dues this year, Virgil. What we have in the bank won't even cover what we owe the Dolly Madison."

"Then borrow. I'm sure you'll have no trouble finding a bank to mortgage the dues of a union the size of ours. It would be bad politics to raise dues before winning a contract.

"But back to the Cardinal. He's dilly-dallying, Mary, hoping that if he can only hold off doing anything long enough, our support will trickle away. And he's right. We've got to show the union that we can get things done. Our membership is at its peak and it will never again be so enthusiastic. We've got to make the big push this fall. But how?"

Mary Ellen picked a crumb from the table and dropped it into one of the dishes that she had stacked neatly to the side for easy retrieval. I closed my eyes and propped my furrowed brow on my hand, slipping naturally into the pose universally assumed by men immersed in thought.

"A demonstration," Mary Ellen said with conviction. "Everybody demonstrates nowadays."

IF THE CARDINAL had taken PEONY seriously, the spectacle to follow might never have occurred, and he would have avoided the embarrassment of seeing his teachers romp before the city's millions in a barbaric display of justified pique. I had outlined my demands and sent them to the Cardinal in May. We were a month into the new school year and still no word from the Chancery. The Cardinal's silence angered and confused me. Was there no limit to his arrogance?

For much of the following weekend, the time I was not on my knees praying for guidance, I was deep in meditation. I did not read my mail. I unplugged the phone. By Monday I was ready and I called Mary Ellen.

"It's time to step up the pressure."

"I'm ready, Virgil. I've been expecting your call."

I felt a rush of tenderness. "Without your support, Mary Ellen, I could not go on."

"Without your inspiration, Virgil, I'd still be the clone from Middle Village."

"Ours *has* been a fruitful partnership, hasn't it?"

"The best, Virgil. Just set the date."

"Friday the twelfth," I replied in a more business-like tone. "That's Columbus Day and a school holiday. Perfect for what we have in mind. Can you meet me later at the Polsky? We'll work out the details there."

"Certainly. I always think we do our best work when we're alone, don't you?"

"Five then?"

"I'll be there."

WHEN MARY ELLEN and I arrived at the Polskyrama, the dinner rush had already begun. The babble of Eastern European voices and the clatter of china made conversation difficult. I spooned up the last of my noodles and gravy and suggested to Mary Ellen that we try to find someplace quieter where we could talk.

In those days, because the Polish and Ukrainian inhabitants of my neighborhood preferred to socialize in their churches and private clubs, the Polskyrama neighborhood, which was my neighborhood as well, offered few amusements to the public. I did recall a little basement bar on Sixth Street where I sometimes stopped in for a shot or two of iced vodka. Not recently though. My arthritis was acting up and I was avoiding hard liquor, but I saw no particular hazard in entering a bar tonight, not with Mary Ellen along as chaperon, so we walked the two blocks to the Cellars of Kiev and took a quiet table at the front.

By the time Mary Ellen and I got around to working out the details of the upcoming demonstration, we were both on our fourth or fifth beer. I was perfectly lucid. Mary Ellen, on the other hand, had begun to giggle. When she ordered a pitcher for the next round, I raised an eyebrow in concern. She scoffed at my caution.

"Relax, Virgil. Nothing like a beer or two to get the creative juices flowing. Now let's get down to work. What do you have in mind for the Cardinal this time?"

"The demonstration you spoke of."

"Just what I've been waiting for," Mary Ellen shouted jubilantly. "A chance to shed a few more inhibitions."

I was not sure of the wisdom of using political action as a vehicle for personal therapy, but I did not say so. I did, however, adopt a serious tone to dampen Mary Ellen's levity. "Since Friday is a school holiday, we'll call the meeting for two in the afternoon. That will give me an hour to work them up for the demonstration to follow."

"Not a meeting, Virgil. We need a good turnout. Schedule a party, but only for those who've picked up their admission ticket at the union hall. After the demo, we'll move down as a group to the Dolly Madison."

"Perfect, Mary Ellen. Not a word then in your announcement about a demonstration. Wait until we have them inside and revved up, then we'll tell them. And no permit. We'll have to risk it. The Cardinal's spies are everywhere. If he hears what we have in mind, he'll make a point to be out of town and we don't want to play to an empty house.

"We'll leave Gomper's Hall at three, quietly, in small groups, and be in front of the Cardinal's mansion by four, just in time to catch the after-work crowd. We've got to reach the people, Mary Ellen, steal the Cardinal's constituency. And

of course, a good audience never does a demonstration any
harm. Everyone dreams of running off to join the circus.

"Now for the party. We need a new theme."

"October. Halloween," Mary Ellen mused. "How about
a costume party? We haven't used that yet."

"No ghosts or goblins. Something appropriate to teachers."

"A Thousand and One Nights?"

"They've already done that number, spontaneously. Recall
Mary Katherine at last year's 'Labor of Love.' The creative use
to which she put the hotel drapes was shocking."

"The Greeks. Let's do ancient Greeks, Virgil. I'll come as
a slave—to my passions." Mary Ellen jumped up, hiked her
skirt up between her legs, balanced the pitcher of beer on her
head and began to sashay around the room.

"Sit *down*, Mary Ellen. People are staring. All right, but
not the gods or they'll all come in robes and chitons. Myth-
ological flora and fauna, Greek or Roman. We'll call it the
Autumn Bacchanal. We can bring our costumes to the hall
and leave them in the vestibule. Later…"

But Mary Ellen wasn't listening. She was thinking out
loud. "Animals. Plants. Now whatever shall I be? Leda, Virgil? To your swan? Leda and the Swan…" Mary Ellen gave
me a suggestive look, the first of our relationship. It marked,
I suppose, the end of innocence. "If I can't come as Leda, I'll
come as the swan. And why not? We live in an age of gender reversals." She flung her arms into the wings of a swan,
spilling her beer.

"I think it's time we go now, Mary Ellen. Lots of work to
do tomorrow." I gave her my arm for support and we stumbled to the door of the tavern.

Mary Ellen was in no condition to travel the subways alone
and I considered putting her up at my place for the night. I

decided against it, however. If it became known that the president and the vice-president of PEONY had shared a room on Avenue B, it would cause scandal in some quarters. And so I had to deliver her safely to her parents' house in Middle Village, a round-trip that took me well over two hours and which I hope never to repeat. On the long ride home I promised to keep a closer eye on Mary Ellen's drinking before it became a problem, as it does with too many women caught up in high-powered jobs.

THE AFTERNOON OF the big union meeting at Gomper's Hall, I decided not to make my usual entrance down the aisle, but to spring upon the seated membership directly from the stage. I entered through the stage door, made my way past unused dressing rooms—Gomper's Hall had been built for vaudeville—to the dusty velvet curtains that concealed the wings from the stage. I paused for a moment to reflect, mumbled an ejaculation to St. Lucy, parted the curtains and burst on stage, arms thrown up in the universal gesture of triumph. I—

I closed my eyes so as not to see what I had seen. Oh, the horror of it! How could she have? How could Mary Ellen have been so negligent? All those pitchers of beer. Whatever had she said in her notice to the members? The hall was packed, row upon row, until the exotic shapes, nearly all animals, disappeared into the shadows at the rear of the hall, back where the light bulbs were never replaced. I looked for Mary Ellen among the menagerie of union officers on stage. Was she the unicorn? The many-headed hydra? I had no way of knowing. The herd began to chant, grotesque heads bobbing and swaying. "Vir-gil, Vir-gil, Vir-gil…"

Well, a crowd's a crowd, and I took my cue from the ghosts of the gutsy hoofers who must have played to some tough houses when Gomper's Hall served as one of the city's major houses and the most important venue on Fourteenth Street. And so I began.

During my opening lines, in which I outlined PEONY's attempts to work out a negotiating arrangement with the Cardinal, I kept my eyes on a sacrificial lamb seated in the front section of the auditorium. As I hammered home the Cardinal's refusal to respond to union demands, I shifted my gaze to a cluster of satyrs seated in the left mid-section. I spoke at length on the tortuous summer I had spent on Fire Island, waiting for word from the Cardinal, and focused as I did on a huge eagle sitting next to Prometheus in Chains. My eyes roamed the vast collection of dragons, scapegoats, sacred cows and Minotaurs. I began to shout a series of rhetorical questions:

"How long are we to wait for the Cardinal's answer?"

"How long are we to wait while the Cardinal dines in luxury?"

"How long are we to wait while our bills pile up?"

"We've waited. We've waited patiently. We've waited, oh, brothers and sisters of PEONY, for... far... too... long. We've been waiting for nearly six months now, and the Cardinal chooses not to answer. It is time, therefore"—and my eyes focused on the head of a fierce gorgon crouched in the shadows of the back rows—"to tell the Cardinal we are tired of waiting, that we have used every civilized method at our disposal to get him to act and he has not done so.

"It is time now to bring an end to his procrastination, to do what no parochial school teacher has dared to do in the past. It is time to act! We must act and we must do it now.

We must take to the streets and wrest from the Cardinal, by force of public opinion, that which he should have granted graciously."

I paused. By arrangement, Mary Ellen had scattered trusted workers throughout the hall. Right on cue, each began to chant, "To the streets! To the streets!" until the call was taken up by the packed hall, becoming a unanimous chant rolling through the membership. "To the streets! To the street! To the streets!"

Mary Ellen, dressed as she said she would be as Leda's seductive Swan, stood in the vestibule surrounded by stacks of posters on sticks. With a feathered hand she took a placard from the top of the pile. It pictured a vicious caricature of the Cardinal fastening a lock to a huge peony in chains.

"Nice, Mary Ellen. Who made it?"

"Mary Margaret. She's so good at—"

"Did they even bring along street clothes?"

"Oh, Virgil, I'm so sorry. All those beers at the Polsky. I forgot what you said about not getting costumed up until after the demo. I didn't think of it until the members arrived at the hall. Now what can we do? It's too late to change into street clothes." Mary Ellen was close to tears.

"No matter, Mary Ellen. I should have thought of this myself. Get someone else to hand out these signs. You get to a phone. Call every TV station in the city. Tell them you just saw a thousand mythical animals marching up Madison Avenue. We're going to get more coverage out of this than the St. Patrick's Day Parade. Even the *Times* won't be able to back-page us this time."

The cameras caught up with us at Fifty-first Street. Someone from one of the TV crews asked if I would detour the march of beasts around St. Patrick's Cathedral. He wanted the church in the background as a symbol of the Cardinal's power.

Great crowds of pedestrians accompanied us as we made the loop around the cathedral and came to a halt below the Cardinal's windows. They applauded as we shouted for His Eminence to come down from his rooms to hear our demands. They applauded again as the satyrs, may of whom I believed to be members of the Club House group from our party days, lined up below the Cardinal's windows and began a ribald little chant scored to the kick of a cloven hoof and the bump of an equine hip. Recognizing the opportunity we had to reach people as yet ignorant of the PEONY cause, I instructed Mary Ellen to round up her feathery flock of girls and begin to work the crowd.

The police arrived, responding, I supposed, to a call from the Cardinal. His alarm was understandable; a mob such as ours had never before besieged the mansion, at least not since the Irish Riots a century before. I was approached by the officer in charge.

"Mr. Quinn?"

I nodded. "And your name, Officer?"

"Sergeant O'Neill. I've got orders to disperse your group."

"You'll do no such thing, Sergeant O'Neill. We have a permit." I waved a spurious piece of paper.

"Nonetheless," O'Neill replied, "orders are orders. Mind you, this isn't my idea. I'm a union man myself. But, if you leave quietly, I'll see to it that there are no arrests."

Before bringing the demonstration to a close, and in a show of contempt for the Cardinal's agents who had infiltrated the crowd, I ordered all demonstrators to remove their masks and painted heads. Mary Ellen had remembered to bring my party costume from Gomper's Hall and I donned it now, a gorgeous narcissus in blossom, artfully created by Mrs. Goldberg out of bolts of genuine flawed silk she had picked up cheap from a merchant in Chinatown. Yellow petals arched from a shoulder ruffle of spring green. From the center of the petals, my head protruded to complete the flower. For twenty-one blocks I smiled, my arms raised in the V of victory, the membership chanting my name in a frenzy of allegiance: Virgil! Virgil! Virgil! Crowds of spectators cheered my passing. Through it all, behind the heroic façade I presented to the masses, I remained unmoved. The flowering of a hero, Sister Philomena used to say, is as fleeting as a daffodil in springtime.

The Cardinal did not respond.

27

I was lecturing my senior boys on the South's refusal to bow to Northern corporate greed when I received Brother Principal's summons. The note was brief and uncommonly dictatorial.

"You'll report to my office at the beginning of Sixth Period, no later than 1:15 P.M."

Sixth period was my free period. Brother Principal practiced economy in all things.

I was further alarmed when I entered the outer office and found Mrs. Mulcaney absent from her desk. I waited, unsure what to do. Should I knock on Brother's closed door? Or wait it out, make him come to me. I was still undecided when the door opened and he asked me—ordered me—to step inside.

A strange cleric sat in Brother Principal's chair behind the Great Desk. I ignored the man and turned to Brother with a questioning look.

"This is His Excellency, Bishop James F.X. McGee, Auxiliary Bishop of the Diocese of New York and chief assistant to His Eminence, the Cardinal."

The Bishop, dressed in undercover black devoid of the purple piping symbolic of his rank, leaned well back in Brother Principal's chair. He held a burning cigarette uplifted in his right hand.

His Excellency heaved himself to his feet and extended his hand across the desk to be kissed. I took the hand, bowed to kiss the ring, and marveled as the huge gem in its antique setting came into focus. My bowed head halted ten inches from the Bishop's hand. I gasped in astonishment. Could it be? Could this blood red stone the shape of a chicken's heart and equally large be what it appeared to be? From a distance, and given the gem's size, I had passed it off as a common spinel. I was wrong. The huge thing was a genuine cabochon ruby. Even without my loupe I could see directly into the ruby's fiery heart.

"Only rarely, Your Excellency, have I seen such a superb stone." My voice was hushed, reverent. "And the setting! Seventeenth-century Dutch, surely. Only the goldsmiths of Antwerp could have wrought gold filigree to such perfection."

The Bishop responded by snatching his hand from mine, then used the hand that had revealed his pique to reach for another cigarette. After a puff or two, he regained his composure and began on an amiable note.

"I was once a classroom teacher," the Bishop told me, "but not in a high school. I taught first year seminarians to look at their vow of obedience not as an obstacle to personal expression, as adolescents do, but rather as a guide to spiritual fulfillment, as do the saints."

I looked over my shoulder for Brother Principal, but Brother was not there. How quickly rats desert a sinking ship! Three years of loyal service, he might at least have stood by and lent me moral support.

Mrs. Mulcaney absent from her post; Brother Principal sent somewhere out of earshot. Obviously the Bishop wanted no witnesses. I was alone with the Cardinal's emissary, and he gave me no time to muster my courage.

"Obedience, Virgil. The humble acceptance of authority ordained by God and sanctified by tradition. From obedience, order; from order, a harmonious Church triumphant in a chaotic world. Maintaining order requires constant vigilance. Throughout its long history, disenchanted men have tried to sway the Church from her divinely assigned mission. They choose to forget that Christ founded his church not as a vehicle for social and economic reform, but as the receptacle of truth and the instrument of personal redemption. These impetuous men have even turned at times to the secular world in search of redress from real or imagined wrongs. I think of Voltaire, of Joyce, without suggesting for a moment that those who led that rebellious mob up Madison Avenue belong to the distinguished company of the two mentioned reprobates. We sincerely hope that the misguided souls who took pleasure in abusing the Cardinal have not cast a blind and arrogant eye upon the consequence of giving scandal to Holy Mother Church. We pray, too, that they have not construed our silence as unwillingness to act."

The Bishop raised his hand to forestall a rebuttal that I did not in any case intend to make.

"Although the Church's ultimate justification for demanding obedience is transcendental," the Bishop continued, "we do not deny the obedient earthly rewards. In choosing her leaders, the Church considers for advancement only those who have first demonstrated their willingness to serve. In this

she is no different than any other institution, secular or religious. Talent alone is not sufficient qualification for positions
of power. Unless power is accountable, it is nature run amok."

I waited for His Excellency to come to the point. Deliver-
ing homilies on obedience to recalcitrant schoolteachers is a
task typically assigned to monsignors, not to bishops. That he
had come at all, and that he ran on at such length, suggested
that the Cardinal saw me as a force to be reckoned with.

"You must be aware, Virgil, that the proportion of lay
teachers in the schools of the diocese is constantly on the
increase. As the number of teaching religious declines—a
temporary setback, but one that will continue until new social
upheavals throw more desperate souls into the arms of the
Church—we will be required to replace them with dedicated
laymen. The Cardinal does not wish for a condition to arise
where the schools are lay taught and exclusively administered by religious. This could lead to accusations of elitism,
charges that we have denied in the past and wish to avoid in
the future. For this reason, His Eminence has been on the
lookout for laymen of sound religious and philosophical disposition willing to share the burden of running our schools.
Which brings me, Virgil, to the purpose of today's visit."

My small sigh of relief did not go unnoticed by the Bishop.

"The Cardinal has been observing you for some time. He
is aware, for example, of your zealous commitment to your
vocation. You appear to be willing, judging from your years
here at St. Lucy's, to go to any means to achieve the goals
you set for yourself. You give generously of your time and
expect modest financial compensation. And perhaps most
important, you have a knack for management, demonstrated
by your organization of PEONY in less than one year's time."
Here the Bishop paused to give weight to what followed. "It

is for all these reasons then that I, as the representative of the Cardinal, am prepared to offer you the position of vice-principal—in a school of *our* choice, of course, and not here at St. Lucy's. We would start you out smaller than that."

The Bishop paused to receive a word of gratitude, which I denied him.

"I do not think it far-fetched, Virgil, not if we consider what I had to say about the unfortunate drop in religious vocations, to see you someday soon in charge of your own school. His Eminence has long been toying with the idea of opening what we've chosen to call an 'alternative school,' something less structured than our traditional schools and designed to appeal to parents of boys we've expelled but whom we would like to keep in the Church. Again, considering your performance here at St. Lucy's, you would seem particularly well suited for such a post."

The Bishop lit another cigarette, his third since the interview began. After several draws in rapid succession, a drooping column of ash formed at its tip, fluttering during my silence onto the black dickey strapped over the Bishop's protruding stomach. He did not bother to brush away the ash, but left it there to be smudged into cloth dappled from previous negligence. When I did not reply, the Bishop continued, and his words took on a familiar, almost wheedling tone.

"Think of it, Virgil. A vice-principalship today, and tomorrow? A school of your own! The power, perhaps, to influence the direction of parochial education. We are not reactionaries, Virgil. The Church is not opposed to innovations, not if properly thought through and carried out under the guidance of older and wiser churchmen. Yours would be a unique and enviable position and more desirable, I should think, than inciting union rabble to shut down our schools."

The Bishop paused, attempting to gauge, apparently, the extent of my greed and ambition. He had offered me power; he would tempt me with more.

"As a further inducement to become one of us, Virgil, we are prepared to create a post tailored particularly to your political aspirations. Large urban school systems such as ours can benefit from the services of a skilled coordinator. As Coordinator of Diocesan Lay Faculty, you could continue your close association with the teachers of all our schools. You would hold this post in conjunction with your principalship, and the position would carry with it a generous stipend."

The Bishop had offered me wealth and power. I did not respond. To gain time, I prayed to St. Lucy. When I got no response, I prayed to Sister Philomena as well, confident that it was no longer blasphemous to do so. Had I not seen her, embraced her even, the woman risen body and soul and clothed in the shining garments of the Elect? I heard the bell ring to announce the end of the school day. The signal. Philomena was on her way. When she spoke, it was from a tiny hole in the plaster wall just to the left of the Bishop's ear.

"Remember what I taught you. Always hold out for a better deal. Think of your comrades. Think of your girls. What would they say to such a cheap sellout?"

His Excellency took my silence for vacillation and made his third and final offer. "Of course, Virgil, you have a following whose financial needs must be considered. We have not overlooked their just demands, or your responsibility to bring home the bacon. Beginning with the next school year we will be offering all the teachers throughout the system a substantial raise in pay. Something, we thought, in the neighborhood of six hundred dollars a year, although the sum is negotiable, fifty dollars either way. We would indicate as well, in ways and words yet to be devised, that this substantial increase in salary was due in large part to the continuing efforts of Mr. Virgil Quinn. We would *imply*, at least, that it was you who sensitized the Chancery to the needs of its teachers. A man as clever as you can see the political importance of such an admission."

Since I remained silent, the Bishop continued. "So much is offered, so little expected in return. We would not, for example, even demand that you dissolve your union. The Church no longer requires the public humiliation of princes as a condition for readmittance to the Kingdom of God.[1] We ask no more of you than your resignation as President of PEONY. The rank and file, it can be presumed, will follow your return to the fold. With the goals of PEONY attained without time-consuming negotiations and the financial hardships following a possible work stoppage, you could accompany the news of your resignation with an announcement that Holy Mother Church in her compassionate wisdom has seen to the needs of her children. It all makes such good sense, Virgil. That is, if you are what they say you are, a God-fearing man."

Principal of my own school. Coordinator of Lay Faculty with a sizable stipend. A raise for the rank and file. Three substantial offers.

As much as I subscribe to any school of thought concerned with immortality, I feel closest to those who believe in reincarnation. The Bishop was offering me power, wealth, glory. All he asked was that I bend my knee. Hadn't I—or Someone like me—been tempted like this before? Who was I this

---

1 This was not true as we shall see. The Cardinal's notions of atonement were medieval.

time? Lifted to the pinnacle by the Bishop's persuasive terms, I looked down on all that could be mine and I was tempted.

I stared at the hole in the wall, hoping to see it transformed into the pink petal lips of Sister Philomena. I saw nothing. I heard nothing. The saint was silent. I didn't despair. Knowing she had got me through two temptations, she perhaps saw no compelling reason to dilute her powers by seeing me through my third. I wish she had held off on her advice until now, not left me twisting in the winds of indecision. It was very clever of the Bishop to couple my advancement to that of the rank and file and make this last temptation the most difficult of all.

Through clouds of rising smoke the Bishop searched for some sign of assent; I hid my thoughts behind a Buddhist mask.

Silence. The Bishop lit up again, forgetting the cigarette still burning in the ashtray. A cockroach emerged from the hole in the wall made holy by the words of Sister Philomena. It waved its antenna about, took a reading of the smoke-polluted air, and returned from whence it came. I wanted to speak, to say, "Yea, Your Excellency," and stoop to kiss the Bishop's ring. But I could not enunciate the words; my back would not bend. And so it is with man. We cannot expect, after a lifetime of saying "No!" to suddenly reverse ourselves the first moment it would be to our advantage to do so. We can only go on doing as we've done in the past, and instead of acquiescing to the Bishop's command to obey, I fell victim to what Sister calls my 'habit of overbearance.' I said nothing at all.

As the Bishop puffed, an ugly purple began to stain the unhealthy pallor of his cheeks. He butted his cigarette, noticed the one still burning and butted it, too. He placed his hands flat on the desk and stared with eyes enflamed by smoke and anger. He rose to his feet. When he spoke, his words were tightly spaced, an angry man but still in control.

"Come down from the cross, my son. If you know what's good for you, come down from the cross."

28

P RIMO WAS SITTING ON the stoop when I returned to my
   apartment. He was wearing the magenta silk shirt I had
given him some weeks before when we celebrated his eighteenth birthday with a quiet dinner at my place.

"You're not looking so good, Mr.Quinn. To tell you the
truth, I've never seen you look worse, not even back when
you used to hit the bottle."

Primo had never looked better. It was the third week in
October, but still too warm for a jacket, and he wore his shirt
tucked into white duck trousers. The cobra link gold chain
around his neck was a gift from me as well. I had selected the
trinket from several I owned. This particular one came from
some old admirer whose name I no longer recalled, I supposed, because the chain's weight and karat were surpassed
by those received in successive years.

"It is better, Primo, not to comment on a friend's misfor-
tunes, real or imagined. But if you must, then avoid allusions
that suggest he brought it upon himself. You would not say to

a friend dying of cancer, 'If only you hadn't smoked so many cigarettes.' Have you been waiting long?"

"Not so long. Hey, Mr. Quinn, I'm sorry about saying you don't look so good. It's just that you always—here, let me carry your briefcase and that bag of groceries."

I unlocked the street door, stepped back, and let Primo precede me up the five flights of stairs to my apartment. I followed at a slower pace.

"These are difficult times for me, Primo," I said when we were seated. "Heavy burdens, heavier than I've ever been asked to bear."

"Do you want to talk about it, Mr. Quinn?"

I took note of his solicitude. Three years before, when he first entered my classroom, he would not have been capable of expressing such sentiment. "You can tell me if you want," he concluded. "Sometimes it's better to talk these things through."

I felt a rush of tenderness. "After all these years, Primo, perhaps you could call me Virgil now." With Primo in his senior year, little harm could come from lowering my standards forbidding intimacy with students. We were partners in reform. We were friends. And he would make sure he passed my course in American History II even if he had to sacrifice all his others to do it.

I told Primo of the Bishop's visit. Not all of it, of course. Primo was not a Kevin O'Connor. For the boy to have understood the implications of the Bishop's satanic summons and the direction it took, it would have been necessary to start at least as far back as the gospel story of the temptation of Christ and then proceed through the pageant of history, noting episodes that bore witness to my mission. In conjunction with my classes in yoga, I had tried to instill in select pupils the more accessible principles of reincarnation, intending to give the boys an alternative to the salvation theory. Alas, I was not particularly successful here. Primo and the others clung to concepts of life, death and the hereafter, in as much as they gave thought to any of these, typical of the Christian culture they were born to. Trying now to explain how I had watched the purpose of my mission change in recent months from finite to eternal (and my person from human to perhaps divine), I was taxed to find terms he would understand.

"It's as if I've been through all this before, Primo, perhaps more than once and at critical times in history. It's as if I've been born again—and again and again, each new manifestation more ambivalent than the last until I am awash in ambiguity.

"But whoever I was in the past, it's certain I'm now Virgil Quinn, and the Cardinal has given me an ultimatum. Either I join his administration and turn PEONY into a company union or—" But I could not spell out my fears to this boy who knew nothing of my past.

"Are you clean, Mr. Quinn?" Primo asked. One would assume from the manner in which he asked the question, most men are not. "Does the Cardinal have anything on you?"

"If you mean, have I committed some crime, no, I have not. Necessity has required me, however, to live at times beyond the pale of respectability. What prophet has not? I think of John the Baptist…"

Primo appeared no more interested in the Baptist's fate than he was in the particular pattern of my checkered past. He did not ask for details. No doubt his family had taught him not to inquire too closely into the lives of those close to him, and he approached my life with the same discretion as he did his father's.

"I have to decide, Primo, and very soon."

"So what's the problem? Take the new job. You deserve it."

"To accept the Cardinal's bribe, Primo, would be a betrayal of my principles, to say nothing of the teachers who support me. My professionalism and high ideals persuaded them to create PEONY. How can I desert the teachers now, so close to victory?"

"I don't know these teachers," Primo replied, "but if they're anything like the ones we got at St. Lucy's, you're not deserting much. I didn't see anyone help you out when you busted the Greek or the Brooklyn Hitter."

"But things have changed, Primo. I've taught them the power of numbers. When I give the word, every teacher in PEONY will walk out of the classroom. Knowing we can now achieve our professional goals, I can't—"

"Professional goals?" Primo gave me a dubious look. "Do you mean money?"

I turned to Primo with a tired smile, all I could muster at the time. "You must understand that good teachers expect more from their careers than increasingly higher salaries. They want the right to choose their textbooks, to make school policy, the power, in short, to control their work lives."

Primo was not convinced and I did not have the energy to further argue the point. I slipped lower into the loveseat and propped my feet on the hassock.

"Oh, Primo, I wish this trying time were behind me."

Primo got up from the desk on which he had been sitting and walked over to where I slumped. He had continued to grow into his eighteenth year and now towered over me. If not for my coaching in dance and yoga, he would have grown into an awkward man.

"Don't worry, Mr. Quinn. You'll find a way out. You always have in the past." And then he stooped, I closed my eyes, and—Oh, Christ be praised!—I felt the brush of Primo's cheek as he kissed me first on one cheek, then the other, in the Sicilian fashion.

For a moment the Cardinal's threats seemed distant thunder. The moment passed.

"Now I got to go," Primo said without embarrassment. "I got a date with this girl. She's the jealous type. If I don't pick her up on time, she'll be calling my mother."

And so it would always be with Primo, torn as are so many men of his race between the demands of wife and mother.

"Go, Primo. Go and enjoy yourself." My words were brave and dripped with a mother's love. I didn't tell the boy what joy he had given me. It was enough to know that he sufficiently understood the intent of my years of instruction to give his teacher support during a critical episode.

Primo paused at the door. "If nothing else works, Mr. Quinn, let me know. Me and my friends will think up something to bring the Cardinal around."

"Thank you, Primo. I'm sure you would try. But in dealing with this particular cardinal, you might find yourself at war with your own."

Primo gave me a quizzical look. I did not explain. Some things cannot be taught. From now on Primo had to go it alone.

THE THREAT IMPLICIT in the Bishop's parting words disturbed me, but I did not lay around the house paralyzed by fear and foreboding. Not at all. I had denied the Bishop satisfaction. The Cardinal would have no choice now but to see me

himself—hadn't he granted audiences to men far less powerful than I?

I prepared for the long-awaited summons. After an hour
of prayer and recollection, I looked over my wardrobe. Finding nothing appropriate for an audience with a cardinal, I
placed an order with Mrs. Goldberg.

"Affluent clerics," I advised my tailor, "shop in Rome. They
buy their clothes from the House of Gamarelli."

Mrs. Goldberg was not impressed.

"They never did in Rome what can't be done for half the
price on Orchard Street," she said, and cut me a suit so austere in line, so somber in hue, yet so rich in detail, it might
have been worn first time around by a rich and fearful peni-
tent summoned to confess his sins to the pope.

A week passed, and still no word from the Cardinal. It
was time to act.

SEAN, THE BARTENDER at the County Cork, warned me. Mary
Ellen gave me less than total support. Sister Philomena refused
to answer my prayers. But what was I to do? The Cardinal
was intransigent. He simply *must* be forced to recognize my
position and power with a summons to his mansion where we
would sit down as equals and hammer out a contract.

I had, I believed at the time, only one card left to play
before calling a strike. If the Cardinal, arrogant man, feared
anything, it was publicity that he was anti-union. When the
diocesan gravediggers, all of whom were members of the flock,
pulled a work stoppage in their demand for a living wage and
the Cardinal drafted his seminarians to dig the holes, the city
was up in arms. Certainly the man would not be so foolish
as to repeat his error now.

I made my decision the day word reached me through unofficial channels that the Cardinal had no intention of backing down on the autonomy issue.

"Let Quinn negotiate," the Cardinal's cook overheard him say, "with every school in the diocese. That should keep him busy for the next decade."

Mrs. Coogan, the Cardinal's cook and the mother of Andrew, that most difficult boy whom I had put up with when the rest of the faculty wanted him expelled, passed this information on to me in gratitude for pleading the boy's case with Brother Principal. Mrs. Coogan went on to add that the Cardinal meant to use his negotiate-with-them-all ploy to avoid accusations of union busting.

All the major dailies sent minor reporters to the press conference I called to expose the Cardinal's stonewalling tactics. The reporters returned to their papers to write brief 'stalled negotiation' articles and hid them on back pages dominated by ads. No mention was made of my charges against the Cardinal. Apparently the city's editors were unwilling to enter the fracas until public events compelled them to do so. There was nothing else to do. If I expected to be heard, I would have to buy space I had hoped to get free.

ADVERTISING SPACE IS major metropolitan dailies does not come cheap. To pay for the full-page ad I ran in the *News* informing the Cardinal's blue-collar flock of the cynicism behind his no-negotiation policy, I had to levy a propaganda fee on every member of the union.

AUTONOMY IS AUTOCRACY my statement began in the largest print that would fit on the page, and then went on to define these terms for the union audience I hoped to reach.

EVERY WORKER DESERVES A BOSS, I pleaded, ONE
BOSS, NOT 400. In a few crisp sentences set in oversized
type, I pointed out the hypocrisy of a church hierarchy willing
to wax fat off the donations of its highly paid union member flock while refusing to negotiate with its own employees.

Leon, my restless friend and one-time consultant on
urban affairs for the left-wing journal, *East-West Review,*
had recently moved over to the *News.* Leon told me that
letters to the editor were running eight to one in support of
my allegations.

I waited a week, and when I did not hear from the Cardinal, I called Mary Ellen.

"D-Day, Mary Ellen. Time to call a strike."

We scheduled it for Monday, November 2, the feast of All
Souls. On Friday afternoon I returned from school and did
what I have always done to prepare for events that require
great spiritual energy. I went into seclusion for the weekend.
I did not pick up my mail. I unplugged the phone, knowing Mary Ellen would be calling for last-minute instructions
on matters she was perfectly able to decide herself. I tore up
Saturday's shopping list; I would fast for the weekend motivated by the conviction that the spirit flourishes when the
flesh is weak.

Perhaps fasting had left me dizzy, but the whispering of the
saints that filled my head in recent weeks grew in pace and
volume as my struggle with the Cardinal escalated. Chatter,
chatter, advice on any number of subjects from how to act to
how to dress. The afternoon of the strike vote I chose to wear
the austere outfit created by Mrs. Goldberg for the audience
the Cardinal refused to grant me. Lucy thought that after
seventy-two hours of fasting, the outfit made me look too
emaciated for a successful union boss. The Sicilian thought

I would look my best in white linen and a Panama. Can you believe it? This in New York City, where no one wears white after Labor Day?

I walked the five blocks to Gomper's Hall, timing my entrance ten minutes late. I would enter through the street doors and make my customary entrance. I would stand for a moment at the back to the hall until heads began to turn, then descend the long aisle to the stage. The applause would begin in the back rows and roll forward as each successive row of devoted followers recognized their leader. When I reached the pit, I would climb to the podium to a deafening crescendo of support.

I paused in the vestibule to straighten my tie, brush back a wisp of hair. I listened. The hall was silent, waiting. I took two steps, pushed open the doors and—The whole of life does not flash before the eyes of a drowning man, only the evil he has done. I heard again the cruel words spoken to Brother Bob at the height of the struggle, my words to Harry when he demanded what I could not give. I saw the frightened face of Orfeo Animan and recalled the means I had used to gain his support. Followed by the recollection blotting out all the others: Kevin in the late night coffee shop begging me for help, the echo of his hollow laugh, his sudden shift from fearful child to cynical adult when he learned that I, too, had shut him out.

A small cluster of men and women filled the seats immediately below the podium. The semi-circle of folding chairs on the stage reserved for union officers were mostly empty. Mary Ellen sat in the first seat of the row, the one to my right when I faced the audience. The empty aisle beckoned. As I descended to the podium, my footsteps echoed through the cavernous hall.

I climbed the steps to the stage and gestured to Mary Ellen to follow me into the wings.

"The Cardinal?" I asked when we were out of earshot.

"Who else? I've been trying to reach you all weekend. We got the news in Friday's mail, special delivery. Have you been out of town?"

"I was fasting, Mary Ellen. I never take calls when I'm preparing myself, I don't read my mail. Depth of meditation is proportional to lack of distractions. Money?"

"What else?" and she handed me a single sheet of the Cardinal's heavy linen bond containing a few lines of typed copy. I scanned the note looking for dollar signs.

"Nine hundred a year and a retirement plan worth peanuts! They sold out for this?" I continued to read and discovered 'how much the Church values your sacrifice for all these years, and how happy we are that the diocese is now in a position to properly compensate you for your years of privation.'

"Such a pittance! And for this they surrendered the right to control their classrooms?"

"Maybe it isn't power they want, Virgil."

"So the Cardinal says, between the lines."

"If you would rather I spoke to the members, told them that in light of the Cardinal's offer and such a small turnout, we've decided to cancel—"

"Cancel, Mary Ellen? Cancel? The people are waiting, the only people who count." I took Mary Ellen by the arm and led her on stage.

When it was over, those present cheered, but not for long and not with much conviction. A nun, one of those who had signed an affidavit promising to support PEONY, shouted from the floor. "I'm with you, Virgil! Say but the word and my feet shall be yours."

"Thank you, Sister Fulgensia. Thank you for your support. God will reward you."

Others rose, one by one, to swear their loyalty.

"Thank you. Thank each of you. But without the membership behind us—"

I could not go on. For the first time in my public career my voice broke and I could not go on.

My followers bowed their heads to leave me alone with my shame.

"Come, Virgil." Mary Ellen tugged at my arm. "Come. You've done all you could. Now let's go over to the Polsky for a plate of piroshki."

29

L IFE AS I HAVE lived it has left little time for moping and none for regret. My more charitable critics say that if the first ad in the *News* was justified, my decision to run the second revealed a regrettable lack of common sense. I must remind these well-intentioned people that if John the Baptist had possessed the good sense to gratify the lust of Salome, he would not have lost his head. What would they have me do? Conceal the truth? For men in power, sins of omission equal those of act.

I did not tell anyone, not even Mary Ellen, where I raised the cash to expose the Cardinal. Did I, when I decided to make my move, know myself? The Cardinal had destroyed my union. That he must not go unanswered, I knew very well. The money would come from somewhere.

I WAS BY now in constant communication with the saints. Bells, bells, shouts and hisses, always voices whispering in my ear, a blizzard of voices over which I had no control.

St. Lucy suggested where to get the money for my next assault on the Cardinal. While walking home from the subway stop where I dropped off Mary Ellen, a delivery boy on a bike came careening toward me. He rang his bell, I leaped to the side, tripped on the curb and fell, hitting my head on the sidewalk. How long did I lie there, stunned? I can't be sure, but the next thing I knew I was in conversation with Lucy. I was reminding the saint that if the Cardinal's power remained unchecked, within a year the teachers in her school would be back to their old tricks. Lucy mentioned several sources of funds—the Ford Foundation, a pyramid scheme—all hopelessly impractical. And then, in passing, she suggested my *'ill-gotten gains.'*

"Ill-gotten, Lucy?" Sister Philomena caught her up. *"Hardly. I would say hard-earned."*

Hard-earned or ill-gotten, both women were referring not to my one-time account at Dime Savings and Loan that I had run through during the profligate years of my second career, but to my considerable collection of expensive baubles given me over the years by patrons with more money than emotional control, the same collection I had pawned to get Channing off the hook and which he in time redeemed. Besides Axel's lavish gifts, I had been given quite a few other trinkets wrought from gold, silver and precious stones. There was the jewel-encrusted, fourteen-karat pillbox meant to hold mood-altering pharmaceuticals, a sybaritic practice popular with George and his group. The always unimaginative Gerhard gave me a two-ounce bar of pure gold hanging from an eighteen-karat cable-link chain, blind to the fact that not only did I possess several chains already (and wear but one, a simple sterling chain from which hangs an image of St. Philomena with a reliquary on the reverse side holding a genuine lock of the virgin's hair), but that I would as soon hang such a symbol of conspicuous consumption as Gerhard's gold ingot around my neck as wear gaudy polyester shirts unbuttoned to the navel, as Gerhard did. The chain, however, would equal half the weight of the pendant. And with the price of gold rising...

When I rented the deposit box to store this expensive junk, I hardly saw it as a war chest. I regarded my hoard more as a supplement to Social Security, much as courtesans in past centuries hung on to their jewels as a cushion against the deprivations of time. But such are the vagaries of life that I now found myself thumbing through Black Books I and II looking for the number of the Columbian, Pepé Gracus-Almundo, my jeweler friend and a man whom I could trust to give me the best price.

CONTRARY TO WHAT my pressroom critics have said, there was nothing reckless about my second ad, no defamation of character, no innuendo lurking between the lines. The ad, filling only half a page and all I could afford, began with an inch-high headline: CARD PLUCKS PEONY IN THE BUD, and descended to a thrifty but still easy-to-read twelve-point type detailing the Cardinal's offer to buy me off with sine-cures backed by dire threats of reprisal if I did not comply.

Only the truth, nothing more.

30

S EAN, MY FRIEND THE bartender at the County Cork, was
telling me that man has nothing to fear but respectability.

After pausing to recharge my ginger ale—it had come to
that—he leaned closer and lowered his voice. "Are you prepared?" he asked. "You must be prepared for the worst, you
know." His voice was mellow, avoiding unnecessary alarm.
"No one challenges *this* cardinal in *this* town and escapes
unscathed."

I put Sean off with a cautious smile. He was not deterred.
After years behind the bar, Sean's experienced eye could penetrate a troubled man's façade to discover the fear that drove
him to seek solace from the bottle.

"More than the loss of his youth or his mate or even his
soul," Sean confided, "bourgeois man fears most of all the
loss of his respectability."

The Cardinal knows. Sean was telling me the Cardinal
knows and will use what he knows to ruin me. I reassured
myself with the thought that respectability was a virtue at

343

which I never excelled and aspired to only in moments of weakness. Then I took a close look at myself in the cloudy mirror of Sean's darkened bar and searched for the source of the fear I saw reflected there. Mary Ellen. Threatened by the Cardinal, a single fear dominated all others, and that was for Mary Ellen. Our work at PEONY had bound her name inextricably to mine. Would she be able to deal with scandal-by-association? She came from Middle Village, Queens, not Avenue B, and must return to face a community that had recently felled every tree in its only park to destroy the cover of midnight sodomites said to gather there. Would she, when asked, do as Peter had done and deny she had ever known me?

I did not know, but if my... *other lives* were to become the subject of public gossip, it would be better if Mary Ellen heard it first from me.

The following morning I called Mary Ellen. Her mother said she was away on a weekend retreat of prayer and fasting. I left a message. She did not receive it until Sunday evening and by that time I was on the front page of the *Daily News*.

"MEAT LOAF OR beef and noodles, Mary Ellen. We have no other choices." The Polskyrama served as an accurate barometer of the city's economy. Even in good times the place did a prosperous business. In bad times the crush of hungry patrons soon reduced the restaurant's selection of four substantial entrées to one or two.

"Whatever you are having will be fine for me."

Usually Mary Ellen elevated the simple experience of selecting a dish to the level of discovery. Tonight's indifference increased my apprehension.

"The meat loaf then," I told the waitress, "and a *fresh* bottle of ketchup."

Throughout dinner Mary Ellen used apathetic chitchat of family affairs to avoid what both of us knew we had come to discuss. I continued to look for openings. She presented none.

I called for the check, foregoing the vanilla pudding included in the price of the meal, and suggested we move on to the Cellars of Kiev. A beer or two might induce a confessional mood on my part and a more sympathetic ear on Mary Ellen's.

As we sipped our beer I fought down anxiety while watching Mary Ellen for a sign to begin. After the third glass and still no lead from her, I made up my mind. To delay longer might leave both of us in a state where it would be difficult to discuss anything.

I gazed up through the window to Sixth Street, avoiding Mary Ellen's look of indifference.

"You have, of course, seen the story in the *News*?" I asked. I had rehearsed my opening line and I got through it without faltering.

"Who hasn't," Mary Ellen replied. She continued to study the glass that she cupped in both hands.

"And what do you think of it? I mean, its general thrust?"

"Like most stories in that paper, it says too little and suggests too much." Her tone was detached, noncommittal. Like me, she avoided eye contact.

"And if the article were true?" I asked. "At least in part? What then?"

"I think, Virgil," Mary Ellen raised her eyes to meet mine, "it's time you told me everything there is to tell."

I ordered another pitcher and began with Omaha.

"...She was my life, Mary Ellen, my heart and my soul. Other boys my age dreamt of becoming baseball stars, racecar drivers, men of fame. I worshipped the lovely Sister Philomena and dreamt of becoming a nun. And when He took her away—oh saddest of days—I swore that if I could not become what she had been, I would at least bring no other woman into my life. Until I met you, Mary Ellen, I kept that promise."

I began my confession with the death of Philomena and my love for her because it is best, I think, when you have a difficult story to tell and wish to render your listener sympathetic, to begin with a poignant episode. It's true I depicted the story of Philomena's tragic death in greater detail than the reported facts allowed, but who would begrudge me this license? The story in the *News* was misleading, even erroneous in one important respect. I was now a desperate man. Would the Cardinal rob me of everything, even Mary Ellen?

"So sad," Mary Ellen agreed when she had heard Sister Philomena's story, but she did not raise her eyes from the empty glass.

"You must not believe everything the *News* has said of me. There are errors and omissions. The report, for example, that I was expelled from the Mercerian Brothers. If those reporters had bothered to do a little research—but then the Cardinal has had ample time by now to falsify the records.

"The truth will hardly be easier for some to understand. But please try, Mary Ellen, while keeping in mind that the decisions I've made throughout my life have rarely been mine to make. Once I received the Call, the direction my life would take was largely up to Them."

I refilled Mary Ellen's glass, then my own.

"Go on," Mary Ellen told me, although she did not seem particularly curious to hear what I had to say.

"My sixteenth summer. A painful time, the most painful I've been asked to bear. Sister Philomena's shocking death left me in deep despair. I spent the first weeks following her death trying to sort out fact from fiction. At that time newspapers in Omaha had to be concerned with taste and not only with sales. They didn't report the violent deaths of distraught nuns. The Church concealed Philomena's death behind a wall of silence. The papers printed what the local bishop told them to print, that Philomena slipped in the bathroom, knocked herself unconscious, and drowned in the tub. Preposterous. Sister chained an anchor to her neck, leaped from the Missouri River bluffs and drowned herself because she could not resolve the dilemma posed by her love for one of her students (who returned her love), and her vows to uphold a moral code that forbade it. Sister's life, at least the manner in which she ended it, was the stuff of literature, and I spent the remainder of the summer composing an epic poem in her memory. At another time, Mary Ellen, you may want to read *Philomena of the Plains*. In concept, and perhaps in execution, it remains the seminal work of its decade."

"And what decade is that, Virgil?"

"Writing is a sedentary pursuit and should be balanced with physical activity. To lift my spirits and maintain my physical health, I began constructing a shrine to Sister Philomena. My father was at that time a sanitation worker with the City of Omaha and had salvaged an old bathtub from the city dump. The tub was quite small with a curved and gently sloping backrest. I buried the tub, faucet end down, to form a vaulted shrine in a corner of Mother's garden. There were, of course, no images of Sister Philomena. In fact, the saint who was her namesake would soon be struck from the rolls of the sanctified by a reformist pope more concerned with purging ecclesiastical history of presumed myths than inspiring his flock by venerating pious exemplars. Statues of St. Philomena were already collectors' items, hard to find and expensive if you found one. So I made do with a snapshot of Sister Philomena taken at a happier time. I encased the photo in glass and ornamented the frame with sea shells sent to me by a missionary priest all the way from Pago Pago. I propped up this icon in the bathtub grotto and planted the now sacred place with a twining virgin's bower of forget-me-nots and n'er-do-wells."

"N'er-do-wells, Virgil? I don't think I've ever heard…"

"Common in Omaha. The shrine completed, I lit the stub of a dining room candle before the snap of Phil. The flame flickered, caught, and Lo! The holy woman spoke! It was the first time I heard a voice from the Other Side."

I studied Mary Ellen for signs of awe or disbelief. Her parted lips, calm and fixed, revealed neither. She did, however, reach for the pitcher of beer, filled her empty glass, hesitated a moment as if wondering whether to top off mine or if the gesture might be misinterpreted as a return to our old intimacy, then allowed kindness to overcome her fears and performed the little service. She did not go back to staring at her glass.

"Do you believe in reincarnation?" I asked Mary Ellen.

"I don't know. I've never thought much about it."

"I do. And the conviction that we have lived in a different place and at a different time gives some of us the power to conjure up lives we may—or may not—have lived before, and these lives become just as real as our own.

"The Sisters of Mercy of Baton Rouge wore a huge rosary— the brown beads were the size of hazelnuts—hanging from their wide black leather belts. Sister Philomena had the characteristic habit of twirling the crucifix that hung from her wooden beads with one hand while she flipped back her veil with the other. As I knelt before her photograph, I saw her execute the gesture—she had come, as I knew she would. All she needed was an invitation and a home proper to a saint.

"When Sister spoke, I fell into a swoon. Swoons induced by apparitions do not, however, impair the senses. The history of heavenly visitations bears this out. I heard Sister's words just as clearly as I hear my own now. An important point because later on, Philomena would say I got things confused.

"She thanked me for what she called her 'quaint summer cottage' and told me how clever I was to have thought of recycling that old bathtub. Her next words, that she would later deny, I heard plain as day.

"'Pity you were born a boy,' she said. 'The Sisters of Mercy are as much in need of your gifts as they were of mine. The order deserves someone of your unbridled imagination. If only we could...'

"Because of the tragic manner of Sister's death, I heard the note of irony. Sister might disagree with my interpretation of why she chose to end her life—her unrequited love for me— but she had never denied she did it. Why was she so willing now to send me into the lion's den? Just one more thing about the woman I was not meant to understand.

"I remembered Sister's words so well because she knew I had already made up my mind to join the Mercerian Brothers, the male counterpart of her own order, the Sisters of Mercy. The Mercerians wore a simplified habit similar in style and color to Sister Philomena's. This made them my first choice. If I could not become the nun I loved, I would become the next best thing, dress like her and become her Brother in Christ.

"Why, I wondered, was Sister confusing me now with what-ifs and maybes?

"Sister interrupted her fantasy of the unsettling effect my presence would have upon the Sisters of Mercy and looked at me closely. She smiled in a way that told me she had something up her voluminous sleeve. I focused my eyes on hers, attempting to read her thoughts as she had tried to teach me to do. No! She could not be planning what her thoughts said she was. Not since medieval times had such scams been perpetrated. 'On the other hand,' Sister continued aloud, 'with your flawless skin and graceful figure...'"

"Oh, Virgil!" Mary Ellen moaned. "How could she be so cruel!"

"Not cruel, Mary Ellen. Saints are never that. She was only carrying out her mission as she had taught me to carry out mine. I would call her devious. My idea to become a nun came from Out There. Who else but Sister Philomena? Later, when my reputation hung in the balance, she could at least have admitted her folly.

"Life grew more perplexing. After coming out of the swoon, I was a changed man. The constrictions of reality loosened and I discovered that almost anything was possible. I no longer put much faith in appearances. Brothers, nuns, Mercerians or Sisters of Mercy, distinctions, it seemed to me, that were largely a matter of perception.

"Snip snip, falling falling, my luxuriant jet black hair shorn and swept disdainfully aside by a mistress of novices I choose to call Sister Mary Mirabelle to conceal her hand in the affair of my transformation. To grow such hair I had refused to cut it all during my junior and senior year at St. Martin Maimed. This was a far more conservative era than the pagan age we live in now, Mary Ellen, and as a result I suffered torments inflicted by the brothers too beastly to relate. They demeaned me. They went so far as to question my sexual identity. I grew bitter. But through prayer and fasting, I found the strength to suffer their insults and beatings in the spirit God no doubt intended them, as preparation for my mission. Henceforth, I would be the Sacrificial Lamb. Persecution became my personal passion, and I assumed the pain my oppressed brothers and sisters were unable to bear."

"Virgil," Mary Ellen broke in, "tell me. How did you get into the convent in the first place? They must do medical exams, certificates and all that."

Doubt, a pernicious sin synonymous with our time. Would Mary Ellen make faith subservient to reason?

"Proof of the miraculous, Mary Ellen. It took a miracle to get me through those convent doors, and Sister Philomena engineered it.

"I was not particularly popular in the convent, at least not with the other novices. They thought my humility false and my appetite for penance excessive. I paid them no mind. It was my ambition to reach the top. And my superiors, taking note of my zeal, began to see me as I saw myself, as an exemplar sent to revitalize an order grown lax. I received the Veil of Christ, and in six years time, in spite of my youth, I became Mistress of Discipline. If not for the accident, who knows how far I would have risen in the order?

"The accident. Sister Philomena's recollection of what happened differs from my own. The way *I* remember it—

"Lent was approaching, and as penance I had assigned myself the task of scrubbing the three flights of stone steps leading from the refectory to the floors above where we nuns had our cells. The Sisters of Mercy of Baton Rouge is an elitist order. Nuns of rank do not scrub floors. However, a missionary priest had recently visited the convent and in a fiery sermon proclaimed, 'The only way for a nun to get to

heaven is on her knees.' To give new meaning to this old
adage, I decided nothing could be more effective than for
my novices to see Sister Mary Virgilina scrubbing steps like
a scullery maid.

"Even as early as Holy Week the weather in Louisiana can
be quite warm. To compensate for the heat and in violation
of convent rules, once the weather changed I no longer wore
intimate apparel.

"On the final day of my Lenten Penance and with the
entire convent assembled in the refectory for Good Friday's
meal of bread and water, I meant to scrub the stairs as the
nuns and novices looked on and then conclude, when I had
finished my scrubbing, with a little homily on humility.

"I started at the top, intending to scrub my way down. The
first flight of stairs went well enough. Because the steps were
washed daily, very little scrubbing was necessary, and I gave
each step no more than a symbolic sweep of the brush and
concentrated instead on style. I had reached the second-floor
landing and was maneuvering to make the ninety-degree turn
when I stepped on the bar of yellow soap, lost my balance
and tumbled skirt over veil down the steps to the flagstone
landing below. I can only guess at my position as I lay unconscious at the foot of the stairs."

Mary Ellen blushed, and rather than allow her to dwell on
my sad position and slip, perhaps, into immodest thoughts, I
underlined my shame by riveting my eyes on hers.

"For three days I lingered in a coma, near death. On the
Third Day, Easter morning, the day we celebrate the Risen
Christ, I awoke at dawn from my sleep of the dead. To my
horror I was dressed in black trousers and white shirt, the uniform of a Mercerian novice. I put my hand to my face and
discovered the beginning of a sparse beard. I felt a dull pain

centered on my bandaged nose. I looked about the room—pale green paint, plastic curtains hanging to either side of the room's single window—a room typical of public sanatoriums in the South.

"Another beer, Mary Ellen? I will, and perhaps a shot of bourbon. All this talking has left me dry."

Mary Ellen did not reply. She sat motionless, her expression sad, a little anxious, inscrutable.

"I wasn't angry with Sister Philomena, not at first," I said as I resumed my story after being served, "or at least no more than I might have been had we had a lovers' quarrel. My cover was blown, as they say in clandestine circles, through no fault of hers. Nuns worth their rigorous training do not shed their underwear at the first trickle of discomfort. Sister had put great trust in my commitment to discipline and graceful carriage and I had let her down. If I had been paying more attention to the job at hand, scrubbing steps, and less to the image I wished to project—an elegant woman *electing* to perform a menial task—I would have taken care to avoid that bar of soap.

"Anger came later. With my broken nose and bruised bones still aching from my fall, psychiatrists working on me night and day, Sister began pressing me to search out another order less alarmed than the Mercerians with occasional falls from grace.

"'Mercerians? Whatever are you talking about,' I demanded of Sister Philomena. 'Fall from grace? A strange term for a tumble down the stairs.'

"'Accurate in both senses of the term,' Sister insisted. She never cared to have her diction questioned. 'What you did with Brother Felix was indiscreet to say the least.'

"'Sister,' I said with more kindness than she deserved, 'I don't understand a word you're saying.'

"Sister gave me a sympathetic look. 'That's what the doctors say, you don't understand a word they're saying.'

"For several moments we stared at each other, Sister with her knowing smile, me with my determined denial.

"Then Sister said, 'It would be better for your mental health, Virgil, if you owned up to it. I'll understand. The Church will understand: Love the sinner, hate the sin. On the other hand, you must learn to be more careful. When you first cast a lustful eye on handsome Brother Felix, when you felt that first illicit tug.... But such things happen—who should know better than I?—and you are now suffering from what your doctors call *reaction formation*. It's a classic Freudian defense, I'm told, and not all that uncommon to men and women of rigid moral pretensions. Sometimes our exalted sense of dignity prevents us from admitting to the unacceptable. To mask our shame we create a new reality altogether that precludes the possibility of having done what we are accused of doing.

"'But why,' Sister Philomena asked, 'that elaborately conceived convent story? Even if it's partly true, given a change of place and gender, wasn't there a simpler way out?'

"'Like suicide?' I reminded her. Cruel of me, for sure, but I had called on Sister for support. What I got was collusion with the enemy.

"'If you had got me into a monastery instead of a convent,' I continued, 'there would be no owning up for me to do.'

"'Oh, dear,' Sister sighed, 'as bad as that, is it? The doctors said nothing about amnesia. But just allow me to recall what really happened to you one more time and then we'll leave it at that, okay?'

"You see, Mary Ellen, Sister had got me confused with some unfortunate soul under her care—I suppose she has many, most saints do—and this sadly repressed brother committed an... an indiscretion with a fellow Mercerian and was, well, dismissed from the order."

If Mary Ellen was not convinced, she at least did not protest.

"Could it be," Mary Ellen asked, always the peacemaker, "that both your and Sister Philomena's interpretations of the story were right? Perhaps Sister doesn't understand all the ins and outs of reincarnation—certainly I don't—and you do. I mean if you really were Sister Virgilina all along, and you... committed an indiscretion with Brother Felix,"—here Mary Ellen gave me a most perplexing look—"then that would throw a different light on the whole affair, wouldn't it? Indiscreet, yes, even morally wrong, but not unnatural."

Clever soul, my Mary Ellen. She could split hairs with the best of them.

(After I left the convent, Philomena and I did not speak for many years. We remained estranged because she would not accept her responsibility for my disgrace and held to her cock and bull story of my making a pass at that Mercerian brute Felix, who threw me down the stairs and broke my nose.)

"My sudden release from my vows, Mary Ellen, began one of the more desperate periods of my life. I arrived in this city on a Greyhound bus with nothing in my purse but the hundred dollar bill defrocked nuns customarily receive from their order. I had no one to turn to. And so I put to use the skill acquired by most nuns, and the one which, if it had been performed in a less careless manner, might have prevented my ignominious fall.

"I placed an ad in the *Village Voice*: 'Young woman, strong, will do cleaning, laundry, shopping. Windows extra.' When placing the ad, I wore a simple cotton housedress and Aunt

Jemima headgear, for you see, I had worn skirts so long I was not yet comfortable in pants.

"I hadn't reached the door of the classified office before I was stopped by two members of the staff *begging* me to take them on. I'm quick to see an opportunity—a virtue of mine, Mary Ellen, that should not be overlooked—and I set my fee a dollar an hour higher than I had intended when I entered.

"There's simply no reason for anyone in this city to starve, not unless they suffer from a severe physical handicap. In a week's time, after I had winnowed out the crank calls from perverse men and women who read into my ad services offered that I had no intention of performing, I had far more work than I could handle. There's no end of working householders in this city who will not or cannot clean up their mess.

"I was, however, not meant to be a cleaning lady. It was not my calling. It wasn't the work I minded; what I couldn't bear was the isolation. Why should a man with my gifts, even if a sacked nun, hide behind the dumpy dress of a charwoman? Who was I hiding from? What misguided notion of humility was I trying to uphold? And for whom? Certainly not Sister Philomena whose advice had always been, 'Go for the top, Virgil. You've got what it takes.'

"Although we were not talking, I've always believed Sister had a hand in arranging the introduction that led, eventually, to my next career. She has never admitted as much, but the coincidence of a man of my attributes and obscure connections meeting a designer of Lyle's reputation must have involved some heavenly machinations. I suppose it was Sister's way of saying she had been wrong about my making a pass at Brother Felix and wanted to make up for it.

"I've already mentioned that my cleaning schedule was filled a week after placing the ad. Calls, however, continued to come in. One intrigued me. The voice on the line was male. His questions concerned my competence as a cleaner. 'What is the proper method of cleaning a parquet floor? What polish is best suited to chrome?' But his tone of voice suggested an interest in activities unrelated to scrubbing and waxing.

"I had by this time scrubbed and waxed acres of vinyl tile, polished a third as much window glass, washed tons of soiled linen. I had no social life. I dined at the lunch counters of neighborhood bars. To pass the evening hours I gazed into shop windows at clothes I could not afford to buy. I finally agreed with Sister Philomena. I was meant for something better, and I accepted the caller's invitation for drinks and dinner at Les Trois Amis.

"Kiril, for that was the name of my blind date, turned out to be a Bulgarian who had fled his homeland when the Communist Party took notice of the correlation between his flamboyant life style, for a Bulgarian, and the declining receipts of the People's Potato Cooperative that he administered. Kiril spent a fearful month in West Berlin, dodging assassins wielding poison-tipped umbrellas, while waiting to be admitted to the United States as a political refugee.

"As I got to know Kiril better I let on, discreetly, that there was a bit more to me than met the eye. As is so often the case with friends to whom we choose to confess our deepest secrets, Kiril had already looked beneath my skirts, so to speak, and was pleased by what he saw.

"Kiril delighted in large parties. It was at one of these, attended mainly by men and women in the high-end rag trade, that I met Lyle. Lyle was instantly taken by my looks, build and movement, nurtured no doubt by a defining word or two from Kiril. Lyle saw me as a crossover possibility, a mannequin who could combine the gait of Greta Garbo and the allure of Lauren Bacall. Lyle made offers, all above board. I declined, reminding him of my sheltered past that had not prepared me for the sophisticated world in which he moved. I was playing for time. If I were to conquer the world of fashion, I had to absorb its style in motion as well as dress. It would not do to stumble on my first walk down the runway. Two months later, when Lyle repeated his offer, I accepted."

"Oh, Virgil!" Mary Ellen moaned and shook her head, begging me to say what she had read in the *News* wasn't true.

"Outrageous, Mary Ellen? But you must have guessed. That afternoon at your parents' house when I taught the PEONY girls how to move with purpose, didn't you wonder then where I had learned my skills?"

"Maybe I did," she answered sadly. "Maybe I suspected something. But I didn't know, didn't want to know, I suppose. I couldn't ask, and if nothing was said, well, I didn't have to think about it."

I reached for Mary Ellen's hand to console her, but stopped halfway, fearing rejection.

"Look at it this way, Mary Ellen. What else *could* I do? Convent life does not prepare one for the world. I had an all but worthless associate degree in elementary education granted by the order. It consisted of a handful of courses similar to those offered by higher education schools that neither teach one how to teach nor prepare one for any other occupation. It was either live off Kiril's largess, running up debts that I would eventually have to pay,"—and I paused to allow Mary Ellen to determine the coin in which men like Kiril expected payment—"or accept Lyle's offer to make me a star.

"Most of what the *News* says about this period of my life is accurate. With so much documentation so easily checked, even that dreadful tabloid could not go wrong. It's true that for my first season before the cameras I played it straight in plaid shirts and blue jeans, boy stuff popular that year with the Fire Island crowd. Lyle said I had to get the feel of the runway before attempting to show more exotic costumes. You see, he did not know—no one was ever to know—that I had years of experience showing one of the most exotic costumes of all time, the habit of the Sisters of Mercy of Baton Rouge, a creation so elaborately tangled that snide commentators have been heard to refer to the nuns as the Order of the Unmade Bed.

"My ambition from the very start was to hit the top. In-demand models of women's wear were far better paid than their male counterparts. Female mannequins played to packed houses dressed in creations as ridiculous as the best male minds could get by with. I was a good deal younger then and my body was still as slender as a girl's. I finally convinced—"

"How old *are* you, Virgil?" Mary Ellen interrupted without changing her position of head on hand.

"Why, Mary Ellen! I'm surprised you should be interested in something so completely personal—and irrelevant—as my age! But since you ask, I am not as young as I appear. Would you guess twenty-nine? No? So few do. Correct diet, plenty of sleep…and of course I drink very little nowadays. You are, by the way, the only person to have asked my age and received an answer—any answer—and I ask you to treat such information with the confidence in which it was revealed."

"Of course, Virgil," Mary Ellen murmured. "All your secrets are safe with me."

"I finally convinced Lyle that it was a simple matter, a mere change of clothes and a touch of makeup, expertly applied, to cross the line and join those loose and lanky mannequins who worked the runways of his Seventh Avenue salon.

"I won't go into the harrowing experience of my years
before the camera. That would require hours and constitute
another story altogether. I should mention, though, that I
became an overnight sensation. Lyle's best collections were
mine to show, and my ability to project a unique combination of austere power, masked by an alluring vulnerability,
made me his highest paid model of town and country wear.

"Oddly enough, it was during these frivolous years, when
my days—and nights—were barely long enough to include
both work and study and the hectic play it took to spend my
inflated wages, that I began my political education. Radical
chic was sweeping the fashion world and I was chosen to be
its most visible exponent. Did you by chance see the cover of
Vogue where I was done up in camouflage fatigues, boots to
the knee, a cartridge belt slung low on the hips and a bando-
leer across my chest? Oh, tasteless times!¹

"But such foolishness introduced me to people and ideas
new to someone from my sheltered background. It was during
this period of incognito—that is, in pants—that I surrendered myself to the seductions of the crowd and was swept
away by the mass movements of the time. I marched. I demonstrated. I gamboled naked down the mall of our nation's
capitol. An episode of pagan abandon is necessary to one's
political evolution, at least in a society such as ours, inflicted
as it is by the Puritanical Ethic. We must first free the soul

---

i   All this preceded by a decade the rise of the famous Brazilian
queen, Liberada (no last name). He launched his career in a series
of TV ads for a retailer of closets ('Don't be fooled by appearances,'
he cooed while showing viewers how to tell a genuine, imported
Armario de la Reina from a competitor's fake). Liberada went on
to become a high fashion model and the international star we
know him as today.

from the strictures of tradition before we can hope to build the New Man. Don't you agree, Mary Ellen? Which is the reason, as much as any, why I got PEONY started off on the right foot by staging healthy, repression-releasing bacchanals.

"As I shed my inhibitions, encouraged and comforted by the crowd, my residual integrity found space to reassert itself, and I cast off pretentious boots and bandoleers and took up plot and intrigue, caustic wit and venomous asides, weapons better suited to a man of my disposition.

"As I cleaned up my life, my righteousness grew apace and I began to hear a voice other than my own."

"Philomena?" Mary Ellen asked, almost hopefully I thought.

"No, we were still not on speaking terms, but it was a woman's voice. First I'd hear the bells and then the whispering in my ear. When the woman finally raised her voice to audible level, I discovered that she was speaking an antique Italian dialect, the mother tongue of the Italian I heard spoken on the streets of New York.

"My private life began to change. Perhaps the woman's persistent whispering was responsible. Whatever the cause, I found myself spending my leisure hours increasingly in the company of strangers, lonely men in need of an escort. I was driven to give of myself in a more personal way than I had in a crowd. I gave what I could, which was rather less than they wanted, and I met a great many men who would be of use to me when I took up my true vocation, to clean up St. Lucy's School for Boys. When I realized I could never give enough to fulfill my clients' needs, I turned my thoughts to pursuits more appropriate to my intelligence and learning than hustling frivolous garments designed for expensive women or keeping bored company with sex-starved men. I did not say, I will teach the young, and then promptly desert the showrooms of the Seventh Avenue for the classrooms of St. Lucy's. No, I said nothing at all. I simply unplugged the phone, avoided the mailbox, stopped eating and sat on the floor, staring at the wall.

"Word came, as it always does to those chosen to lead. This time St. Lucy spoke in English, but I knew from her Sicilian accent it was the same voice I had been hearing for some time. After exclaiming why she had come—that her school had fallen on bad times—her directive was clear: 'Clean up the mess, Virgil Quinn, and you don't have to be too particular how you do it.'

"Blindly I went in and crucified I came out. When Lucy assigned me to her school, she didn't have a thing to say about consequences. Not a word on the Cardinal and what I might expect from him. Early on in my campaign, I voiced my fears to her. She brought me up short by pointing to the trials of Joan of Arc. As if I had anything in common with that sensational virgin reformer whose marvelous psychic resources have been laid to everything from religious delusions to sexual hysteria. It's incidents such as these, Mary Ellen, that have led me to believe the saints are not to be trusted, not entirely. They are all too ready to send us into the lion's den without an exit plan other than the crown of martyrdom. And that's just what Lucy did. She took me by the hand and led me from the church into her school. What could I do but follow?"

31

"AND THE REST, MARY Ellen, is history."

For several moments Mary Ellen remained as she was, her head resting in the cup of her hand. As my story had unfolded, her attention intensified each time I touched upon the direct intervention of the saints in the development of my careers. She looked at me now, however, with pale blue eyes that told me nothing. I had nothing more to say. I had told it all—well, all that could be told—and if she could not find it in her heart...

The barmaid totaled our bill and left it up to Mary Ellen and me to determine our shares. Mary Ellen's lack of response, when I paid the entire bill myself, was a measure of her preoccupation.

She returned to staring at her empty glass. Moments passed. She said nothing. I studied my shoe. I looked up through the cellar bar's sidewalk-level window, counting the legs of passersby. When I could bear her silence no longer, I reached for my umbrella.

"Does anyone know," Mary Ellen suddenly asked, "about the saints?"

"No," I replied. "Until you entered my life there was no one to tell. No one I know believes in the supernatural."

"Just as well you keep it to yourself, Virgil. Few today would understand."

This followed by another long silence.

"Well," I said as I rose to go. "I suppose it's time to call it a night. It's nearly ten and you have a long ride home. I have a busy day tomorrow, lectures to—"

"Oh, *do* sit down, Virgil. *I* have something to say."

Her words were a command and I obeyed. It was the first time she had spoken to me in such a voice and I recovered from my shock by flippantly asking what secrets could be hidden in *her* gentle past.

"None, and that's what I want to talk to you about."

I beckoned to the barmaid for another round, and Mary Ellen abruptly began what she had to say.

"I'm not pretty, Virgil. I'm not particularly bright, and the saints don't talk to me the way they do to you. I'm thirty-three years old and I've lived all my life in Middle Village, Queens with parents who should be able to take care of themselves but don't. My friends, the few that I have, are women much like myself. On Saturday nights we go to Shamrock Village and dance with men who look like us, talk like us, work at the same socially meaningful but uninspiring jobs. They differ from us only in gender. On Sundays I return from Mass to fix roast beef and mashed potatoes for my family that gathers each week to talk about lives as familiar to me as my own.

"Until I met you. No, not met you; the change came later when we were thrown together during the organization of PEONY. I was content, more or less, to go on as I had for so many years. Then we had our fist date. Do you remember the day we walked like half the way from Transfiguration to the Polskyrama? Me in heels? I thought my feet would never be the same. That was over a year ago, and the better I came to know you, the less willing I was to accept my predictable life.

"When I read what they said about you in the *News*... I was angry. And confused. I felt—well, I suppose I felt what any woman in my position would feel. I felt betrayed."

"Love the sinner, hate the sin, that's what the Church says, Mary Ellen. I might have had a little drinking problem, but I didn't, ah, go all the way."

Mary Ellen looked at me with just a squint of disbelief. "Now, I would find it less difficult to accept if you had. Who am I to preach the rewards of...?" Mary Ellen had hesitated to speak the word, but I knew what she meant. "Ever since grade school I've been told to save it for marriage. And what has it got me? Not marriage, although there was a boy once—And now? Well, some things don't seem so important anymore. I don't need to know just who you are or what necessity—or loneliness—might have led you to do in the past. The man I know is not the person they say you are. For me you've been an inspiration to try new lives, shed old habits. And listening to you tonight—well, you don't just dream, Virgil, you live your dreams and put them to work. The rest of us indulge in fantasies, for pleasure's sake. For you, today's fantasy is tomorrow's goal. More than any other man I've known, your life demonstrates that anything is possible."

Mary Ellen continued to talk until she had touched upon all of her failings, none of her accomplishments, and most of my virtues. She was, I was certain now, going to follow her revelations with a proposal that, if I accepted, would mark the end of our carefree camaraderie and the

beginning of a deeper commitment. Startling words that
I had prevented from being spoken before by manipulating our private conversations to avoid the subject. Had I
prepared my answer if ever she should ask? I'm not sure.
In proposals effecting the direction of one's life and work,
what one answers, yes or no, is determined to a large extent
by one's needs when the question is asked. Revolutionaries cannot afford the luxury of sentiment. I was certainly
aware of Mary Ellen's attributes and did not find them
undesirable. If she was plain, I did not consider her looks a
liability. I find beautiful women threatening. If two people
are to live together in harmony, one beauty in the house is
sufficient.

Will you marry me, Virgil? I waited for her to say the
words I would never have the audacity to speak. I concealed my fear and turned to practical considerations. I
tried to project the pattern my life would take now that my
dismissal from St. Lucy's was certain. I would lose everything that once engaged me—a classroom full of boys
eager to learn, days of fratricidal combat. I would become
one of those unemployed men one meets at liberal cock-
tail parties, sitting in a chair well beyond and below the
aggressive conversation carried on by standing men and
women with careers. 'And what do you do?' someone asks.
The man without a label takes too long to answer and loses
his impatient listener to others who can answer in a catego-
rizing word or two.

In my day and in my circle I had been the chief practi-
tioner of the art of tantalization. I had shown my patrons,
all of them who wished to learn at the foot of the master,
the delightful torments of unconsummated lust. (And if,
after a night of drinking, I slipped from time to time, such

falls from grace need not be mentioned.) In a world where everything has its price, I withheld the ultimate favor for reasons that encouraged my more analytic clients to reconsider the purpose of their demands and the nature of their desire. In their haste to possess me they would have, without my patient instruction, merely made of our encounter a jaded repetition of what they had already known too much of. Physical couplings, I warned them, lead inexorably to ennui. Man, unlike the lower animals, thrives on frustration. He cannot sustain a sexual interest in objects once possessed. Long after the sexually active man has forgot the names—and yes, even the delights—of old conquests, those few he desired but failed to possess remain forever fresh in his mind and subject to frequent recall.

Nearly all of my patrons came to accept the wisdom of my thesis, at least inasmuch as it defined our own relationship. Tortured and tormented, they came back for more. Axel did not, but then Axel was very rich and men of that sort are often beyond instruction of any kind.

My work, as consort, had been dependent on my anonymity. I was a public figure now. It would not be the same. The purity of my motives would be suspect. My clientele would see my behavior as just a game, the famous Virgil Quinn playing hard to get. I could not go on as I had in the past.

Will you marry me, Virgil? Would she ask?

Mary Ellen had talents essential to the efficient operation of a conventional household. Her thrifty administration of PEONY had been remarkable even for a woman accustomed to the economies of the upper working class. She was an excellent seamstress if the salt-and-pepper tweed pants suit she wore today was typical of her craftsmanship. Mrs. Goldberg was no longer young. She could not ply her needle forever. And with my fortunes, financially speaking, on the wane, having an in-house tailor of Mary Ellen's ability would enable me to continue to look my best.

Projected on any level, mine would be a hard life riven with insecurity, one of sporadic activity interspersed with idleness, self-doubt and nights of loneliness, the life, in short, of the dissident in any repressive society. Mary Ellen continued to live at home long after most women seek independence. Her purpose was not only to economize but to manage the household of parents who could not cope. To a man burdened with mission, no qualities in a partner are more important than loyalty and self-sacrifice.

Will you marry me, Virgil? Mary Ellen opened her mouth as if to speak but kept her stubborn silence.

And then there was the Other Woman. What of my long-standing relationship with Sister Philomena? How would the loving and much-loved nun react to a transfer of fidelity that threatened her hegemony and implied a denial of my vows? I had pledged myself to Philomena forever. Would Mary Ellen make demands? Did she have procreative expectations?

"Will you marry me, Virgil?" Mary Ellen finally asked, brushing her hair aside, much as Philomena did her veil.

I hesitated for several moments, acting as if the suitor's question came as a surprise, as anyone put in my position is expected to do.

"I… I'm not sure. What if—"

"I do not intend to make demands."

Demands. She means sex. "There could never be anything… carnal, Mary Ellen. I've taken the vow."

"I know."

"Sisters."

"Brothers."

"And still you wish it?"

"It is your soul and not your body that I long for."

"Repression can lead to madness."

"Heavenly madness."

"You were meant to be a bride of Christ, Mary Ellen."

"Times change."

"Indeed, they do."

"And time changes... things." Mary Ellen gave me a pointed look that spoke her mind.

"Don't bank on it."

Far off I heard the tolling of bells that I first took to be the announcement of my betrothal. The bells faded into voices, first faint, then those of two women raised in anger.

"I died for virtue's sake. Those pagan men of Sicily plucked out my eyes because I would not submit to their beastly desire. And now Virgil is prepared to surrender his Flower of Great Beauty. Why?"

Philomena, calmly: *"The last time you spoke on this subject, you said he had already lost it."*

"Not with a woman."

"You have a narrow definition of virginity, Lucy. Anyway, he's made it clear: No sex."

"If he marries her, she will not give up until she's bedded him. Women are like that. And when she has, he will belong to her, not us."

Lucy began to weep. Tears welled up in eyes loaned to her until the Final Days when all of us will be recombined, body and soul, and assumed into heaven.

"Oh, do stop pitying yourself, Lucy! He made no promises to you. For reasons known only to He Who Crowns, you reign as

the ranking virgin martyr in this celestial asylum." In an aside, Sister Philomena whispered to me, *"Saints. Over-reactors, all of them, subject to these maddening fits of hysteria.*" Then Sister returned to berating the out-classed Lucy. *"Your martyrdom was years ago. We're approaching the second millennium. You can hardly expect Virgil to adhere to mores centuries old. He has his own needs to look after. Besides, you knew very well that the sacrifice of your eyes meant an instant passport to heaven. In Virgil's time—or mine, for that matter—who has enjoyed such assurance? So let the boy be. And now, if you'd step out of ear shot, I'd like a word with Virgil—alone.*"

Lucy floated obligingly into the background and Sister wheeled on me. *"OK, Virgil. Level with me! I want to know exactly what you have in mind regarding that woman's proposal. Because if you are so much as thinking about dumping me for that... that uninspiring woman—*"

When Sister was truly angry she used a tone of voice capable of turning a child to stone.

"Never, Phil. Never! It's just that Mary Ellen is here and you're there. Life is getting tougher and I'm getting older. In a few days' time, when the Cardinal has done with me, I'm going to be out on the street. No job, no boys, no platform—whatever will I do with myself?"

"Having second thoughts, Virgil? A week ago you put yourself above the fears of respectable men."

"I'm going to need companionship, someone to come home to. Mary Ellen will give me that."

"I'm always with you," Sister murmured.

"Someone, well, more tangible. I should think a woman with your past would understand these things."

"I do, Virgil. Really I do." Sister's voice was no longer that of a paramour threatened by the marriage of her lover, but

that of a woman who knew she was still number one. *"I just had to be certain of your commitment to me. And now that I am, I leave you to her. But if you really do go through with this, I wouldn't, if I were you, mention our... exceptional relationship. Nothing in the girl's upbringing has prepared her for the delights of a ménage á trois."*

32

My story broke in the *Daily News*, but it was soon picked up by the city's two other major dailies. The *Post*, like the *News*, put me on page one with photos; the *Times* gave me respectable coverage further back. Terrance X. Callahan moralized in the *Brooklyn Scroll* on the many roles I had played and concluded that no one with a biography such as mine belonged in a classroom.

So much coverage, yet not a line about my mission. Taken out of the context of my calling, playing so many roles made me appear just another hustler, which was, I suppose, the Cardinal's intent all along.

And to all these omissions and distortions I could not reply in the press because I had nothing left to sell, nothing, that is, except what Lucy calls the Flower of Great Beauty prized by many but pledged forever to the beguiling Sister Philomena.

My following alienated, my jewelry sold, I responded to the Cardinal in the only way left to me. I took my message to the streets in the most direct and cheapest manner possible.

I moved fast. I had to get to the people before my story grew cold and my name forgotten.

Days after the press wrote me off as just one more city character of whom there was nothing left to be said, I was again in the news and back on the small screen. With my last check from St. Lucy's, I purchased two light-weight bulletin boards, shoulder straps, hooks, tacks and a ream of newsprint. These I assembled into a sandwich board. Each evening I compose a short chapter, very short: It has to fit on two newsprint pages and be written in letters large enough to catch the attention of a distracted passerby. I've chosen as a theme my odyssey from innocence to power—there will be nothing about a fall—a text whose appeal has been demonstrated by centuries of storytelling. Each segment, when read consecutively, will constitute an abridged version of the story I am now concluding. Each morning at nine I catch the bus to Forty-second Street, tack the day's installment to the cork, shoulder my boards and set out. I can be found almost any workday on the busier streets of the city. If my following is not as large as those of the television soap operas, it's nearly as dedicated. Often a reader will miss me at Times Square and hurry over later in the day to catch me at the Madison Avenue mansion where I appear promptly at noon to disrupt the Cardinal's lunch.

The articles in the papers with their accompanying photos did wonders to revive my old career. For weeks the calls poured in, far more than I could answer. Although I had sworn never again to flaunt my body in a public way, I did, out of desperation and with my old flamboyant presence recreated with artfully applied makeup and a seductive black wig, accept a discrete job or two. The pay for a model of my reputation allowed me to make enough in a playful romp before the cameras—I will never again walk the ramp—to fund my real work of harassing the Cardinal for a month or more. And the parties! In the world of glitz and fashion, there's nothing like a scandal to put you in demand.

But I couldn't go on behaving in this manner. One of the liabilities of high moral development is the discomfort it brings when we ignore contradictions inherent in old ways of living. Nevertheless, for a time I tried to re-experience past pleasures. I suppose I was no different than any other young man who feels the shrouds of domestic life about to enfold him. Despite trivial nuances in disposition and demeanor, I am not unlike my more conventional brothers. We all want one last flirtatious fling. I had mine and learned I could not go back. The world might still be waiting for me, but I could no longer wait upon it. My heart wasn't in it. I took a certain pride, justified I think, in knowing when to step down. How much more dignified to retire from the world rather than wait for the world to tire of you.

I have much to look forward to in my life with Mary Ellen. After so many years of coming home to an empty house, it's such a pleasure to find Mary Ellen waiting for me, dinner in the oven and a hot Epson Salts bath in which to soak my aching arthritic feet. We were prepared to move to a fifth-floor walkup down on East Fourth Street, way over by the river, the only suitable flat—two bedrooms, of course—we could afford. When I told Lyle of our prospective new address, he said, "No way will you move into a neighborhood like that," and he offered to rent us an apartment in Chelsea—he owns several—just around the corner from St. Lucy's, for a sum we could afford. We could never have managed market rent on a single salary, Mary Ellen's, out of which she has generously offered to pay household expenses while I relentlessly pursue my mission, to reform the schools (and bring down the Cardinal).

I bumped into Brother Bob this morning at the candy store. I had gone down for my usual—coffee light, hard roll and the morning papers; he for a Snickers Bar and a Baby Ruth.

"And how are things at school?" I asked. "The boys...?"

"All there and all the same. We have a new principal though. One of the best of the Little Brothers. Sent down from St. John Bosco's."

I was aghast! "St. John Bosco's Home for Incorrigible Boys?"

"The same," Brother replied with a smile. "Brother Ivan—that's what the boys call him—did great work up there."

"And Brother Principal? Where is he now?"

"Back at Our Lady of Angels Elementary."

I lowered my eyes in sympathy.

"Don't blame yourself, Virgil. Brother Principal understands, just as I do. We all have a job to do. Yours is just tougher than most."

Brother Bob placed his hand on my shoulder and squeezed, searching, I suppose, for the calluses of a sandwich man.

I said goodbye to Brother and returned to the apartment I share with Mary Ellen. I sat drinking my coffee and munching a hardroll, dreaming of old times, of the many battles I had won and the one I had lost. I laid my thoughts aside and picked up the morning papers. I was gone from the pages of each, replaced by politics in one and rape and pillage in the other. The Russian bear on the prowl again. China in turmoil.

Social upheaval in Central America. Hmmm. Warring oligarchs? Or were those much abused Latinos determined—this
time—to build a just society? And so I read on until, fired by
the day's events, I shouldered my boards and headed uptown.
Each in his own way, we must join the struggle. Reform, like
gender, is a concept in constant need of reinvention.

ABOUT THE AUTHOR

HUGH MAHONEY taught History and English for several years in New York City, an experience which served him well in writing *Virgins & Martyrs*. As a teacher in the city, he helped organize a union of the parochial school teachers, the first in the nation, a struggle that figures prominently in his satirical novel. The movement that he helped further spread to Philadelphia and Chicago, then to many other cities where it met with great success.

Reading Group Questions
and Topics for Discussion

1. VIRGIL QUINN casts himself as a reformer, and he fights a seemingly end-less stream of battles—anti-Semitism, bullying, animal abuse—and often scores a win for his cause. His methods are both inspired and questionable; however, Virgil believes the end justifies the means. Do you agree?

2. VIRGIL LIVES a double life. He is a fastidious teacher by day and, by night, he spends much of his time increasing the number of contacts in his notori-ous Black Books—contacts he uses in sometimes nefarious ways, if to ideal-istic purposes. Discuss the logic Virgil uses in his on-going quest to explain himself to himself. Is it self-serving? Delusional? Accurate?

3. VIRGIL HAS a close, personal relationship with St. Lucy who, along with his deceased elementary school teacher, Sister Philomena, seems to take a special interest in his life and welfare. What does it say about Virgil that he is so "of the world" and, yet, absolutely does not question either wom-an's directives?

4. BULL BELLOLI would likely not be a teacher for very long today. Discuss how our collective expectations of teacher/student behavior have evolved since 1968, the year around which *Virgins & Martyrs* is set.

5. VIRGIL'S GENDER ambiguity is central to his life choices—from nun to su-permodel to fashionable man about Manhattan. Discuss how it informs his understanding of and compassion for the students in his charge.

6. KEVIN O'CONNOR's tragic death is a catalyst for Virgil, who feels keen guilt for having not taken action to prevent it. What could Virgil have done to prevent it? What options would a teacher have today to act?

7. VIRGIL'S RELATIONSHIP with Mary Ellen begins as a completely professional alliance and develops slowly. When did you first notice that they were each, in his or her own way, falling in love? Do you think they will have a happy marriage? A satisfying one?

8. HUGH MAHONEY was a key player in organizing the first parochial school teachers' union in the United States, a struggle that prominently figures in his satirical novel, as the lay teachers try to get the Cardinal to negotiate fairly with them regarding salary and working conditions. Discuss the pros and cons of teachers' unions. Are unions still necessary? Viable?

RECEIVE 10% OFF YOUR FUTURE WATER STREET PRESS E-BOOK PURCHASES.

Thank you for purchasing this book from Water Street Press. The publishers and authors of Water Street Press would like to express our gratitude by offering you 10% off your future Water Street Press e-book purchases. Simply use the code below when you place an order for any e-book at www.waterstreetpressbooks.com and 10% of the purchase price will automatically be deducted. With over twenty books planned for publication in our first year alone, that's lots of exceptional, exciting and provocative reading coming your way!

Stalking Carlos Castaneda
Joan Wulfsohn
NON-FICTION
Available Fall 2012

In 1972, professional dancer Joan Wulfsohn underwent a double mastectomy. And her soon-to-be-ex-husband abducted their three children and spirited them away to a foreign country. "I should have died," Joan writes. But she didn't. *Stalking Carlos Castaneda* chronicles her journey back to life by way of lessons learned from stunning trans-vestites and music hall dancers, teen porn stars, a brain damaged boy, Eastern holy men, Western supermodels and a certain aging sorcerer. It is the story of how one woman learned to live a magical life—bound not by spells and hex-es but rather filled with wonder and transcendence.

Manhattan Gothic
James Howard Kunstler
FICTION
Available Fall 2012

A children's story for grown-ups.

"...amongst their own kind, children are the world's most thoroughgoing skeptics."

But not eleven-year-old Jeff Greenaway. When his parents suddenly come into possession of hard-to-get tickets to the smash musical *How To Succeed in Business Without Really Trying*, but can't find a babysitter, Jeff ventures out in the Manhattan night to meet his hero, Count Zackuloff, the mad, moldy host of Channel Five's Midnight Mystery The-ater, a horror movie program. Amazingly, the Count takes Jeff along on a publicity stunt in costume to the Horn and

Hardart Automat, drawing crowds of curious fans. Next, the Count takes Jeff to a double feature horror matinee at the 58th Street Translux. An unusual friendship develops between the boy and the ghoul. Through it all, Jeff nutures dreams of becoming the Count's on-screen sidekick. But the Count has his own dreams—and they do not include a lifetime of introducing old horror movies on a third-rate New York TV station.

James Howard Kunstler's charming tale takes us back to an age when New York City was a natural playground for a little boy and his own, personal vampire hero—a time when it seemed possible that all of our dreams could come true.

The Happy Party of Honorable Women
Cate Quintara
FICTION
Available Fall 2012

Jill's daughter is getting married. The two women with whom Jill has been best friends since they were little girls—Deanie, a successful novelist, and Trick, who struggles with bipolar disorder—arrive to help celebrate the happy event. The bride, however, has a bigger role than "wedding guest" in mind for them all—she has decided she will make up her wedding party by honoring the women who raised and nurtured her.

Throughout the week of pre-nuptial parties, Jill and Deanie and Trick relive the events that have shaped their lifelong friendship—their marriages and relationships, the births and losses of their children, the tragedies and joys that have forged their bond. The women discover the true depths of this bond—and how the wish of one unconventional young bride has transformed them all.

Cate Quintara invites you to be a guest at a unique and wonderful wedding, and to celebrate a jubilant life milestone—one made possible only because of the lifetimes of ordinary, everyday love that have preceded it.

The Muffia
Ann Royal Nicholas
FICTION
Available Fall 2012

Madelyn Scott-Crane is a smart, 42-year-old professional mediator and single mom who's having the best sex of her life—after twenty-two months of self-imposed abstinence—inspired by the ladies of her book club, The Muffia, and the Muff's latest racy read. But on their second date, as Maddie and her mysterious Israeli heartthrob, Udi, come together in orgasmic splendor that may or may not also be actual love, Udi collapses on top of her. Dead. When Udi's "friends"—who resemble large appliances— arrive to claim his body, the Muffs decide that Udi had secrets, and they need to know what those secrets were. That's when these well-read women put down their books and set out to expose the truth—whatever the dangerous truth might be. International intrigue combines with literary pursuits, lots of home-cooked food, and a little vibrator shopping. One book club, seven women with seven stories, more than seven fabulous meals and at least seven sex scenes all wrapped up in one smart, sexy novel that's just this side of scandalous.